Bro Smooth

Bro Smooth

The Bro Series

Alby Blake

Content Expectations

- Foul language, dirty talk, and spicy situations
- Spicy to-do list
- Sharing, including one-on-one sessions and group sessions

Chapter One

I do up the top button on my blouse and pull down the sun-visor mirror to check my lipstick. The reflection staring back, with buttons up to my chin and my tortoiseshell glasses, looks stuffy. Like I'm trying too hard to be professional. I undo the button again.

A quick swipe of lipstick and a check that there's none on my teeth, and I step out of the beat-up red car my roommate Ronnie borrowed for me off another girl in our dorm, adjusting my top to show only the barest hint of cleavage before pulling my coat tight against the frigid January air. I toss the key into my bag and take a steadying breath. I can do this. Journalists do this all the time, and that's what I'm going to be—a journalist.

At least I don't falter in my kitten heels as I cross the parking lot to the high school entrance. The lot isn't full—there are only maybe twenty or so cars here—but it's still early. I wanted enough time with the competitors beforehand to ask all my questions and find a good seat to see the whole event from beginning to end.

This is my first write-up for the *Sunshine Tribune* after having been there for almost five months, and I'm determined to make my mark even though technically I'm just a work-study intern and not an actual writer for the paper. I have been trying to get the editor to take notice of me and have been suggesting story ideas to him. I figure if he uses one of my ideas, even if he assigns the story to someone else the fact that he liked it means he might remember me the next time and eventually he'll let me report one of the stories myself. And yesterday, that plan finally paid off.

I had seen a flyer for a "cube puzzling club" on the notice board at the library a few times over the past few weeks, and curiosity finally got the better of me. My research showed that it's solving Rubik's Cubes, and it just so happens that there's an all-ages regional competition at a nearby high school this weekend.

And when I suggested the story in our staff meeting yesterday, my editor begrudgingly admitted that the "fucking higher ups wanted more fluffy local interest stories." It was the first time he didn't shoot me down.

I mean, he wasn't exactly *excited* about it, and neither was anyone else when he asked if anyone had any interest in covering the story, but when I said I did, he didn't say no. He said, "Fine, whatever," which is the closest I've ever gotten to a yes from him about anything.

So here I am, ready to take on the world of cube puzzling competitions and show my editor that I'm an amazing reporter. Otherwise, they'll have me doing nothing but fetching coffee the entire semester, which is hardly the sort of on-the-job training I want from this internship. I know I can do so much more if they'll give me the chance.

My glasses fog up as soon as I walk through the door into the heated indoor air, and I pause for a moment to let them clear. There's a small table in the middle of the hallway, and I nearly walk right into it. They should really move it back a few feet. When people start showing up, the narrow space between the doors and the table is going to get really crowded.

But it's not my job to figure out where to put the table, it's my job to cover the competition for the newspaper. So I pretend I didn't just whack the table with my bag, plaster on my most professional smile, and greet the kind-looking woman behind the table.

"Hi, I'm Rebecca Flynn. There should be a press badge for me." I'm not sure how big this competition will be, and I wanted to ensure I have the full access I'll need to speak to all of the competitors, so as soon I got the go-ahead (or, okay, the "fine, whatever") from Carl, I called the number listed on the cubing club's website and requested a press pass for the event.

"Welcome, Rebecca!" The woman's smile grows even bigger, if that's possible. "We're so excited to have you here today, writing this article about us. It'll be good for more people to learn about our little competitions."

Everything she's saying sounds good, but it's making me nervous. The fact that she called the event "little" doesn't bode well for its importance. And if they need me to write about it for anyone to know it's happening, maybe it's not as big a deal as I had thought it was. Which means anything I write up about it will be that much less impressive to my editor.

I look back out at the mostly empty parking lot. Maybe this is really it, those twenty cars are all that are coming. My stomach sinks. No wonder none of the other reporters wanted to cover this event for the paper.

"Here's your badge." She hands me a sticker name tag with the word "Press" handwritten in Sharpie. I'd been imagining an actual badge with a lanyard, something professional-looking that I could take home as a memento of my first real newspaper assignment. I try to keep my disappointment off my face. "Karen is straight back through those double doors, and she'll show you around."

"Thank you." I head toward the double doors labeled "Competitor Entrance".

Just past the table is the door to the auditorium, next to which is a handwritten sign reading "International Cubing Federation Regional Competition" taped to a music stand. *If I can't write about the crowd size in my article, at least I can mention that the signage is clear*, I think. I sidestep towards the door to take a peek at what kind of crowd has already arrived to watch the competition.

The space is a standard school auditorium with stadium seating, absolutely nothing special about it. There aren't even any decorations to mark the occasion. If the parking lot looked sad, this is downright depressing. There are maybe a dozen or so people scattered around—mostly families, probably of the competitors, although there look to be one or two friend groups who've come out to lend support.

I'd only had a night to cram in all my research about the world of competitive cube puzzling, but from what I could tell, most of these competitions are geographically rather spread out. This is the only one happening within a three-hour radius. Traveling so far would be a challenge to any friends coming to support someone and would force families to all come together.

But this isn't something I need to be worrying about right now. I have an article to research and write, and an editor to impress. Even if this event is the most lackluster thing I've ever seen, I'm going to do my best work and make it exciting for our readers.

Stepping back into the hallway, I head through the double doors to the backstage area of the competition. There are more families here than were in the auditorium, and there are kids everywhere. Some of them are running around playing tag and being generally disruptive, some are pacing as they solve Rubik's Cubes, and others are standing in a corner, talking themselves through tough pattern solutions.

I suppose this is one way to tell the competitors from the siblings.

In the midst of this havoc is a woman in a purple polo and matching visor carrying a clipboard and trying to direct people as kids run in circles around her. She must be the one in charge. Or at least she's trying to be.

"Are you Karen?" I paste another smile on my face. If I start out friendly, people are usually friendly back, and I need her on my side if I'm going to get full access to write my article.

"Can I help you?" Karen glances quickly between me, her clipboard, and the swirling chaos.

"Hi, I'm Rebecca Flynn." I hold out my hand, but she just stares for a moment before looking back to what's going on around us.

"Sammy! Tommy!" yells Karen. "What did I tell you two about sword fighting? It's not for hallways! If you want to do that, find an adult to go outside with you."

Dropping my hand, I clarify, "I'm the reporter sent by the *Sunshine Tribune* to cover today's competition."

"Fine, that's fine." She does not sound as excited for me to be here as the woman out front did. "You can watch the competition from the auditorium or backstage. Don't get in the way, and don't talk to any of the competitors without their parents' permission."

"Are they all underage then?" Looking around, I do see a lot of kids. It makes me feel a little bit better. At least I'll be older than everyone I'm interviewing, which will hopefully make them see me as more professional. It'd be more awkward interviewing people my own age or older for my first reporting gig, a thing I hadn't thought to worry about until just this moment.

"Most of them, but we do have a handful who are older." Karen really looks me over for the first time. "Maybe about your age."

"Okay, thank you."

"Brandon, what did I tell you about throwing that ball inside?" Karen hurries off in the direction of a boy who has been whipping a tennis ball against the cinderblock wall since I walked in.

I turn around and really take in the scene in the hallway. This is my first time—both at an event like this and writing for a professional paper—and I'm not completely sure where I should start.

Pulling out my notebook, I jot down the name of the coordinator and take a guess at how many people are running around the hallway.

I have to start somewhere with my interviews, though. I straighten my spine and walk over to the mom closest to me.

"Hi, I'm Rebecca." I go through my whole writing-an-article-about-the-competition spiel, then ask, "Would you mind if I asked your son a few questions about the competition?"

"Sure." She laughs. "Alex, this nice lady has a few questions."

Alex doesn't even glance up at me as his mom pulls him into her side. He continues working through different solutions on a type of cube that I've never seen. Instead of the normal cube shape, it has twelve sides, all different colors.

"Hi, Alex." Alex ignores me, and I glance nervously back at his mom, who just shrugs. "How are you feeling about this competition?"

"Fine," says Alex, eyes on his weird cube.

Okay. So, not a chatty kid, then. "That's pretty confident. How long have you been competing?"

"Seven years."

"Wow. And you're only how old?" Yeah, he's definitely a little man of few words. And not particularly cooperative.

"Twelve."

Oof. This is not going well. When I look up at his mom, she just has a small smile on her face like this is completely normal. I decide to find another interview subject, one who will maybe give me *two* whole words in a row between questions.

"All right. Well, thank you, Alex, for letting me talk to you. Good luck today."

If they're all like this, this whole interview thing is going to be a lot harder than I thought.

I try interviewing two more competitors, with the same result. If I'm lucky, I get a few words in response to my questions. Sometimes they just ignore me completely. Now I really know why none of the staff journalists wanted to come out and cover this competition. Which just makes me even more determined to find a way to make this work.

I know that if this article gets published at all, it'll only be a small piece. Probably too short to print many quotes or anything, but I want to be thorough anyway. If I can write something really amazing, my editor may give me more inches than I expect.

I head back to the seating area of the auditorium and find a seat with a perfect view of the stage that is far enough from the other spectators that I'm not self-conscientious about taking notes.

A few minutes later, a short, balding man steps out onto the stage and looks around, finally noticing the podium on the other side. The audience watches politely as he crosses the entire stage, stepping up to the podium and adjusting the microphone down to his height.

"Welcome everyone!" There's a little feedback on the microphone and I wince at the sound, but it soon dissipates. "Most of you probably know me, but for anyone who doesn't, my name is Eric Kellan. I'm the Algebra teacher and speedcubing club sponsor here at West Boston High. I'm glad to see such a great turnout, and we've got a tough competition for you on the stage today. It'll be exciting to see who qualifies and goes on to represent our area at ICF Nationals!"

There's a smattering of applause around the cavernous room. It doesn't look like anyone's joined the crowd since I'd peeked in here earlier. When I look back to the stage, four adults with clipboards and large cups, each crossing to one of the small tables on the stage and taking a seat at the chair next to it.

"Let's give a round of applause to our judges," Mr. Kellan suggests, and the audience once again claps politely.

Karen comes onto the stage carrying a large opaque blue plastic bin. She goes from table to table, and each of the judges reaches into the bin and scoops something into their giant cup. They all place the cups upside down on the tables in front of them.

"All right, folks, let's give a warm welcome to our first competitors of the day, in the Pyraminx event."

A group of kids troops out to sit behind the tables.

"You will each have fifteen seconds to inspect your Pyraminx," Mr. Kellan tells the kids. "Remember, you may inspect it, but you may not begin to solve it until you have placed your fingers on the pads and the timer light turns green."

The judges each murmur to their assigned kid, and the contestants all reply "Yes" to whatever they said. Each adult holds up a stopwatch, and I hear the beeps of the timers being started as the judges lift the buckets off the tables.

Under each is a Rubik's Cube, only it's not a cube, it's a pyramid. I'm still puzzling over why it looks like that when each kid grabs their pyramid and begins turning it over in their hands, their faces as determined and concentrated as I've seen in any athlete.

After a few seconds, they all put the pyramids down on the tables and place their hands in front of them. As they do, the timer device in front of each of them sets to "oo:oo". A nanosecond later, each kid is spinning and flipping their pyramid, tossing it down and putting their hands back in front of them once they've solved it. This appears to stop the timers. The judges jot something down on their clipboards and hand the clipboards and pens to the contestants, who each glance at their paper, write something down, and hand it back to the judge.

The entire thing took less than a minute.

Holy shit, that was fast. Even the kid who took nearly thirty seconds to solve it.

As someone who is completely incapable of solving even a normal Rubik's Cube, I'm impressed. Not only did they solve it, but they did it *fast*. I've never seen anyone's fingers move that quick.

Karen collects the papers and sorts through them, then hands them to Mr. Kellan before disappearing backstage and reappearing with the blue bin that I now know is full of cubes—er, pyramids. The judges scoop new pyramid-cubes out of it as Mr. Kellan announces who is advancing to the next round. Those whose names aren't called exit, their expressions ranging from disappointed to angry to completely devoid of emotion. A couple minutes later, all of the cubes have been solved just as lightning-fast as the first time, and Mr. Kellan is announcing the winners of round two, the kids who will move on to Nationals.

I note the names of the winners and how they each placed as they tromp off the stage, looking pleased with themselves.

The next phase of the competition uses a different type of cube, one that looks more like if a ball had flat sides. It looks more difficult than the pyramid one did, but now that I know what to expect, my eyes dart around the auditorium to assess how the other attendees are reacting to what's happening onstage.

The adults in the crowd are glancing between the stage and the kids sitting around them. These kids must be the siblings, and they're definitely not paying any attention, mostly playing on computer tablets.

I kind of feel bad for the competitors. They're doing this impressive thing, and nobody really cares.

After a couple more events, though, I begin to understand why even the families are zoning out a bit. Watching kids solve these weird not-cubes isn't exactly riveting entertainment outside of the handful of seconds that their fingers are flying over the puzzle.

My own attention begins to wander a bit, and I notice a group of four guys sitting in the back of the auditorium on the far side from me. I wonder what they're doing here. They look about my age, so they can't have any kids in the competition. All but one of them are in T-shirts with their feet resting on the seat backs in front of them as if they're super comfortable in this type of venue. The fourth guy is in a dark button-up and sitting up perfectly straight. Maybe they're the older brothers of some of the competitors?

I can't get a good look from this far away, but they're kind of cute from what I can tell. And I can't resist checking them out. I'm only human.

I must have been staring, because one of them catches my eye, then swats the guy next to him and nods in my direction.

My head snaps back to the stage so fast I'll probably have whiplash. I'm supposed to be here in a professional capacity, not checking out hot guys. But I've been working so much lately, taking a full load of credits and putting in extra hours beyond what's required at the *Tribune* for my internship. I decide I'm allowed a moment of weakness to acknowledge a group of attractive men.

If I had met them at a party, I might have tossed them a wink or a wave in hopes that one of them would cross the room to talk to me. Not that I go to parties very often. That's more Ronnie's territory, although she has managed to drag me along to a few when I've had some extra time between work and studying.

I sneak another glance, and they're all watching me now. The way they're staring sends a shiver down my spine. Especially because they're clearly talking softly to each other. And I'm certain they're talking about me.

"All right folks!" Mr. Kellan's voice jolts me back to the competition and what I'm supposed to be doing. "We're going to take a thirty-minute lunch break. When we come back, we'll have the Skewb, Square-1, and three-by-three-by-three events."

I stand and hurry out of the auditorium, ready to sit in my car with nobody around for a bit. Unfortunately, I ruin my moment of escape by glancing one last time over my shoulder to see if any of the guys I was checking out is coming over to my side of the auditorium to chat me up.

They aren't. They're slowly filing out of the other side of the auditorium, and each of them is solving a Rubik's Cube, which answers the question of why they seemed so comfortable here. Maybe they're coaches or something.

I should head back and interview a few more kids, but I just can't handle the thought of more one-word non-answers to my questions. So I head out to the car to have a few minutes to myself and eat the lunch I packed this morning. Besides, as much as I want to do my best work for this assignment, the bare minimum is probably still more than my editor expects. There's no reason to force a bunch of kids to talk to me when they clearly don't want to.

Chapter Two

As soon as I shut myself in the car and crank the heat, I pull out my phone and call my roommate.

Ronnie answers on the second ring. "Hey, bitch."

"Hey to you too." I roll my eyes and put her on speaker.

"How's it going being a big-time reporter?"

I laugh, but there's no humor in it. "It's not. This competition is tinier than I thought it'd be. I'll have to keep my article short if I don't want to annoy Carl by making him have to cut it down." Licking the inside of my yogurt lid, I look around the parking lot, but no one else has come out here. "Though I have to admit, these kids are pretty impressive. They're solving these puzzles in like ten seconds or less."

"At least it's good practice, and maybe you can use it for class or something too." Ronnie sounds far away, like she's trying to multitask in our tiny dorm room.

"What are you doing?"

"Painting my nails. I'm hoping Trevor calls me later."

"Make him take you out on a date first this time," I say. "Anything other than just taking you straight back to his place."

"You're so boring." Ronnie is probably sticking out her tongue at me, which makes me smile. "But lucky for you, I love you anyway."

I consider telling her about the four guys I was checking out inside, but there's no real point. There's not really anything to tell.

"No, you're lucky I love you." I finish my yogurt and stuff the trash back into my lunch bag. "I'll see you when I get home."

"Hopefully you won't." Ronnie giggles and hangs up.

As I get out of the car, I can't help but smile. I definitely got lucky when I was paired to live with Ronnie last year as a freshman. We had immediately become best friends, and it'd only made sense to continue our awesome duo situation into our sophomore year.

When I head back inside, I return to my same seat in the auditorium. Partly because it really is a good seat, but in the back of my head is the little thought that this way those four guys will know exactly where to find me if they want to.

"I hope everyone had a good lunch," says Mr. Kellan after taking his place at the podium again—from the correct side of the stage this time. "Our first event of the afternoon will be the Skewb."

The last few events before lunch looked like normal Rubik's Cubes, just with more than three rows, but these are weird ones again. They're almost normal, but with pieces randomly poking out, making them less cube-like. The following event, which Mr. Kellan calls "Square-1," is similar.

"All right folks, it's time. The events you've all been waiting for. The traditional three-by-three-by-three cube events, beginning with the one-handed solve."

The competitors file out onto the stage and take their

seats, and I sit up a little straighter when I see two of the guys from earlier walk out. They're the oldest competitors in the group by a good amount; the others look to be in middle school or younger.

"Judges, you may begin inspection when your contestants are ready."

All of the competitors grab their cubes, which are the typical Rubik's Cubes that I'd been expecting to see all day, and start their inspections, then set their timers and begin solving. I'm nearly holding my breath, watching them twist the cubes one-handed with such speed that their fingers are a blur.

The guys win first and second place, followed by a boy who can't be older than nine. They're all going to Nationals, and I learn that the tall guy with dark hair in a button-down is named Elliot Carter and the blond with red-framed glasses is Felix Grey.

For having just won their event, they don't look overwhelmed or excited, only determined and certain.

Next up is the blindfolded round, and the other two guys are in this one. They're once again the oldest guys up there, but this time it looks like a few of the other kids are at least in high school.

As soon as they have completed their inspections, they pick up their blindfolds from the table and tie them around their heads, and the judges confirm that the blindfolds are completely covering their eyes before allowing the competitors to set their timers.

As the competitors begin solving the puzzles, I'm in awe. I'm not even sure how they're doing it. They're not as quick as the other rounds, which makes sense given the additional challenge of the blindfolds, but it's pretty close.

One of the guys in the group I'd been checking out finishes first and the other finishes third. I note down their names, Lukas Wagner and Sebastian Lange, too. For the article, of course. Absolutely not because I want to cyberstalk them later and find out everything I can about these good-looking Rubik's Cube wizards.

The next event is the 3x3x3 individual category. The guys don't compete in this one, which surprises me. And disappoints me, a little.

"Our final event for today's competition is the team relay," says Mr. Kellan as covered cubes are placed on each table. "Teams, if you could please come to the stage."

All four of the guys enter alongside three other teams of four. I'm certain they'll feel how hard I'm staring at them and try unsuccessfully to make myself look at something—anything—else, but they don't appear to realize I'm out here ogling them. Which is both disappointing and reassuring.

The teams all sit down at the small tables, one team per row, one cube per person. The inspection stage goes exactly as it has for all of the events, each competitor quickly looking over their cube before setting it down and placing their hands palms-down on the table, the timers setting to zero.

Elliot, the dark-haired guy who had taken first place in his solo round, is the first up from the guys' team, solving his cube in seconds. As soon as he drops the cube on the table, Lukas grabs his own and his fingers begin to fly over it. Felix goes third, and tensions are high when Sebastian snatches up his cube at the exact same time the fourth member of one of the other teams does.

I hold my breath until Sebastian slams his solved cube down on the table a literal second before his competitor. The other two teams finish moments later. But it seems in these competitions, seconds matter. A lot.

The judges do whatever it is they do on their clipboards and deliver their papers to the podium.

"Congratulations to our winners!" Mr. Kellan holds his arm out to indicate the guys as the audience, half of whom have already begun to gather their things to leave, applauds. "Not just in this event, but throughout the day. Let's have all of today's winners up here onstage."

As the winners from each event file up onto the stage and stand in a disorganized clump, Karen comes back out with a box of prize ribbons. Mr. Kellan reads out the winners' names again and passes the ribbons out, gifting each competitor a handshake as well.

"Thank you again for coming out to support our competitors, and we hope to see you all at ICF Nationals to support our solvers there as well," he says. "Let's give all our winners and competitors a final round of applause."

We all clap, louder than any of the previous times, but there's still not very many of us in the auditorium and it's a big space to fill with our tiny sound. Especially because some of the parents get distracted by the little kids they're sitting with, who are tired of being quiet and cooped up inside for so long, and have to abandon their applause in favor of sibling wrangling.

Slowly, I stand and follow everyone else out of the auditorium and into the front foyer, where they mill around, congratulating the winners and consoling those who didn't place. It must be hard for some of the participants to not win, since they're so young.

I eye the front doors and consider slipping out, but I need to at least attempt to interview those four guys. Not only did they all win, but they're also the oldest competitors here. Surely there's a story there, even if it's not a very exciting one. Plus, if there does end up being room for a quote or two in the article, I haven't gotten anything from any of the kids that I can use. Probably the older guys will be a little more forthcoming. As much as I don't want to end up embarrassing myself after they caught me staring earlier, I need to do this if I'm going to write this story.

They're huddled in a corner with well-wishers surrounding them. Standing back, I watch how they handle interacting with these people. They don't shrink back like some of the kids I spoke with, but they don't encourage anyone to stay and chat. They're not even smiling, as if their win here today doesn't even matter to them. They just nod their acknowledgement of the congratulations, hands busy twisting their cubes.

I'm staring again, and Lukas notices. Just like before, as soon as he does, he nudges Felix, and before I realize it the others are clued in as well.

Well, now I really have no choice. I walk over to the guys as everyone else drifts away. I force myself to go into professional mode. I'm a reporter and this is my job. This isn't personal, this is business.

Even though they're even cuter up close than they were from a distance.

"Hi, I'm Rebecca Flynn, a reporter with the *Sunshine Tribune*," I say, sticking out my hand to none of them in particular.

The guys all look to each other as if waiting for one of them to make a decision for the whole group who will respond to me.

Lukas finally reaches out and briefly shakes my hand. His long fingers envelop mine for the briefest second before letting go. The others just watch this exchange, still fiddling with their cubes. I wonder if they even know they're doing it, or if it's an unconscious habit.

"You look too young to be a reporter," says Lukas, his hand returning to his own cube.

I grimace. "Okay, you caught me. I'm an intern with the

Tribune through my university. They needed someone to cover this event, and I volunteered."

I don't want to make them feel like no one wanted to come and watch today's competition, even though that's the truth. The lack of crowd here is sad enough that they surely already suspect the full-time reporters weren't exactly fighting each other for the assignment.

When none of them says anything, the awkwardness of this exchange creeps over me. I push it aside and pull out my little notepad. "Would you be willing to give me a quick interview? I talked to some of the other competitors backstage, but didn't really get much from them."

They all glance at each other again, shrugging.

"Sure," says Sebastian.

"Great!" I beam at them, pen poised. "So how does it feel to qualify for Nationals?"

"This will be our tenth year competing at Nationals," says Elliot.

"Oh, wow, that's a lot." He didn't answer my question, but now I know why they don't seem more excited to have won. Going for your tenth time must be a lot different than winning and going for the first time. Maybe I should have asked their background before I started in on the questionnaire I'd prepared last night.

"Then it'll be our tenth time at Worlds, although it should be our eleventh, but Lukas's fingers were stiff last time," says Felix.

Lukas's face darkens. "It was the cube, I'm telling you," he grumbles.

"It was regulation and you know it," says Felix.

"The past doesn't matter." Sebastian interrupts before they really get going with what I suspect is an argument they've had many times before. "This is our year."

"So last year was the only time you didn't make it all the

way to Worlds?" I clarify. That explains why I hadn't seen their names or faces during my quick research last night. I'd only looked up who the winners were last year.

They nod solemnly, but I swear they're spinning the rows and columns of their cubes with more ferocity.

If their annoyance is with me, I don't want to force them to talk, even though I'd like to learn a bit more about them. And not because they're hot. I just think my article could use a bit more substance beyond a list of winners, that's all.

"I just have a few more questions, if you don't mind."

Two kids choose that moment to start chasing each other through the crowd, their screams echoing off the tall ceilings of the foyer. We all wince at the auditory assault.

"This way," says Lukas, leading us through the double doors to the backstage hallway where some of the volunteers are packing up. It's not quiet, but it's not nearly as loud.

"This is perfect." I take a seat at one of the round tables so it'll be easier to take notes. Volunteers are stacking chairs and folding up the other tables, but I don't think we'll be here long, so I hope we aren't in the way.

The guys sit too, and I can't help but blush as my knees bump into Sebastian's below the table. He doesn't move away, but I shift so we're no longer making contact ... even though I very much would not mind if his leg continued to press against mine. They all rest their forearms on the table, and this table is so much smaller than I realized. Maybe we should have stayed standing. Our hands all rest so close together, they're practically touching.

They're still fidgeting with their cubes, but I can feel how heavy and direct their attention on me is. It's a little disconcerting. I'm the type of girl who fades into the background and likes it that way. I'm not used to being anyone's focus, much less having the complete attention of four good-looking guys.

"Okay, ask your questions." Lukas sets his cube in front of Felix to his right and takes the cube from Sebastian on his left. Felix passes his to Elliot.

Elliot sets his cube in front of me.

I stare at it, unsure what to do. Do I pass it to Sebastian on my right? The table is so small that if Elliot had wanted Sebastian to have it, he could easily have reached over my notebook and set it in front of him. Surely he can't mean for *me* to solve it. I'm suddenly buzzing with nerves. I look at my notebook sitting under the cube, but the words on the page blur together. I can't remember a single question I have written down to ask.

"I ... don't know how to solve it," I say finally, sure they'll laugh at me or get up and leave in disgust at my ineptitude.

All four of them look back at me, obviously confused.

"It's easy," says Lukas. "There is a solution to each pattern, so you simply assess what the configuration is and then apply that solution."

"That doesn't sound easy at all," I say, trying to sound unbothered that I've clearly just failed some sort of test.

Sebastian snags the cube from in front of me and solves it slowly. Well, slowly for them. It's probably nearly a minute or so, but he's being very deliberate with his motions, tilting the cube towards me so I can watch each twist and click. It's kind of sweet, that he's trying to show me how to do it, even if I still have no idea how he's doing it.

The others are also solving theirs slowly, giving me the chance to watch and magically deduce how it's done. Like it's that simple.

Clearing my throat, I pull my focus away from how smoothly their fingers manipulate the cubes and redirect my gaze to my notebook, forcing my brain to make sense of the words.

The questions I'd written down last night all seem so ordinary now. *How long have you been solving cube puzzles competitively? What's your favorite event in the competition?* These may have been perfectly fine questions if I was still interviewing twelve-year-olds with zero interest in me or my article, but they seem silly and amateurish to ask these guys.

"So, the four of you were the oldest people in today's competition," I hear myself say. Why did I say that? It wasn't even a question. They stare at me, waiting to see if I'm going to ask them something or just keep stating the obvious and wasting their time.

I've got to get it together.

"Do you know why that is?" I add.

"When you're young, you have lots of time to practice," says Lukas. "When you're older, you have more commitments."

"We're still in college, so we still have a little bit of time to practice, but this will be our last year probably," says Felix.

"Oh? What college?" They look my age, but I hadn't put it together that they would also be in college. Maybe even my college. I don't know very many people around campus, unless they're in my classes. I don't have the social battery that my roommate does.

"MIT," says Lukas. "And you?"

"BU." I'm not sure if it's smart to give them this information—it's definitely not professional—but what could the harm be? It's a big campus and it's not like I told them what dorm I'm in. I'm just making conversation.

I ignore the little thrill that runs through me at the idea of these four guys tracking me down and showing up at my dorm. I'm supposed to be working right now, and anyway, who fantasizes about four strangers stalking them online and knocking on their door unannounced? *Get it together, Rebecca.*

"And what do competitive Rubik's Cubers typically study?" I'm not flirting, I'm researching. Asking questions. Like the journalist that I am.

Okay, maybe I'm flirting a little. Which is completely unlike me. Ronnie must be rubbing off on me after a year and a half of us being joined at the hip.

"Not all cubes are Rubik's Cubes," Sebastian says. His tone tells me that this is not the first time he's had to correct someone, and every time he has to say it, it weighs on him. "It's a brand name. Like Kleenex."

"Oh."

"We study different types of mathematics. I do applied," Lukas tells me.

"Theoretical," says Elliot.

"Pure," Felix mumbles.

"Philosophical," says Sebastian.

I wasn't aware there were so many different types of math. I decide not to delve deeper into that topic, lest I disappoint them again. "You must get sick of each other, practicing for these competitions together and taking classes together."

"We also live together," says Felix.

"That's a lot of togetherness."

Lukas shrugs as if to say, *This is totally normal for us, and we don't care if you think it's weird.* "We like to share."

Okay, living with Ronnie has absolutely been affecting me, because that statement combined with the way their fingers are moving so quickly over the cubes sends my thoughts to a place that is for sure not anywhere they'd have gone a year ago and should not be going in the middle of an interview. I'm sure Lukas didn't mean it like that at all, and my face heats as I shove the thoughts back into the depths of my psyche to be explored later. Much later. Without an audience.

Or never. Never is probably the better option.

Their cubes go silent, and I realize that I've just been sitting here frozen, my impure thoughts probably written all over my bright red face.

"Did you want a picture?" asks Lukas.

"A picture?" I'm struggling to breathe and pull my mind out of the gutter. I'm not sure how I ended up there. I make a mental note to tune Ronnie out the next time she starts detailing her sexcapades.

"Of us with our ribbons," he says. "For your paper."

"Oh! Yes! That's a great idea." I stand and pull my phone out of my purse, glad to have something to do that doesn't involve making a fool of myself. "Why don't the four of you stand against that wall there and hold up your ribbons."

They line up, shoulders touching, and it's weird how much they're all dressed alike. It makes me wonder if they share a single closet too. Graphic tees, jeans, and Chucks. Although Elliot in his button-down kind of ruins that theory.

"One, two, three." None of them are smiling, but at least they're all making eye contact with the camera. I still doubt my editor will dedicate more than two inches of column space to this event, and he definitely won't include a picture. But they don't need to know that. They just won the qualifiers for Nationals. They may not seem like they care, but I'm sure they do, and I don't want to put a damper on their day.

"Are you going to write an article about Nationals for the *Tribune* too?" asks Felix.

"I don't know," I tell him. "Where are Nationals happening?"

"New York," he says.

"Oh. Probably not, then." I bite my lip, feeling bad that I'm disappointing them when I just made an effort *not* to do that. Which is crazy, because I don't even know these guys. I'm not sure why I care so much about how I'm making them feel. "I don't think I could convince my editor to let me travel outside of Boston."

"They were in Boston last year, so we wouldn't have had to travel if we'd been able to go." Felix shoots a glare at Lukas, who returns the look.

"That's a shame," says Elliot, ignoring them both. "It would have been nice to see a friendly face in the audience."

Now I feel even worse, but that stupid little thrill runs through me once more. *They want to see me again.* "I mean, I suppose I could ask," I offer.

"If you want to," says Lukas. His watch beeps, but he turns it off quickly and tosses a hand up in a half-wave. "We'll see you around, Rebecca Flynn."

The guys all disappear back through the double doors, and I look around at the now-empty backstage space. The volunteers have all left, so it's just me and a bunch of stacked chairs.

I take an uncertain step after them. That whole last bit of the conversation happened so quick. If they'd stuck around, I would have shoved my sort-of-dirty half-thoughts to the recesses of my mind and come up with more questions.

It wasn't even a very good goodbye. *"We'll see you around, Rebecca Flynn"*? See me where? When? At Nationals, maybe, if I can get my editor to let me cover it— which is truly doubtful—but was that all he meant? Or is the knowledge that I attend BU actually enough for them to find me on campus? They're math guys from MIT, for all I know they have some sort of elite stalking program on their computers, and my name and college is more than enough to track me down.

I'm being ridiculous.

I straighten my back and follow the guys through the doors. I'm a professional, representing my newspaper. I need to act like it.

When I return to the foyer, the guys are nowhere to be seen. In fact, most of the people are gone, with the exception of the woman from check-in and Karen, who are chatting as they stack plastic bins into a wagon.

I head outside to my car. Ronnie will be out with Trevor by the time I get home, so I'll be able to grab a snack and get started on this article. I shove all thoughts of handsome cubers with their fast hands and awkward goodbyes out of my head and crank the volume on my favorite playlist, psyching myself up to write the best article on competitive speedcubing that the *Sunshine Tribune* has ever seen.

Chapter Three

My article is fantastic. I spend the whole next day drafting it, and it turns out exactly as I'd hoped. I even wear my lucky flowy floral skirt to work today to get my editor's feedback. I'm sure he'll have some feedback and tweaks to tighten it up a little bit, but I'd expect no less. Carl won a Pulitzer Prize for a piece he did on the housing market crash of '08 so I'd be shocked if he's not able to make my article even better.

Straightening my shoulders, I walk right up to his office door and knock. This is the official beginning of my reporting career. I'm about to have my first article accepted into a real city press.

"Come in!"

I take a mental snapshot as I push the door open. I want to remember everything about this moment. The stacks of papers nearly overflowing his desk. The faint smell of cigarette smoke. The bitter smell of coffee in the air. Even the way Carl doesn't even acknowledge me when I walk in. Once he realizes it's me, the intern whose story about the cubing competition surprised him with its attention to detail and thoughtful execution, he'll be delighted that I'm here, and I want to remember the way his expression transforms.

"Good morning, Carl," I say, grateful that my voice doesn't shake even though my hands do. "I just wanted to let you know that I emailed over the story I wrote about the Rubik's Cube competition last night. Just so it doesn't get lost in your inbox." I eye the chair in front of his desk, considering sitting down, but there's a smear of something that might be ink from an exploded pen and might be ketchup on the seat. Whatever it is, it looks like it's dried, but I don't want to risk getting my skirt dirty. I guess I'll just stand here, awkwardly hovering, waiting for the praise that I'm sure is coming.

"The what?" Carl glances up, his forehead wrinkling in confusion.

I remember what Sebastian said about not all cubes being Rubik's Cubes. "The speedcubing competition. The story I suggested Friday? That you assigned me?"

Probably he's just distracted by whatever he was doing when I came in. Any moment he's going to remember my article and recall that he read it when it arrived in his email last night, and that it's fantastic. That it should be top of the fold. Maybe not on the front page, but the sixth wouldn't be too bad. I'd take that. It is my first piece, after all, and it was a small competition. I'm not so delusional as to think an article about a local cubing event would be more important than something like a fire or a little kid who saved his elderly neighbor by calling 911 when they had a heart attack at his front-yard lemonade stand.

I'm lost in these thoughts when Carl, who had returned his attention to his computer, looks up again to see me still waiting. "What are you still doing in here?"

"I ..." My hand slowly raises, about to point at the

computer, where my article is waiting for him. I'm revising my earlier assessment from "read my article immediately" to "is going to read my article now", since it's clear he hasn't actually read it yet. If he had, he'd be offering gentle critique sandwiched in praise.

"Go get me a coffee." Carl shoves his empty mug across the desk at me and turns his attention back to his computer.

Okay. He just needs a little jolt of energy to revive him. He wants to start my article with an awake brain so he can devote his full focus to every word I've written. I take the mug and scurry to the break room.

The coffee pot is empty. Because of course it is. Pulling out a new filter and pouring in the grounds, I grind my teeth a little. Given the number of journalists here who drink coffee and how many degrees they have between them, you'd think they would know how to recognize an empty carafe and brew a new pot. I feel like I do it way more than everyone else. In fact, I know I do. I can't remember the last time I saw anyone else rinse the pot, dump the used grounds, or hit the start button on the machine.

"We're out of creamer," says Brad, coming into the break room and shouldering past me to move the pot out of the way so the fresh brew drips right into his cup. There's a sizzle and the smell of burning coffee as a few drops hit the burner before he gets his mug situated.

I wish I was more comfortable standing my ground and not letting him just move me aside like a misplaced semicolon, but I know it's not worth it. I'm just the intern, and I don't want to make waves with the actual staff. I open the cupboard below the coffee pot, where the spare supplies like filters and creamer live. I've never seen anyone else open it, so I don't trust that Brad actually looked for more creamer before announcing we were out, but he's right. The box of extra creamer is empty. I chide myself for my uncharitable thoughts towards Brad. I should be nicer. He probably already saw earlier that there wasn't any in the cabinet, and he probably doesn't know who orders it to tell them. He's a big shot reporter whose story is nearly always front page, above the fold. He's got more important things to worry about than where to find coffee creamer.

Hoping Brad puts the pot back when he's done filling his own cup, I grab the empty creamer box from the cabinet, toss it into a trash can, and head down the hall to the office admin's desk.

"Hey, Ashley."

"What can I do for you?" Ashley doesn't look away from her computer screen as she keeps clicking away on her mouse, but at least her words and tone aren't harsh. Ashley is always super busy, but she doesn't take it out on me like some of the rest of the staff do.

"Do we have any more creamer?" I drum my fingers on the top of the cubicle divider that gives her some semblance of privacy from the rest of the office.

"Loading dock," she says quickly, grabbing a green folder from her desk and handing me a paper from it. "Haven't had a chance to go grab it yet."

"I'll go pick it up for you." It's not how I imagined I'd be spending my morning, but what else am I going to say? She's already given me the printed ticket to claim the shipment, so she clearly expects me to go get it.

By the time I make it back to the break room, there is a coffee spill on the counter that wasn't there when I left, but at least Brad put the carafe back. I refill the drawer with creamer pods and put the rest of the box in the cupboard before washing my editor's gross mug out and filling it with fresh coffee with exactly one creamer and two sugars.

"Took you long enough," Carl says by way of thanks as I set the cup on the edge of his desk.

I hesitate before turning and heading for the door. He had plenty of time while I was making coffee and fetching creamer to read my article, but if he had, he'd say something, right?

I've got one foot out in the hallway when I stop and turn back to him. "When you get a chance to look at my story, I'd love to hear any feedback you have." There. That doesn't assume anything, but makes it clear that I want to hear what he has to say.

"It's in your inbox."

"Oh. Okay, thank you!" I force myself not to run back to my cubicle to check my email. There it is. I click on it and read what he wrote.

"Edits attached. Fix it and send it to copy."

My hands shake as I open the attachment and see what he meant by "edits attached." He used track changes, and the page is mostly red. No, it's almost entirely red. He's crossed out practically everything I wrote, distilling the piece I toiled over down to two sentences: *Local International Cubing Federation competition winners include MIT students Elliot Carter, Lukas Wagner, Felix Grey, and Sebastian Lange. They will advance to Nationals.* He also deleted my name and left a comment: *No byline needed.*

Tears sting my eyes. I'd thought my article was good. Not hard-hitting news, but a solid community piece. Surely it was at least worth keeping *some* of it. He didn't even leave a single sentence intact, he just mashed pieces of a few of them together to get those two measly lines that barely even acknowledge that the competition happened, much less offer anything to indicate that it showcased some truly incredible puzzle solving by a bunch of very smart people, many of whom are local kids.

Those kids deserve more than two lines that don't even mention them. I go back to Carl's office, not even knocking this time before walking through the half-open door.

"Carl, do you have any feedback on my article?" I ask. "So I can do better for the next one? Obviously I wrote more than you were looking for, but—"

He sighs and leans back in his chair, exasperated with me. I don't think he has any right to be, I'm just asking for guidance from the person who is supposed to be guiding me in this internship, but clearly he's got no interest in mentoring me in this moment. "No one cares about some stupid Rubik's Cube competition. Frankly, the fact that we're even announcing the winners is overkill, but you told them we're running an article so now we have to print something."

"It doesn't even name all the winners anymore, though. Most of the competitors were kids, I thought it was a good community feature," I say. "That's why I took the initiative …"

"I want initiative in filling the coffee pot and helping out around here, not stepping into roles you have no business being in. I have real reporters to write the stories, I need you to get the coffee and file paperwork. I don't recall even telling you that you could go to this thing."

"You said 'fine,' so I thought—"

"You thought wrong. Now go accept my changes to make it into an announcement and send it to the copy desk like I told you to. Or is that too much for you to handle?" His voice has gotten louder with each sentence, and I'm sure everyone in the office can hear him.

"I can do that," I mumble, turning away before I do something to further humiliate myself, like burst into tears. I shuffle back to my desk, face flaming and eyes burning. I can hear the other journalists snickering around me.

I accept Carl's changes and send the sad little non-article over to the copy desk. I can't bring myself to completely delete my original story, though. I move it, along with the photo of the four relay winners, into the "Research" folder on my desktop. Maybe the next intern who sits here will see it and think it's worth reading, at least.

Chapter Four

My dorm room door flies open and Ronnie comes in like a whirlwind, blond waves haloing her head and her signature perfume clinging to her clothes. I drop my phone on the quilt next to me so she doesn't see the picture of the hot cubers that I've been staring at. I can't get them out of my head, and I don't know why. No guy has ever had a hold on me like this before.

"Were you staring at your phone again?" Ronnie kicks her shoes off and climbs up onto my bed, bouncing up and down on the mattress in her socked feet. "What is in that magic little box that is sucking up all your attention?" She gasps and claps her hands together. "Is it a guy? Do you have a secret boyfriend you're texting?"

"What? No! Nothing like that," I insist, then let out a groan when she pins me with a look that says she knows I'm keeping something from her. She's caught me staring at my phone all week and has threatened to pry it out of my hand so she can see what has me so captivated.

"I'm going to get it out of you at some point. You might as well make it easy on yourself." Ronnie drops to her knees and sits facing me. "Come on, talk to me about it. You've been more miserable than usual this week."

"I haven't been miserable." I can't make eye contact, instead pretending to be very interested in a loose thread on my bedspread.

"Clearly you are if other people are asking me if your mom died or something," she argues.

"I haven't been that bad."

If I don't give Ronnie something, she's going to keep pestering until I confess that I've been staring at the photo of the Rubik's Cube team on my phone, daydreaming about my article having been a hit, Carl sending me to cover Nationals, and them looking out into the audience and seeing me, their faces breaking into big grins as they wave from the stage, then leaping off the stage after they win and wrapping me up in a huge group hug before taking me up to their hotel room to ravish me. And I am absolutely not going to tell her all of that, because it's weird and pathetic, and I don't even know why I keep doing it, so I lean over and grab my laptop off my desk.

"It's not that big a deal," I tell her. "It's just my article from last weekend." I pull up the story and hand the computer to Ronnie.

Ronnie tilts the screen so she can read it easier, nodding as her eyes scan the article.

"This is really good. It actually makes a Rubik's Cube competition sound fun to watch, which is something I never in a million years thought I'd say." She hands the laptop back to me. "What's the problem?"

"My editor ripped it to shreds." I open a browser window and tap out the address for the *Tribune*. The full URL for the final version of the cubing story auto-populates from my browsing history, and I hand the computer back to her. "This is the published version."

Ronnie's eyes widen as she reads the two sentences that made the cut. "Yikes."

"I didn't even get a byline for it," I groan, falling back against my pillow and flopping my arm over my eyes. I don't even want to see my ceiling right now. I need darkness to wallow in my failure.

"Well, that's not fair! You did all that work, suggesting the story and going out there and spending all day at the competition and interviewing all those people. And your original article is good! They should be thanking you." Ronnie closes the laptop and slides it back onto my desk, her eyes dark with indignation.

"Welcome to the world of unpaid internships," I mutter. "And the way it's going right now, I'm not sure they'll let me come back for a full reporting internship next year. Or even give me a good reference letter."

Maybe I should start looking for a backup plan. I just can't see myself graduating in two years with a job offer from the *Tribune* like I've been imagining since I was accepted to the internship. I've only just started my sophomore year, so there's plenty of time for me to figure something else out, but still. I feel the pressure.

"Okay, first, your editor is an ass," says Ronnie, holding up a finger.

"Carl is a Pulitzer Prize-winning journalist," I counter.

"Doesn't matter. Still an ass," she says, shaking her head. She puts up another finger. "And second, we need to get you out of this funk. Get up." She climbs off my bed and goes to her wardrobe, rifling through it and pulling out dresses and tops.

"No thanks," I tell her. "I like where I am. It's comfortable."

"Nope, we're going out to a party, and we're going to have fun." Ronnie tosses an armload of clothes on my bed, then disappears back into the depths of her wardrobe. "We'll get you all un-funkified, and then we're going to come up with an awesome plan for you to show your asshat of a boss that he's a fool to keep using you as nothing but a coffee runner."

"A plan? Like what, hacking into the paper's website and replacing the online version of the article with my original?"

Ronnie spins around and points at me with both hands. "Yes! That! Do that!"

I pull the pillow over my face to hide from my roommate and her criminal intents. "Absolutely not. Even if I knew how, it's probably a felony."

I hear her deflate. "Yeah. Probably." She bounces back almost immediately, though. "But there's got to be something you can do to show him what he's missing. Get up and let's find you something to wear, and then we'll go to the party, and we'll let our good friend White Claw help us figure something out."

"It's not like I'm going to get a second chance on the article," I insist. "And he's definitely not going to let me go to any other events to represent the paper. In his mind, he didn't even sanction me going to this event. Apparently when he said 'fine, whatever,' he didn't mean 'fine, whatever, you can cover it if you want,' he meant 'okay, I heard you, stop talking.'"

"Well, we'll just have to find you something else to write about," says Ronnie, yanking the pillow off my face.

"Anything he's going to like is already being assigned to the staff reporters," I argue. "That's why I suggested this one, and why he hated it. Said Rubik's Cube competitions aren't interesting and nobody cares." I reach for the pillow, but she's keeping it just out of reach.

"Okay, enough shop talk. You need to shake all of the

woe-is-me off and I know exactly what will do it." She crosses to my dresser and starts shuffling through drawers. I watch her, assuming she's looking for something skimpy and sexy she can force me into, although I don't know why she thinks she'll find anything like that in my stuff. She knows me better than that.

Ugh. I really don't love the idea of going out. I want to keep wallowing. And not wearing lip gloss or whatever Ronnie will slather all over my face. And daydreaming about the hot cubing team being glad to see me again and ... I don't even know what comes next. I've only ever dated one guy, in high school, and all we did was kiss a couple times. I mean, I understand how sex works, I've watched porn a couple times and it's not like I've never touched myself. But when it comes to this fantasy, the part where we go up to their room for "I just won a cubing competition" sex is fuzzy. Would it be all four of them, or just one? Which one would I want it to be? If it's all of them, is it all at once or one at a time? I'm out of my depth here, so things always just sort of fade to black once they take my hands and lead me into their hotel room.

"Aha!" Ronnie reaches into the back of my sock drawer and whips out a folded piece of pink paper. "I knew you'd kept this!"

My stomach sinks and I fly off the bed, grabbing for the paper, but she holds it out of my reach. "Ronnie, give it back."

"I saw it in there when I borrowed your fuzzy socks the other week and knew exactly what it was. It's the only time I've ever seen you write on pink paper."

"I don't even know why I have it still, just throw it away."

She points a finger at me with the hand that isn't holding the paper high above her head. "You want to complete this list, don't you, you little minx. Why else would you have kept it?"

"I forgot about it."

"You brought it with you when you moved home over the summer, and then brought it back when you moved into this dorm. There's no way you'd have done that if you'd forgotten about it."

She's right, but I refuse to admit that the list of sexual acts we thought we should attempt before we graduated that we'd written up at the beginning of freshman year is not only a thing I kept on purpose, but a thing I take out and read over at least once a month, wishing I knew how to go about checking any of the items off. I'm interested in sex, but not enough to break my no-dating rule, and I don't want to randomly hook up with guys I meet at parties and never see again like Ronnie and her friends have done. I don't feel comfortable giving that degree of power to some drunk idiot I just met. What I really need is a fuck buddy, someone I trust enough to not hurt or embarrass me, but who understands that the sex does not mean we're in a relationship. But where the hell would I even begin to find someone to fill that role? I don't get out enough for that.

"Let's go to this party tonight, and we'll find you a cute guy, and you can do a couple of these things and take your mind off that loser boss of yours." She scans down the list. "It doesn't even have to be anything too major. Look, you've got 'make out' on here, and 'dry humping,' you could do both of those with some random nice-looking guy tonight and check the boxes and never have to think about him again."

"I don't want to dry hump some random drunk boy at a party tonight. Or any night."

"Well, you're not sitting here feeling sorry for yourself." She folds the list again and tucks it into my purse. "You're coming to this party with me, and you're bringing the list just in case you meet someone who's worth dry humping, and if you don't then you don't. No big deal."

I hate that I'm actually considering her suggestion.

"Come on, Becks," wheedles Ronnie when I say nothing. "Please?"

I can feel myself being pulled into this. If I keep fighting it, it'll only be worse when I do eventually cave. I sigh and shake my head in acquiescence. "Where's the party?"

Her eyes light up. She knows she's got me. "Over near MIT. Those girls down the hall, Callie and Reyna, are going too and said we can catch a lift with them, but they're so annoying. You have to come. Even if you completely ignore the list and don't talk to a single guy, you can't leave me alone with them."

My ears perk up when she says "MIT." That's where the cubing guys said they go to college. They didn't seem like the type to go out to parties, and even if they were, there are probably a lot of parties at MIT on a Saturday night. But what if …?

Also, I know Ronnie isn't going to let up. Sometimes she does, if she has other friends to go with, but if she thinks the girls she's going with are annoying, she's going to push until I give in. May as well not drag it out any longer.

"Okay, fine. Let's go to a party, I guess," I tell her. "But you do not get to try to find me someone to make out with. That is not why I'm agreeing to this."

"Yay!" Ronnie jumps up, clapping, and dances back over to our wardrobes. "Now we just need to find you something awesome to wear."

"Can't I just wear this?" If Ronnie dresses me, I'm going to be tottering around in heels and a miniskirt, completely miserable. If I have to go to this party, I don't want to spend all evening tugging on my clothes and trying not to break an ankle.

"There is literally an iron line down the front of those pants, so no." Ronnie pulls out a tiny black dress from her wardrobe. "How about this?"

"I'd like to keep breathing tonight." I pull myself out of bed and join her at the wardrobes, reaching into mine and pulling out a dress with a bold sunflower pattern all over it. It's not really a winter dress, but it's one of my favorites, and I can always pair it with a cardigan and tights to make it less summery. "What about this dress? It's bright and fun."

She wrinkles her nose. "Maybe if we were going to a family barbecue. We're trying to attract guys tonight, not drive them away. You need to look sexy."

"Fine. How about this?" I reach into the back and pull out a pair of tight black pants Ronnie made me buy last year, "because you need *something* besides khakis and pencil skirts." I never did end up wearing them to anything. The tags are still on them.

I know the pants aren't the vibe she's going for, so I'll have to compromise a little on something else, but a) it's freezing out, and b) I want to keep some of my dignity tonight. Even if the only reason I am going to this party at all is to maybe see a group of guys I've only met once and who probably won't be there.

"Let me wear these, and I'll let you pick out the shirt to go with them," I tell her.

"Not bad. I could allow it if you paired them with ..." Ronnie steps over to her own wardrobe and pulls out a slinky, sparkly pink tank top. "This."

I grit my teeth because I don't do sparkly. It draws way too much attention. But if I don't want to freeze in a miniskirt in January, I need to let her pick the top.

"Deal. But I'm wearing my own shoes." I grab a pair of black ballet flats out of the wardrobe.

It's Ronnie's turn to sulk. "Fine. At least in those you're short enough for most guys to get a good glimpse of your cleavage and want to chat you up."

I hadn't thought of that, but with the neckline on Ronnie's top, it's sure to happen. Great.

I try to snag a sweater on our way out the door, but she catches me and throws it back in the room at the last moment.

"We're trying to meet boys and have fun, not be warm," she says, dragging me down the hall to find our ride. "Besides, if you're cold when you get there, you're doing it wrong."

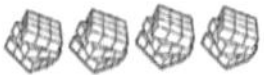

The other girls from our dorm heading to the party are dressed in even less clothing than I am, and I suddenly feel lucky Ronnie let me get away with wearing so much. I suppose I should thank her for not letting me go in what I was wearing, because I'd probably have attracted more attention in my normal clothes than I will dressed like every other girl at the party. Plus, I have to admit this is a pretty cute outfit, and if by some miracle the cube guys are there, I'll be glad I look like I put in some effort.

By the time we park down the street from the party, it's beyond freezing, and misting to boot. We race up the sidewalk and across the lawn to get inside, the other girls all squealing about their hair and makeup getting ruined by the rain, but I'm just annoyed my glasses are all misty-wet. Inside the house, it's packed and smoky and I hate to admit that Ronnie really was right. It's almost oppressively humid in here with so many people. I'd have roasted with more layers on.

Still, I'm glad I didn't let her pick my shoes. She and the other girls barely made it across the lawn in their strappy heels, and their toes have to be like ice cubes from tromping through the wet grass.

"I'm going to grab a drink and see if Trevor is here yet. Maybe let him talk me into finding a private corner or a room upstairs." Ronnie winks at me, then squeezes into the crowd and disappears, leaving me alone in a room full of drunk strangers just like I was afraid she would.

And she wonders why I don't like going to parties with her.

Edging around the crowd, I scan it for another familiar face—hoping, even though it's unlikely, to find the guys from the cubing competition. I'm not surprised when I don't see them in the sweaty mass of people dancing and drinking. They're brilliant mathematicians from MIT, a loud house party like this one is almost certainly not their scene. If they even go to parties at all, they're probably only ones where my cardigan would have been appropriate attire. I chide myself for even looking for them and decide I'm going to put them out of my mind and stop obsessing over them like a weirdo.

I make my way to the kitchen, where there's a keg and coolers full of canned drinks, but I don't see Ronnie anywhere around. I accept a plastic cup of beer from the guy manning the keg and shuffle over to a corner to keep an eye out for any of the girls I came with. They'll all have to get thirsty at some point.

My moment of quiet personal space is short-lived.

"What's a pretty girl like you standing over here looking so lonely for?" A guy whose whole look is so generic-college-guy that I can't tell him apart from any of the other men around leans against the wall next to me, standing a little too close as he peers down at the cleavage Ronnie made me display.

Glad as I was for my flats a few minutes ago, I now have to admit she was right. I should have worn the heels so this guy doesn't have a perfect view right down my shirt.

"Not lonely. Just enjoying some peace and quiet." I can barely stop myself from rolling my eyes. Even his pickup line is generic. I can't imagine it's ever actually worked for him. "And some breathing room," I say, hoping he'll take the hint.

My eyes keep roving over the crowd, searching for any familiar faces. I come to these types of parties so infrequently, I don't know any of these people. Ronnie probably knows half of the people here. She goes to a lot of parties, and she's such a people person, always chatting up literally anyone who looks at her at these things. Whenever I try it, I end up sounding like I'm interviewing them for a newspaper story because that's the type of interaction where I feel safest.

"Cool, cool," the guy says, the hint bypassing him entirely. "You know, if you're interested in quiet, maybe we should go upstairs?" He gestures around the room with his beer, sloshing some of it on my shoe. Gross. "I can barely hear you. Although I bet in the right circumstances, you can be loud." He grins as if this is actually a clever thing to say.

This guy isn't bad-looking. In fact, I'm sure most girls would consider him quite attractive, with his floppy dark hair and square jawline, but his attitude is so smarmy it detracts from his looks. I don't care how hot a guy is, if he's going to be a pervert right off the bat, I'm not interested. I can't believe this type of behavior actually works on some girls.

"Umm." I need to get away from this guy, but if I just walk away, I bet follow or try to herd me upstairs. If only Ronnie would come into the kitchen for a drink right this moment, she could rescue me, but of course she doesn't.

Somebody shouts something from the other side of the room, and the guy, who still hasn't introduced himself—such an asshole move, if you're going to stare down a girl's shirt you should at least tell her your name—turns a little to call back at them. His shift in position leaves me just enough space to look past his shoulder, and there's a gap in the crowd that gives me a perfect view into the next room.

There, at a table, is a guy with blond hair and red glasses whose face I know almost as well as my own reflection, because of how much I've been staring at his photo all week. As soon as I see Felix, though, Mr. Generic turns back to me and blocks my view again.

I can't believe it. They're actually here. It's like I willed them into existence, and the timing couldn't be better.

"Actually, I see my friends are waiting for me. Excuse me." I slip past the guy, curving my body so no part of me brushes against any part of him. Then I hurry through the crowded kitchen, hoping he doesn't follow me or catch up to me before I can reach the other room.

And as I suspected, it's not just Felix. Lukas spots me when I'm halfway there and nudges his friends to look my way. Felix only glances up briefly before focusing back on the cards in his hands, but the others keep their focus on me.

I know it's pathetic how much I've been staring at their photo, and driving across town on the off chance of running into them (because I have to be honest with myself, I don't think I'd have let Ronnie talk me into this if the party was near any other school) is worse. And borderline stalkerish. It would definitely not be my best moment if they found out.

Stopping a couple steps away, I stare up at them. Only Felix is seated, and I have to crane my neck to see the others' faces. Why does everyone have to be taller than me?

"Hi." I'm not sure if Lukas and his teammates can hear me over the music, and now that I'm standing in front of them, I'm not sure what to say. Do they even remember who I am? I put a hand to my chest. "Rebecca. I interviewed you at your competition last weekend."

And, I realize, now I've reminded them about the article that Carl edited down to nothing. Do I apologize for how short it was? Maybe they didn't see it so they don't know, and it'll be weird if I bring it up. I shouldn't have said anything.

"We remember," Lukas says, and I register that he says "we," not "I," like he speaks for the entire group. Which, thinking back on my interview with them, I guess he kind of does a lot of the time.

I notice their hands moving in front of them and glance down. "You brought cubes to a party?"

"Yeah." Lukas frowns a little and glances between me and the group of guys in shirts with Greek letters on them sitting across from Felix at the table.

The frat guys do not look happy. In fact, they look downright pissed, and without even knowing what game they're playing, I can tell from the pile of crumpled bills in front of him that Felix is winning. There's another pile of money in the middle of the table.

I'm not sure what type of situation I've walked into, but I'm pretty sure my presence is making an already tense situation worse. I should just say it was nice to see them and leave, let them get back to whatever they're doing and go find a quiet corner to look up bus schedules or order a rideshare to get myself back to campus. I'm not going to see

Ronnie again for hours anyway, so it's not like she'll miss me.

That's what I should do. Instead, I keep talking.

"That's cool." If they want to bring their cubes everywhere, who am I to judge them? "It's probably why you're all so good at the competitions. Always practicing." I hope that will placate them, and it seems to. Their shoulders relax, and the furrows between Lukas's eyebrows disappear.

"Yeah," agrees Elliot. "We have a lot of classes right now so we have to squeeze it in when we can."

"But you're still making time to come out and party. Multitasking. Good way to fully experience your college years." I sound so stupid, congratulating them on actually getting out of their rooms as if they're normally hermits.

Especially because they could say the same thing right back to me if they knew. I'm one hundred percent a hermit and not fully experiencing my college years, but it's only because I want to make sure I'm fully set up for life after college. I don't want to screw around now and pay for it later.

The guys all cock their heads, confused about why I'm congratulating them. It's a little funny, the way they react as a group instead of as individuals.

"Sorry." I laugh a little and shake my head, trying to make it look as if I'm laughing at myself, but really I'm panicking and embarrassed. *Cut your losses, Rebecca,* my brain is screaming at me. *Just say goodbye and remove yourself from this awkward situation.* But I can't. I don't know why, but I don't want to stop talking to them. I want to remove my foot from my mouth and start over and act like a normal human. "I'm just surprised to see you here, is all."

"Why? This party is closer to our school than yours,"

Lukas says, that line between his brows making another appearance.

Now I feel judged, like they're wondering why I'm here instead of at a party closer to my own school. They probably think I'm banned from BU parties for being so awkward. This is not the way I wanted this conversation to go. Why am I failing so badly at this? It's not like I can tell them I was hoping to see them here because for the past week I've been writing mental fanfiction about them and in it I've thought of them as nerdy, not the type of people to frequent college house parties.

"Good point," I admit, watching Felix push more money into the center of the table. Another card gets turned over. I rack my brain for something else to say, but I come up empty. And I can't just stand here awkwardly anymore, saying nothing, feeling smaller by the minute. "Well, I should probably go find my friend."

I'm about to follow it with, "It was good to see you all again," and slink off with my tail between my legs to delete their photo and make a vow never to think of them or this interaction ever again, when Felix shoves his pile of crumpled bills into the center of the table.

"All in." He sits back in his chair and pulls a cube from the pocket of his red zip-up hoodie. He turns the cube quickly as he flicks his eyes up at me, then back to the guys across from him.

"Fuck you!" His opponents throw down their cards and stand up. They're jacked, more than a little drunk, and they look ready to fight.

"Sorry, Lady Luck was on my side." Felix nods toward me—am I Lady Luck in this scenario?—and stands as well, pocketing his cube again and scooping up his winnings. "Until next time."

"Fuck no, sit back down." The guys flex their muscles,

like they're ready to throw some punches if Felix doesn't comply. "We're winning back our money."

I'm suddenly terrified that they're going to hit him, but Felix doesn't appear to share my concern.

"Not tonight." He shakes his head and keeps organizing his pile of cash.

The now-penniless frat guys splutter and grumble, slamming their chairs into the edge of the table as they push them in, but for whatever reason they decide to cut their losses and wander off into the kitchen, probably to drown their anger in cheap beer.

"Congratulations on your win, Felix." I can't believe I've just said his name out loud. It's surreal to be standing here speaking to all of them. The tension in the room has gone down significantly now that the guys Felix was playing with have left, and all four of them have turned their attention to me. And of course, I can't think of anything to say.

"You don't want to stay and see if you could win even more?" I wave my barely-touched drink at the table.

"I want to hang out with you now that you're here," says Felix. "Unless you really have to go find your friend right now."

"Um." I've been thinking all week about the moment I would see these guys again, and in my head I expected I would be confident and cool, but now that I'm actually face to face with all four of them, towering over me with their fingers flipping their cubes so fast they're a blur, I can barely string together a coherent thought. And it's so hot in here with all the partygoers and smoke, and so loud, I have to force myself to focus and not get all jumbled up in my head, lost between my fantasies about this moment and the reality of it. "No, she's probably fine. She can text me if she's looking for me."

I have the same feeling I get before a big test or interview, like there's a little flutter of hope inside my chest, and I'm worried I'm going to screw up and it's going to be crushed.

But these guys want to hang out with me. That's what I'd hoped would happen when I came over here, so why am I lowkey panicking right now?

Maybe I should have positioned myself where they'd be able to see me and let them come find me instead. But because I sought them out, it feels like they have the upper hand, and at any moment they could change their minds and say, "Just kidding."

We've all been standing here not saying anything for too long. I'm trying to think of something else to say when Lukas breaks the silence. "You didn't use our photo."

Well, there goes my hope that they hadn't seen the article. Of course they saw it. They probably were excited to see themselves in the paper, and I let them down. I glance away, not wanting to see the disappointment or anger or whatever other emotions are playing across their faces at my failure to do what I had said I would.

I spot Ronnie in the crowd, one hand possessively on Trevor's chest and the other holding a drink. When she catches my eye, it's questioning. *What's going on? Who are those guys and do I need to come save you from them?* her expression is saying.

Little does she know, it's not the guys I need to be saved from. It's myself.

Shaking my head slightly to reassure her that I'm okay, I turn my attention back to Lukas and his friends. I don't need to be saved. I need to acknowledge that I made them a promise I couldn't keep, and I need to apologize. I force myself to breathe, wishing their gazes weren't so penetrating.

"My editor cut the story down by a lot. I'm so sorry." And I really am. It's not fair that they shouldn't be recognized properly simply because my editor just doesn't care about what they do, and assumes most of our readers won't care either. But there's no way I'm going to say any of that to them.

"The article I wrote included a lot from the interview we did." Like how many times they've won and how long they've been cubing.

"Do you still have the picture though?" asks Elliot.

"I bet she does," says Sebastian, studying my eyes.

"Um." Do I admit that I do? And that I look at it every night before I go to bed? And first thing in the morning when I wake up? And maybe a few times throughout the day?

Absolutely not. No way. I am never telling them that. My face heats just thinking about what they would say if they knew what a weirdo I've been about that stupid picture.

"What are the journalistic ethics of keeping our photo if you didn't use it in the article?" asks Sebastian. He doesn't look like he's accusing me of anything, but more like he's genuinely wondering. Or studying me and trying to figure out who I am.

I'm not sure what he's trying to get at with this line of questioning. As a reporter, I should be able to follow the thread of a conversation and anticipate where questions are leading to, but for some reason I can't with Sebastian.

Or maybe it's not him. Maybe it's the feeling of his three teammates' eyes on me all at the same time. Or, quite possibly, it's the pressure I've put on this entire interaction by building it up in my head since the first time we met.

I've been acting like a flake all evening, and I really need to get it together. I force myself to focus.

"It'd be fine, ethically, to retain a photo that wasn't run with an article for use in a future story." That sounds right, anyway, or at least feasible. It's definitely better than, "I don't care if it's ethical or not when the subjects of said photo are really cute and have an inexplicable hold on my brain."

"Do you look at it?" asks Elliot.

Now, how am I supposed to answer that? I could say no, but for some reason, I don't want to lie to them. And something about the way they're looking at me says that if I say no, they'll be disappointed, which churns up a flurry of butterflies in my belly.

"Yes." I want to see if those butterflies are telling the truth. I'm a terrible liar, anyway.

The competitors all nod and exchange a look that says they expected me to say that, even as they continue to solve and scramble their cubes.

Relief floods through me that they don't jump down my throat and accuse me of being creepy. For a split second, I wonder if they'll move in closer, taking the admission that I look at their photo as proof that I'm attracted to one or all of them. If they'll hit on me. Maybe ask me to go upstairs with them.

Lukas's words from last weekend slip through my mind. *We like to share.*

I don't know how it's possible, but my face flushes even hotter than it already was, and I bring my beer to my lips in hopes that the liquid will cool me down. I don't even know which part of this is more ridiculous, the idea that not just one, but all of them would be interested in me, or the realization that I might ... be into that.

What am I even thinking about this for? Yes, they're all hot, and yes, they seem to like the idea that I look at their picture, but I'm not interested in dating even one person, let alone four at once. I promised myself that I would focus on school and not on boys, that I wouldn't let my future be jeopardized because of a nice smile or broad shoulders or quick fingers. I don't want a boyfriend, and I really don't want four boyfriends. Even if they are good-looking and brilliant and driven.

"Well, if you still have a picture of us," says Lukas, pulling out his phone, "it only seems fair that we have one of you."

Chapter Five

I choke on my beer. Surely I misheard him. This is the absolute pinnacle of embarrassment in an evening rife with humiliation. Everyone around us is staring at me as I cough. This is the absolute pinnacle of embarrassment in an evening rife with humiliation.

"She needs water," says Elliot, disappearing into the crowd of onlookers. More liquid is probably not what I need as I continue to sputter on the beer in my airway, but I'm too busy coughing to protest.

"We'll be outside," calls Felix, taking one of my arms while Lukas takes the other to steer me out the back door. Sebastian strides ahead of us, clearing a path to the back door.

Ronnie is halfway to us with a concerned look on her face, but I wave her off.

"Fresh air," I mouth in between coughing fits so she knows where I am. Not that she could possibly miss the spectacle of me hacking up a lung as I'm escorted outside by three tall, attractive guys.

There's a small porch on the back hosting a few smokers, but once they hear my coughing, they clear out pretty quick, leaving the guys to settle me on the bench swing.

Felix sits beside me and Lukas and Sebastian hover around us as I try to regain my breath. I try sipping a little beer to see if it helps, but it does not. It really is disgusting beer, even for a frat party.

It's freezing out here. The sweat on my skin from inside began to dry as soon as the cold air hit my skin, and Ronnie's strappy little glitter top isn't doing anything to keep me warm. I rub my hands over my arms, and Lukas takes his sweatshirt off and drape it around my shoulders.

"Thanks," I rasp out, still fighting a coughing fit, and slip my arms into the sleeves and zip it up. It's warm from his body and smells like boy, in a good way. I'm tempted to bury my nose in the fabric and inhale, but that would be really weird of me, so I staunch the desire.

"Sorry it took me so long," says Elliot, stepping out the back door and closing it behind him. "They're out of cups and the glasses in the cupboard did not look clean, so I had to wash it first. Here you go, this should help."

I accept the glass and take a sip. The water is much better than the beer. The only reason I'd been drinking it in the first place was to give my hands something to do and to not look out of place. Looking around, I realize that none of them have a drink in their hands. They can't hold a beer and solve their cubes one-handed, after all.

Wait, actually, they can. I've seen it with my own eyes.

But for whatever reason, they're here, completely sober, and want to spend time with me.

"Thanks, I needed that," I say to Elliot, once I've drained half the glass.

"What did you answer about the photo?" asks Elliot. "I wasn't here to hear it."

"We're still waiting for an answer," says Lukas, leaning

against the railing across from the swing and pinning me with his gaze.

The other guys fall into line on either side of him, Felix standing to join them. It's a little intimidating, all four of them staring at me from the railing, solving their cubes almost in tandem.

"Why do you want one?" I sip more water instead of the beer, which I set on the table next to the swing as I have no plans to consume any more of it tonight. Even if it doesn't try to pour itself into my lungs, I don't want to fit in badly enough to force any more of it down. Not to mention, I've embarrassed myself plenty tonight stone-cold sober. The last thing I need is to get tipsy and make it worse.

"Fair is fair," says Sebastian, echoing Lukas's words from a few minutes ago.

"Exactly," agrees Elliot. "You have one of us."

They do have a point. I've been looking at their photo all week, and it's not fair for them not to have the same opportunity.

I can't believe I just had that thought.

"Why? Other than to be fair?" I ask. "Because I could delete your photo from my phone right now, if you want me to."

I don't want to delete it, but if they're uncomfortable with me having it and this is their way of telling me, then I will.

Their hands still on their cubes. It appears I've alarmed them with my suggestion.

"Don't delete it," says Sebastian quietly.

"Yeah, don't. We like you having it," Felix tells me.

Elliot is the first to resume his cube-fidgeting. "We could send you better ones."

I chug the rest of my water to avoid eye contact with any of them, so they don't see how much that idea appeals to me. They do look sort of stiff and awkward in the picture I took of them with their prize ribbons. I wouldn't mind having better photos of them. I'm not prepared to fully examine why I want them, though.

Lukas, apparently taking my silence for agreement, pulls out his phone. "What's your number?"

The back door opens and Ronnie pokes her head out, her gaze sweeping from one end of the porch to the other before her eyes land on us.

"There you are," she says, stepping out and immediately wrapping her arms around her shoulders to stay warm. "I'm going home with Trevor, are you cool out here?"

Ronnie's eyes shift, questioning, to the four tall guys leaning against the railing with their phones out. If I said anything, she'd jump in and drag me out of here with her. Sure, she might then make me hang out in Trevor's living room while she spends time with him in his bedroom, but she would rescue me if I needed her to.

"We'll bring her home," Elliot tells her.

"She'll be safe with us," adds Felix.

Ronnie eyes them, solving their cubes one-handed with their phones in the other, and grins at me.

"Okay, I'll tell Callie. See you in the morning!" She disappears back into the house, the door slamming shut behind her.

Wow. Normally when she ditches me at a party it takes ages to convince her I'll be fine catching a ride back to the dorm with any of the other girls on our floor. Turning back to the guys, I take in the way they fidget with their cubes and realize that she probably assumed they're harmless nerds. Or maybe she's engaging in her favorite activity: Meddling in Rebecca's Love Life (or Lack Thereof). Knowing Ronnie, that's the more likely scenario.

"Okay," says Lukas, straightening from the railing. "Do

you want us to take you home now, or do you want to stay for a bit longer?"

"Oh, no, you don't have to do that. I'm sure I can find one of the other girls from my dorm to drive me back. We all came together, they'll text me when they want to leave." I don't want to make them drive all the way to my college just to turn around and drive right back here. Well, not here, specifically. I'm not sure where they live, but I'm pretty sure it's not in this frat house.

Elliot looks baffled. "Of course we need to," he says. "We promised whoever that was we would take you home."

"That was my roommate, Ronnie." I steel myself for them to start asking more questions about her. People are always asking about Ronnie because she's so fun and outgoing and pretty. She makes an impression.

"Okay, well, we don't want to have lied to Ronnie. We want her to like us. If your friends don't like us, they won't want you to date us." Lukas hands me his phone. "I opened a new contact so you can easily put in your information."

He steps off the back porch into the yard, and starts making his way around to the front of the house. The others follow, shepherding me along with them. I let them guide me, because my brain is still back on the porch trying to wrap itself around what Lukas just said.

They ... they want to date me? These guys, these four good-looking, obviously brilliant guys, want ordinary, boring me? I know I've been flirting with the idea all week, with my tame little "they win and run offstage to have behind-closed-doors celebration sex with me" fantasies, but I haven't fully acknowledged even to myself that I've developed a huge crush on them.

I only glance back at the house once before following them, Lukas's phone still in my hand. I could go inside and look for Callie and Reyna, but I doubt they want to leave yet, and I'm over this party. Besides, the guys are surrounding me, corralling me to wherever they've parked their car.

Looking down at Lukas's phone, I see he already started the phone contact for me, putting in both my first and last name. All I have to do is put in a number.

Girls in college do this sort of thing all the time. They meet a guy, give him their number, he texts them, and they go out on dates. Maybe they even sleep together. This is all completely normal.

It's just that this is new to me. I'm not the type of girl to sleep around, or even date. I don't think I know how to do this. Especially if, as Lukas implied, they *all* want to date me.

How would that work? Would I be dating them all individually, just with the understanding that they're all okay with it? Or would I be dating all of them together, at the same time? And beyond dating, if we get to the point where we're having sex, is *that* going to be a group activity, or individual?

I'm getting ahead of myself. I haven't even typed my number into Lukas's phone yet, it's way too soon to be thinking about sex.

But now that I've started, I can't seem to stop imagining what each of them is like between the sheets.

Sebastian doesn't talk much but I can feel his eyes on me, the way he notices every detail, every movement. I bet he'd be attentive in bed. He'd make sure I came first.

Lukas, on the other hand, is pretty vocal about what he wants. He'd tell me exactly what he wants me to do. And probably manhandle me into every position he can think of to try. I think he'd still make sure I was having a good time, but he'd be a lot more take-charge than Sebastian.

Felix probably really would want to try everything. I bet

he has a running to-do list of every position and location that occurs to him, so he can tick them off one by one.

And Elliot, he's just plain sweet. He's probably a slow, gentle lover. Eager to please. Probably gives hours of oral pleasure before even getting to the main event and his own release.

We arrive at their car, a small black SUV, and I blink back into focus. I don't remember the walk from the house to here, distracted as I was thinking about what kind of sex they each like. Lukas opens the back door and gestures for me to climb in.

"Check your assumptions there, Lukas," says Sebastian. "Fair is fair."

Lukas hesitates a moment, then nods. "You're right," he agrees.

Confused, I watch as all four of the guys scramble their cubes and pass them around the circle to the right. I've seen them do this before, when I interviewed them, but why are they doing it now?

Lukas solves his cube first, a smug smile on his face. Felix completes his puzzle just barely after him, followed by Sebastian and Elliot.

"Looks like I'm driving," says Elliot, sounding resigned. "Who has the keys?"

Felix tosses him the keys before circling around to the other side of the car and settling into the backseat. Lukas holds a hand out for me to climb inside too. Looks like I'm in the middle then. I don't even mind, I'm so charmed by the fact that they just competed to see who gets to sit next to me. It was probably the nerdiest competition ever, but that makes it all the more adorable, and it's all I need to finally type my phone number into Lukas's phone.

I pause before handing it back to him, though. Sebastian had a point earlier. Fair is fair. So I go to the home screen, smiling a little at the wallpaper, a big logo for the International Cubing Federation World Championship, and open up a text message to myself.

I'm certain Lukas is going to share my number with the others, and if their entire team has my number, I should have at least one of theirs.

I hit send on the text and hand the phone back to Lukas. When he glances at the screen there's the barest hint of a smile at the corner of his mouth. He taps the screen a few times, and I hear buzzing and text notifications throughout the car a moment later. I can only assume he's forwarded my number to the others.

They really do share everything.

"Are we taking you straight home?" asks Elliot. His driving is smooth, and the way he grips the gearshift reminds me of the way he wraps those same fingers around a classic cube.

"We said we would." Sebastian fiddles with the radio dial until something soft and symphonic hums quietly through the air.

"It's still early, we could go to our place and watch a movie," suggests Elliot, rolling up to a stop sign. He turns his head to look at me. "If you would like that."

Would I like that? Going with four guys I barely know, to a strange house where they live, and no one knows where I am? I suddenly feel claustrophobic, boxed in by Felix and Lukas in the backseat of this SUV. Ronnie didn't balk at them giving me a ride home so I didn't either, but it occurs to me now that they could stop anywhere and brutally murder me. I could become a cautionary tale. A statistic.

I want to write the headlines, not be one.

I've never tried being like other college girls, dating and partying and focusing as much on the "college experience" as on my schoolwork, because I've seen the damage that can do years down the line. I've lived it secondhand, watching my mom fawn over my narcissistic dad and struggle to stretch his single income with no work experience or degree of her own while he womanizes in every bar across town. I've played it safe all through high school and the first year and a half of college, but now look at me. I've gotten in a car with four guys I don't know just because they showed me some attention.

My breathing quickens and I eye the windows. They're all closed. This is a very small space. I can feel Lukas and Felix's body heat and I start to sweat, feeling warmer than I did in the crush of bodies at the party. Is this what a panic attack feels like? I fight the urge to flail my arms out, climb over Lukas's lap, and launch myself out of the moving car.

Things are not that dire yet. There are other ways out of this. I could text Ronnie an SOS, but Lukas and Felix would see me do it, and that might send them all into a rage and speed the murdering process along. But if I don't try, it won't matter how fast or slow my impending demise comes because no one will know it's happening.

I slip my hand into my purse and wrap my fingers around my phone, then pause. Ronnie probably won't see my text in time if she's in the middle of hooking up with Trevor. I should also include Callie and Reyna on the message. I don't know them all that well, but I do have their numbers. I can share my location and they can leave the party and come find me, assuming they're not also having too much fun to bother checking their phones to see my plea. I try to think if there's anyone else and come up empty. It never occurred to me until now that my all-work-and-no-play approach to life means I've made very few friends, and therefore have no one to help me when I'm about to be murdered and dumped in a ditch somewhere.

Felix must realize I'm spinning out, because he puts a

hand on my back. "Hey, it's okay." His palm is hot on the skin exposed by Ronnie's stupid sequin top. "You don't have to come over tonight."

"Yeah, we can do a movie night another time," agrees Lukas, squeezing my shoulder.

Elliot locks eyes with me in the rearview mirror for a moment before returning his attention to the road. "We didn't mean to spook you. I thought it might be nice to hang out, get to know each other a little without all those people around, but if it's too much for one night, that's okay."

Sebastian turns to look at me, and the concern on his face helps to ease the anxiety wrapping around my chest. "We shouldn't have suggested it. You don't know us very well yet, and we said we would take you home. We shouldn't have tried to change the plan."

It seems that my fears of being gruesomely dismembered by them are unfounded. Real murderers probably wouldn't be trying to make me feel better and promising that they'll take me home after all. They probably are just nice, nerdy, normal guys who really do just want to watch a movie together.

Glancing out the window again, I realize that we're only about two blocks from my college. How did we get here so quickly? It feels like we've only been driving for a few minutes. I guess time flies when you're convinced you're about to die.

"Which dorm do you live in?" asks Elliot, switching lanes and preparing to turn into the drive.

"How did you know I live on campus?"

"You told us earlier that you could get a ride from someone in your dorm," says Elliot, then parrots back verbatim what I had said on the porch at the party.

I can't help but be impressed. Is that really how his brain works, able to recall exactly what someone said or did, no matter how innocuous? No wonder he's so good at solving his cubes so fast, he can recall all the patterns after just a glance.

"So you're taking me home?" My thoughts are moving like sludge through my own brain, probably a result of the fading adrenaline from thinking the situation was more dire than it is. I'm so confused. My feelings have been all over the place since I spotted them across the room at the party. This whole situation is moving so fast. In the past two hours they've gone from faces on my phone screen, to saying they want my best friend to like them so they can date me, to maybe being about to murder me, to dropping me off at my dorm. I've got mental whiplash from it all.

"We said we would." Sebastian turns around in the passenger seat again to give me a questioning look. "Unless you changed your mind about coming over to watch a movie."

Felix brushes a strand of hair off my forehead. "Are you feeling okay? You're all flushed."

"I'm fine." A tingle spreads through me at his touch. "I live in The Towers, on Bay State, but actually, um." Would it be terrible to change my mind when they're already practically at my dorm? "We could go back to your place and have a movie night." Just a movie night. This is me taking the leap. Letting myself have a small taste of what Ronnie and all those other girls get to experience. One movie night won't derail my entire future.

"Yes!" Elliot pumps his fist in the air. It's the most emotion I've seen any of them show about anything. "Movie night! Let's go!"

"Okay, wait," I say, laughing and tugging his arm down. "Just to be clear, this isn't a date. I don't date."

"You don't?" Felix looks surprised, and I think disappointed.

I shake my head. "I'm focused on school and work, I don't really have time for dating. But hanging out tonight, that I can do."

"Sure," Lukas says smoothly. "We'll just hang out and get to know each other."

"Did you have a specific movie you'd like to watch tonight?" asks Felix.

I'm glad they aren't going to push back on the not-a-date thing. "Not really. I'm good with just about anything so long as it's not scary."

Elliot's face in the rearview is very serious as he asks, "How do you feel about superhero movies?"

"Good?" I don't have an opinion on superhero movies, because I haven't watched any, but maybe it will turn out that I like them.

"Good, good." Sebastian looks back over his shoulder at me again. "We're making our way through the MCU right now."

"That's a bad idea," says Lukas, shaking his head. "It'll be too confusing for her. We should start again from the beginning."

"Then our watch numbers will be uneven," Sebastian protests.

Lukas purses his lips. "Good point. We could give her some other options from our collection to pick from, how does that sound?"

The guys chorus their agreement with this plan.

"That works for me," I say.

"Okay, now that that's settled, we have the real question," says Elliot. "Rebecca, what is your must-have snack for movie watching?"

"Anything salty. I usually eat pretzels when I watch movies in my dorm. My favorite is microwave popcorn, but people kept burning it and setting off the smoke alarms in the dorms so we're not allowed to have it anymore. And pre-popped popcorn just isn't the same." If I can't have my favorite food, I'd rather have something else altogether than a subpar version of what I really want.

"Okay." At the next stop sign, Elliot looks to Sebastian, who nods. Elliot flicks on the turn signal and the car turns right.

A moment later we're pulling into a grocery store parking lot. Felix turns to me. "I'll be right back."

He climbs out of the car as Elliot pauses in front of the store. As soon as Felix's door closes, Elliot pulls out of the loading zone and finds a parking spot close by.

Lukas shifts in his seat next to me, his thigh pressing against mine. "Our preferred movie snacks are nachos."

"Oh, okay." The heat of his leg against mine is doing things to me. I am keenly aware of my inexperience with guys in this moment. A boy's leg touching mine should not be making my pulse throb between my legs and my brain go fuzzy.

"Here he comes," says Sebastian a minute later, pointing at the store.

Elliot pulls back up to the front to pick up Felix, who is not carrying the makings for nachos. Instead, he's holding a bag of pretzels and a box of microwave popcorn.

Chapter Six

"You didn't have to do that," I say as Felix buckles himself back in. "But thank you. It's very sweet." The fact that they made an entire stop just to get me snacks, really is incredibly nice of them.

"The correct snacks are important for the full movie night experience," explains Elliot as if it was a given that they'd go out of their way to get popcorn for me.

"You're right. That's very true," I agree, smiling. A small part of me wishes I were interested in dating them, because these four guys are so sweet. But I know it probably wouldn't last. If my mom's love life is any indication, men are sweet at the beginning when they're reeling you in, but it's not long before you're waiting on them hand and foot, putting your entire life on the back burner for their comfort, only for them to get bored and cheat behind your back.

Elliot pulls into the driveway of an old New England-style house, the type usually chopped up into a bunch of tiny little apartments and then shoved full of students.

Lukas opens the door and gets out of the car, then holds out his hand to help me out. It's such an old school move, but I have to say, it's cute.

This feels like magic. Taking a man's warm, callused hand as he helps me from his car and guides me up the steps and into his house, like I'm a princess in a fairy tale. Except I can't think of a single fairy tale that has three other men waiting for the moment I step over the threshold and into their private space.

For a moment, I wonder how many other women they have done this same thing for, made to feel special and welcomed into their home. But as soon as I have the thought, I remind myself that I'm just here to watch a movie, so it doesn't matter.

They lead me into the house, all of them stopping as soon as they step into the little hallway to toe off their shoes and line them up neatly on a little rack against the wall. I can tell these guys like things neat and orderly in their lives.

"You can have whichever of the empty spots you prefer," Sebastian tells me, pointing to the shoe rack. "It can be your permanent spot."

I don't know that I'll be here often enough to need a permanent spot, but I get a little thrill thinking about it. "Thanks."

"Once you've taken off your shoes, we'll give you the tour," says Lukas.

I quickly take off my shoes and set them in the empty spot on the top of the shoe rack. The tile floor is chilly under my bare feet, and I wish I'd known this was how the night was going to end up. I'd have tossed socks into my purse.

At least my toenails are painted so they look cute.

"Okay, ready." I stand up straight and put on my best smile. Inside I'm nervous, but I tell myself to knock it off. This is going to be fun. This isn't a date, and there's no pressure, and we're going to watch a movie and have a good time and get to know each other and I'm in complete control.

Lukas leads the way through the small foyer and past a set of stairs, pointing out the half bath, then down the hall and into the kitchen, which is painted a soft sage green. It looks nice against the white cabinets. The kitchen is very clean, no dirty dishes in the sink or crumbs on the table, and I wonder if this is normal or if they clean three times a year and today just happened to be that day. We turn right into a dining room, furnished with an entire table and chairs set that looks like it's never been used as a beer pong table, then right again into the living room, which boasts a large sofa and larger television. Lukas names each room as we pass through it, which I find oddly charming. It's cute that they want to show off their house.

It doesn't look like any college dorm room or even share house I've ever seen, especially considering it's inhabited by guys. Everything is spotless and tidy, not just in the kitchen. I peek back into the kitchen, something I'd half-noticed earlier snagging at the corner of my mind. Sure enough, all of the countertop appliances have tiny little labels on them.

"Your house is really nice. Lucky you don't have to stay in the dorms." I would love to move from the dorms to an apartment at some point, especially if it meant having this much space. Although living in a house this big would also mean having to share it with several other people, which would mean I'd have to find several other people to live with. Although no doubt if and when we move off campus, Ronnie'll have a whole list of potential roommates lined up.

"And all of the bedrooms are upstairs," says Elliot, gesturing over to the foyer and the stairs I can just see through the archway.

Bedrooms feel like a dangerous topic, so I indicate the shelves against one wall. "Are these all of your trophies?"

Way to be Captain Obvious, Rebecca.

"Yes," says Felix, taking my hand and leading me across the room. "Come look."

The others follow, clustering around me as I let my gaze wander over the shelves, which are organized largest to smallest, left to right. Felix drops my hand now that we've reached our destination, and I tamp down the disappointment that pings in the back of my brain, refusing to examine why I felt it.

"Which one is your first trophy?" I ask as I peruse the display. "How far back do these go?"

"This shelf is mine, and this one was my first." Felix points out a small bronze cube about the size of my palm on the top shelf. "I was eight."

"That's very young to start competing." I don't remember what I was interested in at that age, but competing and winning at anything wasn't even on my radar.

"Not really," says Felix, nodding his head towards Elliot. "Elliot started competing when he was six."

"Really?" Who discovers their passion in life that young and then sticks with it? Most people can't commit to anything, yet here these guys are, still working towards one of the first goals they've ever had in life: to win the world speedcubing competition.

"Yes," says Elliot, stepping up to the shelves and reaching a hand out toward them. "Let me show you my first trophy."

Elliot systematically names each event each trophy came from, moving right to left. I'm calculating how many years he's been competing, and there don't seem to be enough trophies. And hasn't named any event twice.

"Are you only going to each event once?" I ask.

"No, we keep all of the extra trophies in our rooms," he explains, straightening one of his trophies on the shelf.

"We only keep the highest trophy from each event on the communal display shelves," adds Lukas.

He and Sebastian show me their shelves, and I really am impressed with the number of awards they've all gotten. And knowing that they have more in their rooms? I guess that happens when you've been competing since elementary school, but it's still cool to know that they have all this to prove how good they are.

"Okay, movie time," says Lukas, pointing to a different set of shelves, this one lined with movies. "Sebastian and Elliot can help you pick something, Rebecca, and Felix and I will go prepare the snacks."

Sebastian pulls out a few movies and sets the cases face out on the shelf. I'd thought they were going to have me pick a superhero movie, so I was expecting something with Batman or Superman or another character I'd know, but none of these options appear to be superhero movies. In fact, they all look more like sci-fi than anything.

I shake my head and shrug helplessly at Elliot and Sebastian. "These are all new to me. Which would you recommend?"

"You've never seen any of these?" Sebastian looks downright shocked. It's kind of amusing that me not having seen a couple of movies is the thing that shakes him to his core.

Even Elliot turns slightly to stare down at me in surprise.

I feel like I owe them an explanation. "Ronnie and I tend to mostly watch rom-coms, and I don't watch a ton of movies on my own."

"Well." Elliot pauses and I'm not sure if he's trying to assess how he feels about my ignorance or make a game plan for dealing with it. "Then I say we go with one of these two. They're TV series, not movies, but we could watch an episode and see how you like it. This one is a classic, it's set in space and has great phaser shootouts, and this one takes place on Earth and involves paranormal antiques."

"And since they're both series, we'll be able to watch more episodes at future movie nights," adds Sebastian. His optimism about the likelihood of a repeat of tonight is cute.

"Let's do whichever series is longer, then." I don't know what more movie nights will look like in terms of interacting with them. Given my body's response to Lukas's leg touching mine in the car, there's a good chance I'll have to tap out of future hangouts just to keep myself from doing something embarrassing like kissing one of them just to see what it feels like. Especially with them having mentioned wanting to date me, allowing myself to explore my physical attraction to them feels like a terrible idea.

Both Elliot and Sebastian smile brightly as if I've just made their entire day.

Lukas and Felix return, carrying bowls of freshly popped popcorn and pretzels and a towering tray of nachos.

"You don't have a movie queued yet?" asks Lukas, setting the popcorn on the coffee table.

"Are you still trying to decide on one?" Felix deposits the nachos next to the popcorn and begins to pull bottles of water out of the pockets of his hoodie.

I realize I'm still wearing Lukas's sweatshirt. I should probably give it back, but it's so comfortable I decide to keep it until it's time to go home or he asks for it back, whichever comes first.

"Rebecca picked *Star Trek* and said we can watch more episodes in the future, so we'll have to arrange our movie night schedules to coincide," says Sebastian as he puts the disc into the player. He sounds ... almost proud? Like my agreeing to future movie nights is a huge win for them. And actually, it probably is.

Sebastian glances over his shoulder at me as the DVD player drawer closes. "We may have to pause the list we were working on on our own, but I'm fine with it if it means we get to do more movie nights with you."

Well, that's incredibly sweet, not least because I get the feeling that breaking routine is not something Sebastian typically enjoys.

The guys all hover around the coffee table, arranging the snacks and drinks, then stand back and stare at me expectantly.

"Have a seat," says Lukas, waving to the sofa.

I sit on the end, but they all look at each other and I fear I've done something wrong. "Should I move? Is this where one of you usually sits?"

"No, but ..." Felix's fingers twitch at his sides even though he's not holding a cube. "Would you mind sitting in the middle? That way two of us can sit by you instead of just one."

"It's more fair that way," says Sebastian, nodding.

"Oh. Sure. Sorry." They all watch as I scootch over to sit as much in the middle as possible. I'm sitting right on the crack between two of the cushions, it's the only way I think we'll all fit. This is a decent size sofa for four people, but five will be a bit tight. There will be no way to avoid touching each other. That pulsing thrill between my legs begins to beat again at the thought.

Elliot and Sebastian slide in to sit next to me. I realize that they're taking turns. Lukas and Felix already got to sit next to me in the car, so now it's Lukas and Felix's turn. Is this how they all date the same girl? By making it all a rotating schedule? They do like fairness, after all.

Lukas starts handing out plates. "Help yourself, Rebecca."

They're digging in and the popcorn smells incredible, so

I scoop up some popcorn and pretzels. It'd be rude not to since they went to the store specifically to get it for me. I just hope I don't get any kernels stuck in my teeth. Having to ask them for dental floss is a level of embarrassment I'm not sure I can handle tonight.

"All right, we're all set," says Elliot, clicking through on the DVD so the episode starts. "This is a utopian futurism science fiction about space explorers boldly going where no one has gone before."

"Hey, no spoilers," says Sebastian, cutting him off. "You're going to ruin the episode for her."

"I can't believe you haven't seen it before," says Lukas, dishing some nachos onto his plate. "We feel lucky that we get to experience your first time with you."

As soon as he says it, I nearly choke on my popcorn. I can't believe Lukas just said that. None of them seem to realize the probably unintentional innuendo, though. They are only showing concern about me and the bit of popcorn trying to take up residence in my lungs. This is so embarrassing. This is now the second time tonight that I've choked in front of them. Is my body just determined to give up on breathing around these guys?

"Are you okay?" asks Felix, patting my back.

Elliot uncaps a bottle of water and hands it to me.

"Thank you." I take a cautious sip after coughing the popcorn back out of my airway. "I'm okay. Really."

"Do you want anything other than water?" asks Elliot. "We don't have any alcohol, but there's juice in the fridge. Or energy drinks or tea?"

"Water is fine. Thanks." I take another sip to show my appreciation and then set down the bottle on the coaster Felix immediately slides in front of me.

"Are you sure you're good?" asks Lukas.

"Yeah, let's start the show. I'm excited for my first time."

I use Lukas's words because I want to test their reactions, see if me saying the same thing registers for them the way him saying it did for me. But they all just settle in around me to munch their snacks and turn their focus to the TV.

"You won't regret it. This show is awesome," says Felix.

"Life-changing," agrees Elliot.

I'm sure they're hyping up the show way more than it deserves, but as I lean back against the sofa cushions, Elliot and Sebastian's arms brushing mine, I let myself imagine for just a moment what it would be like if I did try to date them. Every weekend could be like this—popcorn and movie nights, cuddled up on the sofa with them, being introduced to all sorts of new things ... now *that* would be life-changing.

Chapter Seven

A buzzing interrupts the sound of the TV. We all look around for the source, and Sebastian hands me my purse. I pull out my phone, setting the bag down behind me on the sofa.

"I'm just going to step into the hall a moment." I hold up my phone, which is still vibrating in my hand. The screen is lit up with Ronnie's name and picture.

"We can pause the show," says Sebastian, already grabbing the remote.

"Thanks." It probably doesn't matter as I probably wouldn't be any more lost if they were to keep watching, but it's sweet of them to do anyway.

I swipe the phone screen to answer the call once I'm in the hallway. "Hey, is everything okay?"

"I'm fine, but I heard there was a fight at the party," says Ronnie. "Did those guys take you home? Are you okay? Do you need me and Trevor to come get you?"

"I'm fine. Must've happened after we left I'm actually," I look back to make sure the guys can't overhear me, "at the guys' house to watch a movie."

"Oh. Wow. But you're okay there? Can they bring you

home later? If so, I'll stay the night with Trevor." Ronnie's voice drops to a whisper. "I think things are starting to get serious between us. He told me he's not seeing anyone else right now."

I'm not going to ask Ronnie to come get me mid-episode, even if I'm kind of confused by the plot. Especially if she's still with Trevor. I already don't think he likes me much, and if he thinks I'm cock-blocking him I've got no hope of him ever coming around. I don't care if he likes me for my sake, but if he and Ronnie do end up being serious, her life will be easier if Trevor and I get along.

"I'm good. I'll get a ride. Don't worry about me, go have fun with Trevor."

Ronnie squeals with glee. "Thanks! Don't wait up!" The line goes dead.

I stay in the hallway a moment, looking back toward the living room archway. The show might be kind of silly, but the guys are nice.

When I return to the living room, however, I nearly trip over my own feet in shock.

Felix is holding a piece of pink paper in his hand, and the others are all reading it over his shoulder.

It looks like my purse has fallen over on the sofa, spilling some of its contents onto the cushion. Including, it appears, the stupid sex list Ronnie had slipped in there earlier. I'd completely forgotten about it, and now my heart plummets into my stomach as I watch the guys' intense perusal of the evidence of my sexual inexperience.

I should call Ronnie back and beg her to come get me, even if she is with Trevor. Even sitting in the back of Trevor's car knowing they're both thinking about all the fun naked things they'd rather be doing won't be anywhere near as bad as this moment right here. But it will take her at least fifteen minutes to get to me. I have no quick way out of this scenario. Even if I order a ride off a rideshare app, I'll have to wait for it to get here. Any amount of time is too much.

But as I head back into the living room to retrieve my bag so I can run far, far away from here, my humiliation morphs into anger.

"What do you think you're doing?" Even if it did fall out of my purse, what makes them think it's okay to read it?

Reaching over the coffee table, I grab the list out of Felix's hands. I'm glad for the piece of furniture between us. All trace of embarrassment has temporarily left me, and I'm seeing red.

"Your bag tipped over when you got up," explains Sebastian, fanning his hand toward the now empty cushion. "We were picking your things up."

"When did picking things up start to include reading other peoples' personal papers?" I fold the list in half, then fold that in half too. I keep folding, making it smaller and smaller until I can't fold it one more time. My fingers curl around the small pink square, and my cheeks flood with heat as my shame returns full force as quickly as it fled.

I wish I could fold up this moment just as small as the paper and hide it. Or better yet, throw it away like I should have done with that idiotic list last year when I first wrote it.

"There's no reason to be embarrassed," says Lukas.

"I'm not embarrassed." It comes out louder than I mean it to, and I know my face looks like a tomato right now, which only intensifies my mortification.

Great, now they think I'm either some sort of sex-crazed pervert who carries around a list of sex acts like a shopping list, or so inexperienced I have to keep my sex study guide with me at all times, and on top of that I'm also standing here looking like I've got the world's worst sunburn.

"Okay," Felix says. His voice is calm, like he's trying to

soothe a feral animal. "Good. Because you don't need to be. You just ... look like you are."

"I'm not embarrassed," I repeat, and this time I mean the force I put into it. More quietly I add, "I'd like to go home now. Please take me back to my dorm."

This was supposed to be a nice, casual way to get to know them better. A movie, some popcorn, and a plate of nachos. But instead, I just want to throw up and then hide in a hole for the rest of time.

This was a bad idea. As soon as I get home, I'm going to crash into bed and pretend like this never happened. I can block their numbers, and I'll never have to see them again.

"Okay." Sebastian hunches his shoulders, his expression morphing from intrigued to defeated. "If that's what you want."

"We'll put away our snacks and then drive you home." Elliot turns off the TV and picks up the tray of partially-eaten nachos.

He looks so sad and heartbroken I almost feel bad for him, except that all my sympathy is directed at myself right now. So instead of consoling him, I merely step to the side to give him more room to bring the tray into the kitchen. The other guys move to help while all I do is stand there wishing the floor would swallow me whole.

"You don't all have to drive me," I mumble. "It only takes one person to drive a car."

Sebastian stops in his tracks on the way to the kitchen. "That's not how we do things."

There's that doing-everything-together thing again. If you'd asked me an hour ago, I'd have said it was cute, if a little weird. But now, I'm finding it nothing short of maddening.

"You know," says Lukas, coming back into the living room, "we didn't lose our virginity until college."

"Statistically, most women don't have sex until just after high school, so you're not far from the average," adds Felix from the doorway. "There's nothing to be embarrassed about."

"I'm not embarrassed," I reiterate. "I'm mad. You violated my privacy." Do they really not understand that this was a serious overstep? That I have every right to be mad at them for reading something that was obviously not meant for them to read?

"We're sorry," Sebastian tells me, his tone and expression earnest. "You're right, we shouldn't have read it, even if it did fall out face-up and we couldn't help but see the title and it got our attention."

He has a point, not that I'll admit that to him. If I saw a piece of paper titled "Sex List: Things to Try Before Graduation," I probably would have a hard time looking away too.

I look down and realize I'm still wearing Lukas's sweatshirt. I shrug it off and drape it over the arm of the sofa, missing its warmth but not about to give them any reason to contact me ever again once I'm safely delivered back to my dorm.

"You know." Lukas glances around the room, holding a silent conversation with each of his friends before continuing. "If you want, we could help you."

I stare at him, not comprehending.

"With your list," he clarifies. "We could help you cross a few things off it."

"Or all of them," adds Felix softly. The lenses of his red-framed glasses glint in the light from the TV, and something about him reminds me of a large cat, a panther or a lion. He looks soft and sweet, but there's something else coiled beneath the surface. Something intense, and animalistic, and thrilling.

Something I am one hundred percent *not* going to think about, now or ever again.

"Absolutely not." I shake my head, my own glasses sliding down my nose with the force of the movement. It was stupid to write out that list in the first place, and stupider to carry it around with me instead of tearing it into a million tiny pieces and flushing it down the toilet. I don't even really want those things I wrote down. Sure, I'm curious about sex, but there will be time to explore that after I graduate. "Nothing about that is a good idea."

"Why not?" asks Sebastian.

"Because …" I trail off, not sure what to say. Because if I'm being completely honest with myself, I don't have a good answer. Something about these guys makes me want to know more about them, and it's not even worth denying my attraction to them. The fact that Lukas's suggestion has my blood racing and tingles spreading through my lower belly is proof enough of that.

"You have a list of sexual activities you would like to partake in," Sebastian states. "And we would like to partake in those activities with you. You said you're not interested in dating, and we'll respect that, but you can explore sex without dating."

"And if you change your mind and do want to date us, we're amenable to that," says Elliot.

"One thing at a time." Sebastian tells him, and smiles at me. I realize that I don't think I've seen him smile before, at least not like this. They've all always been so serious and straightforward, but Sebastian's grin is bright and totally changes his face, making him look more boyish and playful, and … fun. But it's short-lived, his no-nonsense mask falling back into place almost as quickly as it lifted.

I let my gaze fall on each of them in turn even as I'm mentally yelling at myself. *Why are you hesitating? You cannot possibly be considering this. Say no. Say* hell *no, and get out of here, and block their numbers, and maybe consider transferring schools and legally changing your name.* But I can't help letting myself half-imagine it for a moment. Me, naked and on all fours, with Felix kneeling behind me as he pounds into me with that cat-like control, shoving me forward so that I take Elliot's cock deeper into my throat with each thrust. Elliot's hands buried in my hair, holding my head right where he wants it as he fucks my mouth. Sebastian underneath me and bucking his hips against his own hand, his lips locked around one of my nipples, sucking, as he pinches the other between those dexterous fingers. He twists them just so and bites down gently, sending a bolt of pleasure through my body so I come hard, my whole body shaking with the effort to keep sucking Elliot off instead of collapsing on top of Sebastian. And Lukas, fisting his own thick length as he watches his friends and me pleasuring each other, whispering "Good girl" in my ear and triggering a second orgasm for me as they all find their release simultaneously.

I force myself out of the fantasy, dropping my gaze to the ground and gathering my hair into a low ponytail over one shoulder just to have something to do with my hands. What am I *doing*, thinking about that, right in front of them, and in such graphic detail? All week I've been looking at their pictures and refusing to let my fantasies turn fully sexual, and then I choose this of all moments to fling open the door? What is wrong with me?

"Can I think about it?" My voice comes out hoarse, barely above a whisper, thanks to the lust now coursing through me.

Their expressions all sharpen for just a moment into ones of hunger, allowing me another brief glimpse of exactly how different they can be from what they've shown me up until now.

"Of course," says Felix. The others nod in agreement.

If I say no, what will happen? Will they give up on me forever, move on and find some other girl who already knows what she's doing and won't need to be taught? I'm not ready to commit to this yet, but the thought of someone else taking my place in that fantasy I just had almost has me agreeing to this ridiculous proposition.

"Okay."

"Okay, you'll do it?" Elliot looks even more excited than when I agreed to come over for a movie night.

I shake my head, my eyes wide. "No! I mean, okay, I'll think about it." Yikes, if I do go through with this, I'm really going to have to watch my words moving forward. They take everything so literally.

Chapter Eight

The ride back to my dorm is so uncomfortable, given everything that has transpired in the last half hour or so. Elliot is driving again, with Sebastian in the front passenger seat, since they both sat next to me on the sofa for the little bit of their nerdy space show we watched. So I'm squeezed between Lukas and Felix again.

Technically it's fair, but I'm wondering if they've ever taken into consideration the time length of their switching. We only got through part of one episode of their show, and the drives from the party to their house and their house to my dorm add up to at least twice that. That means Lukas and Felix are sitting next to me longer than Sebastian and Elliot, and I'm surprised they're okay with that, given how focused they are on fairness. Maybe they're thinking it'll even out in the long run, or that trying to keep track of the amount of time each of them gets to sit with me is too much of a hassle. Though I suspect that type of math is as simple for them as counting to two is for me.

If they've thought through something as small as the rotation of sitting by me, I have to assume they've also fully discussed their offer to help me check things off on my sexual to-do list, although I wonder how, given the short amount of time there was between them finding the list and me finding them with it. But they seem able to have entire conversations silently and in a manner of seconds, so probably they just used that mind-meld power to decide while they were reading over the list before I came back from my call with Ronnie.

I also wonder if they'll truly be able to compartmentalize and separate their supposed desire to date me from their offer to help me with the list. I've told them I don't want a relationship, and while I want to trust that they'll respect that and be able to keep this whole sex-list thing strictly that, I can't help but be skeptical. Especially because I don't know that I can trust myself to keep from developing feelings for them once we start. I've always been worried about my ability to separate sex and emotions, and seeing how obsessed my mother is with my father, I haven't even tried, just in case I'm not able to compartmentalize.

I suppose I can't keep that up forever, though, and perhaps now is the time to test myself. These would be the perfect men for such a trial. I'll probably never have a similar chance.

I note how Elliot's fingers wrap confidently around the steering wheel. If they can manipulate a cube so well, they must be able to do other things with their fingers too. The thought makes me blush, unable to stop my brain from imagining the possible ways in which we could explore their dexterity. Ronnie has told me before about her first time and how awkward it was, but somehow, I don't feel like I'd have that problem with these guys. They're goal-oriented, focused, and competitive. Surely that will work in my favor.

Felix's hand brushes against my thigh. Was that

intentional? I look up at him, and his eyes are on me. Focused. Assessing. Analyzing.

Silently, Elliot pulls into a parking spot just outside my dorm and we all sit in the stillness for a moment. I can practically feel the guys' hesitation to open the car doors and say goodnight. I completely understand. Once we step outside of this car, am I going to see them again?

The very idea makes my lungs constrict. I'm not sure that any of us is going to be able to navigate a strictly platonic, non-sexual relationship with one another, so it seems like saying goodbye forever and letting them teach me about sex are my only two options.

Finally, Lukas eases open the door and steps out of the car. I slide with him across the back seat, and Felix scootches across as well to exit through the same door even though it would have been much easier to get out on his own side.

The four of them walk me to the front door of my dorm. It's a tight squeeze to walk three abreast on the sidewalk, but their shoulders pressed against mine help to stave off the January cold.

We pause in front of the door, and I dig in my purse for my key card that will let me into the building. I don't immediately swipe it and rush inside, though. It feels like if I let them walk away without an answer, I'll be letting them leave for good.

Another girl from my dorm comes up and slides past us. She raises her eyebrows at me like she's not sure if she should intervene or not, so I give her a smile to let her know I'm safe. There's a lot I don't know right now in life, but I do know that these guys will not hurt me. Not intentionally at least.

As soon as she disappears inside and out of sight, Felix

asks, "It's probably too soon to ask, but have you made your decision yet?"

I sigh. "I'm still thinking about it." I'm going to have to pull out some paper and list the potential benefits and problems of this whole thing as soon as I get upstairs.

"But you haven't ruled out saying yes, right?" asks Sebastian.

"I'm going to give it fair consideration, if that's what you're worried about," I assure him.

"In that case, can we kiss you goodnight?" asks Felix.

I should say no. I should tell them that until I decide, there will be none of that. I should swipe my key card and go inside and forget any of this ever happened.

"On the lips, if that would be okay," says Elliot, jumping in before I can say anything.

"That would give you an idea of what you could expect," agrees Felix.

"Don't push her," counters Lukas.

I'm probably going to regret this, and it certainly isn't going to help me make an unbiased decision, but I find myself agreeing. All night, every brush of their hands or press of their legs against mine has made me buzz with desire, and at this point my body is begging for some sort of release. I'm not even aware I'm going to say yes until the words are already leaving my lips.

"Okay, but this is not a promise that I will say yes to the overall proposal."

Sebastian immediately steps forward, lifts my chin with his knuckles, and kisses me, hard, full on the mouth. When he pulls back, my lips want to follow him but when I open my eyes, he's grinning as if he knows he's leaving me wanting more.

As Sebastian steps back, Lukas slides right into the place he vacated and sweetly tucks my hair behind my ear before leaning in to brush a soft kiss across my lips. It's teasing in a completely different way from Sebastian's kiss, and once again I can't help but lean in, trying to chase Lukas's lips as he too steps away.

I'm pretty sure they're trying to show me what I could have, if only I agree to their terms. And, heaven help me, it's working.

Felix steps forward, his hand sliding around the back of my neck to angle my face up to him as he pulls me in. I can tell he's holding himself back as he presses his lips to mine, and I wonder what it would look like if he didn't restrain himself. A thrill runs through me at the thought.

By the time Elliot has teased a kiss over my lips, I'm lightheaded. If I were a weaker woman, I'd fling myself right into their arms and declare their proposal accepted. But I'm still aware that we're in public and another student could walk by again at any moment. And more importantly, I need to make my decision with a clear head.

"Good night," I choke out, swiping my card through the reader and practically fleeing inside.

I race through the lounge, ignoring the girl who walked past us outside. Has she been sitting in here waiting for me? She is clearly trying to get my attention, but I pretend I don't see or hear her. I recognize that it's sweet that she wanted to make sure I'm safe, but I don't know her, and I don't want to be around anyone right now.

As soon as I reach my dorm room, I fling myself down on my bed and toe off my shoes, glad that Ronnie isn't here. While I could easily ignore the stranger downstairs, Ronnie would make it her duty to force me to divulge exactly what just happened. Even if I'm not fully sure myself.

If I were the type of girl who dated, they would be the ideal guys. They're ambitious, dedicated, goal-oriented.

And they're obviously smart since they're all studying mathematics at freaking MIT.

But even if they are the perfect guys on paper, that doesn't mean they wouldn't distract me from my own goals, or end up hurting me in the long run. My dad didn't always take advantage of my mom's love for him. There used to be a give and take to their relationship. Now, however, her entire life revolves around him, and he barely gives her the time of day.

Something scratches against my leg, and I look down to see the list poking out of my purse. I pull it out and smooth it open, looking over the list of sexual activities freshman me wanted to have completed by graduation. Or at least, freshman me thought she was supposed to complete them. Even at the time, I didn't really intend to actually do anything with the list. It's not even an exciting list. It's pretty basic, things that I'd assumed just about everyone will have done before they graduate college.

Things like giving and receiving oral sex, sixty-nining, vaginal sex, and maybe, if I'm brave enough, try out a toy or two. I couldn't think of anything super kinky to add because my experience is so embarrassingly limited.

If the way they kissed me is any indication, I bet the speedcubers would have a few ideas of things I should experience.

There's a sharp peal of laughter from down the hall, pulling my attention away from my handwritten list. Even though it's late at night, other girls are up and having fun with friends, enjoying their college experience, and probably there are at least a handful of couples having sex in this building right now. And yet here I am alone in my dorm room, just me and my stupid list of stupid boring sex things I still haven't tried despite being halfway through my sophomore year. I'm so far behind my peers on this, and I hate feeling like I'm behind the curve. I feel that way when I go to parties with Ronnie and don't know how to just have fun like everyone else. I feel that way at work when Brad tells me to refill the coffee creamer instead of actually teaching me what I need to do to be a reporter. And now I'm feeling it when I think about all the sex everyone else is having without me.

Yet again, I'm being left behind. But at least this is something I have some control over.

Reaching for my phone, I open up the message I sent myself from Lukas's phone earlier, still feeling the whispers of the guys' kisses on my lips.

Okay, I text. *I'll do it. You all can help me check off items on my list.*

Dots immediately appear, then disappear, then appear again. As I watch Lukas try to figure out how to respond, I feel confident in my decision. I'll check off the items on my sad little list and go into life after college with at least some semblance of experience under my belt so that when I am ready for an actual relationship, I'll have some idea what I'm doing. And maybe I can use this to my advantage even further, too.

Finally, a new group chat pops up with Lukas and three unfamiliar numbers.

You won't regret this decision – Felix.

It's cute that he signs the text so I know who it's from, since they know I don't have all their numbers saved.

Will you send us a photo too? You never did give us an answer about that, and fair is fair – Sebastian.

He's right. And at least if I send them a photo, it will balance out the stalker-y feeling I've had, staring at their faces all week. I scroll through my camera roll, trying to find a picture that's decent enough to send them. I finally decide on a selfie Ronnie took of the two of us on my camera. I'm more in the background of it, but it's not a bad picture. I crop it so I'm the main subject of the picture, then send it to them.

They respond with a group photo of all of them, with a message saying, *You have two photos of us now. You should even things out.*

I giggle at that. This could become a truly ridiculous game if I choose to let it, and the idea isn't unappealing. *That's a tomorrow problem*, I tell them, and set the phone down to get ready for bed.

Once I'm in pajamas and snuggled under the covers, I allow myself to imagine what, exactly, this thing I've agreed to will look like. Group sex? Or will they pass me from one of their beds to the next? Will they all watch, or will it be totally one-on-one? Will they touch each other, or only me?

No. I shake my head, shutting my own thoughts down.

I will not lie here thinking about four guys running a train on me. I haven't even had sex with one guy, I have zero business thinking about having sex with four at once. Or four in succession. I promised myself that I would not let boys distract me from my studies and my work. Having sex with four different men would be way more of a distraction than I could ever have imagined.

Chapter Nine

The door to my room slams open, but I barely look up. I'm trying to focus on my homework, but my phone is sitting right next to my books on the desk and it's all I can think about. When will I hear from the guys again?

Ronnie throws herself down on her bed and stares at me. Waiting.

After thirty seconds or so, she tosses her pillow at me to get my attention. "Aren't you going to ask me how my night was?"

"Oh, yeah." I give up on trying to focus on work and turn my full attention to Ronnie. "How did things go with Trevor?"

"So amazing!" Ronnie stretches her arms above her head and does jazz hands. Last night's mascara is smudged under her eyes and her hair is thrown up in a messy topknot, but she looks happy. "He even made me coffee this morning, so I know he's taking things seriously between us."

"That's awesome. Congrats!" I say it with as much enthusiasm as I can muster, but I must not be very convincing because she just rolls her eyes and holds out her hands for me to toss her pillow back to her.

"Okay, fine tell me about *your* night. Did anything happen between you and one of those guys you were with last night? Who were they, anyway? And which one are you into?"

Yikes. Ronnie figured out with just a glance what I am still trying to wrap my head around. If the crush I've been harboring is that obvious to her from seeing me with them for two seconds, it's no wonder they offered to help with my list. They probably picked up on something I wasn't even aware I was putting down.

"Those were the Rubik's Cube guys from my article." I don't want to tell her about their offer. I want to keep that close to my chest for a while. Maybe I should tell her—after all, she's my best friend and she probably could give me some advice—but something in the back of my mind is whispering to me to stay quiet for now.

"Oh?" Ronnie's eyes widen and she sits up straighter, settling in for a gossip session. "Oh. They did look kind of nerdy, but they are way cuter than I thought they would be for people who compete in something so lame."

"It's not lame," I protest, offended on their behalf. I mean, yeah, I thought the same thing at first, but now that I've spent a little bit of time with them and watched them compete, I don't think it's lame at all. It was bad enough when my editor said it, I don't like hearing Ronnie voice the same opinion.

She ignores my objection. "Well, you were vibing with them. I never see you chatting with guys, but it looked like there was something between you and at least the one in the purple shirt. That's why I left you there last night. I was hoping you'd get lucky for once."

I frown. I know I'm not nearly as social or experienced as her, but she knows why I don't seek out relationships and hookups like so many other girls. Her saying she was hoping I'd "get lucky for once" is so dismissive of that, and it stings.

"But since you obviously seem to click with them," Ronnie continues, shoving off her bed and gathering up her shower things, "maybe you should talk to them about doing another article about their whole cube thing. Don't you have an assignment for one of your classes where you have to write a series of related articles? You could use the one your editor didn't publish and then do some others about cubing. You definitely have chemistry with those guys. Maybe you can take that connection and make it work for you."

"I did think about that," I confess, setting aside my bruised feelings. "It would be a good series idea, and if it turns out well I can show it to Carl and maybe he'll admit he was wrong about the cubing *and* about me. I mean, he probably won't, but it's a nice fantasy."

My phone vibrates with an incoming text, and Ronnie dives for it, snatching it off my desk before I can turn around.

"Are they texting you?" she singsongs.

I grab for the phone, but she dances out of my way, staying just close enough to use my face to unlock the screen and start reading the message.

"Invasive much?" I make a halfhearted attempt to take the phone away, but she spins and drops onto my bed. Accepting that she's already read it and I can't make her un-read it, I lean over her shoulder to see what it says.

We had a good time with you last night.

Another pops up. *When can we see you again?*

The third comes through right on its heels. *Movie night this weekend?*

And a fourth. *We could come pick you up.*

"You should let them help you out with that sex list,"

says Ronnie, handing me the phone. "Sounds like they'd be into it."

I stare at her, slack-jawed. She hit the bullseye and has no idea, and I'm not about to tell her.

"I'm heading to the shower." Ronnie retrieves her shower caddy from where she had dropped it when she grabbed the paper from my desk. "If you're gonna sext with them while I'm gone, put a hair tie on the door so I don't interrupt."

I glare at the door as it closes behind her, then return my attention to the phone screen. I need to answer, but I'm scared. I know they're not just offering a movie night.

I sit there long enough that the door opens and Ronnie strides back in, wrapped in a bathrobe and hair dripping over her shoulders.

"Did you text them back?" she asks, setting her shower caddy on her desk and reaching for her hairbrush.

"Not yet."

"Rebecca June Flynn, you text those cute nerds back right this minute and tell them you want another movie night, and this time you want it naked."

I roll my eyes at her, and she grins cheekily and fluffs up her wet hair, attempting to gain a little volume. My phone buzzes again, and I dive for it.

"Don't even try to tell me you haven't thought about it." Ronnie blows me a kiss as I check my phone. "I think you should go for it."

The message, from Elliot, sends a swirl of butterflies through my midsection. *We don't want to pressure you. We're just excited.*

I take a deep breath and tap out a response. *Movie night sounds great. I'll bring the list.*

Chapter Ten

It's been a week since I saw the guys, and even though we've texted every day since I agreed to their sex list plan, I'm still nervous about meeting them. I'm not fully confident in how this whole arrangement is actually going to go.

When they text me to arrange a time to pick me up, Felix says, *You can stay the night, if you want.*

Do I want that? Do *they* want that? I hadn't thought about what would happen after the sex stuff.

He sends a follow-up text while I'm thinking. *We'd like it if you stayed, but if you don't want to, we understand and will bring you home whenever you're ready.*

They're so sweet. I don't know if I'm ready for any of this, but I guess if I'm going over there to fool around, it can't hurt to plan to stay the night. If I change my mind, I'm sure they'll bring me back to the dorm.

I can stay the night, I tell them.

The typing bubble appears and disappears a few times before Lukas finally responds. *We're looking forward to it. See you at seven.*

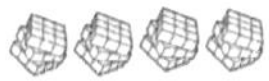

The guys had agreed to let me interview them for the article series I'm working on for class before driving over to their house for movie night, so we meet up at a coffee shop near my dorm after my last class. It's much louder and harder to have a proper conversation than any of us expected it to be, so as soon as we're done with our coffees we leave.

The drive over to their house is fairly quiet. They don't talk much because I think they just need to decompress after the loud café and a full day of classes, and I'm quiet because without my interview questions to drive the conversation, all I can focus on is the rest of the evening. I'm nervous. I know what's happening tonight, and I feel like I'm going to vibrate right out of my own skin with the anticipation.

Lukas won't let me carry my own overnight bag in from the car, and I can feel my heart pounding as he sets it down at the base of the stairs, but then he walks right on into the kitchen as if this is the most normal night in the world.

"I'm glad we're home where it's quiet," says Sebastian, following him into the kitchen. Felix and Elliot are close on his heels, so I trail behind them.

"I didn't think the café would be so loud on a Friday night," says Elliot, pulling nacho fixings out of the fridge and laying them out on the counter. "I expect that when we go to a party, but a café?"

"Next time we research better," agrees Felix, grabbing a baking pan from the cupboard.

Sebastian pulls a bag of chips from the pantry and pours them onto the pan. Watching them go through the motions of their Friday night nacho routine, is fascinating. The way they move around each other in the kitchen, everybody knowing exactly what their job is and where they need to be to avoid running into someone else, it's almost like watching a choreographed dance.

"Normally we go to a library to study, and it's much quieter," he tells me. "You should join us next time."

"We could still bring in a latte for you," offers Lukas, grabbing a packet of popcorn from a different cupboard and laying it out flat in the microwave.

All eyes are on me as they wait for my response.

"We wouldn't be able to talk much for me to ask you questions for my article, though, if we're at a library." Not that the article is the only schoolwork I have, but it's the only schoolwork I need their help with.

"We're just thinking that we all have rigorous school schedules right now and figured we could see each other more regularly if we include studying and homework time when we get together," Lukas tells me. "And maybe we can't do a full interview at the library, but this would let you ask us the questions slowly and decide exactly what you need answered as you write out the article instead of feeling pressured to get through every possible question all in one sitting."

"Yeah, that way it's less pressure each time. We know you have a lot on your plate right now too," agrees Felix as he slides the nachos into the oven that Elliot started preheating when we first walked in.

They're right that it's difficult to generate all of the questions that might be helpful for my article in one go. It'd be easier to ask them as I need them, since I'm sure I'll think of a hundred more that could be helpful as I'm writing.

"And if you have other homework, you could do that too," Elliot points out. "It wouldn't have to be just your article. But it would be nice to hang out with you more, and this would be an easy way for us to all spend time together."

"Okay, we can try to do that." I mean, I need to study anyway, and if they want to sit near me while I do it that's not a big deal. It might even come in handy, if I need help with some particular math issue.

I normally study alone, or occasionally with Ronnie, but there could be a lot of benefits to having study partners who actually take their schooling seriously.

"I was kind of surprised that you wanted to go to the café and do movie night tonight," I say, watching the four of them continue to move around the kitchen efficiently, getting down plates and pouring drinks. "I thought you normally go to parties to play poker on Friday nights." That's what it had sounded like when we were texting earlier in the week about our weekend plans.

"Normally, yes, but we voted and decided that going out with you tonight was worth missing one of our poker nights." Felix carries the stack of plates out to the living room and sets it on the coffee table.

Wow. To have them prioritize me over one of their work sessions is unexpected.

"Don't worry," says Felix, grabbing two oven mitts and clapping them together, which snaps me out of my mental spiral. "We're working on paying our rent for six months from now, so it's not a big deal to skip a night."

"Besides, if we're seeing each other more often, we can schedule around the poker," adds Lukas. "You could maybe even come with us to the parties and be our good luck charm."

"You know," Sebastian tells him, "good luck charms aren't really lucky. It's just that the idea of having that luck calms your nerves and lets you think clearer and make better, more logical decisions."

"Yes, but in movies, whenever there's a poker scene, there's usually a woman who the hero says is his good luck charm," says Elliot. He looks at me. "So if that's something you'd like, you can come be our good luck charm even if good luck charms don't actually bring us luck."

Sebastian looks thoughtful as he considers this. "I suppose that even if we know the good luck is actually just a placebo effect, it can't hurt to have you as our good luck charm," he concedes. "Maybe the placebo effect will work even though we know to expect it."

"I think it could be a fun experiment to try," I tell them. I take the bag of pretzels from Elliot and go into the living room to deposit them on the coffee table, if only for something to do with myself.

Lukas comes into the living room with the bowl of microwave popcorn and offers it to me.

"Thank you for making popcorn," I say, taking the bowl from him and setting it on the table next to the pretzels. I can't spot a single burnt kernel. Of course they're able to make perfect popcorn. They probably ran an analysis to determine the perfect microwave setting to ensure every kernel pops and none of them burn.

Felix carries the hot nacho tray out to the coffee table and sets it down on the hot pads they put there earlier. "Don't forget, you're sitting in the middle."

"Fair is fair," I say with a smile as I settle into position.

"Exactly," says Sebastian, grinning as he sits on one side of me and Felix sits on the other.

Elliot starts up the show before he and Lukas join us on the sofa, and everyone starts to plate up their snacks. We all have a little bit of everything, and they were right about nachos being a superior movie night snack to popcorn, not that I'll admit it out loud.

As the first episode winds down, I start to wonder

what's going to happen next. Are we going to stay up late, watch more TV, and not actually tackle the list at all tonight? Will they want to go to bed right away? Where will I sleep? In one of their rooms? On the sofa? I'm assuming they don't have a guest room.

And if they do want to try something from the list tonight, will I be able to wash my hands first? Because right now I have grease from the popcorn and cheese and I don't want to get that everywhere.

Maybe I should go brush my teeth.

Finally, I can't take it anymore. I cannot be the only one who feels a mounting tension.

"So what's the plan for tonight? Are we checking off any items on that stupid to-do list, or are we just hanging out?" I reach for a napkin to wipe the snack grease off my fingers, and also just to give myself something to hold onto. My hands are shaking, I'm so nervous. Maybe I shouldn't be; we've been having a good time and they've put no pressure on me. But I can't help it. This is a big deal, and the build-up is really starting to make me spiral.

Felix shifts so he's angled a little more toward me and puts a hand on my knee. "We would like to cross at least one thing off the list," he says. "If you're up to it."

"We didn't want to make you uncomfortable by moving too fast," Lukas tells me, and the others nod their agreement.

"So ... just one thing? We can't get through the whole list in a night?" From what Ronnie's said about her nights with certain guys, they can really cover all the bases in just an evening. It sounds intimidating, but at least it would get it all over with and I could stop being so nervous. I pull my hair out of its ponytail and begin to finger-comb it, just to give myself something to do with my hands.

Felix swallows, his eyebrows inching above his glasses.

"We agreed that since it would be your first time for a lot of this stuff, it'd be better to go slow. We don't want to make you feel ... used, or like we don't care about you, or anything."

"Or overwhelmed," adds Elliot.

"Besides, you should enjoy the experiences," says Sebastian, sliding a hand across my thigh so his fingers rest very close to the spot that begins to dampen at his touch. "Which will be easier if we don't rush through it all."

"I would enjoy this a lot more if it weren't so stressful." I sweep my hair into a ponytail again, making sure there are no bumps before looping the elastic around it.

"This shouldn't be stressful, it should be fun," says Felix, tugging me closer and pulling me onto his lap so I'm straddling him. "We can help you relax."

He cups the back of my neck and pulls me down for a kiss. It's not polite or sweet like when we've said goodnight outside my dorm. This kiss takes the promise from the last one and makes good on it. It's slow, deep, and I can feel something more simmering under the surface, but Felix isn't letting it through yet. His lips part against mine, his tongue asking for more, and I open up, letting him explore.

It's not that I've never been kissed before. I'm not exactly experienced with it, but those goodnight kisses the other day weren't my first time kissing a boy. But none of the kisses I've had prior to this could have prepared me for the swooping sensation in my belly, the feeling of being off-balance that makes my fingers clutch Felix's shirt to stay upright. I had no idea a kiss could make a person feel this way.

I feel hands settle on my waist, pressing me down against Felix's lap. "Lower your hips more," says Sebastian. "Sit your whole weight on him. See how much you affect us and our bodies? Nothing here is stressful. You're wanted. We all want you."

Felix shifts his hips and I can feel him hardening beneath me even through our layers of clothes. It's kind of exciting that I'm making that happen, that his body is responding to *me*. I grind my hips against his, testing, and he groans, his fingers pressing into my nape as he deepens the kiss even more.

"That's with one guy," says Lukas, gripping my ponytail and pulling gently to break my kiss with Felix. "Now feel what it's like to grind down on Felix's cock while kissing someone else."

He catches my lips in a sweet kiss, coaxing them to open for him as Felix's hands wrap around my waist and guide me, dragging me forward and back so I can feel the pressure of his hardening cock sliding along the front of my jeans.

I'm the one who takes the kiss deeper with Lukas. I don't even mean to do it, it just happens. I'm gripping Felix's shirt with one hand and Lukas's with the other, as though I'm worried one or both of them will disappear if I don't hold on tight.

"My turn," says Sebastian, sliding me off of Felix's lap and onto his. "Show me what Felix just taught you."

A bubble of need has been building up in my chest, and my entire body feels electric in a way that I've never experienced. So there's no hesitation on my part as I grind my weight down on Sebastian's lap and start rolling my hips exactly the way Felix just taught me.

Sebastian doesn't let me catch his lips with mine, though. Instead, he presses them to my jaw, feathering kisses along my skin in a way that feels good, but isn't enough.

"You can now check dry humping off your list, and from the looks of my friends, you've done a very good job," says

Elliot. His voice is husky, like I've never heard it before, and I feel dizzy with the knowledge that it's because he wants me. "And good students get rewarded. Would you like your reward?"

All of my focus is on the pressure building between my legs as I grip Sebastian's shoulders to steady me as I move against him, so all I can do is murmur, "Mm-hmm."

"You can stop me at any time. You're in charge here," says Elliot, coming to kneel behind me.

Elliot reaches around me to undo the button and zipper on my jeans. I suck in a breath as his palm slides under the hem of my shirt, along my stomach, and his fingers reach inside the denim to cup me.

"An excellent student and a very good girl," says Elliot. "You're so wet for us."

He rubs all four of his fingers over the front of my damp panties, emphasizing his words.

I lean back against him, thrusting my hips against his fingers, silently begging for more. I've never had a boy touch me there before, and I definitely never imagined it would happen while I simulate a sex act on top of a second guy while two of their friends watch from beside us on the sofa.

"Are you ready to check off another item on your list?" asks Elliot, moving aside my panties until he is sliding a single finger along the seam of my pussy.

"Yes." I gasp out the word. I take back every thought I ever had about the list being stupid. It's not stupid, it's perfect. It's genius. Who knew checking items off a list could be so sexy? Especially with the way I'm staring into Sebastian's hooded eyes, and can't see Elliot at all.

Elliot circles his finger around my entrance, and I bite my lip to not cry out. I'm so close, I don't know why he's teasing me. Especially as his thumb brushes across my sensitive clit, causing my hips to buck and allow his finger to slip into my entrance.

"So eager to begin, I see." Elliot leans down to whisper in my ear, but he doesn't let his finger retreat. If anything, he presses it in deeper. To his friends, he adds, "Rebecca here is desperate to continue. She wants to race through this list, but I'm not sure we should let her."

He pulls his finger back, withdrawing almost completely, and my hips follow him of their own accord. I nearly whimper at the thought of Elliot and his friends taking me this far and then not following through with their promises of pleasure.

"No, we should make the list last the whole semester at least," says Lukas, a wicked grin on his lips.

"We could calculate the number of weeks and then divide the list by that number," says Felix, brushing the backs of his knuckles along my cheek.

I lean into his touch even as the lower half of my body squirms against Elliot's hand, seeking more contact.

"Taking into consideration the number of steps each list item could also be broken down into," Lukas agrees, nodding.

"Fair," I say, panting as I reach out to rest a hand against Sebastian's chest, right over his heart. "Be fair, now."

"That's true. Fair is fair." Sebastian rubs his thumb along the inside seam of my jeans on my thigh. Such a simple touch shouldn't do anything for me, but I'm in such a heightened state of arousal that even that small movement lights a fire under my skin. "We should at least let her come tonight."

"True. We don't want to be rude hosts on her first overnight in our home," agrees Elliot, adding a second finger alongside the first and pressing gently into me.

"Yes." I barely register the conversation around me,

with my entire focus on Elliot's fingers, but I'm aware at least that it's in my favor.

Elliot works his fingers in and out of my throbbing pussy as his thumb does something magical to my clit. My breath comes quicker and my eyes begin to roll back in my head as he applies a little more pressure.

My other hand comes up to join the first, gripping Sebastian's shirt. If I let go right now, I'm certain I would fall over to the side, right into Felix's lap. As soon as Elliot curls both of his fingers inside of me, pressing the heel of his palm against my clit, I gasp and lean forward to hide my face in Sebastian's sweater as my orgasm rips through me. I knew from watching Elliot play with his cubes that his fingers were dexterous, but I didn't fully understand the benefits of all that play until right this moment.

"Good girl." Elliot kisses the back of my neck as he eases his fingers out of my still-fluttering pussy.

All I can do is lay there against Sebastian's chest and let the tingling settle over my entire body. I feel so relaxed right now. We could lay here and watch several episodes of their space show and I wouldn't even mind. It wouldn't even matter that I can't see the television from my current comfy position.

"Not bad," says Lukas. "But I could do it faster."

"You really think so?" asks Elliot, rising to his challenge.

"It's simply a matter of finding the right patterns. Instead of aligning the colors, you have to monitor her breathing to measure her reactions," says Lukas, confident in his assessment.

"Prove it," dares Elliot.

"Oh, I will." Lukas moves to sit next to Sebastian, then wraps his arms around me and lifts me onto his lap, turning me so my back rests against his chest.

Elliot is standing next to the sofa, looking pretty proud

of himself. I glance down to the bulge tenting his pants, and think that maybe I should feel a little proud of myself too. And I will, as soon as I'm done floating on this little bit of heaven that's still hovering around in my veins.

"Think you can take one more?" asks Lukas, rubbing his wide hands up and down my sides reassuringly, letting my shirt lift a little and then settle back down with each change of direction.

"Mm-hmm." This is so relaxing, laying here and feeling Lukas's confident hands on me. I'd probably agree to just about anything right now.

This time when Lukas's hands make their way back down my body, he slides one into my pants and immediately slips two fingers right into my pussy. Thank goodness I'm so relaxed because I can feel the stretch of taking two fingers at once again so soon. I'll probably be sore later, but right now it feels good, and that's all I care about.

Pressing his palm against my clit at the same time that he moves his fingers inside of me, Lukas takes me from nothing to everything so quickly, I can't breathe. As he works his magic on my pussy, my own fingers clamp down on his forearm, holding him in place. Because if he stops, I just might keel over.

The second orgasm comes so fast, it crashes over me before I know it's approaching. "Fuck!" I pant, gasping as the air returns to my lungs.

Even in high school when I had enough privacy to touch myself, it never felt like this. Like the orgasm is literally being ripped from my body, painful and sharp and oh, so delicious.

"What was my time?" asks Lukas, sliding his hand out of my pants and leaving a trail of my own juices along my stomach. "That was definitely faster than Elliot."

I lay there panting for breath, held in Lukas's arms, and

their voices all blur together as they argue about whether or not Lukas should have time automatically added because I was already sensitive from the orgasm that Elliot gave me. I could probably fall asleep right here if they were just a little bit quieter.

"At least we've made a good start on the list," says Elliot, beginning to gather the remains of our movie snacks to take back to the kitchen.

I should get up to help, but my limbs feel like rubber and if I stand up right now, I'm just going to fall right back over. Besides, I'm warm and cozy wrapped up in Lukas's arms right now.

My brain feels like it wants to form a question about sleeping arrangements, but my mouth isn't cooperating.

As if he can hear my thoughts, Lukas says, "You can sleep in my bed." He kisses my cheek. "I'll sleep down here on the sofa."

"Not fair to you." There should be more words there, but I can't figure out what they are right now. I'm about eighty percent of the way to asleep.

"If you want, you can sleep in my bed next to me," says Felix, stroking his fingers along my arm. "We could add sleeping next to someone to your list and cross that off tonight too."

"Okay." Sharing a bed actually sounds nice. Warm. Cozy.

"Wait, why do you get to sleep next to her?" asks Sebastian. "As of right now, our tallies are equal, and we're both behind Elliot and Lukas."

"Fine, cubes?" asks Felix, reaching for one of the cubes on the side table and mixing it up. He tosses it to Sebastian as Sebastian tosses a mixed-up cube to him, and their fingers begin to fly.

"I win," says Felix smugly, setting the solved cube on the coffee table with a loud *snick.*

"At least it was fair," Sebastian grumbles, setting down his own cube.

"Nothing is fair if I'm the only one taking care of these dishes," calls Elliot from the kitchen, where I can hear the sounds of plates being rinsed and put into the dishwasher.

"We'll help," says Sebastian, taking up the nacho pan and carrying it out of the room.

"I'll show Rebecca upstairs and then come back down to help." Felix helps me up and then stands himself.

I should say something, offer to help clean or say I can find my own way upstairs, but I'm not sure my limbs could manage anything at the moment. And I have no idea where Felix's bedroom is. I can't pick the wrong one. Not after he and Sebastian competed to see who gets to sleep next to me.

I dimly wonder if we really will only be sleeping, or if Felix is planning to cross something else off my list tonight.

I'm not sure I can manage anything else in that department.

"Come this way, Rebecca." Felix wraps his arm around my waist and guides me into the front hall.

I should call out goodnight to the others, but I'm so sleepy, and my voice doesn't want to work. At least Felix is tall and solid beside me so I can lean against him as he grabs my bag and helps me up the stairs.

"This is my room," says Felix, turning on the light and setting my bag at the foot of the bed. Crossing the hall and turning on another light, he adds, "Here is the bathroom, if you want to get ready for sleep. I'll leave a towel on the counter for you."

I manage to find my voice and croak out a thank you.

"See you in the morning." I can hear Felix's steps bounce down the stairs again.

I'd turn to call good night as well, but my focus is centered completely on the double bed in front of me. The bed I'm about to share with him for the entire night.

I tear my gaze away and dig through my bag for my toothbrush before heading to the bathroom. As I brush my teeth I can't help glancing at the mirror, at the reflection of the big bed across the hall.

I take off my glasses and begin to wash my face. When I glance up after drying my face with the towel Felix set out for me, Sebastian's face fills the mirror next to my own. He silently puts toothpaste on his own brush and then stands beside me to brush his teeth as I finish drying my face and slide my glasses back onto my nose. All this without a word between us as if we've done this a hundred times before. As if we've always completed these little domestic tasks together.

As soon as I'm done, I scurry across the hall to Felix's room to find him already in bed. Where did he come from? He wasn't in the bathroom with me and Sebastian, so I wonder if he used another one or if he just crawled into bed without brushing his teeth or anything. I hope not.

"There are T-shirts in the drawer," says Felix, pointing out a dresser in the corner. "If you need something different to sleep in."

"I brought my pajamas." I pull my sleep clothes out of my bag as evidence. I should have brought them into the bathroom with me to change, but I wasn't thinking.

"Oh." Felix folds his glasses and sets them on the nightstand. "I forgot about your bag."

I hesitate, debating if I should go back across the hall to change. But Sebastian is in there now with the door closed, so I'd have to wait and I really would like to just go to sleep already. Besides, Felix has already taken off his glasses, so he probably won't see much. And he'll see everything at some point. May as well rip off the Band-Aid.

I take a deep breath and turn my back to Felix to change as quickly as possible. I'm not brave or confident enough to simply strip in front of him. It may happen by the time I get to the bottom of the list, but not yet. I'm glad the T-shirt I grabbed to sleep in is long enough to cover my butt when I shimmy my jeans down and pull on my sleep shorts. All he really got to see was the back of my bra when I changed shirts, and my legs.

I unclip my bra and tug it off through my sleeve, wadding it up and shoving it and my glasses into my bag before flipping off the light and skirting around the bed to slip into the empty side. I try to make myself small, to stay on my side as much as possible, but I am very aware of Felix's body next to mine on the mattress.

"Would you mind if we did one more thing tonight?" asks Felix in the darkness, rolling to face me. "It's not on your list, but I'd really like to do it."

Excitement and apprehension war within me. On the one hand, I wouldn't mind another orgasm, now that the haze from the first two has worn off, but I also now have the clarity to be nervous again.

"What is it?" I ask, trying to keep my voice steady.

"Can we snuggle?" Felix's own voice is so soft and low, I can barely hear it.

That's it? Nothing sexy, just snuggling? It sounds nice, but it also sounds like something a couple would do, and I don't want to muddy things up in that department.

I must take too long to answer, because he says, "We just gave you two orgasms, and I don't think I'm wrong to suspect it was the first time someone else has done that for you. It feels kind of shitty to just roll over and go to sleep after that. I want you to feel cared for." I open my mouth to protest that we're not dating, it's not his job to make me feel that way, but he seems to anticipate this because he says, "I'm not trying to act boyfriend-y, or anything. You've made it clear you don't want that, and I will respect it. But I think you deserve to be held, and I'd like to hold you."

That's ... actually really sweet. And even though he says he'd like to do this, I know that if I say no, he'll accept that. Which makes me not want to say no. "Okay."

I can hear the smile in his voice when he says, "Come here," and pulls me across the gap between us, turning me so my back is against his chest, until I'm ensconced in his arms. "Good night."

"Good night," I reply, relaxing into him. I didn't think I would like this. So much touching, and it seemed like not nearly enough space to sleep, but before I know it, the dark and quiet soothe me into sleep.

Chapter Eleven

The room is still dark when I wake up, and this bed is super comfy, nothing like the bed back in my dorm. I should get up, but I feel like I could sleep forever.

I roll over to ask Felix if he's awake, but the words die on my tongue. The bed next to me is made up as if no one had slept on that side of the bed all night. Well, that answers that. I'm certain I fell asleep in his arms last night, so he's obviously just already up.

Slipping out of bed, I peek into the hall. I don't see any of the other guys, so I tiptoe across the hall and brush my teeth. We may have gotten intimate last night, but there's a limit to intimacy and avoidable morning breath is it.

As I brush, I wonder what their morning routine is. Are they all early risers, or just Felix? Are they still in pajamas? Are they itching to drive me back home so they can return to their routine undisturbed?

There's only one way to find out.

Quietly, I slip down the stairs. I don't want to draw attention to myself. As soon as I'm near the foot of the stairs though, the most wonderful smell comes wafting through the hall. Coffee. I follow it to the kitchen and peek through the doorway.

Lukas spots me first. "Good morning," he says, coming over to plant a quick, hard kiss on my lips before pulling me into the room.

I'm definitely glad I brushed my teeth now.

"I should go back upstairs and change." They're all in normal day clothes, sweaters and jeans, and now I feel completely underdressed. I do have a fresh outfit I'd packed in my overnight bag because I hadn't wanted anyone to see me come home in the same clothes and think I'm doing the walk of shame.

"Later," says Sebastian setting out the plates at the kitchen table, where they've squeezed a folding chair in to accommodate having an extra person. "Breakfast is ready. The eggs will get cold."

"Yeah, and you look cute in your pajamas," agrees Elliot.

"The fabric of her sleep pants is soft too," says Felix. And when the others raise their eyebrows at him, he adds, "We cuddled last night. It wasn't on her to-do list, but I felt it should be."

The rest of the team nod in agreement as they start passing the plates of eggs, bacon, toast, and fruit around the table for everyone to serve themselves.

"Did you sleep well last night?" Elliot asks me. "If Felix's bed wasn't comfortable enough for you, you can pick a different bed to sleep in next time."

"True, we'll have to start a rotation," agrees Sebastian.

"I slept fine." I'm not sure what the point of asking me was for if they're just going to start a rotation anyway. I haven't even agreed to a next time yet. Sleeping over regularly feels awfully relationship-y.

"We can put it in our shared calendar so we don't get it

confused with the rotation of who gets to sit by her," adds Elliot. "Or any other rotations."

"There's a calendar for who gets to sit by me?" I do love a good calendar, but this seems extreme.

"Of course," says Sebastian. "Text us your email address and we'll add you to it."

"It's not just for that, though. It makes it easier to keep track of all of our classes, poker nights, appointments, that sort of thing. It can be hard to maintain it in our heads when there are five of us to keep track of," explains Lukas.

"Four," I correct automatically.

"What?" asks Lukas.

"There are four of you." These guys are literal math geeks. How could they miscount?

"Oh, yeah." Lukas glances around the table. "Four. Of course."

Yikes. Time to change the subject.

"So, what's the plan for today? You're all dressed, so you could drive me back to my dorm after breakfast." I pause. "Which is delicious, by the way. Thank you."

"You're welcome," says Elliot, blushing as he cuts up his sausage patties into tiny little squares.

"We were actually thinking," says Felix, "your school stuff is all here."

"And we usually spend Saturdays studying," continues Elliot.

"Would you like to study with us today?" adds Lukas. "We usually do it in our rooms, but we could sit down at the table today."

I chew at my lower lip. I usually spend most of Saturdays studying, too—or at least as much of the day as Ronnie lets me before deciding that we need to do something "fun." But my routine is to study in my dorm, and part of me wants to stick to that pattern.

The other part of me says to break the routine and stay here, because they look so hopeful that I will. And it might be nice to switch things up. I might even get more work done with them than I would with Ronnie bugging me to finish up and go do something with her. I bet they'll actually let me study in peace.

Oh, what the hell. "I suppose I could stay and study for a little while."

"We usually study for the entire day since our classes can be a bit intense. So perhaps you should just stay for dinner and another movie night," suggests Felix, dancing his fingers along the edge of the table. "Then we could take you back to your dorm tomorrow."

"Or Monday morning, depending on your class schedule," adds Elliot, glancing away from the table.

I'm certain I misheard him. Felix's suggestion of staying one more night isn't *not* tempting, considering how last night went, but staying until Monday is ... a lot.

I won't promise to stay till Monday, but there shouldn't be any harm in staying a few more hours, and we can play tonight by ear.

"Okay." At the very least, I'll get some homework done. And if we end up doing more than studying, well. The flutter of excitement low in my belly at the memory of what we did last night says that maybe that would be okay, too.

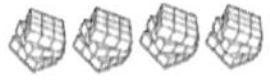

It's weird showering in their shower, seeing around all of their toiletries instead of mine. Of course, I didn't realize I'd be staying long enough to need to shower, and I didn't bring any of my things so I have to use theirs. Now I smell like them. All morning as we sit around the big dining table, I keep catching whiffs of myself. It's weird to smell them on me so strongly.

But they've been quiet enough that I'm able to get through a lot more work than I usually do at the library. It helps that the guys would occasionally get up to refill everyone's mug of coffee. I don't pay enough attention to notice if there's a pattern to it, but I'm sure there is. I wonder if they have a calendar for that, too.

Even the gentle clicking of them solving their cubes one-handed as they go through their own homework is kind of soothing.

Before I know it, the guys are closing up their books and standing to stretch.

"Lunchtime," announces Lukas, straightening his books in front of his seat before pushing in his chair.

"It's not fancy," says Sebastian, "but we hope sandwiches will be okay."

"Sandwiches are perfect." I close my own book and notebook.

"You'll have to tell us your food preferences, and we'll put them on the shopping list," says Elliot as we head into the kitchen.

"We do have a good selection of sandwich stuff though," says Felix, "so hopefully we'll have something you like."

"I'm sure it will be fine." I trail behind them and stand back to watch as they pull out chips and pickles and condiments for their sandwiches, randomly tossing scrambled cubes to each other and solving them like they don't even realize they're doing it.

I don't know how they can do that.

"I still don't think I could ever solve a Rubik's Cube like that." I don't mean to say it out loud—if there's anything I've learned from my mother it's that if you admit to a weakness, men will exploit it—but they all perk up, like this is an exciting moment for them.

"Here, we'll show you," says Sebastian, gently placing his scrambled cube in my hands. "You just have to recognize the patterns and recall the algorithm to achieve the desired outcome."

"So basically, you're just analyzing a problem without even having to think about it. Just doing it by rote?"

"Yes, and for us, it's mostly about doing it faster than anyone else," says Felix. "But you don't have to worry about speed at this point."

"Uh, okay, so where do I start?" I'm not even going to try to solve the cube one-handed like them. I can feel a blush creeping up my cheeks as a flash of memory from last night springs to the forefront of my mind, reminding me just how dexterous their fingers are. Trying to focus on the task at hand, I wrap both hands around it and feel the way the mechanisms swivel a little under the pressure from my fingers.

"The easiest way for beginners is to first make a white cross here on the bottom," says Lukas, moving to stand behind me and wrapping his arms around me to guide my fingers on the cube. "Once you have that, you can solve the corners, like so. Then you'll make the yellow cross next."

It's difficult to pay attention to the way Lukas is guiding my fingers because my body is reacting to the way his arms feel around my body. The flush from a moment ago begins to creep down my neck and chest, and that excited swoopy feeling in my belly returns. How am I supposed to focus on the cube when he's so close to me? This sort of feels like snuggling with Felix last night, having Lukas's arms around me from behind. Or maybe like he's hugging me. It's a nice feeling. I can never remember my dad ever hugging my mom, not even when he's trying to manipulate her.

My phone buzzes on the table. Saved by the vibration.

"I need to get that." I ease out of Lukas's hold, glad when he lets me go instead of holding me captive. "You all get started on lunch."

I grab my phone and go out into the hall, glad for the escape. I need to get my mental state settled, and maybe my physical state too. I can feel my heart pumping harder than usual.

I'm still holding Sebastian's cube, and I stare at it for a moment while my phone buzzes away. Finally, I snap out of it and swipe across the screen to answer just before it sends Ronnie to voicemail.

"Where are you?" Ronnie sounds vaguely panicked, completely skipping over the pleasantries and getting right to the point. "I'm at the dorm and you're not here. You weren't even in the cafeteria when I went to look, or the library."

My stomach drops and I cringe. "Sorry, I thought I'd be home before you got back." I should have messaged Ronnie this morning to give her a heads up, but I wasn't even thinking about her, I was so focused on my homework and the copious amounts of coffee the guys kept pouring for me.

"That doesn't answer the question," Ronnie points out, irritation creeping into her voice as the panic ebbs. "Where are you? Did something happen?"

"I'm over near MIT. They were helping with my class article, and then we watched more of the show we started last time but it got late, so I crashed here, and then they offered that I could stay with them and study today."

I drop my voice when I mention my reason for staying the night, moving into the living room and away from where the guys are so they don't overhear me making it sound like I slept on the couch after working on my story all night. It's not entirely a lie, it just … omits some of the more interesting parts of the evening.

"Wait," Ronnie interjects, then in a quieter voice adds, "Did something happen with one of the cute cube guys? Girl, you need to give me the details! I give you details all the time!"

"You give me too many details," I counter, hoping the guys don't decide now is the moment to come tell me lunch is ready. With my luck, though, that's exactly what's about to happen.

"You're not denying it," Ronnie sing-songs. "It's finally happening! My little Rebecca is growing up, and soon she'll have her first boyfriend, and then she'll finally get *laid*! I'm so proud!"

"No comment," I say dryly. The guys have accepted that I'm not interested in a relationship, but Ronnie will be much harder to convince. I'm not sure I'll ever be able to get her to believe that I'm not, in fact, dating any of them.

"That means it's true!" she squeals in my ear. I hold the phone slightly away from my head, wincing. "In that case, stay at their place as long as you want, but as soon as you do come home, I'm going to get all of the details out of you."

I groan inwardly, because she's right. Ronnie is a pro at prying information out of people, and I'm a terrible liar.

"Which one is it? Take a picture of him," she adds, not giving me a chance to answer the question before barreling on into the next thought. Which is good, because I have no idea what to tell her. "The last time I saw all of them it was too dark and quick for me to remember what they look like. Posed is ideal, but I'd take a candid. Just make sure I can see his face."

"You're annoying."

"You love me." Ronnie makes confident kissy sounds at me through the phone, then hangs up.

"Everything okay?" asks Elliot as soon as I return to the kitchen.

They're all sitting around the little table in the corner, elbow to elbow, since the extra chair has made space tight. I almost point out that we could use the bigger dining room table, but it's so filled with homework that it would be silly to put it away only to pull it right back out again.

"Yeah, I just forgot to tell Ronnie I was staying over, so she freaked out thinking I'd been kidnapped."

"We should have reminded you," says Lukas, shaking his head. "We'll do better next time."

I'm about to point out that it's not their job to make sure Ronnie knows where I am, but before I can say anything, Felix speaks up, sounding sad but resigned.

"So do we need to take you back now? Does she need you?"

"Nah, once she realized I'm alive she told me to stay here as long as I wanted." Technically, it was more like *she* wanted me to stay here so I can eventually get lucky, but I'm not going there right now.

"Oh, perfect," says Elliot, adjusting his food on his plate but not actually eating any of it. "You must be hungry. We wanted to make you a plate, but didn't know what you'd want."

Felix adjusts his napkin and the rotation of his plate too, and I realize that all of their food is untouched.

"That's okay, I can make it. You don't have to wait for me, you can start eating." It's sweet of them to want to wait, but there's no reason for it. This isn't a formal dinner or anything, we don't need to be beholden to etiquette to that degree.

I survey and the sandwich fixings arranged on the counter. There's ... a lot of options. They must take their sandwiches seriously. Although I suppose there isn't anything they *don't* take seriously.

"It's nice that Ronnie called you to make sure you're okay," says Sebastian. "She's a good friend."

"Mm-hmm." I pop two slices of bread into the toaster and pour some chips onto my plate. I still don't hear any chewing or even any movement behind me. "Really, guys, it's fine, you can eat. I'll be there in a minute."

As soon as the toast pops up, I hurriedly assemble my sandwich and carry my plate over to the table. This time Elliot is sitting in the folding chair. Felix was there for breakfast, so I'm sure it's yet another rotation they're going to track somehow.

All eyes are on me as I pick up a chip and take a bite. That was obviously the signal because as soon as I start to chew, the guys all immediately pick up their own sandwiches.

We spend a few minutes just eating, and I watch in fascination as Elliot takes a bite of his sandwich, sets it down, makes sure there is a perfect empty line between his sandwich and his chips, selects and eats a chip, and then picks up his sandwich again. He does this in rotation, chip, sandwich, chip, sandwich. I'm so curious what his criteria is for the order in which he eats his chips, because he's considering the pile before selecting one each time, but it would probably be rude to ask him.

"Did you see that Fredrik is working on the Collatz Conjecture?" asks Elliot. "He's posted about it on the message boards."

"He's never going to solve it," scoffs Felix. "He doesn't fully understand the parity cycles."

"The bigger reason is that the math hasn't caught up to that equation. We don't have the math to prove it, and he's not going to be the one to push it. He's not creative enough," Lukas agrees.

"I didn't say he was going to prove it. I said he's working on it," Elliot clarifies. "Besides, it'll be a cuber who solves it, and he couldn't solve his way out of Schrödinger's box."

The group chuckles at this, so I guess it's a funny joke. But the entire conversation has gone right over my head. I have no idea what a Collatz Conjecture or parity cycle is, and while I have heard of Schrödinger's box, all I know is that it has something to do with a dead cat, and I'm not sure how that connects to cubing.

I knew they were smart, but this is beyond what I can even fathom. I'd been thinking I could have them help me with my math homework, but my gen ed math class would look like child's play to them. If they find out I'm in such a basic math class, they'll probably think I'm stupid. I'm not, it's just that my brain is wired for words, not numbers, and I don't see the graphs and equations in my head the way they probably can.

While I've been thinking about this, they appear to have run out of things to say about Frederik and his inevitably doomed attempt to solve whatever the Collatz Conjecture is. The conversation fades as they all return to eating, and I notice that their hands are empty except for their sandwiches.

"Where are your cubes? Wouldn't this be a perfect time to get in more practice?"

Elliot shakes his head. "No cubes at meals."

"It's a newer rule," adds Sebastian.

"I'm telling you, it was an accident." Felix glares at them all.

Elliot shudders, his expression haunted. "The intent has no weight on the outcome."

I lean forward, grinning. "This sounds like a story."

"Someone," Lukas says, giving Felix the side-eye, "sabotaged us for all upcoming group challenges involving the cubes."

"It was not sabotage!" Felix insists. "It was an accident. I was looking for my own cube, but you'd all left yours lying around instead of putting them away."

"We all leave our cubes out, even you, so you can't push back on that," argues Sebastian.

"But what happened, exactly?" Watching them get heated is kind of entertaining, but I'm not getting any information. I'm a reporter, I live for the details.

They had told me last night at the café that before joining the cubing community, they all felt a sense of loneliness, a lack of belonging when it came to their peers, because most of their classmates just didn't have the same interests or, let's face it, the same smarts as they did. Seeing how they joke and bicker together, I'm struck by how comfortable they are with one another. Almost more like brothers than roommates. I'm taking mental notes for my article on their camaraderie, how they interact with one another in different scenarios, because it could work really well to juxtapose these types of interactions with their previous feelings of being outsiders.

In his irritation, Felix is gripping his sandwich so hard his fingers are leaving deep impressions in the bread, and mustard is beginning to leak out from the crust. "I *accidentally* got syrup on their cubes. Which made the gears stick the barest amount."

"Speedcubing is all about the microsecond. You could have given yourself an advantage, since yours was the only cube that wasn't affected," Lukas points out.

"Exactly," agrees Sebastian. "It's unfair."

"And syrup is really difficult to clean out of gears."

Elliot shudders again. "It was so sticky. Just awful. All that lost practice time too."

"I did say I was sorry." Felix whips off his glasses and begins to aggressively polish them with the bottom edge of his T-shirt.

"And we accepted that," Sebastian reminds him. "And then put a rule in place to ensure it doesn't happen again."

"I didn't say it was a bad rule," grumbles Felix, sliding his glasses back on. "I just don't like that you guys think I would sabotage you. You know I wouldn't."

"Rebecca," says Lukas, cutting off any further arguments and looking over at me, "we've unfairly been monopolizing the conversation."

"No, no. I'm loving this. It's like watching siblings give each other grief." I'm hoping to keep them talking about themselves so they don't start asking me for fun anecdotes about my own life. I don't have any. I don't have siblings, and I've always spent most of my time studying. Any fun stories I could tell are more Ronnie's than mine. Even if I was there for them, the funny things always happen to her, not to me.

"Still," says Sebastian, "why don't you tell us about the homework you're working on today?"

It's not exactly a riveting topic, but at least it's something I can talk about. "I've been working on my psych assignment this morning, but I'm nearly done. And I have the book I'm reading for my lit class, so I'll probably read some of that this afternoon once I finish with psych. I'm pretty much caught up, but it won't hurt to read ahead."

"True," agrees Sebastian, nodding sagely. "It gives you a buffer if you have a day when you need to take it easy."

"And you're working at the newspaper as well?" asks Felix, leaning forward to look at me around Elliot. "Your schedule sounds very busy."

"Well, it's an internship, so I'm only part-time for college credit," I tell him. I don't want to really let them know how rough the job actually is or how much my editor dislikes me.

"What's your work schedule then?" Lukas pulls out his phone, his thumbs hovering over the screen.

Is he adding my work schedule to his calendar? Or, more likely, their joint calendar? That's ... I'm not sure how to feel about that. "Uh, Sunday afternoons. And then I usually go in again on Mondays and Wednesdays for a couple of hours too."

"Is it the same time every time or does it change?" asks Lukas.

"The same time. Sundays I'm there from two to five but a lot of the time I stay longer. During the week, I usually go after my last class for the day. So four to six."

"Is the newspaper close enough for you to walk?" Felix asks.

"No, I normally take the bus." I'll need to save up and buy my own car after graduation, especially if I don't get a position at the *Tribune* and end up moving somewhere else, but luckily right now there's good public transport.

Elliot frowns. "You're taking the bus by yourself a lot?"

I huff a laugh. "I mean, not really by myself. There are other people on the bus too."

Racking my brain for a way to turn the conversation away from myself, I come up empty. I haven't had a chance to compile more interview questions yet, and my on-the-spot thinking is failing me.

I'm saved by their internal clocks. They all get up from the table at the same time and take their plates up to the sink, rinse them off, and place them in the dishwasher. I stand to carry my own plate over to the sink, but Sebastian takes it from me.

"You're our guest," says Sebastian. "You shouldn't be cleaning up."

I stand there stupidly in the middle of the kitchen while Sebastian puts my plate in the dishwasher and Lukas and Felix put away the food and Elliot wipes down the table.

I feel useless, and I don't like it.

Once the kitchen is reset to perfect condition, Elliot pulls me into his side and kisses the top of my hair. Assuming this is a precursor to more checklist activity, I feel my body tighten with a combination of nerves and excitement. Elliot guides me back into the dining room and over to the chair where I was sitting before, then pulls it out for me. Okay. I guess ... we're just going to go back to studying? No list-checking-off? I'm surprised to find myself disappointed.

The others all file in and take their own seats at their homework stations, opening up their books and pulling their notebooks closer. Guess it was just me who felt that moment of possible tension in the kitchen, and then had the thought that we'd be fooling around now.

I absolutely cannot start going boy crazy now. Or ever. But I have to finish my psych homework and read part one of *1984*. I need to do well in my classes so that I can graduate with honors to compensate for the likely lack of recommendation from my editor.

The guys are all studying now, so I drag my laptop closer. I can always ask them about the list later. I'm sure they've already scheduled out the timeline on their calendar, and a rotation for it too. At least if I know when to expect the next encounter, I'll be able to relax until then.

Maybe.

Chapter Twelve

An alarm going off breaks my focus, making me jump in my seat. None of the guys seem bothered, though. Lukas pulls out his phone and turns off the alarm before they close up their books and stack up their notebooks.

I guess study time is over. Now what happens? I glance at the time on my own phone. Five p.m. Wow. I hadn't intended to stay this late at all.

They had suggested that I stay for another movie night, but just in case they've changed their minds, I should give them an out. "If you guys want to drive me back to my dorm now, you can still be home before it's too late."

They all frown at each other.

"It's been great spending the day with you," I add quickly. I don't want them to feel like I'm trying to leave because I don't like them or I'm tired of them. Quite the opposite, in fact—normally I'd be itching to get back to my own routine, but I really have enjoyed spending the day with them, and I'd be lying if I said I didn't sort of want to see what other checklist items we could take care of tonight if I stayed. I just don't want them to feel like they have to honor their earlier suggestion if they would rather get back to normal. "I just … you know, if you're ready to have your house to yourselves again. My feelings won't be hurt."

"Not really," says Lukas, his frown clearing a little. "We like having you here."

"We want you to stay," adds Sebastian, "but only if you want to." He sounds like he means it.

"I just don't want to overstay my welcome," I tell him. "I know you said I could stay another night, but I don't want you to feel like you have to stick to an offer from hours ago, if you're ready to just get back to your normal routine."

Sebastian's brow is furrowed, as though he's trying to work through a complex math problem. "So … you don't want to go, but you're willing to if we want you to leave?" he asks.

"We'd like you to stay for another night," Elliot tells me.

"We wouldn't have asked if we didn't want you to," Felix says, reminding me of what I already know but haven't quite been able to convince myself of despite all evidence pointing to it being the truth. "We wouldn't have asked if we didn't want you to."

"You don't have to be anywhere until your internship tomorrow, right?" asks Lukas. "Let us prove to you that we want you to stay."

Men proving themselves is, in my experience, usually bullshit. My dad has "proven" to Mom so many times that he's sorry for being a terrible husband and human, but it never means anything. He's still the same piece of shit as always, just with a shinier coat for a week or two until things blow over and he can go back to his old ways.

And the guys Ronnie has dated in the past wouldn't even try to prove themselves to her. If they did something shitty and she called them on it, they'd just break up with her after gaslighting her into thinking she was unreasonable for being upset that they cheated on her, or whatever.

However ... I may not know these guys well, but I do know that unlike my dad and all of Ronnie's exes, they don't say things they don't mean. What I see is what I get with them. So I should give them the benefit of the doubt. "You don't have to prove anything. You're right, if you didn't mean it, you wouldn't say it. I shouldn't have even questioned it."

"Still," says Sebastian, wrapping his hands around my waist and lifting me up to sit on the dining room table. "We'll show you, if you'll let us." He steps closer, wrapping my legs around his hips so we're pressed together.

It clicks into place then exactly how they plan to show me they want me to stay. Flashes of last night ping through my head, and I arch closer to him, that nervous-excited thrum kicking up in my bloodstream again.

"Okay," I whisper, tilting my face up to his.

"Can I kiss you?" asks Sebastian, biting his lip. His pupils are dilated, making his hazel eyes appear dark, and I yearn to pull him closer, to feel the bulge forming behind his fly against the ache beginning behind my own, but I can tell that he wants to be in charge here, so I resist the urge.

"Okay," I repeat, my voice husky with want. It's sweet of him to ask in spite of the fact that we've kissed before, but right now the need building inside me at the thought of what's to come has me wishing he'd stop being a gentleman.

Who even *am* I right now? I don't recognize this version of myself. I'm not a person who throws herself at boys, but right now I think I might die if he doesn't make his move.

But he just stands there, looking down at me like we've got all the time in the world and he's in no hurry to get started. Finally, I can't take it anymore. My entire body is electric with anticipation, and even though I know he's supposed to be driving this encounter, I'm done waiting. Gripping the edge of the dining table, I let my gaze fall to each of the other three guys, all watching this play out from a few feet away, before gathering my courage and leaning forward to kiss Sebastian.

Who leans back, just out of my reach.

"Not here," he says, tapping my lips. His hand moves to my inner thigh, just above my knee. "Here."

It's a weird place to kiss me and not at all what I want right now, but I'm sure he's got a plan. These guys don't do anything without intention.

"Okay?" It comes out as a question, and a slow smile spreads across his face. It's not his normal sweet, shy smile, nor the one that lights up his face like a kid in a toy store, but one of a man who has just been granted his greatest wish and who is going to savor the experience.

His fingers slides along my hips to the top button of my jeans, but pause as he stares down at me, silently asking for permission to continue. I nod, and he deftly flicks the button open and slides the zipper down. He tugs at the waistband, and I lift my hips as best I can so he can slide my jeans down over my hips and down my thighs, dropping them to the floor of the dining room.

I'm now sitting in my underwear and a T-shirt on a cute guy's dining room table, with his three roommates watching, and his fingers are skimming along the edge of my panties as he sinks slowly to his knees without taking his eyes off me. I've imagined a lot of things for my future and my life, but never once did I imagine this.

"Just relax and enjoy this," says Sebastian, wrapping his hands around the backs of my calves. "If you feel uncomfortable or want to stop, just say so and I will, okay?"

I nod, my breath catching in my throat. I've never had a guy on his knees before me. Is he going to beg for me to stay the night? Or ...

Sebastian's lips graze the spot he had tapped a moment ago, and I feel my face heat. *Oh.*

Lukas clears his throat, moving towards the table. "May I also prove to you that I'd like you to stay tonight?"

Before I can respond, Elliot comes closer on my other side. "Me too?"

"I think you should let them," says Felix, stepping between me and Elliot so that the fabric of his jeans almost-but-not-quite brushes against my bare thigh.

"Okay." My gaze flicks from Felix, to Lukas, to Elliot, letting them know that this is my response to all of them.

"Thank you," says Elliot.

"And like Sebastian said, if you want us to stop, just say so and we will." Lukas pulls my T-shirt over my head so I'm sitting on the table in just my bra and panties, Sebastian's hands lightly stroking my calves.

I feel completely exposed, aware of every nerve in my body screaming for contact, but other than Sebastian, none of them are touching me.

Until Felix hooks his finger under my chin and turns my face toward him. "Thank you for trusting us."

Slowly, he leans in until his lips brush against mine. I may be mostly naked in front of four men, but I am too turned on to be embarrassed and can't help but follow as he pulls back slightly to look down at me. He grins, his expression turning wolfish, and captures my lips again in another kiss.

This one is more insistent than the first, and I don't even register that he's pressing me backward until the cold wood of the dining table against my shoulder blades sends goosebumps pebbling along my skin. The hardness of the tabletop contradicts the softness of Felix's lips. When I part my lips and my tongue darts out, asking entrance, he again leans back with another wicked smile. I can see myself reflected in his glasses, my dark hair splayed out on the wood where textbooks were only a few minutes ago.

"Just relax and let yourself go." Felix leans in again for another quick kiss before moving around to the other side of the table so his face is upside down in my vision.

He runs his fingers through my hair, gathering it into his hands. I close my eyes, letting his touch relax me, almost forgetting that I'm mostly naked and they are all fully clothed.

I feel hands on my shoulders, but I don't open my eyes. The hands stroke down my upper arms, lowering my bra straps, and then fingers hook into the cups of my bra and flip them down to reveal my breasts. I gasp, my eyes flying open to see Felix still smiling down at me. I keep my eyes on his as warm breath ghosts across my breasts—Lukas? Elliot? both?—making me shiver, my nipples hardening. I've never had a man so close to my breasts before. Part of me is desperate to cross my arms in front of my chest, but I keep my hands flat on the table.

"You're beautiful." Felix presses his forefinger against the bridge of my glasses to slide them back up my nose, exactly the same way he does for his own glasses. I'm not used to being called beautiful, and I part my lips to protest against the compliment. But there's nothing in his expression to indicate he's lying, and when I glance down at Lukas and Elliot, who are leaning over me, their lips inches from my bare breasts and the same intensity on their faces that I see on Felix's, I remember that they don't lie. None of these guys ever says anything they don't mean.

And the knowledge that they mean it, that they find me beautiful, makes me *feel* beautiful.

I arch my back slightly, lifting my breasts the tiniest bit closer to their faces. The anticipation of what's to come heightens my awareness of where they are in the room:

Felix above me, Lukas and Elliot hovering over my exposed breasts, and Sebastian kneeling between my legs.

Lukas and Elliot lower their faces in tandem, mirroring one another's movements, and I've never realized two people could be so in sync with each other.

Their warm breath disappears, replaced with the sensation of tongues flattening against my erect nipples, before their mouths move to explore the undersides of my breasts, leaving the wet nipples cold and wanting. One of them tugs my bra further down, the lace scraping gently against my skin. It's such a contradiction to the teasing softness of their mouths.

I shift underneath them, arching my back again to try to get their mouths where I want them—on my nipples. It was only one stroke, but it was enough to know that I want the attention focused there. Lukas and Elliot must understand what I'm silently asking for, because they flatten their tongues against the sensitive tips of my breasts again before circling them around the erect points. I hadn't realized how hard they were until right now. I let my eyelids drift shut and focus on all the fluttery feelings they're eliciting in my body right now, the swoopy feeling in my stomach and the pressure building between my legs. It's similar to the feelings that were building in me last night when Elliot and Lukas reached down into my pants. I'd had no idea that merely playing with my nipples could do that.

I wish I had something to hold on to. My fingers itch to grip anything to ground me, but all I can do is press my palms flat against the dining table as Lukas and Elliot latch their lips around my breasts and scrape their teeth delicately along the delicate skin until only my nipples are caught between their lips. The way the sensations alternate between hard and soft has my breath coming faster, and I bite my lips against the panting.

When they start sucking, I nearly come off the table. The only thing keeping me in place is Felix's hands, massaging my shoulders and upper arms. The pressure builds with each hard suck of their mouths, and then suddenly it's there—a burst of ecstasy that spasms through my entire body, making me cry out, before reducing to gentle waves of pleasure, leaving me a pliant puddle on the table.

After a moment, Sebastian speaks, and I can hear the awe in his voice. "That was beautiful to watch."

Slowly, I open my eyes to find Felix grinning down at me.

"It really was," he agrees.

Sebastian kisses the inside of first one knee, then the other, before slowly tracing his lips up the inside of each thigh. My legs are shaking from the final tremors of my nipple orgasm—who knew that was even a thing?—when his warm breath lands on the fabric of my panties.

The breath changes to the flick of a tongue. There was probably already a damp spot on the cotton from my orgasm, but with the press of Sebastian's tongue, it's even bigger. When another breath blows over the wet fabric, I shiver.

I inch my thighs a little farther apart, giving Sebastian more access. I'm not even embarrassed by my own wanton behavior, I'm so desperate to find out what he's planning to do next. This time when Sebastian leans in, he drags the flat of his tongue along the entire gusset of my underwear, and when he presses it against my sensitive clit, my hips jerk of their own accord.

He chuckles as hooks his finger around the fabric between my legs and pulls it to the side, baring me completely to his gaze. No one has ever seen my pussy before, and for the briefest of moments I consider closing my legs. But before the thought has even fully formed in my head, Sebastian is draping my left leg over his shoulder and his mouth gets to work. Again, he flicks the tip of his tongue over my clit, then pulls it into his mouth to and sucks just like Elliot and Lukas did to my nipples moments ago.

My hips move against Sebastian's insistent tongue of their own accord, and I hook my right leg around his other shoulder, my heels pressing against his back and holding him closer.

The pressure builds, and I press my pussy against Sebastian's face as everything inside of me explodes. My eyes roll back into my head behind my still-closed lids, and my hands come off the table to grip Felix's forearms, my nails digging into the muscles as the orgasm tears through me. I'm dimly aware of the fact that I'm whimpering, but I don't care. Sebastian keeps his tongue flattened against my clit as I writhe against it, allowing me to control the pressure to prolong the bliss coursing through my body.

"But that," he says when I have gone quiet and still, "was even more beautiful." He presses a kiss to my hipbone as he stands up, and I open my eyes to stare down my body at him. His mouth glistens, and I can't help but notice that his pants are tented, and there is a small wet spot near the fly.

I'm certain that I know what's coming next. I wait for him to unzip his pants and pull out his cock. My body feels like I'm floating on air, so if he does fuck me now, I'll be too spaced out on my double orgasm to feel the pain that I hear usually accompanies a first time.

We're really just plowing through the items on my list, but in this moment, I'm okay with it.

But instead, he takes a step back, and Felix comes around the table and take his place between my legs. Of course, he hasn't gotten to do anything but kiss me, so they'll let him be the first one to fuck me. That would be fair, after all. Except that he doesn't move to take off his pants either. He reaches for my hands and slowly lifts me into a sitting position, brushing my hair out of my face and kissing my forehead.

"Let's get you cleaned up." He lifts me off the table and places me on my feet, one arm around me for support when my legs wobble like jelly. "Then by the time you come down, food will be here." He leads me into the hallway and up the stairs.

"Do you have any preferences for dinner?" he asks once we're upstairs.

"Um." I barely have the mental faculties at the moment to put one foot in front of the other, and he wants me to come up with a dinner plan? "No? I don't know. Pizza?"

"We can do pizza," he agrees easily as he turns on the bathroom light.

I lean against the wall as he starts the shower and gets the water to a comfortable temperature. Then he kneels in front of me and drags my ruined panties down my legs, lifting my feet to step out of them. When he stands, he moves behind me to unclasp my bra, and I look up at the mirror to find him watching me in the reflection. His fingers skim over my breasts as the bra falls to the floor. My pulse kicks up in anticipation, but instead of getting naked himself, he just slides my glasses off my face and sets them on the counter before helping me step into the hot spray of water. He tugs the shower curtain closed and I hear the door snick shut behind him when he leaves.

I slowly begin to lather boy-scented soap over my skin, wondering what I'll do for clothes after the shower. I only have that the clothes that are currently in a pile on the dining room floor, and what I wore yesterday.

I suppose I could duck across the hall in a towel and

grab my pajamas from last night. That doesn't solve the problem of what to wear to work tomorrow, but I'll worry about that later. For now, I just have to get clothes on my body so I can go downstairs and eat pizza with the guys.

I huff a laugh as I think about how many sanitizing wipes Elliot will have to use on the table before he'll be willing to sit there again to do homework, let alone to eat.

I don't regret what just happened at all. It was, in all honesty, one of the most amazing experiences of my life. Never in my wildest dreams could I have anticipated that I would end up spread out on a table, coming my brains out from the efforts of three different tongues. That's a thing that happens to other girls, not to me.

When I turn off the water and push the curtain aside, I realize there's no need for me to go across the hall for clothes at all. Sitting on top of the counter is a folded pair of Superman pajama pants and a T-shirt from a speedcubing competition.

Smiling, I put on my borrowed clothes and head downstairs for pizza, and probably another evening of that nerdy TV show. These guys really are sweet, and I decide to do my best to pay attention and try to enjoy the show that obviously means so much to them. I'm glad they want me to stay, and even gladder that they insisted on proving it to me.

Chapter Thirteen

"Can we at least walk you to the door?" asks Lukas, climbing out of the car to let me out.

We've spent so much of this weekend together, it's almost weird to say goodbye in the parking lot of the newspaper office. They had spent a good amount of time this morning debating if they were going to bring me to my dorm so I could drop off my bags and then bring me to work, or if they should bring me straight here. But I eventually put us all out of our misery by informing them that I wanted them to just take me straight to the newspaper.

So they've dropped me at work with both of my bags. They tried to argue with me about how I'd have to then carry them home on the bus later, but it's just a backpack and a small duffel bag, not giant suitcases. Besides, I didn't want them to have to go even more out of their way.

"I think I can manage to walk twenty feet up a sidewalk," I point out. "You can see the door from here, you'll even know I got inside safely." I don't roll my eyes as I say it, even though I want to. I know their insistence on making sure I'm safe comes from a good place.

Sebastian frowns as he holds my backpack out for me to

slip my arms through the straps. "I thought men were always supposed to walk women to the door."

"At the end of a date, sure," I correct him, taking my overnight bag out of Felix's hands. "This is just you guys dropping me off at work. Totally different."

"We did spend the weekend together," he points out.

"Studying," I say. He looks like he's about to protest, so I add, "And yes, movie night and ... other things. But it wasn't a date, remember?"

Sebastian looks to his roommates for support, but they don't say anything. Eventually, he nods in agreement.

"Good. Now get home safe, and watch out for deer," I tell them, spouting the line my mother always says to Dad whenever he gets in the car. I'm not sure there has been a deer in Boston in at least a century, but it's ingrained in me. It's what I get for growing up outside of the city instead of in it.

I turn and begin to make my way up the sidewalk, bracing myself for whatever my editor has to throw at me today. I've had such a good weekend, I'm not sure I even care if Carl acts like a dick to me, and that's a pretty good feeling.

"Wait," calls Lukas. When I turn back, he says, "We didn't get to give you a goodbye kiss."

I sigh. So much for us not treating this like a date. But I don't have time to argue with them.

"Fine, one workplace-appropriate kiss each." The last thing I need is for one of the reporters to tell Carl they saw me making out with four different guys in front of the office.

One by one, the guys line up and kiss me chastely before returning to stand beside their car doors. None of them are in the same place they rode over here in, so they must have a different rotation for when they drive somewhere with just them. Exactly how many of these different rotations are they keeping? Their minds are fascinating. Weird and a little exhausting at times, but fascinating.

Squaring my shoulders, I head into work, feeling their eyes on me as I walk through the front doors and into the empty lobby. When I'm far enough from the front doors that I think they can't see, I turn back around so I can watch them drive away. But they're still sitting there, waiting.

Shaking my head, I call the elevator with a small smile on my lips. While I'm waiting, the front door opens. I turn, expecting one of the guys to be running in with something I left in the car.

Instead, that smarmy asshole Brad is walking toward me. I see him register my slightly wrinkled clothes, which are much more casual than I ever wear to work even though pretty much everyone else is in jeans and T-shirts most of the time. His gaze drops to my overnight bag, and I steel myself for a gross comment, but he doesn't say anything. Just steps past me onto the elevator and pulls his phone out and scrolls until the elevator opens on our floor, which is just fine by me.

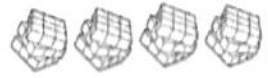

As usual, I spend my shift restocking the break room and seething about the lack of real work Carl offers me. When I ask him for something to do, the best he can come up with is delivering a folder to one of the reporters whose desk is ten feet from his office. I finally give up trying to find something newspaper-y to do and instead take a deep dive on the creation of Rubik's Cubes and speedcubing competitions. I did some bare-basics research for the article I wrote for the

Tribune, but my new one for class is going to need a lot more.

Just before 5:00, I start wrapping up for the day. On the weekends, buses don't come super often, so I have to make the 5:15 one or I'll be stuck here for ages.

"We're out of coffee." I'm shutting down my computer when Brad leans against my desk, practically hovering over me as he checks out my computer screen. "We're out of coffee."

"I need to catch my bus," I tell him.

"Well, then. You better hurry up." Brad doesn't make a move, just stays leaning against my desk, waiting for me to do his bidding.

I fear that if I don't just go start a new pot, he'll manage to hold me up so I miss my bus, so I speedwalk to the break room. I'm really cutting it close though, so as soon as I hit the start button on the coffee pot, I spin around to dash back to my desk for my things and nearly run straight into Brad.

"You should watch where you're going." Brad smirks and doesn't move out of the doorway.

"Excuse me. I'm going to miss my bus," I say, exasperated. Not just with Brad for blocking my way, but at everything about this stupid job. Working at a newspaper is my dream. This internship is supposed to be fun for me, and I hate that it isn't.

He doesn't move. "You're not even going to say please?"

I grit my teeth. "Please."

Slowly, Brad inches a little to the side, forcing me to make entirely too much bodily contact as I squeeze past him. Everything about him is just so smarmy. If I hadn't read about his awards and all the impressive stories he's covered with my own eyes, I would never believe this man was capable of doing anything other than being a misogynistic asshole.

"Don't forget your overnight bag," calls Brad, stopping me in my tracks.

Unease settles into my body. I didn't realize he'd been paying attention to me earlier, but I guess he was, at least enough that he saw that I came in with an extra bag. But why would he assume it's an overnight bag? It could be a gym bag.

Unless ... did he look inside it just now when I wasn't at my desk? The very idea gives me the ick something fierce, but I don't have time to worry about it now.

I force myself to keep moving, grabbing both of my bags and hightailing it out of the office. I don't want to give Brad the satisfaction of letting him know he got to me, but I can't help looking over my shoulder as I get on the elevator, and again when I get outside. Brad isn't following me, but the windows of the building are tinted so for all I know, he could be standing up there watching me.

Why can't I just have a normal internship, without creepy assholes who ruin everything?

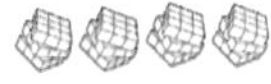

I drop my bags as soon as I shoulder open the door to our dorm room.

"Good! You're finally back!" Ronnie jumps up off her bed and practically ushers me into the room and to my desk. "I brought you a sandwich and some chips."

She gestures to the packaged cafeteria food on my desk as if it's a prize and not the same thing we eat every day.

I eye her with concern. "Is everything okay? Did something happen to you while I was gone this weekend?"

"No? I don't think so. Why?" Now it's Ronnie's turn to sound worried.

"Because you brought me back food from the cafeteria and you've set it out like I'm an animal you're trying to trap. Or maybe you're trying to butter me up before delivering bad news?"

She rolls her eyes and plops back on her bed. "You're ridiculous."

"Says the girl who practically jumped into my arms, she was so happy to see me," I counter with a laugh. Normally I'm the one who is glad she's back because I spend a lot more time alone in our small dorm room than she does. It feels pretty good to have her get excited over me for a change.

"Okay, fine," she says. "I know you. If we'd gone to the cafeteria for dinner, you would have refused to tell me anything about your weekend, and I want *all* the details. Don't leave anything out."

Tilting my head as though I'm considering where to begin and not just stalling for time, I methodically unwrap the plastic wrap from my sandwich and smooth out the wrapper to use as a plate, because of course Ronnie forgot to get one and while my desk is tidy, I'm not sure it's clean enough to actually eat off of.

I should ask Elliot what type of sanitizing wipes are best and get a pack for our dorm room.

Ronnie is starting to vibrate with annoyance at how long I'm taking to answer. I don't want to lie, but I feel weird telling her all the sexual details of the weekend. What if she judges me? If it was with just one of the guys, I know she wouldn't—but I have no idea how she'll react if she knows I hooked up with all four of them. At once. Multiple times.

"I got through all of my psychology homework and did

my reading for English. Although I just remembered, I still need to write out a short essay on that section for tomorrow."

"Ugh, Rebecca!" She falls back against her pillow and covers her face in frustration.

"It's okay. It's only one page, so I can easily get it done tonight." I know for a fact that she isn't referring to my homework, but maybe if I play dumb she'll leave me alone. Besides, it's kind of fun to watch her squirm.

"Okay," she says in a forcibly measured tone, sitting up and swiping her hair out of her face, "what did you do besides homework?"

Damn. So much for that plan. "We watched a couple episodes of a TV show and ate some nachos. They did a whole layer thing so there weren't any bare chips, and so many varieties of toppings, all warmed up in the oven so there was a nice crunch." I really do think they have the superior movie snack, and now I'm kind of embarrassed I'd told them I like something so basic as popcorn and pretzels.

"No, no, no. You can't distract me with talk of food," Ronnie says, cutting me off. "Although that does sound delicious and we should try it. *But* I want boy talk right now, not food talk. Where did you sleep, at least?"

All I can do is blush and shove a couple of chips in my mouth so I can't be expected to answer.

"I knew it!" She pumps her arm with her excitement.

I take a bite of my sandwich before I've even swallowed the chips just so I don't have to look her in the eye. I'm afraid she'll realize that I'm not telling her the entire truth.

"So which one was it?" she asks, scooting to the edge of her bed in eagerness. "And how far did you go? Do we need to have the safe sex talk?"

"Oh my god." I roll my eyes and groan through a mouthful of sandwich, so it sounds more like "uhmuhguh."

Ronnie tells me every last detail whenever she starts seeing a new guy, but I've never been in this position before, and her getting so excited is making me feel even more uncomfortable.

"This is a big step for you," she continues. "I just want to make sure you're being taken care of, and your first time is memorable. And that it's nothing like my first time."

I know exactly what she's doing. She's trying to use her own bad experiences to get me to offer up details to prove that mine was a good one. And we've been friends long enough that I know if I don't give her something, she's just going to keep pushing until I blurt out everything just to get her to stop. Normally this trait doesn't bother me, but right now I'm really wishing she would read the room and accept that I don't want to share everything with her.

"I slept in Felix's bed," I admit, biting into another chip. May as well start eating at a normal pace, since my attempts to avoid talking by cramming my face full of food don't seem to be working.

"Which one was that?"

"The one in the red." He's always wearing something that's red. I'm pretty sure it's his favorite color. No one wears that much of a color if they don't love it.

Ronnie looks up at the ceiling, searching her brain to remember their faces. "The one with the glasses?"

"Yes, the one in the glasses." I shouldn't be annoyed that his glasses are the feature she remembers, but there's so much more to him than being "the one with the glasses" and I don't like that he's being distilled down to just that. Although I suppose I should cut her some slack since she did only meet them once, briefly, and it was mostly dark. And she'd been drinking.

"He was cute! Did you fuck him? Tell me!" Ronnie claps with excitement, squealing and bouncing on her bed.

"I am really not comfortable with this conversation." Ronnie is my best friend, but I hate feeling put on the spot like this, and I haven't even had a chance to figure out how I feel about the weekend's events without her influence.

"Becks." Ronnie shuffles forward so she can put her hand on my desk and force me to look at her. "If talking about it is this embarrassing, then you shouldn't be doing it."

I scrunch my nose at her. "You're really annoying, do you know that?"

She's not wrong, but at the same time, I think it's valid to be comfortable doing a thing but not want to air all the details about it. Although if I can't talk to her about these things, there's no hope that I'll ever be able to talk to anyone at all about it. I need to just tell her and deal with whatever the fallout is.

"Would you rather I tell you about what Trevor and I did this weekend?" she asks, her voice dripping with fake innocence. "Because I'm completely comfortable with that, and maybe it'll give you ideas of things you could do with this Felix guy," she adds with a little wink.

"No, I do not want to hear any more details of things you've done with Trevor."

"Well, it's that or you tell me about what you did."

May as well just rip off the Band-Aid, I think. Resting my elbows on my desk, I cover my face with my hands as I mumble, "Fine. With which guy?"

I am positive that every dog in a three-mile radius of our dorm hears the shriek Ronnie lets out as she falls back on her bed, kicking her feet against the covers in giddiness.

Well, *this* was not what I was expecting. Even though she seemed breezy about the idea of me hooking up with all of them when she told me to let them help with my list, I was prepared for judgement and condemnation now that it's not a hypothetical, not delighted thrashing and celebrating. I'm not even sure what to do with this, so I take another bite of my sandwich and wait for Ronnie to come back to her senses.

It takes three bites before she regains her composure enough to sit up and speak calmly. "So ... who? Felix, obviously, and which other one?" When I don't respond, her eyes grow wide. "More than one other one?"

In for a penny, I guess, though my voice is barely above a whisper when I answer. "All of them."

Ronnie stares at me, then begins to cackle. "Wow. Your romantic life is crickets for the entire time I've known you, and now your first time out of the gate, you're dating multiple guys at once? When you decide to do a thing, you really go all out, huh?" she says with a shit-eating grin.

I shake my head, my glasses sliding down my nose. "No. No, no, no. We are not dating."

Ronnie's eyebrows are practically in her hairline now. "So, what, you're just fooling around?"

I pick up another chip, ready to shove it into my mouth, but what would be the point? I'm not getting out of this conversation, and I'm no longer hungry. I toss it back onto the desk. "Sort of."

"Sort of?" Ronnie tilts her head in confusion. "What do you mean sort of? You either are or you aren't."

I sigh and shove myself away from the desk and my half-eaten lunch. "Remember that list you found the other week?"

"Obviously."

"It fell out of my purse." I close my eyes, reliving the humiliating moment when I walked into their living room to find them looking at the stupid pink paper. "Right in front of them. And they kind of offered to help me complete it."

"Lucky boys, having that just drop into their laps. Any

lucky you, too, it sounds like. A no-strings v-card punch is not a bad way to do it."

"Maybe," I hedge. "They asked me to go out with them and I told them I'm not interested in dating anyone at the moment, but we could do this instead. They agreed, and I'm really just hoping they don't keep pushing the dating thing."

Now that we've started the list, I wouldn't mind finishing it with them. But not if it's going to get complicated.

"Does that mean you just fooled around the entire weekend?" Ronnie's eyes get big again. "How much of your list did you get through?"

"No, of course not." I have way too much going on to spend an entire weekend just fooling around. My homework would never get done at that rate. "I told you, we also watched a TV show, made meals, and we got a lot of studying done too. They're also really good students, and they're hoping to graduate with honors."

"But you're not dating them," she clarifies.

"No, definitely not."

"I don't believe you, but okay." Ronnie chuckles as she stands to grab her shower caddy out of her cupboard.

"I'm not," I insist. What about that is confusing her? I just said quite plainly that I don't want to date them, or anyone. And even if I hadn't just said it, this is not new information for her.

"As long as you're happy and having a good time, you can do whatever you want," she assures me, snagging her towel off the top corner of her cupboard door. "But you need to leave me a note or text me when you're not going to come home overnight, because safety first."

"I know," I agree. "Even the guys felt bad about that. And they promised to remind me next time."

I can't believe I forgot to tell her this time. It's not like me for something so basic to slip my mind. Although I was thinking about other things at the time. Sexy things. I was distracted.

She snorts. "Yeah, you're totally not dating."

It's clear she doesn't believe me, but before I can respond, she closes the door behind her, leaving me alone with my thoughts and the realization that once again, I have neglected to send a text I should have remembered.

Pulling my phone out of my purse, I pull up the group chat with the guys.

Home from work. I should have texted them right away like I had said I would, but I didn't want to ignore my best friend to text the people I just spent the whole weekend with. Assuming she'd have even let me have the fifteen seconds it would take to type out the message.

Glad you made it home safe, texts Sebastian.

Felix sends, *If you had come here after instead, we could have another movie night.*

Is movie night going to become a euphemism for ticking items off the list? The thought makes me giggle, and sends an exciting little chill up my spine. I feel bad now for judging other girls for hooking up with guys. Now that I've done it, I can see what all the fuss is about.

We could plan something for next weekend? I type out, then immediately regret it. Did that make me look too eager to see them again? I don't want to give them all the power in ... whatever this is.

Lukas replies before I have a chance to unsend the message. *We actually have plans already for next weekend. It's Nationals, so we'll be in New York.*

Shit, it's Nationals already? I had no idea. Why didn't they say anything sooner?

Do you want to come with us? Lukas asks.

Go to New York with them? That feels a lot like

something a boyfriend would suggest, not a guy who's just a casual hookup. I immediately begin to decline, but pause when it occurs to me that this could be really good research for my class series. I may not get another chance like this.

Okay, sure. It'll be a good opportunity to work on my article. I need to make sure they know I'm saying yes because of the work experience, not because of the weird non-relationship we have.

Awesome! texts Felix. *We were nervous about asking you.*

Well, that's flattering. And I'm glad I'm not the only one who is uncertain about things.

But Felix isn't done. *Because you'll have to miss class on Friday.*

Wait, what? What did I just agree to?

We'll pick you up Thursday night after our last class, Sebastian's next message says. *We'll text you when we're leaving. It'll be a late night by the time we get there, but then at least we're there and ready in the morning.*

We'll make sure to have you back on Sunday before your shift at the newspaper though. This is from Elliot.

I'm still focused on the leaving-on-Thursday-night part. The part where I'm going to have to skip my Friday classes because I'll be out of town with them. I've never missed a class in my life unless I was violently ill—like stomach virus levels of sick. But now I've accidentally agreed to skip just to spend time with them.

I'm so glad you're going to be there, Lukas tells me. *This competition will be so much more fun with you in the audience watching us.*

There's no way I can back out without being the worst. I can skip my lit and history classes for one day.

I'm excited to come with you too, I text back.

I hit send before I realize what I just typed, and when it

clicks for me I nearly collapse on top of the remains of my sandwich.

Come. With. You.

Well, I suppose if I spend the whole weekend with them again, it's possible I'll be able to cross that off the list. I mean, two whole nights? Something is bound to happen between us.

Chapter Fourteen

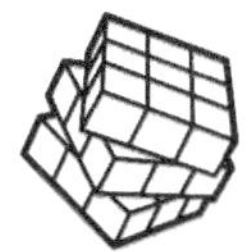

"I never thought I'd see the day," says Ronnie, trotting ahead of me to hold open the front door to our dorm.

"It's not a big deal." I focus on not getting the wheels of my little suitcase caught on the bottom doorframe so I don't have to look Ronnie in the eye. Because of course she's right —this is a big deal. I just don't want to make it a bigger one by talking about it.

"You're the picture of a perfect student, and yet here you are, skipping a whole day of classes to go away for a long weekend with your multiple boyfriends," Ronnie continues, not listening to me.

"They are not my boyfriends," I correct, hushing her. I don't need the guys walking up and overhearing Ronnie making comments about us dating when I've been so clear that that's not what this is.

"I'm just saying, you're doing a lot of things that look an awful like dating," she points out. "Oooh! Are you going to meet their families?"

"No." I can feel the blood drain out of my face. The thought hadn't even occurred to me. Surely they'd have told me, though, if their families would be there. Right?

"Really? Because I'd think most parents would want to be at a competition to support their kid," she says.

"Well, I'm sure the guys would have mentioned it if they were going to be there," I counter.

"We'll see," she says knowingly.

I see them turn the corner and spin to face her. "Best behavior, here they come."

"I have my embarrassing stories at the ready," whispers Ronnie before turning her biggest smile on the guys as they come up the sidewalk.

"You didn't have to come all the way up here," I call out as they approach. "I was just going to meet you in the parking lot."

"That wouldn't have been polite." Sebastian looks appalled at the idea.

"Besides, this way we can help you with your suitcase," says Felix, taking it from me.

"It's good to see you," says Lukas, leaning down to kiss me on the lips, but at the last second I turn my head so his kiss barely brushes against my cheek. I can feel Ronnie's "I told you so" eyes boring into me, but I ignore her. Lukas should have known better than to try to kiss me in public, and I can't believe I almost let him do it. Thank god I came to my senses and turned my head.

"We also get to officially meet your roommate," says Elliot.

"Very impressive memory," murmurs Ronnie, sticking out her hand. "I'm Veronica, but you, handsome man, may call me Ronnie." She winks.

"Thanks." Elliot shakes Ronnie's hand quickly before dropping it like it burned him. He shuffles closer to me, almost using me like a shield between him and my ridiculous roommate.

"Stop teasing them, Ronnie." I tell her. "You're making them uncomfortable."

She laughs, the sound echoing off the dormitory. "But it's so fun."

"Not for them." Usually when she makes men squirm it's funny, because they deserve it. But these four don't, and I don't want Ronnie being mean to them.

"Sorry." Ronnie shakes out her body and stands more naturally, her tone sobering. "You're right. That was uncool of me. It's nice to meet all of you."

"Nice to meet you too," says Elliot, standing straighter and looking a little more comfortable, even if he is shooting glances over to me.

"So," says Ronnie, "you're taking my friend away for a long weekend?"

"It's the International Cubing Federation national competition," answers Lukas, clearly more comfortable with the switch to direct questioning. "We're competing."

"So if you'll be busy competing, will Rebecca be sitting alone in a room full of strangers for the whole weekend?" Ronnie crosses her arms, ready to take them on. I can't tell if she really didn't realize they were competing, or if she's messing with them again.

"She won't be alone, we won't be backstage the whole time, and—" Sebastian starts, but I cut him off.

"Ronnie, be nice. They're doing me a favor by taking me so I can use it as research for my article." There's no reason for Ronnie to be so protective of me. Even if I am sitting alone all weekend, who cares? I'm good at being alone. It's kind of my whole thing.

"She's just looking out for you," says Felix, placing a calming hand between my shoulder blades. "We understand that, and you have nothing to worry about, Ronnie. We only have good intentions."

"Okay, well, don't be *too* nice. Rebecca deserves a little dirty in her life." Ronnie sounds dead serious when she says this, and I purse my lips, glaring at her.

The guys just stare from her to me to each other, uncertain what to do. Felix drops his hand from my back, covering his mouth with it like he's suppressing a laugh, and Lukas also looks like he's amused by Ronnie. Sebastian looks vaguely confused, though, and Elliot looks like he wants to melt into the sidewalk.

"Okay, this has been terrible. You're the worst. We're going to go." I wrap Ronnie in a hug, because she's my best friend and her heart is in the right place even if she is embarrassing as hell.

"Go have fun. Get out of your head," she whispers before stepping out of our hug. To the guys, she adds, "Be safe. I want Rebecca back when you're done."

"Nice meeting you," says Lukas, waving once before settling his hand on my lower back and guiding me down the sidewalk to where they parked.

It's silly—I don't need him to guide me to the car, and it's toeing the line of boyfriend behavior. But it's kind of nice to have the weight and warmth of Lukas's hand on my back. I haven't forgotten all the things that hand can do, and has done, to me, and as soon as I have the thought, my mind starts up a replay of last weekend.

By the time we get to the car, I'm blushing. If they ask, I'll blame it on the weather. Maybe they'll believe my face is red from the cold.

They place my school bag and suitcase with theirs in the trunk. It looks like they've only packed two suitcases for the four of them. I've clearly overpacked, but I didn't know what to bring for the weekend.

Elliot turns around in the driver's seat before starting the car. "You sure you have everything you need? It'll be hard to turn around once we get on the road, and it'll already be late when we get there even if we don't have to come back."

"I think I have everything, yeah."

"If there is anything you're missing, we can always buy a new one there," says Lukas, taking my right hand and lacing our fingers.

Elliot pulls out of the parking lot, and the trip has officially begun.

"How was your week?" asks Felix, taking my left hand. "We haven't heard from you much."

"Fine. Just busy, trying to get a little ahead of things in case I don't have much chance to study this weekend." It's not an outright lie, but it's not the whole truth. I don't want to ruin the vibe for our whole car ride, but this week has been pretty shit. My classes are getting harder. Carl has been belittling as always. And Brad is being even more creepy and rude than usual.

Both Felix and Lukas squeeze my hands. Even though I'm not confiding everything, it's sweet that they're comforting me and it does make me feel better.

I divert the conversation to them. "How have you been? You didn't play a poker game this week, did you?"

They normally play on Friday, but they skipped last week for movie night and they're missing this week for the competition. Working an unpaid internship for college credit, I get how tight money can be. I don't want to be the cause of extra financial stress for them, if they really did need last week's income since they're also missing tomorrow's game.

"No, but we're not worried about it. We have plenty for the next few months, remember? And the competition is more important," says Sebastian.

"And so are you," says Lukas.

Sebastian turns around to frown back at Lukas. "I wasn't implying the competition is more important than Rebecca."

"I didn't say you did," counters Lukas.

"Not specifically, but you implied it," Sebastian shoots back.

Before Lukas can further their argument, I jump in. "I'd love to hear more about this weekend. Do you have a schedule you can show me?"

They both look like they want to continue their little fight, but I know that now that I've asked a question, they don't want to be rude and not answer it.

"I have it right here," says Felix, releasing my hand. He pulls up the document on his phone, which he immediately hands over, no questions asked.

I can't believe how much trust these guys have in just handing me their phones—first Lukas to get my number, and now Felix. Although they've been sitting right next to me so it's not like I can snoop around, but still. My dad never leaves his phone out, and he always leaves the room to take calls. Sometimes he even leaves the house.

"So the first day, you can see here," says Felix pointing to the screen, "is for the next qualifying times. Everyone will have qualified to be there, but only the cubers with times below a certain threshold will get to compete in the actual semi-finals on day two." Felix moves the screen down to show the schedule for the second day.

"So everyone competes on day one, and then only certain people will stay for day two?" I confirm.

"No, everyone stays for day two and day three, because no one wants to miss seeing who wins the national title for each event and they all want to know who is going to go to Worlds," Elliot corrects.

If all of the competitors are also staying, I'm assuming

there are going to be a lot more people in the audience at this competition than at the one where I met the guys. This is good news for my research. My four guys will of course be the stars of the article series, but it'll be good to get some other perspectives.

The car ride lasts four hours, and while they do sneak in a few questions about me, mostly about my internship and my friendship with Ronnie, I'm able to keep the conversation mostly focused on them and the competition.

It's been a long day, though, and eventually I get tired and rest my head on Lukas's shoulder. It's so cozy and warm sandwiched between him and Felix, and once the sun sets and it gets dark, I nod off, lulled to sleep by the car's vibrations.

I'm awakened by a kiss to the side of my head. "We're here," says Lukas, his voice soft.

I blink awake. We're idling in front of a massive hotel. Doormen are already pulling bags from our trunk as another guy in a red jacket slides into the driver's seat, ready to pull away as soon as we step toward the front doors.

"Come on, sleepyhead," says Felix, helping me out of the car.

Yawning, I try to clear my head and take in as much as I can of my surroundings.

"Welcome to New York City," says the doorman, opening the front door for us to walk through. He doesn't give us a second glance, even with my arms hooked through both Felix's and Lukas's.

The entrance is opulent, filled with people even at this

late hour, lots of flowers, and a few cozy little sitting areas tucked into corners. We make our way to the front desk, Elliot and Sebastian behind us with my backpack and our three suitcases.

The woman at the desk takes Lukas's information, then glances at us. "There are two queen beds. Do we need a trundle bed added to the room?"

"No," says Lukas, frowning.

She nods and slides a packet of key cards across the desk.

"Enjoy your stay," she says, but we're already turning away.

"The elevator is over here," says Lukas, pointing.

The guys nod at a few people huddled in groups, many of them solving cubes, but we don't stop to say hello.

We have the elevator to ourselves. Everyone else is probably getting ready to go out on the town, especially since it's New York. But after the long car ride and a full day of classes, I'm exhausted. I really hope the guys aren't going to want to drop our bags in the room and also go out.

Sebastian's hand hovers over the buttons. "Tenth floor," says Lukas.

I wonder if they feel the subtle tension filling the elevator with each floor we go up, or if it's just me. Felix went over the schedule for the competition in the car, but beyond that I have no idea what the guys have planned for this weekend.

Passenger princess all the way on this trip. And whatever is going to happen between us is probably already planned out on their shared calendar. I received the email to join it, but I haven't been able to bring myself to actually open it and look over the details yet. It feels like it toes the line of dating too much to allow myself to be a part of their group calendar.

As soon as the door to the room swings open, there's no ignoring the way the two queen beds dominate the room, with only a single desk and chair tucked into the far corner and a small table under the TV. I'm obviously going to be sharing a bed with two of them. The question is, which two?

I move to enter the room, but Elliot lays a hand on my arm, stopping me.

"Actually, would you mind?" He leans down to unzip the top part of a suitcase.

"Elliot has a routine," Lukas explains when he sees my confused look.

"You have no idea how many germs can be in these rooms." Elliot begins pulling cleaning supplies out of the suitcase. Had I misjudged when I thought they were sharing two suitcases? Maybe they're only sharing one, and the second is for Elliot's disinfecting wipes and sprays. I can't decide if the idea is funny or concerning.

"I'm sure they cleaned the room before we checked in," I tell him.

"Sure, they cleaned it," agrees Elliot easily as he begins wiping things down, "but did they did they sanitize it?"

"I, uh, I don't know." I've never given much consideration to the steps housekeeping takes when turning over rooms for guests.

"Exactly," he says, moving into the bathroom. "And why should we live with uncertainty when we can ensure the outcome we want?"

"If we want it sanitized, we should sanitize it," clarifies Sebastian. "That way we know it's been done."

"Makes sense to me." I've been taking care of things for almost as long as I can remember because if I want it done correctly, I should just do it myself. I've seen what happens when my mom depends on my dad or I depend on either of them, and no thanks.

"Okay, that's the best I can do. I can't clean the carpet, so we'll just have to use our room slippers," says Elliot, setting his cleaning supplies down on the credenza beneath the TV.

"Uh, I didn't bring any room slippers." How was I supposed to know to pack something like that? I don't even know what room slippers are. Are they like shower sandals, but for wearing in the room?

"Don't worry, we packed some for you," says Felix, swinging one of the suitcases up onto the unfolded suitcase rack. He unzips it fully and drops a pair of fuzzy pink slippers onto the floor. "They're washable."

"Thank you." It's both very sweet and very weird that they bought me slippers, not so that I would be cozy and comfortable, but to keep my feet clean.

I grab my own suitcase and am about to lay it on the foot of the bed when Elliot practically dive-bombs me, his eyes wide and slightly panicked.

"You never want to set your suitcase on the bed," he tells me. "You'll transfer all of the germs from the wheels onto the bed."

"Okaaaay." I draw out the word and look around the room for a place to put the suitcase. "I can just keep it on the floor."

"That could be a tripping hazard," Sebastian points out. "And you'd have to bend over all the time to get things out of it. Horribly inconvenient."

"Why don't you put yours on the credenza," suggests Elliot, moving his cleaning supplies over so there's enough space.

"I can call down to the front desk and have them bring up another suitcase rack," suggests Lukas, moving toward the phone.

"No, no, this is fine. There's plenty of space here, see?" I tell him, swinging my bag up to sit next to Elliot's supplies. I didn't think where my suitcase went would be such a big deal.

On the upside, all the tension I'd felt in the elevator has disappeared in the wake of all the room prep.

"I'll make a note of it at least for next time," says Sebastian, pulling out his phone. I wonder if they have a special app for these types of notes, or if he's putting it into their calendar app somehow, or what.

"Thanks?" I'm not sure that we will ever go on another trip together, so his making a note is probably pointless, but if it makes him happy then I guess there's no harm.

"It's not a problem," he assures me, clearly not understanding my tone. Just as well. I don't feel like having to have a discussion tonight about whether or not this will be a repeat occurrence.

"So ... what's the plan for the evening?" I ask as the guys pull out and put on their own room slippers. This is their weekend and their competition, so if they want to go out, I'll rally for them.

But I really hope they don't want to go out. I'm exhausted. That was a nice little nap in the car, but I need some real sleep.

"We usually get an early night's sleep before a competition. Registration starts early," says Lukas.

"Did you, uh, did you want to go out instead?" asks Felix, ruffling up the back of his hair in discomfort.

"No, no, an early night sounds great." I shake my head emphatically, sagging with relief. I don't know that I could have pulled myself together enough to go out without a coffee.

"We're done in the bathroom, if you'd like to use it," says Elliot, after the guys have rotated through, changing into pajamas and brushing their teeth.

If we're staying in, I'm going to get comfy too. I grab my sleep clothes and toiletry bag and slip into the bathroom. It's going to be interesting to be in such close quarters for this weekend. At least at their house we have a little more privacy.

Before I go back into the room, I eye my reflection. It's obvious I'll be sleeping in one of the beds with two of the guys, which is going to be pretty tight, even in a queen bed. My hair tends to get a little wild when I sleep, and I'd hate for one of them to wake up with a faceful of it. I dig into my toiletry bag for a hair tie and braid my hair back off my face. At least this will help keep it from attacking my bedmates while we sleep.

Chapter Fifteen

When I walk out into the room, the overhead lights are off, but the light from the TV gives off enough glow for me to pack my clothes back into my suitcase. Then I just stand there in my jammies and new pink slippers, looking from one bed to the other, where the guys are snuggled under the blankets already.

"We thought we'd see if there is anything good on TV, but if you'd rather just go to sleep, we can turn it off," offers Lukas.

"No, that sounds good." I'm tired, but also hyper-aware of them being in the same room as me, almost certainly with plans for ... things ... after being apart for a whole week. And I can't get Ronnie's stupid words out of my mind, that if I can't talk about something, then I shouldn't be doing that thing. It's probably even more true if I can't talk to the guys I'll be doing the thing with about it. I know we'll have to talk about it eventually, but there's no reason why I can't start small, with a sleeping arrangements conversation, and work up to the big discussion. "Um, so, can we talk about what this is going to look like?"

"Sure," says Sebastian, muting the television.

Now that it's happening, I'm even more anxious than I was a moment ago. Standing there in front of them like this feels very much like being onstage in front of an audience, so I move over to sit in the desk chair. At least this way there's the semblance of more space between us, and I don't feel quite so put on the spot. As I settle into the chair, they all sit up and the blankets drop.

All their chests are bare.

My gaze drops to their laps. Are they wearing underwear still, or sleep pants, or are they completely naked?

Okay, maybe we shouldn't start with the sleeping arrangements. Maybe something even more innocuous.

"I'd rather not everyone here know that I'm a reporter." I link my hands in my lap to give myself the most professional look I can in my pajamas.

If the competitors learn I'm writing an article about speedcubing, they might be awkward around me. Besides, after last time, I don't want to get people's hopes up that the article will actually be published when as of right now it's only for a class assignment.

"Not a problem," says Felix. "We can introduce you as our girl—"

"As our friend," says Lukas, cutting him off. "As our friend who is a girl."

I narrow my eyes at the two of them, trying to assess their faces for any lie. Especially with all the grief Ronnie's given me all week about our little agreement, it's important that they still understand that I'm not their girlfriend. I'm hoping Felix just misspoke, and wasn't slipping up in a "we'll let her think we aren't dating but really we all agree that she's our girlfriend" kind of way.

"Are you going to interview the other competitors for

your article?" asks Elliot, looking down and adjusting the blankets around his waist.

"No," I say. I think I see Elliot's shoulders relax a little against the headboard, but maybe I'm seeing things. "But I would like to talk to some other competitors, just so I have a better and more varied understanding of what the sport means to different people. And how they came to the sport. Things like that."

"We can introduce you to a couple of people," offers Felix, pushing his glasses a little farther up the bridge of his nose.

"That will make it easier for you to talk to them," agrees Lukas, nodding.

"Thank you." That is a relief because if they didn't offer, I would have had to ask. I'm great at interviewing people when they know they're being interviewed, but having casual conversations with strangers is harder.

"Some of them are a little awkward," warns Sebastian.

I start to say something about how awkward all the people at the other competition were, but stop myself. Because really, who is normal? We're all a little awkward in our own ways. "That's okay. That's part of why I'm not going to do actual interviews. That would probably make a lot of them even more uncomfortable."

They all nod, then look at me expectantly. I don't say anything, my stomach beginning to knot itself up again because I have to be a big girl and ask about sleeping arrangements and the list, but I don't want to have to do it. I want to have already done it and be past it.

"Is there anything else you'd like to talk about?" asks Elliot gently when I don't move from the desk chair.

"Yes." Now is the time. I can't put it off any longer. I need to be an adult.

But I can't make myself say the words.

Felix seems to sense my discomfort, and I'm surprised by how in tune with me he is when he says, "Is this about your list?"

"Yes," I say, relieved to not have had to be the one to bring it up. I know I have to be able to talk about it with them if we're going to do it, but talking about it is easier when I'm not the one to bring it up.

"Do you want to stop going through it?" Lukas bites his lip as he waits for my response, and it seems that he's really hoping I want to continue. I can't imagine why, as it's not like they've gotten anything out of the deal so far, but maybe they're hoping I won't bail before we get to the part that gets them off.

"No." I'm not fully sure what I want from these guys—a thing I haven't actually admitted to myself yet, because that would mean admitting that there's a part of me that might not hate the idea of a relationship, and I am not going to even entertain that thought—but I'm certain I don't want to stop going through my list.

They all visibly relax. I hadn't even noticed that their shoulders had all tensed up around their ears. Maybe they don't want to stop going through my list either.

This emboldens me. "Did you make a ... schedule, or a timeline? For the completion of the list?"

I'm certain they have, since they've made schedules and planned out everything else in their lives down to the rotation of who gets to sit beside me in the car, but I'm curious what the timeline they have looks like.

Lukas nods. "Would you like to see it?" He grabs his phone off the nightstand. "We have it fairly optimized, but if there's something you want changed, we can talk about it."

The room had felt so small when we first came in, but it

feels much larger now as I cross from the desk to the bed to accept Lukas's phone. The anticipation of what I'll see on the screen makes each step feel like it takes a year.

I can see the designated color for the sex list schedule—pink—spread over the calendar, but my focus is on this weekend. It's a whole list, not just one or two things, and some of them weren't on my list at all.

Cuddle sandwich. Public hand-holding. Chaste public kiss. Fingering. Eating Rebecca out. Blow job.

I'm surprised they've added so many new things to my list. We've already done two of them and just the memory has me blushing, but they were so fun I won't say no to a repeat. As for a cuddle sandwich, I've got no idea what that is.

"We can't do anything in public," I say, handing back the phone. "I don't want to give anyone the impression that we're dating."

Felix hesitates, but finally nods. "Okay," he says, and Lukas deletes the kiss and hand-holding from the calendar.

I'm glad they didn't put up a fight on that, and some of the tension falls from my shoulders. I appreciate that they're being respectful. It makes me feel weirdly gooey inside, but maybe it's just my excitement at knowing that they're going to touch me again, and soon. And it sounds like this time, they're going to teach me how to touch them too.

"I notice that one of these items has me doing things to you instead of the other way around," I point out. I'm excited by the idea, and I thought my tone of voice conveyed that, but I guess it didn't because they all look worried.

"We don't want to rush you," says Elliot.

"If you want to put that off, we're happy to do that," Lukas confirms.

"It's just that you had sixty-nining on your list as well as giving a blow job, and we thought that the blow job was the logical first step of the two," Elliot continues.

Sebastian, surprisingly, is the one to tell me he'd rather not scrap the weekend's plan completely. "We would still like to touch you again though, if that's all right with you."

"Uh, yes, that's ... that's fine, I'm good with that." I'm not sure if these are the words that will trigger their ravishing me, or if we're going to keep discussing the plan first.

"Good," Elliot says, smiling. "We enjoy doing that a lot."

I blush, and glance down at the list on their schedule again to hide it. There are initials next to a couple of the acts. Elliot's initials are next to "Eat Rebecca out," so I guess he's scheduled to lick my pussy tonight, and Sebastian appears to be fingering me as well. The idea of being touched so intimately in front the other guys sends a flurry of excitement and nerves through my body, though it's weird knowing that they've scheduled and assigned each thing. What if whoever it's assigned to doesn't feel like it that day, will they change the schedule or does he have to do it anyway?

"But we don't have to do anything you don't want to," Felix assures me as I stare at the phone in my hand. "If anything doesn't feel right, or isn't fun, or you just change your mind, just tell us and we'll stop."

I look up from the calendar at him, the glare from the TV reflecting in his glasses. "Thank you," I tell him. "It's good to know that, but I do want to do these things, with you."

They all smile at that. "Good," says Sebastian. "We want to do all of these things with you too."

"And more," says Elliot, his voice husky. I force myself not to look at his lap, where I suspect I'll find a bulge under the blanket.

Clearing my throat at that image, I ask, "So which bed am I sleeping in tonight?"

Funny how suddenly that question isn't scary anymore, after everything we've just talked about.

I have an idea it's the one on the left, since that's where Elliot and Sebastian are and they're the ones who are, apparently, going to be making me come tonight. My thighs clench together, eyeing the space between the guys that is most likely meant for me.

Sebastian pats the empty space between him and Elliot, then tosses the covers back—I'm glad to see he's wearing pajama pants—and stands to allow me to slide in. When he resettles himself in the bed, I realize that even though it's a big bed, we'll definitely be touching all night.

Sebastian hands the TV remote to Lukas. "Why don't you try to find something?" he suggests.

"This is impossible," says Felix, and he sounds so annoyed that I have to assume he's picking up the conversation they'd been having while I was in the bathroom. Wow, that feels like a million years ago now. "Even if we can find one of our shows, we'll be watching episodes out of order."

"Who even watches live television anymore?" asks Sebastian.

Lukas continues to flip through channels, not staying on any one for too long, and the whole time I'm just waiting, wondering when they're going to decide that it's time to touch me.

I've never been a fan of surprises. They just stress me out. Would it be weird for me to just ask the guys to start touching me? Or maybe I should touch them first? Are they trying to find a show because they want to watch something, or just to fill time? They have a lot on their plate with the competition starting in the morning, so maybe they want to relax, but the schedule said we were going to hook up tonight, so I don't know what to think.

"Let's just watch this," says Lukas, pausing his clicking on a show about how things are made.

"Is this the first one in a season at least?" asks Felix.

"They're all individual standalones, you don't have to have seen any of the other episodes for this one to make sense," says Lukas, exasperated.

"It just feels better when we watch things in order, though," grumbles Felix.

"Sometimes things are more interesting when they're out of order," I say.

"Is that true?" asks Felix, suspicion lacing his voice.

I shrug. "Honestly, I have no idea. I also prefer to do things in order," I admit.

At least my addition to the conversation lightens the mood. They all chuckle, and Felix stops grumbling as we all turn our attention to the TV. Or, well, they all do. My attention is still very much on the touching that may or may not be happening soon.

Both Sebastian and Elliot slide down the headboard until their heads rest on the pillows. I feel silly sitting up with them lying down on either side of me, so I do the same. Sebastian pulls me in until I'm tucked into the crook of his arm, and I don't know what to do with my own arms. I finally just tuck them in close to me, between our bodies, though I want to stretch out and hook one around his waist. But I'm not sure if I'm allowed to do that.

Once I'm settled in and stop moving, Elliot scootches closer and molds his front to my back, resting his own arm along the top of my thighs beneath the blankets. The tips of his fingers hover and tease at the bottom hem of my sleep shorts, almost tickling my skin, but in a good way. A really good way.

My arms are falling asleep, wedged between my chest and Sebastian's. I have to move, and if they're touching me now, maybe I'm allowed to touch them back. Only one way to find out.

"May I touch you?"

Sebastian tilts his head to look at me. "Of course you can touch us," he answers, sounding surprised.

It's a relief to stretch my arm across Sebastian's waist and feel the solid warmth of him beneath my hand. I begin to mimic Elliot's subtle touches on my thigh with my own fingers on Sebastian's side, exploring every inch of Sebastian's stomach.

Every few minutes, Elliot inches farther underneath the bottom hem of my shorts, exposing ever more of my own bare skin to his exploration. Every brush of his fingers has me closer to holding my breath. At some point his fingers will brush the edge of my panties, and hopefully even farther, finding the spot where my desire is pooling between my thighs.

I have completely lost interest in the television and its explanation of how sweet corn is tinned due to the hard bulge pressing against my ass. Even as my body wants to wiggle against it, I hesitate. I want more, but I'm not sure how to ask for it.

I've been hoping one of them will show me how to take this further, but they're both just letting me explore as much as I like, Elliot's fingers touching me but not where I want them. I suppose I'll have to take matters into my own hands. Quite literally.

Taking a deep breath, I slowly inch my hand down to

the waistband of Sebastian's sleep pants. The fabric is soft as it brushes against the side of my pinkie. I slide my hand across his skin again, until it bumps against something that is definitely not fabric. I move my hand again, lifting the sheet a bit until I realize what it is that I'm touching, and my hand snaps back up to a spot above his belly button.

There, tucked into the waistband of his pants and visibly sticking out, is the head of Sebastian's cock. I've just touched a bare cock for the first time in my life and it was only sort of on purpose.

Did Sebastian notice the way I jerked my hand away? I hope he isn't offended. I was just surprised.

"You can touch that too, if you like," says Sebastian, his voice gruff.

Okay, so he definitely noticed.

"We've touched you, and fair is fair," he continues.

"Very true," Felix agrees. Neither he nor Lukas are paying any attention to the show anymore either. They're completely focused on the way I'm touching Sebastian.

"Go on, you can do it," Elliot whispers in my ear as his own fingers hook around my thigh and squeeze, his hand very close to the quickly dampening gusset of my underwear.

Tentatively, I reach out and trace the shape of Sebastian's erection through the fabric of his pants. With my head on his chest, I can feel the slow, steady breath he releases.

"Is this okay?" I whisper, sliding my hand away from the thick bulge in his pants. He's so still, I can't tell if he's enjoying this or not.

"Don't stop." Sebastian's free hand reaches down to bring mine back to his dick.

"I'm ... not sure what to do." It's embarrassing to admit,

but it's the truth, and this is what we're here for, after all. For them to teach me.

"Let me show you," says Sebastian, his hand guiding mine up and down his length, encouraging me to add a little pressure.

Each time he guides my hand down, Elliot presses his own hard length against my ass. It's teasing and private, the way he syncs his movement with mine, but we're in a room with two other people.

At least, it's private until Elliot's grip on my leg lifts it up to hook over Sebastian's lap, giving himself better access to the space between my legs and drawing everyone's attention to the fact that something is definitely happening beneath the covers.

Sebastian's guiding hand on mine is much more forceful than I would have expected to feel good for him. His fingers wrap around my hand, making my grip on his cock so tight that as his hips gently rock up against the pressure, his sleep pants tug down until the entire head of his cock is on display, shiny with a little bead of pre-cum.

The memory of our earlier conversation about blow jobs flashes across my mind, and I wonder what pre-cum tastes like. My tongue slips out to moisten my lips, and Sebastian must be reading my mind.

"You can lick it if you like." There's even more tension in his voice now than there was before. "No pressure though," he adds quickly.

"Does it taste good?" I do kind of want to taste it, want to know its flavor. But if it doesn't taste good, there's no sense in my trying it.

Sebastian groans and Elliot chuckles in my ear, but Lukas and Felix are full-on laughing in the other bed, even as I watch them adjust their own hardening cocks under their covers.

"I don't know. I've never tasted myself," says Sebastian, gritting his teeth as my finger circles the head of his cock, just avoiding the drop of pre-cum. "But I know it would feel really good for me."

"Why don't you give it a try and then you can tell us?" suggests Elliot, kissing the back of my neck as his hips rock against my ass.

This is why I'm here. To try new things. So I bite my lips and swipe my finger across the head of Sebastian's cock, gathering up the liquid and bringing it to my lips. The salty tang dances along my tongue. It's not bad. I wonder if it's one of those things where the first taste is okay but the second isn't as good, or if it just gets better the more I consume.

"How is it?" asks Lukas, turning onto his side on the other bed, completely focused on me, and the finger still stuck in my mouth.

"It's … not bad." Are you supposed to compliment a guy on the taste of his pre-cum? This is uncharted territory for me.

"Would you like more?" asks Sebastian, his eyes also focused on my lips.

"Because we have plenty," whispers Elliot. "And it's just for you."

Just for me. The words send a deeper warmth flooding through my body. More than the excitement of his hard cock grinding against me and everyone watching the way I'm touching Sebastian, those three words give me the courage I need to nod.

"Then come take it." Sebastian kicks the blankets down to the bottom of the bed as he helps position me between his legs. Then he leans forward and gently unhooks my glasses from behind my ears to fold them and set them on the nightstand.

I'm now on all fours, face to face with his cock, which is still halfway tucked into his pants. I miss Elliot's warmth spooning me, but he's right there beside us, watching. I could reach out and grasp his hand if I wanted, and that makes me feel a little better.

"So I'll just," I swallow, my hands shaking slightly with nerves or excitement or both, "uh, release it a little more."

I wince as soon as I say it, knowing I sound as unexperienced as I am. When I glance up, though, Sebastian is biting his bottom lip and completely focused on me and my hands. I grip the waistband of his sleep pants and tug them down his thighs, making his cock bob ever so slightly as if it's beckoning me closer.

This is the first time I'm seeing a penis on full display. I'm not sure what I expected, but my eyes trace the slight veining as I try to pair the thickness I felt with my hand to the sight before me.

"You can keep touching it for a bit first, if you want," says Sebastian, his hands moving to his head and gripping his hair. "Give your palm a lick first. Your hand will slide down my shaft easier if it has a little lubrication."

It feels awkward and not at all sexy to drag my tongue along the length of my own hand, but he's the teacher here and I've always prided myself on being an excellent student. Sebastian watches me so closely that I wonder if maybe I'm wrong about this not being sexy. I allow more saliva to collect on my tongue and lick my palm again, my eyes locked on his, and his breath hitches.

Okay, guess I'm wrong. Apparently licking my hand is sexy, at least to the guy getting the hand job.

Tentatively, I lay the flat of my hand on the shaft of Sebastian's cock. It's so warm and silky soft, even in its hardness. I glance up to see that all four of the guys are completely focused on me. It's both thrilling and terrifying to be the center of attention like this, especially when I don't know what I'm doing.

"You're doing great," says Sebastian. His eyes are dark, his voice rough, and that's all the reassurance I need to keep going.

Wrapping my hand around him, I feel the weight of his cock. It's heavier than I thought it would be. More solid. Giving him a few tentative strokes, I remind myself to grip him tight, just like he showed me. But I watch his face the entire time to make sure I'm not hurting him. That would be the most embarrassing thing I could do, more so even than not knowing what I'm doing.

And the more I stroke, the more his tip glistens. I wonder if it tastes different straight from the source than it did off my finger.

"Can I?" I glance meaningfully from Sebastian's face to his cock. I'm not ready to say "taste you" yet. I'm already feeling like my inexperience is showing enough without trying to sound sexy on top of it.

"Always," he says, sounding strained. "Yes. Always."

I suppress a grin. Under other circumstances, I would tease him for choosing that word. I wonder what he would do if I decided to be as literal as he usually is, offering him oral sex at inappropriate times and expecting to be taken up on it.

Obviously, though, I'm not going to do that, so I gather my courage and focus on the task at hand. Some might say this right here is an inappropriate time, with our three friends watching us, but this is how they do things. They like to share. So I bend down and flick my tongue quickly against the head of his cock. His pre-cum tastes a little more salty than it had on my fingertip, but the resulting groan from Sebastian is so rewarding it sends tingles down my spine. Even if it didn't taste good at all, it would be worth continuing just to elicit that sound from him again.

So I try a different method, trailing the tip of my tongue along the side of his shaft just to see if he'll do it again, or if he'll make a different sound. I need to try everything so I can figure out what drives him craziest. Especially because with the way his eyes are rolling back in his head and his hips are thrusting against my tongue, I'm not sure he's going to be coherent enough to actually walk me through the finer points of giving a blow job.

"Can I touch you at the same time?" Elliot leans over to kiss my shoulder and trail his hand down my side until he comes to my hip.

The feel of Elliot's hand on my hip is both heavy and light at the same time, and the tingling between my thighs says I'm game to at least try. I can always say if I don't like it.

"Okay."

I keep my attention on Sebastian's lap, but I can hear the rustling as Elliot moves behind me on the bed and hooks his fingers around the waistband of my sleep shorts while he feathers kisses along my lower back, exposed from the way I'm leaning into Sebastian's cock.

There's a brush of cool air as my shorts and panties are tugged down, over my hips and down my thighs, trapping my legs together. When I shift to help Elliot peel my panties and shorts down past my knees though, he stops me by wrapping his hands around both of my thighs and releasing a breath against my bare skin. They've seen me naked before, up close even, but there is still a strong and new intimacy to it, being bent over and on display for Elliot while Felix and Lukas watch me suck gently on the tip of Sebastian's cock.

Without warning, Elliot runs the flat of his tongue along

my seam and I startle, falling forward onto Sebastian's cock and gagging myself.

"Fuck that's good," groans Sebastian.

"You're doing fantastic," Lukas tells me, his voice rough. "Just like I knew you would."

Their praise makes my blood hum. I've always loved being the best student in a class. And this praise does something to me that no classroom praise has ever done. When Lukas and Sebastian say it, I can feel myself getting wetter, and my clit begins to pulse with need.

As I pull back enough to breathe, I glance over to the other bed to see both Lukas and Felix completely focused on the way I'm speared on both Sebastian's cock and Elliot's tongue. Both of them have their hands down their pants, and I wish they would pull them down a little so I can see the way they're gripping their own dicks.

I must have gotten too distracted by checking out Felix and Lukas in the other bed because Sebastian lifts his hips, thrusting his cock deeper into my mouth and bringing me back to the moment. I like that he's taking control, gently fucking my mouth. I moan when Elliot dips his curled tongue into my pussy so I really am being penetrated by both of them at the same time. And all I have to do is kneel here and enjoy the pleasure that they're literally thrusting upon me.

"Is this okay?" asks Sebastian, his hand brushing a piece of hair back that's fallen out of my braid. He keeps his hand on the side of my head once the hair is tucked behind my ear, holding me gently in place as he fucks my face.

I can't exactly answer with my mouth fuck of cock. So I hum an assent and lean into his thrusts a little more, until he's hitting the back of my throat with each strong stroke.

I'm not sure what Elliot is doing to my clit and pussy at the same time that I'm gagging on Sebastian's length, but it feels fantastic. I try to widen my stance to give him better access, but my panties and sleep shorts, and Sebastian's legs on either side of me, prevent me from spreading as far as I'd like, so I just lean forward as much as possible to give Elliot all the space I can. It feels like there's a spring being wound tight inside of me, just like the other times they've touched me, and I know my orgasm is close. I press back into Elliot, chasing the rush of pleasure building with each stroke of his skillful tongue.

"Do you want to come, baby?" Elliot says against my pussy, the vibrations of his voice spiraling me closer to release.

I can barely nod with Sebastian's cock pressed against my tongue but I do my best, whimpering "mm-hmm" and reveling in the way the vibration makes Sebastian's dick grow even harder just as Elliot's voice stoked the fire between my legs higher.

"She does," confirms Sebastian, his voice more strained than ever. His fingers curl into my hair, not pulling but holding me where he wants me. "So make me come, sweetheart, and then Elliot will make you come too."

With this, Sebastian stops doing the work for me. Left to my own devices, I move my head up and down to mimic the way he'd been thrusting past my lips. Each time I pull back for breath, I swirl my tongue around the tip, and his groans are music to my ears. And each time I bob down on his cock, I go as far as I can until my eyes water, trying to get him into my throat so he knows just how much I want him.

By the third time my mouth sinks down onto him though, Sebastian's grip on my hair tightens and he holds me down, thrusting shallowly and hitting the back of my throat. It's hard to breathe, but just as I'm convinced I'll have to pull away to take a breath, his groan fills my ears and I feel the warm spurt of his cum pouring down my throat.

When he finally lets go of my head, I look up at him, gasping for air. He's looking down at me like I'm the most precious thing in the world, his eyes slightly out of focus as he wipes the tears that leaked out as I gagged on him from my cheeks.

"You did so well, Rebecca." He tilts his head to look past me to Elliot, who I realize has stopped going down on me while I got Sebastian off. "She can come now."

As the words are out of Sebastian's mouth, Elliot returns to his task, thrusting his tongue in and out of me. It's rolled and skinny going in and he widens it as he pulls out, but he does it so fast, and all I can do is rest my forehead on Sebastian's stomach and enjoy the experience. Especially when he brings his finger up and begins circling it around my clit, moving in ever faster and tighter spirals until I come with a choked sob, my fingers gripping the sheets on either side of Sebastian's hips as my own buck against Elliot's mouth.

As the waves of pleasure begin to abate, Elliot continues to lick me slowly, drawing out all of the tingles and vibrations fluttering through my body. And if he weren't holding my thighs upright with his hands, I'd probably collapse right here onto Sebastian.

Slowly, Elliot kisses his way up my spine, before falling to the bed and pulling me against him so we're in practically the same cuddling position we were a few minutes prior. The only difference is that Elliot's cock is even more insistent in the way it's pressing against me, with my shorts and panties still down by my knees and my pussy sensitive from coming so hard only a moment ago. I can feel him, hard against my bare buttocks, and if I wasn't half limp from my orgasm I'd wriggle against him until he was wedged between them. I like the idea of letting him use the crack of my ass to get himself off. Maybe in a minute, when I have myself under control, I'll suggest it.

But for now, all I can do is murmur, "Thank you," to them both. My body is languid with the aftereffects of my orgasm right now, and a variety of thoughts and emotions are trying to poke their way to the forefront of my mind. I'm not in the mood for that though, so I push them aside to sort out later, when I'm not partially naked and in bed with two guys.

"You're welcome," Sebastian and Elliot respond at the same time.

I huff a laugh. They're obviously very good at doing things in tandem, as they've just proven.

I wonder if Elliot is going to ask me to help him come, or if he's going to take care of it himself. What is the protocol for that? I glance across Sebastian's stomach to see Lukas and Felix slowly stroking their still-hard cocks inside their pants. Are they going to come at some point? Will they let me watch?

I open my mouth to ask Elliot if he would like to use my ass to make himself come, but instead what comes out is, "Are blow jobs like your cubes?"

They all go still, the three guys I can see staring at me in confusion.

"What do you mean?" Lukas asks, hand still in his pants but not moving.

I try to explain what I mean, my words coming slowly because even I don't really know what I'm asking. "In your cubing, each scramble requires a different pattern to solve, right?" They nod, so I continue. "Do all of you prefer the same techniques for your blow jobs, or are there different patterns that different people prefer?"

I'm not sure I've explained it clearly, but in my head it

makes sense. It must make some sense to them too, because the confusion on their faces clears.

"Everyone has their own patterns they prefer," says Elliot, pressing a kiss to my neck as his hand skims over my shoulder and down my arm. "Some people require a longer solve, and some people can come with just a few touches. Especially if they're the right ones."

"Can I try a new pattern then?" I glance over my shoulder, down to where Elliot's tented pants press against me. "On you?"

"Of course." Elliot grins.

I start to shift farther down the bed.

"If you really want to try a different pattern," says Elliot, continuing with our metaphor, "you could try it from a different angle, too."

"A different angle?" What other type of angle is there than straight on?

"I'll show you." Elliot helps me sit up and turns me so my ass is more at the top of the bed, then slides down on the mattress to his hip are in line with my face. "Now you can lean down from here."

As I see it, my options are either to straddle Elliot's face, or lay on my side and prop myself up on an elbow. I go with the latter, as straddling his face when he's just had it between my legs already feels like asking him to lick my pussy again, and I don't want him to feel like he has to do that.

I free his cock from his pants and he helps me shove them down his legs, kicking them off. I take a moment to admire his hard penis, which is the same girth as Sebastian's, but perhaps slightly longer, before lowering my head and wrapping my lips around it. It's a little harder to get enough leverage to bob my head up and down on Elliot's cock, so I focus instead on using my tongue to tease the tip.

"You can use your hands too," says Elliot. "Squeeze the bottom a little even as you focus on the head. And use the other hand stroke it like you did to Sebastian."

Feedback, good. I can work with that. I use the hand on the arm holding me up to grip the base of Elliot's penis, and as I bring my other hand up to wrap around him, Sebastian scoots down and turns onto his side, lifting my leg and throwing it over the side of his face so his own face is at my pussy while I'm still trying to find a rhythm and angle to blow Elliot effectively. I hold my leg off Sebastian's face, trembling a little with the effort, but I don't want to smush his head with my leg.

But apparently, that's exactly what he wants. "No hovering," says Sebastian, pulling my hips toward him until my pussy is in direct contact with his lips before pressing my leg down, clamping his head between my thighs.

While Elliot had used his tongue to thrust in and out of me, Sebastian latches onto my clit and sucks hard. It's very challenging to focus on what I'm doing to Elliot's cock when Sebastian has me careening toward another orgasm of my own.

My hand strokes down Elliot's cock to angle it better, and when it reaches the base, I shift the hand gripping him there, causing my palm to ghost over his balls. His hips jerk, thrusting deeper into my mouth to show me exactly how much he liked that. So I do it again, one hand wrapped around his length, squeezing the base as I suck the head of his cock like a lollipop, while my other hand cups his balls, my thumb stroking the soft, loose skin. Elliot's hand grips my hair just like Sebastian's had done earlier as he thrusts into me, again and again, until his cum floods my mouth and I swallow it greedily down.

I pull off of Elliot's cock to lick along the shaft as it pulses in my hand, and Sebastian takes that as a sign and suckles even harder, applying just the right amount of suction to send another orgasm tearing through me. This second one hits me quicker and harder than the first, and my thighs tighten around his head, holding him right where I want him as I ride his mouth, crying out in bliss as his fingers dig into my hips and his tongue flicks against my clit and triggers a third orgasm.

It seems these boys are quickly learning exactly what patterns to use to have me exploding for them with the fewest number of moves.

Chapter Sixteen

When the bedside light is turned on, all I want to do is snuggle deeper into the blankets where it's warm and cozy. But the alarm is also going off and that ruins the snuggle-down vibe. Plus, it's competition day, and we can't be late.

"Do you want to shower first, Rebecca?" asks Felix, leaning over Sebastian to pull down the covers enough to see me. "We're pretty quick in the shower, but we want to make sure you have enough time to get ready before we go down to breakfast."

Ugh. He makes a good point, dealing with my long hair alone probably means I'll take longer to get ready than all of them put together. And they all probably want to make sure they're there early for registration and to mentally prepare for the first day of Nationals.

"Okay," I tell Felix, forcing myself to sit up. "Thanks." I drag the blankets down just enough that I can lift my legs out from beneath the covers and then crawl down and off the bed. A hot shower will help wake me up.

The hot water feels fantastic beating down on me, and I let it run over my entire body as I lather shampoo into my hair. When the door opens, I jolt and nearly get shampoo in my eyes.

"It's just me," says Felix, stepping up to the sink with barely a glance at me through the shower glass as he begins to shave.

After everything I've done with these guys, I shouldn't be embarrassed about Felix seeing me shower, but it's still awfully bold of him to just walk in like this, without even knocking to see if I'm okay with him being in here. I turn a little away from the glass and can't stop myself from casting furtive glances his way as I race through the rest of my shower, any relaxation I could have enjoyed out the window now that I have an audience. It's just as well, given that all four of the guys will also want a shower before we go downstairs.

The towels are just out of reach from the shower stall—a terrible bathroom design, if you ask me—so I have to step completely out of the shower to get one. There's no denying though, the appreciative glance Felix sends my way when I reach for a towel and wrap it around me tight. If he notices my shyness, he doesn't say anything. Or maybe he chalks my slight blush up to the hot water heating my skin.

Moving to the counter, I watch in the mirror as Felix drops his boxers right on the floor and steps into the newly evacuated shower, as naked as I was just moments ago.

Making sure my towel is tucked snug around my chest, I brush my hair, trying hard not to be too obvious as I watch Felix in the mirror. I should leave. It'd be the polite thing to do, but he stood here and watched me shower so there's no reason I shouldn't be allowed to do the same. After all, as Sebastian says, fair is fair.

I thought I was being discreet in my voyeurism, but that thought is thrown out the window when I look up again only to see Felix facing me, one hand on the glass and the other stroking his cock. He's looking right at me, and I know I should look away. I should leave the room. But I'm frozen and fascinated.

My eyes drop to his hand, following the way he grips his cock so hard he looks like he's choking it. His fist starts at the very bottom of his shaft, and then slowly travels up to the tip, rolling his palm over the head before dragging it almost aggressively back down to the base. It's methodical and calm, but vaguely violent all at the same time.

Will I be brave enough to grip him so hard one of these days? Should I drop my towel and join him in the shower?

"Twenty minutes," calls Lukas from the bedroom.

His words are like a cold bucket of water. I don't have time to join Felix in the shower. I cannot be the reason these guys miss out on their dream of being world champion speedcubers.

I run the brush through my hair one more time and then run out into the bedroom so I can trade my towel for clothes and grab my toothbrush. The other guys all go into the bathroom and race through their own shaving and showering. If they're also jerking themselves off in the bathroom, I don't know, because I refuse to go in there to brush my teeth until they're all out and getting dressed. Three hot guys dropping towels, completely unashamed of being naked? I never thought I would find the image so tempting.

Lukas checks his watch impatiently as we all wait for Elliot to make the beds to his standards. Then we troop downstairs.

If I'd thought the lobby was crowded last night, it's nothing compared to how hectic it is this morning. Not just with tourists, but business people who must be here for a conference or meetings, as well as the large number of speedcubers and their families here for Nationals.

Wait. I look around the lobby again, even as Lukas grabs my hand and guides me through the throngs of people, and realize that there are a *lot* of families here. The guys' families aren't here, are they? Ronnie's words from yesterday echo in my mind, and I pray she was wrong, that their families aren't here. They haven't said anything about it, and that's definitely something that they would warn me about, right?

We wind our way through the crowds until we reach the back of a line, and Lukas drops my hand.

"There are a lot more people here than the last time I came to one of these," I say, surprised and impressed at the turn out.

"That was just Regionals," explains Sebastian. "This is Nationals."

"Sure, but it's still surprising to me compared to the last event I attended." I've been under the impression that speedcubing is a niche sport. I didn't think they would be able to get this many people all in one place.

"I thought you'd all retired," says a voice behind us, and we all turn to see a kid in a superhero T-shirt with a lanyard around his neck. He looks like he's maybe a freshman in high school. "Your fingers have got to be slowing down."

I bite back the urge to tell him that their fingers are wonderfully fast and nimble, thank you very much, as I well know. It would be wildly inappropriate for me to say something like that out loud to anyone, let alone a fourteen-year-old kid.

"Hey, Stephen," they all mutter, sounding resigned to experiencing this situation. I'm guessing it's not the first time it's played out at one of these events.

"Maybe you should get out of line. I won't tell anyone you're here, and that way you can retire and not suffer the embarrassment of losing again. Because you're not touching my title."

Stephen is a real dick. Is it wrong to think that about a kid? I don't think I care if it is.

"Statistically, we have a very good chance of winning," says Felix, pushing his glasses farther up the bridge of his nose.

"They've been practicing a lot, and their fingers are faster than ever." They all look at me in surprise. I guess they weren't expecting me to stand up for them. But Stephen is pissing me off. I'm not sure who he is, but there's no way I'm letting him be mean to my friends.

"And didn't you just have two DNFs at your last local competition?" asks Lukas.

"No," Sebastian corrects him before Stephen can respond. "It was one DNF and a flipped equator."

Stephen's face grows red. At any moment, steam might start flowing out of his ears, he's so mad.

A woman appears next to him, placing a hand on his shoulder. "Do you want to wait in line again with your friends, or are you joining your father and I for breakfast?"

Stephen gives his mom a practiced, choir boy smile. "Breakfast sounds great."

The sneer he shoots us behind her back as he turns and walks off is so over the top I can't help but snicker at it.

"Have your parents come say hi to me later," says the woman to the guys, nodding formally before following her son into the crowd.

"Well, now we definitely have to win and prove him wrong," says Felix.

"He doesn't deserve to be a national champion," Sebastian agrees.

"We can't take that title from him," says Lukas, "so we just won't let him become World champion."

I'm barely listening. Stephen's mother's words replay in my head. *Have your parents come say hi to me.*

They would have told me if their parents are coming, right?

"Are you parents here?" My eyes search the room as we move up the line. As if I'd recognize them if I saw them. I've never even seen a picture of them.

"Of course," says Elliot, sounding surprised that I didn't already know this. "Why wouldn't they come?"

"Well, they weren't at the last one." I can feel my breath coming faster. Is the room tilting a little?

"That was a small one-day competition, so there wasn't a point in them flying out just for that," says Sebastian.

"You should have told me." I smooth my hair, suddenly self-conscious about looking frizzy when I meet their parents.

Oh my god, I'm going to have to meet their parents. This is not okay. That's a girlfriend activity, not a whatever-we-are one. My palms begin to sweat and I fear I may be having a mild panic attack.

Felix frowns. "You didn't ask."

"I didn't know I needed to," I hiss as we reach the front of the line. "I'd have thought you guys would have given me a heads up on something like that."

The conversation is put on pause as the guys get checked in for their individual events and their group relay. They're given their own folders and lanyards, and I'm also given a lanyard, in a different color. This must be the guest one versus the competitor one. I slip it around my neck, my hands still shaking with nerves and irritation. I don't know if I'm angry or nervous or both, but I'm definitely not happy.

But the guys probably have no idea why it's a big deal, and may not even register that I'm upset. I don't share their "Of course our parents are here, why is that a surprise?"

attitude, but I know them well enough to understand why they don't see an issue. The problem is that if I don't explain my feelings to them, they probably won't ever see my side of it, and now that the conversation has been interrupted by registration, they may think it's done.

"I'm still upset that you didn't tell me your parents were coming," I say as we walk away from the registration table. I grab the nearest sleeve, which happens to belong to Felix, and lead him over to a quieter spot by the wall, trusting that the others will follow us. Which, of course, they do. "Them being here might seem like a no-brainer to you, but from my perspective, they weren't at the other one, so I assumed it was normal for them not to come."

"But we explained to you why they weren't at that one," Elliot says, clearly not following what I'm getting at.

"I know. But not until after I found out they were coming to this one. So do you see how I'd be surprised to find out they're going to be here this weekend?"

They all think about it for a moment, then begin to nod. "I guess that does make sense," says Sebastian.

"But we weren't intentionally keeping a secret from you," Lukas tells me. "We didn't realize you wouldn't know. That was just a miscommunication."

"And we're sorry that we didn't communicate," Elliot assures me. "Next time we'll make sure to tell you ahead of time if our parents will be there."

"I appreciate that," I say. "But you guys don't understand why I'm upset that you didn't tell me I'd be meeting your parents, do you?" I recognize that they are trying to make amends for what they think has me upset. But I'm not upset that they didn't tell me so much as I'm upset that it didn't occur to them that I would want to know.

They stare at me blank-faced. "Because ... you thought

we were intentionally withholding information from you?" Lukas ventures.

"For which we've apologized," Sebastian reminds me. "And you accepted."

I suppress a sigh, resigning myself to having to spell it out for them. "We haven't known each other for very long. And our"—I swirl my hand around, indicating all of us—"situation is weird, wouldn't you say?"

"I don't think it's weird," Felix says, and the others murmur their agreement.

"What I mean is," I say, trying to infuse my words with a patience I don't feel, "if you introduce me to your parents, they might think we're dating. Which we aren't."

"They won't think that if we don't say it," Lukas assures me. "We'll just tell them you're our friend. Like we said we would do."

"My point is, that if we *were* dating, meeting your parents would be a big deal. And I know we're not dating but we are ... doing other things. Which makes the situation complicated."

"Oh." I look at Felix and can see that things have clicked into place for him. "If we were dating, you would want us to warn you before introducing you to our parents, because you would want to prepare. And even though we aren't dating yet, meeting our parents is still something you need to prepare for because our relationship with you isn't just normal friends, and you're concerned they might suspect something based on how we all act around each other. And us not telling you they would be here means you didn't have a chance to prepare yourself."

I choose to ignore his inclusion of the word *yet* because outside of that, he's spot on. "Yes, exactly that. I'm upset because none of you thought about the fact that meeting your parents might feel weird for me. I understand why you didn't think you needed to tell me, but I want to make sure that you understand why I think you did need to."

"So ..." Sebastian says slowly, clearly puzzling something out. "It's like when we gave you a cube the first time. We didn't know you wouldn't be able to solve it, because it's such an easy thing for us to do. But for you, it put you on the spot."

"And it was probably uncomfortable, having to either admit you couldn't do it or try and likely fail," Elliot adds.

That is actually a surprisingly good comparison. "Right. This is just a little bit of a larger scale discomfort."

"We're very sorry that we didn't think about it being awkward for you to meet our parents." I can hear the sincerity in Lukas's voice, and see it on his face, and my heart melts a little. "We see now why it is, and recognize that it was unfair of us to spring it on you like we did." He reaches out like he wants to hug me or take my hand, but then remembers my no-PDA rule and drops his hand. "Can you forgive us?"

Like there's even a chance I could say no after they worked so hard to understand, and they do really seem sorry. "Yes, of course. Thank you for understanding, and for the apology." I take a deep breath, suddenly drained from the weight of that conversation. "Wow, that was a lot for first thing in the morning."

"Let's get some coffee," says Lukas, placing his hand on the small of my back and pointing to the sign directing people to the continental breakfast. So much for remembering about no PDA, I guess, but his touch doesn't feel like anything more than a friend guiding a friend, so maybe to him it's not PDA and shouldn't be for me either. "Coffee always helps."

"Yeah, coffee would be good." Caffeine may not be the

best idea in my current state, but the familiar routine of it might help settle me.

In the breakfast line, I get yogurt and granola, along with a dish of fruit and a slice of toast and, yes, coffee. I survey the room, but don't see any empty tables. I turn to the guys, the question of where we should go forming on my lips, but Felix is already answering it.

"Over here." He tips his head toward a table where a guy in a black hoodie is sitting alone, and we all follow him over there. "Hi, Calvin. May we join you?"

It takes a moment for the guy—Calvin—to notice us and slip the headphones off his ears. "What?"

"May we sit here?" This time Lukas asks, lowering his tray so it hovers just above the table.

"Oh. Sure." Calvin pops the top on an energy drink and takes a long swallow.

Felix immediately sits across from Calvin, and Lukas sits at the other end of the table. I begin to place my tray in the spot between Lukas and Felix, because I'm pretty sure it's their turn in the rotation given that I slept between Elliot and Sebastian, but hesitate in case I'm mistaken. Maybe sleeping arrangements don't count in the rotation, which would mean the car ride yesterday would be where it left off, and I was between Lukas and Felix for that. But Elliot and Sebastian move to sit across from Lukas and next to Calvin, so I slide into the seat I'd initially selected, pleased that my instinct was correct. Seems I'm picking up on patterns left and right these days.

"When is your first event?" Sebastian asks Calvin, cracking open his juice.

"Not until just before lunch," Calvin replies. He looks over at me, clearly curious about the outsider infiltrating this tight-knit group. "Hi, I'm Calvin."

"This is Rebecca," Lukas tells him, watching as I reach across to shake Calvin's proffered hand. "Our friend."

"Who is a girl," Sebastian adds helpfully.

"Nice to meet you, Rebecca," Calvin says to me, tossing an amused look at Sebastian before noticing something across the room that makes his whole demeanor change. His shoulders go rigid and his face hardens. "Fuck. She's here."

They all look to where Calvin's glare is pointing. I turn to look too, but not knowing anyone here, I don't know who has caught his attention.

"I don't know why you have such a problem with Patti," says Elliot, returning to his breakfast. "She's nice."

"We listened to her breakdown the events for a few of the Southwest competitions," Felix tells Calvin. "She must be here on the commentator team."

"Just my luck," Calvin grumbles. He stands, grabbing up his tray and drink. "See you all in the waiting area."

"What just happened?" I ask, turning back to the table as Calvin stalks away. "Who's Patti?"

"The girl with the pink hair," Felix tells me, nodding back in the direction they'd all been looking a minute ago. "She's one of the commentators who presents for the live streams of the competitions."

I crane my neck again to try to spot her. "Why did he run away when he saw her?"

My gaze lands on a tiny, fairy-like woman in the breakfast line. Her pink hair is cut in a cute bob, with choppy bangs, and she looks more like she belongs backstage at an emo concert than a speed-cubing competition. Which is to say, she looks very cool. My jeans and plain maroon sweater feel incredibly bland in comparison to her cropped lace tank top, fishnets, and combat boots.

Sebastian shrugs. "He just does that when she's around."

"He's always been weird about her, and when she started commentating it got worse," says Lukas.

"He claims she's more critical of him than she is of any other speedcuber," Elliot tells me.

"Is she?" Even though I'm not interviewing anyone this weekend and can't exactly put this information in my article without Calvin's permission—and even if I thought he'd talk to me about Patti, which I doubt he would, I'm not about to turn my article into a gossip column—I can't help the way my reporter brain begins to whir with the possibilities.

"She's generally pretty snarky, so it's difficult to tell," admits Felix with a shrug as his phone beeps with an incoming text. He looks down at the screen. "My mom just dropped her bag at the desk. I'll let her know where we are."

"She's coming here? Now?" I pull out my phone and check in my camera to make sure I have nothing in my teeth. At least my hair isn't as frizzy as I feared.

"Of course," says Felix, surprise in his voice. "She's not going to be able to check in for a few hours, so she may as well come see us before we have to go get ready." He stands and scans the room, then waves slightly. "There she is."

I can't believe I'm going to have to tell Ronnie she was right. She is going to give me so much shit.

The blonde woman walking toward us is all color and pattern. Bold orange and green stripes make up her long dress, which clashes slightly with a bright yellow canvas purse. This is clearly not someone who is used to sitting off to the side, but prefers being the center of fun.

"Hi, Mom." Felix hugs her and kisses her on the cheek. He gestures to the chair recently vacated by Calvin. "Do you want to join us?"

The last parents I met were Ronnie's, the day we moved

into the dorm freshman year, and they were already there when I arrived and they came over to introduce themselves to me. Should I introduce myself, or wait for Felix to introduce us? I'm not sure if I should stand to greet her, to show respect? Would that make me look a little too eager to make her like me? Or make it seem like I'm more important to her son than I really am?

"Good morning, gentlemen," she says, slowly moving around the table and hugging each of the guys in turn as they stand and greet her.

I fidget with my napkin, waging an internal battle with myself over what I should be doing.

"Would you like us to get you something to eat?" offers Felix.

"I didn't stay here last night, so that wouldn't be appropriate," says Felix's mom. She indicates me, still sitting paralyzed by nerves and indecision. "Why don't you introduce me to your friend?"

"This is Rebecca," says Felix.

"It's lovely to meet you, Rebecca. I'm Summer," she says, and I force myself to snap out of it and stand up. I'm thinking I'll just shake her hand, but she pulls me in and hugs me just as warmly as she'd hugged each of the guys before taking the vacant chair across from her son. "What events are you competing in this weekend?"

"Oh, no, I'm not a speedcuber." I'm surprised that anyone would think I'm here to compete. I mean, I know I'm smart, but if I had to say what sort of smart vibes I give off, I'd say *book nerd*. Definitely not *math genius*. "I'm just here for fun, kind of last minute."

I try to pass it off as if it's no big deal that I'm here watching these guys compete for a national championship. That I'm skipping a full day of classes to spend time with them and support them. That I'm meeting their parents and cubing friends like I'm someone who might ever see any of these people again after this.

"Yikes, last minute," says Summer, making a face. "Where did you end up getting a room? When I dropped off my bag to be stored at the desk until check in, they said they were completely full. There's some sort of business conference happening this weekend too."

"Oh, um." I glance at the guys, but none of them offers to help me out, so I guess I'm on my own. "I'm just ... crashing with the guys."

Felix's mom freezes for a moment, and then she smiles like she just won the lottery. "Of course, yes, that makes sense. Even if you could get a room of your own, there's no sense in paying for multiple rooms if you don't have to."

"If you don't want to eat, would you like anything else?" ask Lukas, checking his watch. I don't think he realizes that he's saving me from the inevitable word vomit that would follow Summer's response to my staying with her son and his friends, but I am so grateful that I don't have a chance to embarrass myself. "We have a few minutes before we have to go back to the waiting area before our event."

"Well, I wouldn't mind one of those fancy city coffees," Summer admits.

Felix is already opening the map app on his phone and searching up the nearest coffee places. "There's a café about a six-minute walk down the road." He looks torn, and I'm betting a twelve-minute round trip plus time to order is cutting it too close for his liking.

"Think we can make it there and back in fifteen minutes?" asks Sebastian, also checking his watch. "Maybe if we place a mobile order now so it's ready when we get there?"

Felix's mom waves a hand. "Oh, you guys go do what you need to do. I can go get coffee and I'll be back before your first event." She takes her son's phone from him and glances briefly at it before handing it back, apparently memorizing the café's location in a matter of seconds. Maybe Felix comes by his affinity for patterns naturally.

"You shouldn't be walking around the city by yourself," Elliot says. "Even if it is probably fairly safe this early in the morning."

"It's fine," she tells him. "I'll be back in no time, and when I get back I'll find your parents to sit with them."

It takes a lot of concerted effort to keep moving my hands naturally as I eat my granola and yogurt. *All of their parents. Will be here. Where I am. And I'm going to meet all of them and they'll all realize that I'm sleeping with their sons.* I should run. Maybe to the train station. How much will a train ticket to Boston cost?

Felix must sense how panicked I am because he reaches out and places his hands on my knee under the table, stilling the leg I didn't realize I was bouncing. It calms me a little, but not enough. Maybe I can put off meeting the other parents for a few minutes longer.

"I could come with you." I regret it as soon as the words are out of my mouth, but I can't back out now, and it's probably the lesser of two evils. Fancy coffee sounds way better than the sludge they're serving here, and if I stay here, we are just going to go find the other parents and then the guys will have to go to the competitors waiting area and I'm going to either have to find a way to excuse myself from sitting with their families or I'll be trapped with, well, their families. At least Felix's mom is just one person, and she seems nice. I can walk to get coffee with her and then when we get back I can stay I need to run up to the room and tell her I will find her inside the competition, and then I can just ... not do that. I can hide for a few minutes and then pretend I looked for her and couldn't find her, and then I won't have to sit with the guys' families and have to pretend I'm not having an internal meltdown for the next few hours.

Felix seems to like the idea of me accompanying his mother to the café. "It is better to never walk alone," he agrees, an eagerness in his eyes that makes me wonder if I've made a terrible mistake. Maybe *now* is when I should have pretended I need to go to the room. I could hide before I have to spend any time with any parents at all.

Too late now, though, because Summer claps her hands together and stands, looking as delighted as her son at having me tag along.

"That sounds wonderful."

I silently beg for a sudden disaster to get me out of this, an earthquake or meteor strike or rabid polar bear attack, but no such luck.

At least I'll have a fancy coffee at the end of it. That's something, I suppose.

"All right, I'll see you in there," says Summer, and all of the guys stand up automatically. She walks around the table again and hugs every single one of them as if they were her own son. "Good luck, you're going to do great."

"Good luck," I say, waving awkwardly at them. I'm not about to hug them and give anybody any opportunity to try to kiss me or anything. They agreed to avoid any PDA this weekend, but I can't risk them slipping up, especially not with Felix's mom standing right there.

"We'll take care of your tray," Lukas tells me, and I thank him before hurrying after Summer.

As soon as I make it to her side, she links her arm through mine. Wow, didn't expect that, but okay. "My, it's busy in here. We don't want to get separated."

This is it. Here comes the interrogation. She's going to hold me hostage until I tell her exactly what is going on between me and her son.

Maybe I can distract her and put off having to answer questions for a couple minutes longer. "Do you remember where the café is?"

Already, I'm not sure I can do this for our entire walk. Small talk is not my favorite thing.

"Looked like we just turn right out of the hotel and we'll come to it eventually," she says with a shrug, jostling my own arm.

I keep my eyes straight ahead because I don't want her to see how completely shocked I am that she's just going to walk in the general direction of the café and not use GPS to make sure she does actually know where she's going. I want to pull out my own phone to guide us, but I don't want her to think I don't believe her capable of getting us there. I'm trying to make a good impression on her, after all.

"Is this your first speedcubing event?" she asks as we walk out of the hotel into the brisk winter morning.

"No, this is my second." My response is reflexive, and I immediately wish I'd kept my mouth shut lest she start to ask more questions about how I know her son.

"Ah, so you haven't had time to be jaded by them yet." She laughs and pulls me closer for a moment as if we're old friends sharing a joke. This is something Ronnie would do, but I'm not prepared for it coming from my new friend's mom.

"No." I try my best to smile but I'm not convinced it doesn't come out as more of a grimace. I'm so *nervous*, even though she's being perfectly nice and normal and not asking uncomfortable questions. "I went to a local one in Boston, and this is a big difference. A lot more people."

She nods, not looking at me as she takes in the sights around us. "Then it's still exciting for you. Three days of competition this weekend, and then Worlds will be four."

"You're already confident they'll make it to Worlds?

You're not worried at all?" I've only just met them this semester and I'm super stressed for them. As a mom, she should be a bundle of nerves.

Well, my own mother wouldn't be, but the way Summer hugged all the guys equally makes me think she must be a better mom than mine. It's not like the bar is high though.

"No, they're talented, they're going to do great," she says. "I'm here to let them know I'm supporting them, but that doesn't mean I'm not going to get out and enjoy my vacation a little too." She says it confidently, but stage-whispers it as if we're sharing a secret, which makes me giggle.

"Have you been to New York before?" I ask her. She says she has, and turns the question back on me.

"No," I say. "I haven't traveled much outside of Boston. The little I've done is for work." I mean, technically the first cubing competition was outside of Boston, so it's not an outright lie. And it sounds a little less sad than the truth, which is that until now Boston is the only place I've been besides my hometown, which is less than an hour away.

"Oh, a job that lets you travel is amazing." She's all smiles, pointing to the café up ahead. How about that. She did in fact get us here without GPS. I know it was a straight shot, but I'm still impressed at her confidence in doing it. "What do you do for work?"

I tell her that I'm working at a newspaper, and she launches into a bunch of questions about journalism and my career goals, and I try to gloss over the more unsavory parts of my job and make it sound like I'm actually doing real work there and not just restocking the break room. Before I know it, we've gotten our coffees and are walking back into the hotel lobby.

"Well," she says, bringing the conversation back to where it began, "since you haven't had the opportunity to travel much, and you're not here for work, consider stepping out of the hotel a little. Take in the sights." She had looped her arm through mine again on the walk back, but now she lets go of it. I should be glad to no longer be physically attached to her, but it feels like a dismissal.

Does she not want me to be here and support our guys? Or maybe she's trying to protect me from the other parents by getting me out of the hotel before they can grill me about my relationship with their sons. Maybe the other parents aren't nearly as nice and chill as she is, and she's trying to give me an out so I don't get stuck sitting with them.

"You don't—do you mean now? Go see the city now?" I ask.

"Oh, not right this minute, the competition is about to start. But at some point during the weekend. Don't let the boys hold you captive, you'll be bored out of your mind if you have to spend the entire weekend locked away in that convention hall watching them solve their cubes. You're allowed to go see some of what New York has to offer."

I open my mouth to protest, to tell her that that's the whole reason I'm here, is to watch them, but she's not done.

"Others might be content with just one thing, but you can have all the things. Don't listen to anyone who tells you otherwise." She wags a finger at me, sounding stern. Like she's admonishing me for being boring.

Or maybe she's trying to give me a message. Maybe she's talking about more than just speedcubing or visiting the city. Maybe she's trying to tell me in her own way that it's okay to see more than one guy at a time, like both her son and all three of his friends. Or that it's okay to be in a relationship and have a career at the same time.

Or maybe I'm reading entirely too much into a simple conversation and all she's saying is that I'm in New York for the first time and I should see the Empire State Building before I leave. That makes a lot more sense than Felix's mom not only giving me permission, but practically *demanding* that I fuck her son and his best friends at the same time.

I think I've been quiet for too long, so I frantically look around the crowded lobby.

"I'm not sure where to go." There are people moving in all directions through the hotel and I don't know where the competition is happening, but I'm sure it's got to be about to start.

"You'll find your way. Don't worry," she says, giving my arm a comforting squeeze. "Just follow the signs."

Is this woman really laying some woo-woo stuff on me right now? I'm not judging, I know woo-woo works for a lot of people. I'm just not one of them. I prefer logic and reason. Not to mention I was talking about not knowing where to go for the competition, not in life.

When I turn to say as much, already gearing up to pretend to laugh at the miscommunication, she's pointing at a sign a little to our left tucked against the wall. The sign reads: *ICF Nationals This Way* with an arrow. There is a literal arrow guiding us. She wasn't being woo-woo.

"Oh, perfect." I take back all of my *Felix's mom is being weird* thoughts. Logic and reason really are guiding us at the moment.

We're almost at the competition hall when I remember my plan to run up to the room so I could get out of having to sit with the parents. Shit. It's too late now. If I try to disappear at this point, I'll miss the beginning of the competition, and I don't want to risk missing any of the guys' first events.

Also blocking my plan is the fact that Summer still hasn't released my arm. Still clinging to me like we're bosom buddies in a Victorian schoolyard, she halts us so we can get a good look around the room. It's quite large, with actual bleachers in the back, although they are mostly empty at the moment. The rest of the room looks a lot comfier, with real chairs at various event stations. Even these aren't full though. With all the people at the hotel, I'd thought the place would be packed, and I'm surprised it's not.

I remind myself that it's only the first event of the first day. And like they said, this is Nationals, there are bound to be more people in attendance here than for a local competition. Probably a lot of them are still at breakfast, or sightseeing before their events start, and I bet the families of younger competitors are backstage with them like at the regional qualifier.

A little booth off to the side catches my attention, because I can see a few people standing around it and one of them is the girl with the bubblegum pink hair and edgy outfit I saw when we were having breakfast this morning. *Patti*, I remember, *her name is Patti.*

"Ah, the others already saved us seats," says Summer, gently tugging me away from the booth and up the center aisle between the chairs to a group of people waving at us.

All I can do as Felix's mom practically drags me forward is take a fortifying sip of iced coffee through my straw and hope the caffeine and sugar will carry me through this meeting. I wish the guys were here to act as a buffer.

"Don't worry," Summer whispers, "I'll introduce you."

Unfortunately, that's exactly what I'm worried about. I'm still not convinced that little speech about having it all wasn't a veiled declaration that she approves of the situation between me and the guys, or at least what she's decided is the situation. What if she introduces me as their girlfriend? Or, worse, their fuck buddy? A mom wouldn't do that, right? There's no way a mom would say to her friends, *This is the girl who's fucking our sons.*

"Hi everyone," says Felix's mom, finally letting go of my arm so she can hug the other moms and wave at the dads. When they all look to me, she adds, "This is Rebecca. She's a journalism major at Boston University and came down to watch the competition."

She begins to point to all of the other parents, telling me their names, but I'm barely listening, distracted by the fact that while I told her I'm working at a newspaper, I never said that I'm a journalism student, or what school I attend. How does she know all of this?

I want to be glad that she isn't defining me by my friendship with the guys, but all I can do is panic about the fact that they might all be talking about me to their parents. Why would they be telling their parents about me? I'm not their girlfriend, and the friendship we're developing isn't exactly the sort of thing you share with your families. *Yeah, I met this girl and watched my roommate go down on her on the dining room table while our other two roommates sucked on her nipples. She's a journalism student at BU and likes pretzels.*

"Hi." My greeting is barely audible, partly because I feel like I'm choking and partly because it's surprisingly loud in this room.

At that moment, a woman walks out onto the stage with a clipboard and it starts to quiet down around us. The guys' families all scoot down one seat so there are two chairs instead of just the one they'd originally saved for Felix's mom, and I sink into the aisle seat, grateful that I only have to sit next to the parent I've already spent some time with. Not as grateful as I am to have had the introductions cut short, but still quite grateful.

"Welcome everyone to the International Cubing Federation USA National Championships," she announces with a big smile, and the crowd cheers.

She goes over the etiquette of watching, reminding the audience that they need to keep quiet to allow all cubers an equal and fair chance at concentrating on their solves. Then she checks her clipboard and announces the first event of the day.

Felix comes out for the first round, not looking out to the audience. He is completely focused on the table he's assigned to. I watch as he nods to the judge and flicks his fingers over his Skewb to warm himself up. Once he sets it down and places his hands at the ready, the judge lifts the box to reveal his scramble, and it's a blur as Felix's hands come off the board and solve the cube in less than two seconds.

I lean down to set my drink on the floor so I can clap, but no one else looks like they're going to applaud, so I pretend to scratch my ankle before raising my coffee to my lips and taking a nervous sip.

Lukas's mom leans over her husband to say quietly, "It took me a long time to get used to that too."

I just smile uncomfortably at her before turning back to the stage, where Felix is looking out at the crowd. I can tell when he spots us because his lips tip up in a hint of a smile, and then he's grabbing his Skewb from the table and heading into the back to wait for his next scramble.

Without any of my guys on the stage, I let my eyes wander to the other competitors, noting their times. They're good. Better than most of the competitors I saw at the local one I'd gone to for the newspaper, but that makes sense since these are supposed to be the best of the best in the country.

As I shift my gaze to the crowd around me though, I realize that just like at the local competition, I am one of the few people here who is actually interested and impressed by what's going on onstage. There are a lot of parents in the audience doing things like knitting or reading, only occasionally pausing to check if their kid is on the stage competing.

At the end of the event, they announce who is moving on to the next round and we're allowed to clap. I'm just glad Felix's name is announced. I would feel gutted if he didn't make it to the next round. I want all of the guys to win.

While the organizers and volunteers set up for the next event, I anxiously sip my coffee. Families, including the guys' families, are starting to turn to each other and chat quietly.

I can't hear what they're saying. I wonder if they're talking about me. Then I wonder if it's egotistical to think that, even if it's realistic that they might be chatting about the girl their sons brought along to an important event.

I watch them out of the corner of my eye, pretending that I'm focused on all the happenings around us. They look so comfortable with each other. It's clear they've known each other for a long time. As the volume in the room rises, they have to talk louder, and I can hear them asking about different family members and memorable events. It makes sense that if their kids have been friends for so long and competing together, they would also spend time together and get to know what's going on in each others' lives. And there's clearly not much else to do at these events but chat.

Chapter Seventeen

My phone vibrates in my bag and when I pull it out, I see it's our group text.

Meet in the hall for lunch? texts Lukas.

Can you bring our parents too? Sebastian asks.

"The guys are ready for lunch," I say, turning toward their parents. "They'll meet us out in the hall."

Felix's mom smiles calmly as if everything is going to plan, following me into the aisle to wait for the others. The other moms hustle along, shooing their husbands ahead of them. For their part, the husbands seem perfectly content to be shooed.

It doesn't escape my notice though, that the moms are suddenly looking at me a little more intently for some reason. I sigh, turning away so no one sees. Lunch is going to be awkward, but I've been through worse—like my own family dinners, for example. At least I don't anticipate any arguments breaking out today.

"Ready?" I ask to make sure we're all together. It'd be embarrassing to lose one of their parents on such a short walk. Not that we couldn't find them, but I'd look pretty inept if my one job was to get the parents to their sons and I couldn't even handle that.

I thought heading out into the hallway would be a relief, but I was wrong. Everyone else is having the same idea we are right now. Luckily, the guys are already here, hovering near the wall to our left as soon as we come out.

The moms all race forward to hug their sons. The dads hang back a little to let the moms do their thing, but when they have the chance they move forward to do that hug-and-clap-on-the-back thing that men do. I suddenly wonder what happened to Felix's dad. Why isn't he here?

Am I a bad friend? I have probably asked them hundreds of questions about speedcubing, but how many have I asked about them as people? Or about their families?

Once the parents have said their hellos and congratulated Felix on his win, all four of the guys move toward me, but I take a step back, willing them to understand that they have to act like any normal, non-sex-having friends would. They agreed to no PDA. And their parents are watching us, waiting to see how this will play out, probably hoping they'll get some answers about who, exactly, I am to their sons.

Not even being able to answer that question myself, I know I shouldn't care what their mothers think of me.

But I do. I want them to like me.

There's an uncomfortable moment where the guys and I just all stand there looking at each other, me silently begging them not to be weird and them trying to figure out what to do with their bodies now that the hugs they were obviously primed for aren't going to happen.

Sebastian's mom, Andrea, saves us from ourselves, stepping forward and clapping her hands together once. "Where should we go to lunch?"

"We can go to the hotel restaurant," suggests Lukas.

"I second that," says Sebastian. "Then we'll be close by and can easily get back for our next events."

"Are you sure you wouldn't like to leave the hotel for lunch?" Summer asks. "Go try something new, see a little bit of the city?"

"This is where the competition is," says Lukas, confused and looking to his teammates for clarity. "We don't want to be late or miss something."

"Okay," his mom, Jen, throws up her hands in defeat. I can tell they've been through this before. "Let's go to the hotel restaurant."

"You'll see," says Lukas. "It'll be much better this way. Less stress."

"We've already given in," Summer tells him, but there's not a hint of anything but resigned amusement in her voice. "Let's not beat a dead horse."

We make our way through the crowd. It appears everyone here has the same plan as us, which Lukas declares is proof that it's a very efficient plan.

I don't point out, as we wait for a table, that going to the same place as everyone else is probably less efficient when it comes to the time it will take for us to get a table and eat. They already have enough to think about today without me adding to it.

As soon as we order, Lukas's dad—I think Summer said his name is Neal—places his elbows on the table, looking at the boys over his clasped hands with a stern expression.

Sitting between Elliot and Sebastian, I sit up straighter in my chair. This is it. The official parent interrogation is beginning. My hands feel clammy. I'm going to have to explain that although their sons are great, I'm not dating them, just fooling around with them. Which is going to be very uncomfortable to say out loud to all their families.

"How do you boys feel the competition is going?" Neal

asks. "I know you still have a lot of plays to make, and it's early yet, but how are you feeling?"

"They aren't plays, they're events, and then that's broken down even more into solves," explains Lukas patiently, even though I am certain he's explained this before, probably many times. "But I feel pretty good. The new hand warmers I brought are helping keep my turns smooth."

"The real challenges will come after lunch," Sebastian tells the table. "Statistically, the biggest things we have to worry about this afternoon will be not flipping the equator and making sure we finalize the last permutation before dropping our cubes."

"Well, I hope you haven't been neglecting your studies to practice," Elliot's mom, Mary, admonishes. "Make sure you have your priorities straight."

Elliot nods. "We always block out all of Saturday to study, Mom."

"What about you, Rebecca?" Felix's mom turns to focus on me suddenly. "I imagine your program also means you have a lot of work to do outside of class time."

I feel like a deer staring down an oncoming truck. Why did she have to put me on the spot? I'd just started to feel comfortable. Like we were going to keep the focus on their sons and the national competition, the whole reason we're here.

I should have known my luck wouldn't hold. It never does.

"My studies are very important to me." Why is my stupid, traitorous brain choosing this moment to replay last weekend, when Sebastian splayed me out on the dining table among our books and papers and made me come my brains out? I can feel my face turning scarlet, and can only hope everyone just assumes I'm nervous to have all the attention on me. "I even brought some work with me just in case I had extra time while we're here."

And now I'm imagining dumping it all on the bed upstairs so the guys can lay me out on top of it again for a repeat performance. I think they would agree that practice makes perfect. And my guys love to practice.

"You should have brought it down with you this morning," Elliot tells me.

"I didn't know if there would be much downtime at a competition of this level," I explain, aware that every eye at this table is on me. "Besides, it would feel wrong to be doing homework during the competition when I'm here to support you."

"A lot of families do other things during or between events," Sebastian points out. "There's no reason you couldn't do homework. We wouldn't mind."

I blink at his use of the word *families*. It sounds like he's including me in that group, but I'm sure he's not. It's just that most of the audience is the families of the competitors. It's easier to say that than to say, "the people in the audience." Right?

"When the boys were younger," says Andrea, leaning in so I can see her, "they used to spread out on the hotel hallway floors to do their homework."

"Not me," contradicts Elliot, scrunching his nose. "There's no telling how filthy the floors are with so many people walking around in their shoes."

"No, you never would." His mom laughs. "Not even if we brought a blanket from home."

"You used to stand to read and if you had to write anything down, you'd use the wall," says his dad with a chuckle.

"Fewer people touch the wall than touch the floor," Elliot insists.

"What else do kids do to amuse themselves at these events?" I ask, happy for the chance to deflect the conversation from myself lest I do something mortifying like mention how we amused ourselves in the room last night.

Besides, I kind of like the idea of hearing stories about the guys when they were younger. And I'll likely never meet their parents again, so it's not like I'll have another chance to ask.

"Other kids ran in the hallways, but not our boys," says Lukas's mom. The way she looks at them all, clearly proud, it's as if they're all her sons. I get the feeling all of the parents kind of view the guys that way, and I wonder what it must be like to have not only your actual parents be so obviously proud of you, but to have bonus parents who feel the same.

The servers arrive with our meals, and the parents launch into stories about the boys quizzing each other on the history and rules of speedcubing, having mini competitions in the hallway with ridiculous rules like having to hop on one foot while solving, and—the most annoying thing, according to Andrea—correcting adults.

When we are all finished eating and the check has been paid, Elliot's father leans back in his chair. "So when is your next event?" he asks, checking his watch.

Elliot looks down at his own wrist. "We have two hours."

"That should be plenty of time to check out the museum down the street," Summer says. "Who would like to join me?"

"We would," Mary tells her excitedly. "When are we going to be in New York again and get a chance?"

"We're in too," says Jen. "It'll be nice to get outside, get some fresh air, and have a little walk."

"What about you boys? It's the natural history museum,

not an art museum." Summer seems to think that would be a determining factor, but the guys all shake their heads.

Sebastian grimaces. "That would be cutting it kind of close."

"Agreed," says Lukas. "I'd rather be here just in case something happens."

"Like in case the competition schedule gets ahead for some reason, which it has never done in the history of the sport," Andrea clarifies, the same tone of amused resignation in her voice that was in Summer's when she told Lukas not to beat a dead horse.

The guys all look to Sebastian, who nods. "There's a first time for everything."

"Well, that's all right, you boys can stay here," agrees Felix's mom. "What about you, Rebecca? Would you like to come with us to the natural history museum?"

Under different circumstances, I would love to walk through the museum. Walking down to the café earlier with just Summer was fine, but being alone with all of them without having the guys as a protective barrier is a whole different story.

"If you would rather stay here and do homework, we understand," Mary says gently. "Especially if you don't want to do it during the competition, we'd understand if you wanted to take advantage of the downtime."

I hadn't even considered that I could use the time to get some work done. "That's probably the best idea. I'm missing classes today, and I don't want to fall even more behind."

"No, you definitely don't." Andrea stands, gathering her purse, and the rest of us follow her lead. "In that case, we should get going if we want to be back in time to see Lukas's event."

We head back into the hall, where there's yet another round of hugging. And every parent is hugging every kid, including me, as if it's the most natural thing in the world. I can't even remember the last time either of my parents hugged me. This is probably more hugs in a morning than I've had in a lifetime.

Once they're on their way to the museum, I turn to the guys.

"Where are you hanging out until the next event?" Now that my homework was mentioned, I feel guilty because I haven't planned ahead for how I'm going to make up for being here all weekend. Normally I study on Friday nights and all day Saturday. The main reason I haven't been interested in dating is that I didn't want it to get in the way of my studies, so I can't let the fact that I'm fooling around with guys now affect my GPA. Graduation is still two years away, but one bad grade could take the rest of the semester to make up for, and I don't want to have to work any harder than I already do just because I let myself get distracted.

"We normally spend the entire competition in the competitors' waiting area," says Lukas, tilting his head a little as he glances over at his friends, having one of their telepathic conversations.

"Okay. In that case, I'll head up to the room and get some work done. I'll set an alarm so I'm back for the next event."

"Or you could bring it down here to work on," suggests Felix.

A screaming toddler goes running by, followed by a slightly older kid, not screaming, and finally an adult yelling for both of the kids to stop. We all watch them disappear down the hall, and I look back at the guys.

"No, thanks. It'll be quieter upstairs." Plus, there's no point in bringing my stuff down here if I'll be sitting alone while they're in the competitor area. I might as well take advantage of the quiet solitude of our empty room to really knock out a good chunk of work.

"Or ... we could all go upstairs," Elliot suggests, his mouth slowly forming the words as if he's uncertain about them. "Our room isn't that much farther from the competition platforms than the waiting area."

"And they do have all of our numbers so they can text us if the schedule changes," says Sebastian, equally slowly.

"We can always turn up the volume on our phones and set an alarm," says Elliot.

"Then let's wait up there so we can all be together," agrees Lukas, already heading over to call the elevator.

Unfortunately, we're not the only ones who have the idea of running up to their room after lunch. When we finally manage to find an elevator with space for us, we're forced to stand much closer than we would have normally. I'm not going to complain though. I didn't realize how much I would miss being able to touch them all day. Lukas must have the same thought, because he reaches out to grasp hold of my sweater and gently tug me closer to him. It's only about half a step's worth of distance, but it brings my side flush against his, and his solid warmth makes me feel calm for the first time all day.

I glance around the elevator, but everyone else on it is involved in their phone or simply staring at the doors, waiting for them to open. So long as no one will see, I slip an arm around his waist and give him a squeeze that's not quite a hug before quickly dropping my arm so we're not found out.

When we get to our floor, we weave out of the elevator and down the hall to our room.

As soon as Lukas opens the door, but doesn't go in, I can sense there's a problem. I peer around him into the room. It looks like housekeeping has come through and completely reset the room, undoing everything Elliot did last night and this morning before we left.

I turn to Elliot, whose eyes are wide. He looks like he's just gotten unexpected bad news. "Do you need to clean it again?" I ask.

His expression turns embarrassed, but he nods. "Just a quick one?"

"It's not a problem," I assure him. If this is what he needs to feel comfortable, I'm not about to stop him. Especially when it's so easy to allow him this.

When Elliot has finished resetting the room and we have all changed to our room slippers, I look around until I find the Do Not Disturb door tag half-hidden under my suitcase. "We probably should have put this out before we left." I grab the sign and hang it on the outside of the door. "It probably won't do anything else for today, but it doesn't hurt either. And we'll leave it up the whole time we're here so housekeeping doesn't come in and undo everything again."

Elliot nods as he tucks his cleaning supplies back into his bag, but he won't make eye contact with me.

I hate that I've made him embarrassed. He has absolutely no reason to feel ashamed, and I never want to be the one to make him feel that way.

Acting on instinct, I wrap my arms around him from behind. It's not lost on me that this is almost exactly how he was holding me last night before we knocked a couple of items off my list. The memory sends a tingle through me, and it occurs to me that while I could do homework right now, I could also suggest we tick off another box. The only thing stopping me from reaching down right now and touching Elliot any way I want is my own self.

But he's upset, and I don't want to push myself on him.

So I just plant a kiss against his spine through his shirt and step away, giving him the space he probably wants.

I pull the book we're reading for class out of my bag, resigning myself to actually doing the homework I'm supposedly up here to do. When I turn around, the guys are sitting on the beds, and I look between them, debating. I could sit at the desk, but we've had so much distance between us already today, and will go back to the same as soon as we leave this room again.

"Can I sit with you?" I hold my book to my chest as I wait for their answer. They're under a lot of stress and maybe they need their space right now. I wouldn't blame them if they just want to sit on their own.

But their reply is both affirmative and immediate. "Of course," says Lukas.

At the same time, Sebastian says, "Always."

I could go back to the same place where I slept last night but the calendar rotation would say that I should sit between Felix and Lukas. But if I sit between them now, will that mean I should sleep between Elliot and Sebastian again tonight? That doesn't feel fair. This schedule is supposed to make life easier, but right now it's just annoying me.

The reality is that I spent last night with Elliot and Sebastian, and right now I want to sit with Lukas and Felix. So I clamber over Lukas's legs and settle between them. No one says anything, so they must assume I'm following the rotation. Maybe I can sit with Elliot and Sebastian at dinner and that'll get me on track to sleep between Felix and Lukas tonight.

"What are you going to do while I read?" They can't be planning to just sit here and watch me read.

"We could read to you," suggests Lukas.

"You want to read my book to me?" That sounds even more boring for them than watching me read.

Lukas shrugs. "You have to read it."

"For class," I clarify. "It's not exciting."

Lukas's response is to pluck the book from my hands. He opens the book to my bookmark, respectful of the spine, and starts to read at the top of the chapter.

His voice is quiet yet sonorous, and very relaxing. This is way more enjoyable than reading it by myself has been.

After a couple of minutes, Felix reaches for the book and picks up where Lukas left off.

I turn to watch him read. It's cute, the way he pushes up his red glasses with the back of his hand against the bottom rim.

I'm not sure what comes over me, but I lean up and kiss his cheek.

Chapter Eighteen

Felix looks down at me, and all I can do is stare back, uncertain of what happens now.

I've never initiated with them before. I'm not even entirely sure that's what I was doing when I kissed him, at least not consciously. But the way he's looking at me, all I want now is to kiss him again, properly, and more.

Felix very carefully places the bookmark between the pages and sets the book down on the side table. Then he hooks a finger under my chin and brings my lips back to his for a kiss.

It starts sweet and gentle, but it's been a long day and we're only halfway through it. I can't imagine how stressful it's been for them as competitors. Meeting and sitting with their parents has been challenging enough for me, and I'm sure it's nowhere near the amount of pressure they feel. This is the release we need.

Shifting up onto my knees, I swing one leg over Felix's lap so I'm straddling him. This is a much easier way to kiss, and now my hands can be involved too. They slide right into his hair of their own accord. I love how silky it is, and that he is allowing me to touch him. I'm still learning all of this and I'm not exactly sure what I'm doing, but based on the rapidly-hardening cock twitching beneath me, I think I might be doing okay.

I pull back to look in Felix's eyes. They're dark and appreciative, but he doesn't reach out to bring me back in for another kiss. My eyes slide to Lukas, who is still quietly sitting on the other side of the bed, watching.

Last night, I was touched by both Sebastian and Elliot at the same time. What would it feel like to be touched by Lukas and Felix at the same time too?

But if I want that, I think I'm going to have to ask for it. Especially with the way Lukas is sitting so far away and not taking any initiative.

I trail my hands down from Felix's hair to rest on the lightning bolt slashing across his red shirt. "Lukas, do you want to come closer?"

Without a word, Lukas shifts closer on the bed so he's leaning against the headboard right next to Felix, their shoulders touching.

I hesitate, my previous boldness fading. It's scary to say, out loud, that I want this. I want two of them. At the same time.

Gathering my courage, I drop my left hand to the top of Lukas's thigh. I'm not brave enough to rest it on the bulge in his pants, but I get as close as I dare.

"You can touch me," says Lukas, apparently reading my mind. He moves my hand from his thigh to place it on his growing erection. "I won't bite unless you want me too."

Surely he's kidding. But he winks and smiles before releasing my hand, allowing me to move away if I want.

Glancing back over to Felix, I inch my fingers over Lukas's groin and slowly undo his pants. I have to use both hands, and the zipper is loud in the otherwise silent room, but neither of the guys stop me. I glance back at Felix, who just smiles and rests his hands on my own thighs.

So this is happening. I'm really doing this. Of my own accord and by my own initiative.

Lukas lifts his hips slightly to allow me to reach into his boxers and tug them down in the front. His cock springs free and I wrap my fingers around it. It's a little girthier than Elliot's or Sebastian's, but not quite as long. Bringing my gaze up to Lukas's, I keep my eyes on his as I slowly lick my palm before wrapping my fingers around him again and giving his cock a gentle, testing stroke.

"Look at you, being so brave," he says, leaning over to capture my lips in a searing kiss.

"Such a good girl," agrees Felix, his hands moving to my waist and sliding me forward and back on his lap, right along the length of his cock, still tucked into his own pants.

"Thank you," I murmur against Lukas's lips. The praise makes my chest expand with warmth.

I take advantage of the pause to switch back to kissing Felix. I don't think I have a favorite of these guys to kiss, they're all good, but different from one another. Lukas is teasing me with little nibbles, but Felix is being soft and sweet.

I maintain the rhythm of my hips moving against Felix as he slides his hands up under my sweater to palm my breasts.

"You're so gorgeous," he murmurs, slipping his thumbs beneath the top of my tank to flick over my hardening nipples. One of the perks of having small breasts during sweater weather is not having to wear a bra, and I'm immensely grateful to past me for not bothering with one this morning. "So soft."

"Do you want to fuck me?" As soon as the words leave

my lips, I freeze. My hand stills on Lukas's cock, flying up to cover my mouth. I can't believe I just said that.

Felix, too, is frozen. Can I take the words back? Rewind time and unsay them? I mean, we all know that's where this little list project is going to end up eventually, so it's not like I want to take it back forever, but Felix isn't saying anything and they're all looking at me and suddenly all my bravado from a few moments ago with Lukas is gone, and all I want is to disappear into a hole and never come out.

I shift to climb off Felix's lap. I might not be able to take the words back, but I can definitely go hide somewhere until they leave for their next competition event. It's not a plan, exactly, but it's all I've got right now.

"Wait," says Felix, snapping out of his stupor to grab my waist and stop me from climbing off the bed. "Where are you going?"

"I'm sorry," I whisper, not meeting his eye. My face is hot and tears of embarrassment are stinging the backs of my eyes, but I refuse to let them fall. "I shouldn't have asked."

"You can always ask us questions," Felix tells me, dipping his head to try to catch my eye.

"But if you ask something," says Lukas, taking one of my hands in both of his, "you have to wait for an answer."

"You froze," I mumble, still not able to make myself look up. "You didn't say anything."

"Your question surprised me," says Felix, rubbing his thumbs up and down along the sides of my stomach. "That's all."

"And if he's not interested," adds Lukas, "I am."

"You are?" This is what finally makes me look at them, my eyes snapping up to meet Lukas's green ones. Is he just saying that to make me feel better? He's never lied before that I've seen, so he must mean it.

"Of course," says Lukas, moving to sit behind me,

straddling Felix's shins, and wrapping his arms around my shoulders. "We want to help you cross every item off your list. We just didn't have it on the schedule for this weekend, so we weren't expecting you to be ready for it so soon."

"But it's the main thing on my list," I counter. It feels like they've been inching me along, and I'm not sure how long I'm going to be in their lives. They graduate in a couple of months. That's plenty of time to tackle the smaller items, and believe me, I want to check off as many of those as possible with these guys, but that's the big one and I'm ready.

"Don't you want to ease into it instead? Small steps to the big goal?" Lukas nuzzles kisses along the side of my neck.

"It's like finishing the biggest part of the project before knocking out the extra credit," I tell him. Besides, I've already grown more attached to them in the past few weeks than I ever intended. The sweeter they are, the more chance I have of falling for them. And I can't do that. I need to protect myself. That's the whole reason I agreed to this whole thing in the first place.

"We still have another event this afternoon," says Felix, bringing my attention back to him. "We wouldn't be able to stay in bed the rest of the day cuddling with you."

Sebastian and Elliot have been quiet this entire time, but now Sebastian speaks up. "It wouldn't be fair to you, to do that and then have to go back downstairs right away," he says, shaking his head.

"We want to be able to make sure you feel cared for after." Elliot's face is so earnest, I consider caving, but now that my embarrassment has abated, I'm back to feeling like I want to take charge and get my way.

"How about a compromise?" I ask, rolling my hips so I grind against the bulge in Felix's pants. I'm not playing fair, but I also don't care. "What if we do it now, even though you can't stay after, but then we also do it later and you can take care of me afterward as much as you want?"

Felix groans and grabs my hips to stop the motion. "So your compromise is that we get laid twice instead of once?"

"Yep."

"And there is absolutely no way we can talk you into just waiting until tonight so we can make you feel as special as you are?" His fingers tighten on my hips when I try to rock against him again.

"Absolutely none." I've made my choice, and I'm determined to go through with it. I'm also horny enough that I don't care about cuddling after, I just need an orgasm.

"Okay," says Felix, dropping his hands to his sides, freeing me, and his head back onto the headboard. "I guess we'll fuck you twice today then."

"Really?" I hadn't thought they would give in this easily. I lean forward and press my lips to his, the kiss quickly becoming greedy. When I pull back, I'm breathless. "Thank you."

Felix chuckles, pulling me toward him so our foreheads are touching. "You're welcome," he says, his voice soft. "Do you know who you want to be your first?"

"I have to make that decision?" I'd assumed they would have decided this already since they'd planned out everything else between us. Shouldn't the calendar already have this information? Even if we're moving it ahead by a few days?

"Of course. It's a big decision," says Elliot. "If that means you don't want to do it today, that's okay. You can have a few days to think about it, if you want."

"Maybe next weekend we can sit down and talk about it," agrees Sebastian.

"Felix," I say. As soon as the name is out of my mouth, I

know I've made the right choice. He's always been so sweet to me, cuddling me that first night at their house and helping me to the shower after Sebastian ate me out so good on the dining room table. And I'm sure he'll bring that same caring to my first time.

He's always given and given to me, never once asking for anything for himself. This is my chance to give him a reward for his kindness.

"Me?" asks Felix, shocked. "Are you sure?"

"You." I lean in and give him a long slow kiss, feeling his cock twitch beneath me. When I break the kiss, I look around to the others, suddenly concerned that they'll feel cheated, or like I'm playing favorites. "Is that okay?"

"Of course it's okay," Lukas says, resting his chin on my shoulder. Elliot and Sebastian murmur their agreement. "It's your decision, and we all just want you to be comfortable for your first time."

I turn a little to kiss him on the cheek, and he captures my lips in a slow, deliberate kiss. When it ends, I look over to Sebastian and Elliot, sitting on the other bed. I feel bad that they haven't gotten any kisses yet, and am about to ask them to come over when Elliot speaks.

"Are you comfortable with us watching?" He sounds nervous, although I don't know why he's feeling that way when I'm the one about to lose my virginity with his friend. "Or we could leave, if that's what you want."

It's very sweet that Elliot is offering something I know he doesn't want to do, all for my own comfort. It's a shame I'm not interested in dating them, because they'd probably be great boyfriends.

"You can definitely stay." I climb off Felix, squeezing his hand briefly to let him know I'll be right back, and go over to give Elliot a hug.

I might want Felix to be the one I have sex with first, but

I don't want any of the others to feel slighted. It's because they've been so kind and attentive that I'm ready to take this next step.

"Okay," Elliot hugs me back and then gets up. "I'll grab a towel to keep the bed clean."

Okay, well, that doesn't make me feel sexy. I get it, it would probably be weird if Elliot *didn't* put a towel down as a barrier between the bed and my naked body, but still.

"He means it in the best way," says Sebastian, his hands sliding under the hem of my sweater and across the skin of my waist. "You know we don't expect this of you, right? Just because we're all here in a hotel room."

"I know." I plant a kiss on his cheek and turn back to the other bed, ready to return to Felix's lap, but he's up and digging in his suitcase.

"Here you go," says Elliot, laying out a towel from the bathroom on the bed. "It was in the clean pile so hopefully it's sanitary."

"Thank you," I tell him. I know this is something that Elliot does because he cares, and I'm appreciative of that.

"Come here," says Lukas, still kneeling in the center of the bed, right below the edge of the towel. As soon as I climb up on the bed, his hands grip the top of my pants. "May I?"

This is happening. My heart thuds a little harder in my chest. I nod.

Lukas helps me shimmy down first my pants and then my panties, the cool air of the hotel room making goosebumps race across my skin, and I'm glad to still have my sweater to keep me warm.

And then Lukas grabs the hem and tugs it up. "This too?"

Well, there goes that safety net. I'm not changing my mind, but I'm still nervous, especially now that I'm getting naked and no one else is. "Only if you take yours off too." Fair is fair, after all.

Lukas huffs a laugh and pulls off first his comic T-shirt and then the long-sleeved shirt he's wearing under it, revealing toned arms and chest. He's not muscly and bulky, but there's a solid trimness about him that's not easy to see when he's wearing two shirts all the time. I'm glad that I bargained, because it's a nice view.

I stare down at him as he pushes me gently back to a sitting position and leans down to kiss my knee. I gasp as he kisses his way slowly up my inner thigh, sending sparks of excitement through me. This is familiar, and I know just how pleasurable it is to have their mouths between my thighs. There's no way I'm going to deny either of us this right now, and my legs fall open of their own accord.

Lukas takes his time, keeping me on edge as he meanders his way up my sensitive skin until he hits my center. Even then, he doesn't go straight for the spots that drive me crazy. No, he edges around them, teasing me, hinting at the pleasure my body is craving but never actually giving it to me.

When he finally latches on to my clit, my hips buck against his mouth. I'm practically begging to ride his tongue the way I want. But he pulls back slightly to keep that blissful feeling right out of my reach, giving himself enough room for a single finger to tease around my entrance before sliding inside.

I moan, half in pleasure and half in frustration. It's not enough. I reach down to grip his hair and hook a leg over his shoulder. I need more, and I might not be able to form the words, but my body can definitely convey its desire. I can feel the warmth of Lukas's breath as he laughs softly against my aching pussy before curling his finger and making me writhe as I try to get closer, to make him put his mouth back on me.

Felix, who has shucked his clothes save for his superhero boxers, comes back to the bed and lies next to me. His bare skin against mine is warm, and even through the haze of desire, I can't help but grin as I stroke a finger across his thigh.

"Nice boxers."

"They're my lucky boxers." His voice is dead serious, and I quirk an eyebrow at him.

"Were you trying to get lucky with me, or are they just for your events today?" I doubt he was aiming for more than what's on our schedule, but I'm curious if he was thinking something sexy might happen at some point today or if he was wholly focused on cubing.

"I only planned for the competition," he says, kissing my neck. "I couldn't plan for you."

"None of us did," agrees Sebastian.

Felix hooks his thumb under my chin and brings my lips up to his. It might start sweet, but he's soon matching the rhythm and pressure Lukas is applying between my thighs. I don't know how they do it, but I appreciate every movement and the synchronization as I tumble over the edge into the sweetest orgasm that leaves me floating on air.

My pussy is still pulsing with the aftershocks when Lukas sits up and the chilly air gusts over the wetness slicking my thighs. Before I can even shiver, Felix settles his own hips between my legs. He kisses down my jaw and over the heavy pulsing in my neck.

"Are you still sure?" he asks, his tongue flicking over my pulse. "We can stop at any time."

"Don't stop," I pant. I'm not backing out now. I want everything, and I want it from them.

"Only if you're sure," says Felix, raising himself up slightly and looking down at me as he rolls a condom onto his thick shaft. It's hot, the way he strokes himself to roll down the condom. When he pulls his hand away and I get a good look at him for the first time, my eyes widen.

Whoa. Maybe I should have looked at all of their dicks first to see which one is the smallest, then picked that one to be my first time. Felix might not be as long as his friends, but he's definitely wider. I did not realize that when he was touching himself in the shower this morning.

Was that only this morning? It feels like forever ago.

I look back up at his face. "I'm sure. Stop arguing with me." I'm not going to change my mind. I'm ready for this.

"Yes, dear." Felix smiles as he lowers himself down enough to continue kissing along my neck, his hands planted on either side of me so he's not smothering me with his weight.

I reach down to stroke the pad of my thumb over the tip of his cock. It feels a lot different with the condom on it, but from the way he groans into the crook of my neck, he still loves the feel of me touching him. I trail the head of his cock through my folds, relishing the way he holds himself so still, letting me explore this moment, even though I'm sure he's as desperate to press forward and sink inside of me as I am to have him do it.

The bed dips on both sides of me as Elliot and Sebastian stretch out beside us. Maybe I should be weirded out to have them right here as I'm about to fuck their best friend, but I'm not. It feels right.

I glance over Felix's shoulder and meet Lukas's eyes. He's sitting right there at my feet, hand wrapped around my ankle, mouth shiny from my orgasm. I'm still looking at him as Felix lines himself up with my entrance.

"Ready?" Felix asks, and I turn my eyes to meet his behind his glasses. I nod, and he presses slowly forward, sinking inside me.

Even as wet as I am from the orgasm Lukas gave me, it hurts a little. Felix is so big, and as my body adjusts to take him, I can't help but bite my lip and close my eyes, breathing through the discomfort.

"You're doing so good." Lukas rubs his thumb across my ankle, even as Elliot and Sebastian both lean in to kiss me—Elliot the side of my head, and Sebastian my shoulder.

"You're so tight," groans Felix as he moves the last little bit until he's buried inside me. "You're doing amazing. Are you okay?"

"Yeah," I whisper, and pull his head in for a kiss. "It's just ... weird. Good weird. I've never felt anything like this."

He kisses across my cheekbone until he reaches my ear and says very softly, "I'm going to start to move. Tell me if it's too much."

I nod, and he withdraws his cock, then presses forward again. He slowly drags his thick length in and out, letting me adjust to the feeling of being fucked while he kisses my neck, gently sucking on the spot where my racing pulse flutters under my skin.

"I'm not going to last long. You're too good," says Felix, his voice gruff, like he can't catch his breath.

Reaching between us, his thumb brushes over my clit in tight concentric circles and my hips buck in time to his thrusts, meeting each movement of his own hips. He doesn't let up, continuing to thrust in a slow steady rhythm that contradicts his stressed breathing and frantic fingers.

"Fuck!" The word is ripped from my chest as the orgasm comes out of nowhere, forcing my eyes to roll back in my head and my fists to tighten their grip on the sheets as I quiver underneath him.

As the orgasm subsides, my fingers let go of the sheets and I lie there, panting and shaking. Elliot and Sebastian both take my limp hands in theirs, bringing them to their lips and kissing them as I float on air. Even Felix's change of pace to quick short thrusts feels good, extending the flutters wracking my body.

Felix's face is a tableau of pure ecstasy as he freezes above me and then collapses, nuzzling into my neck.

"That was incredible. Thank you." He plants a kiss on my shoulder and then continues to just lie half on top of me, holding me tight and keeping me warm.

"You were outstanding," says Lukas, leaning over him and kissing my forehead. "I knew you would be."

My brain is fuzzy, and I'm warm and sticky from sweat and my multiple orgasms. But it's so cozy with our little cuddle pile that I don't want to move. Felix is a little heavy, pressing me into the mattress, but I don't care. I want to stay like this forever.

I don't know how long we lie there before an alarm goes off, making me giggle. That's my guys. Always setting alarms.

"It's okay, you rest," says Elliot, sliding my glasses off and kissing my forehead as I stir beneath Felix.

They slowly climb out of bed, but Elliot comes back with a warm washcloth and cleans me up, then gently pulls the towel out from beneath my hips.

"Keep resting," says Lukas, pulling the covers up over me. "Come downstairs whenever you're ready. No rush."

They each lean down to kiss me before making their way to the door. Felix is the last, still fastening his pants as he sits next to me on the bed and brushes his lips across mine.

"You're amazing," he whispers near my ear. "And I'm honored to have you choose me for your first time. Thank you." He moves a piece of hair off my forehead as he stands, and I'm only dimly aware of the door shutting as I drift into sleep.

Chapter Nineteen

When I wake up, the room is dark. I sit up in a panic. What time is it? Did I just sleep away the entire day? Did I miss the guys' events?

I grab for my phone and see that I only slept for twenty minutes. That calms me down enough to realize it's only dark because the curtains are closed.

I pad over to them, still naked, and throw open the blackout curtains, keeping the netted ones over the windows. We might be a ways up and probably no one can see, but I don't want to flash anyone in case someone is able to see in. Elliot had cleaned me up before they left, but I still want a shower. Especially if I'm going to go down and sit next to their parents. I definitely don't want to smell like sex.

Oh god, did Felix shower? I bet he didn't. There wasn't time. I hope that by the time he sees the parents again after the competition, the sex smell has worn off. I don't love the idea of the other competitors smelling me on him and being able to connect the dots from the sex musk to the girl he's hanging out with all weekend, but as long as the parents don't realize, I'll have to be content with that.

I race through the shower, keeping my hair out of the spray and only focusing on the area below my waist. I'm sore, but energized. I'd always wondered why people were so sex-crazed, but now I definitely understand. Sex is great. *I just had sex for the first time.* I don't really feel any different. I mean, I wasn't expecting to suddenly feel like a whole different person or anything, but I thought there'd be something besides a slightly achy vagina to mark the turning point between "virgin" and "girl who has sex."

As far as I'm concerned, the only downside is that I'm down to two pairs of underwear and I'm going to have to put one of them on, which will leave me with one pair for the next two days. I'm going to have to go shopping.

Grabbing my book and glasses off the nightstand, I run my fingers through my hair to make it presentable and race out the door.

Lukas is just stepping up onto the stage for his event as I slip into the audience room. Perfect timing.

Before sitting at his table, he looks out into the audience, eyes crinkling slightly at the corners when he sees me. It's not a smile, exactly, but I know that's competitor-mode Lukas being happy to see me. I give him a small wave and sneak forward to slide into my seat next to the parents. If I don't join them, they'll definitely notice, especially since they're in the same place they were earlier so I can't even claim not to have seen them. But boy, do I not want to spend the rest of the afternoon sitting beside them after I've just fucked one of their sons.

It was nice of them to save me a seat, but I'm glad that the event has already started so I don't have to answer questions about why I'm late or what I did during the break.

"Hi!" Mary whispers, leaning around Summer to greet me.

I smile and offer a little wave, making sure she can see

my book on my lap. Maybe they'll all assume I was just upstairs reading, rather than losing my virginity to Felix while the others watched.

Turning away, I focus on Lukas. It's always so impressive watching his solves. I can never believe how fast his fingers are, even though I've seen and felt them work their magic. Unfortunately, being very fast also means that he's leaves the stage after only a minute, leaving me alone in the audience with all of their parents and no excuse not to talk to them.

While the rotation of competitors changes over, Elliot's mom leans forward again to get my attention.

"How did your homework go?"

I freeze. Were they discussing how I wasn't down here when they returned? Do they suspect we were fooling around upstairs instead of working?

I force a smile. "Good." I hold up my book so they can see where my bookmark is. They don't need to know I wasn't the one who placed it there. Felix was. Right before he fucked me.

Is it just me or is it warm in here?

"How was the museum?" She was super excited to go see the city this morning, so hopefully she'll want to talk about it a lot and fill our time until the next scramble and I won't have to say anything more.

"Oh, it was amazing!" she whispers excitedly before launching into a list of all the things they saw as they walked through the exhibits.

Occasionally, Sebastian's mom also leans forward to add in a tidbit or comment about the museum. As soon as Lukas steps onto the stage for his second cube though, we all sit back to watch. After all, this is why we're all here. To support our guys.

Lukas warms up his hands with a few turns on his

practice cube, and then he's ready. His cube is revealed and we watch his eyes analyze the data quickly before touching his hands to the starting pad and beginning. His fingers fly through the turns, then he drops the cube and resets his hands. It's over faster than ever. When he looks up and meets my eyes, I can tell even he's pleased with his performance.

I'm so proud of him.

When he walks off stage again to wait for his next scramble, I quickly open my book, hoping it will help me avoid additional conversation and possible interrogation by his parents.

"Dear," says Lukas's mom, setting her hand on my forearm to get my attention.

Well, there goes that plan. So much for my book protecting me from deep personal conversations with the parents of the guys I'm fooling around with.

She leans in close to whisper in my ear, "You might want to roll up the collar of your sweater."

I pull back to look at her, and my confusion must be written on my face because she touches a finger to her own neck. I'm still confused.

She looks a little embarrassed as she mouths, "You have a hickey."

Oh, god. I'm certain that my face is turning beet red as I mirror her movement, touching a spot on the side of my neck just above the collar of my sweater. Sure enough, it feels bruised when I press on it. *Fuck.* I quickly flip the collar of my sweater up—thank every god in every pantheon that I put on a turtleneck this morning—and turn to face straight ahead, willing the blush that I know is still turning me scarlet to subside.

As much as I would like to sink into the floor right now,

I am grateful to Jen for saying something. She could have let me walk around all day with a giant hickey just right out there for everyone to see, but she didn't. I can't bring myself to look at her, but I turn my head slightly in her direction and whisper, "Thank you."

She reaches over and places a hand on mine, squeezing gently once. "We've all been there."

Taking her hand back, she turns to ask Mary a question about the next event, allowing me a much-needed moment to compose myself.

I am going to have to have a serious conversation with her son and Felix when we're alone together next. It had to be one of them who did this to me, because it definitely wasn't there until after I fooled around with them this afternoon.

I stare down at the pages of my book, not really reading so much as stewing in anger and embarrassment. I'm certain the moms are going to demand I accompany them to the bathroom or something so they can grill me about my relationship and intentions with their sons, but they just keep talking to one another, and eventually I begin to relax. It seems Jen really was just doing me a solid, and no one is going to make a big deal out of it.

For now, anyway.

I survive the rest of the events for the day, but I barely get any reading done. It was hard to focus when I was so conscious of all of the guys' parents sitting next to me, knowing they all saw my hickey before I covered it up.

Any respect they might have had for me after having lunch together has almost certainly flown right out the window.

We move out into the hallway to wait for the guys so we can all go to dinner together. It's slow going with most of the crowd moving in the same direction, but at least I don't have to meet any of their eyes or talk to anyone as we let the crowd carry us along.

As before, the guys are already waiting for us when we make it out the doors. Elliot immediately comes up to me and lifts his hands to my neck.

"Your turtleneck is flipped up," he says. "Let me fix it for you."

I push his hands away. "No, it's fine. I did it on purpose. I'm ... cold."

There is no way I'm rolling this collar down. I might even have to wear the sweater again tomorrow. And Sunday. I don't think any of the makeup I have with me is going to cover a hickey. Guess I'll just have to be Turtleneck Girl all weekend.

"Oh." Elliot steps back, but he looks hurt and won't meet my eye now. Ugh. Now I look even worse in front of his parents. None of them appear to be paying attention, but still. Maybe they're only pretending to look up dinner places on their phones, when really they're thinking, "Yikes, so she's a slut *and* a bitch."

"Here." Sebastian takes off his black zip up and begins to slide the sleeves up my arms. I'm going to roast in two sweaters, but after my little scene with Elliot, I don't fight him. I'm going to have to apologize to Elliot for hurting his feelings.

As I stand there, beginning to sweat, it occurs to me that between the hickey and the fact that I'm wearing

Sebastian's sweater, the parents are absolutely going to assume I'm dating him, a the very least. Do they know their sons like to date as a unit? If they assume I'm someone's girlfriend, do they assume I'm dating the whole group?

"Well, should we go to dinner?" asks Sebastian's dad, Hank. "What's everybody feeling like eating?"

"Maybe we could go somewhere outside of the hotel since you don't have to be back for more events tonight?" Summer suggests. "We don't have to be out late, and I'm sure Rebecca would like to see at least a little of the city."

"That sounds good to me." I'm ready to agree to just about anything at the moment so long as it means I can escape this uncomfortable moment. "Just let me go put my book back upstairs."

Running up to the room will be a perfect escape. I'll be able to check if my hickey is completely covered by my sweater and put a bit of makeup on it so no one else notices it. I mean, they already saw, but that doesn't mean I need to keep flashing it around, showing them the evidence that I was fooling around with their sons.

I can also claim that moving around warmed me up a little, and I can give Sebastian his zip-up back. It's a win-win-win.

Except that Elliot's mom shoots down my plan. "Oh, you don't need to waste time doing that, I can just put it in my purse." She takes the book from me and drops it into her oversized bag. "See? Plenty of room."

"Oh. I—thanks." I have a sudden flash of inspiration and try again. "But I still need to go up and grab my purse."

I grabbed my phone and key card when I rushed downstairs earlier, but my purse is still up there, offering another easy excuse for going back upstairs.

"No need," says Lukas, moving to put his hand on my

lower back before catching himself and resting it between my shoulder blades instead. "You're here as our guest, so it's our treat."

I make one last desperate attempt and say, "But you all paid for my lunch, you're not paying for my dinner, too."

"Yes, we are," Felix tells me, moving to my other side. "You missed class to come support us, the least we can do is buy you dinner."

"Joke's on all of you," says Hank. "We're paying for all of your dinners. You boys don't really think we came all the way here to watch our kids compete just to make them buy their own meals, do you?"

Everyone laughs, but internally I'm freaking out. Apparently I really don't have an excuse to go upstairs alone for a moment, and they're really acting like I'm their girlfriend. We are definitely going to have to talk about this later.

In the meantime, all I can do is follow the parents as they lead us off to dinner. Most of the guys are in the middle of the group, walking with their own parents, but Felix hangs back to wait for me. As we leave the hotel, he rests his hand on my lower back to guide me through the door, but then leaves it there. As unhappy as I am about the hickey and the boyfriend behavior, I'm so tempted to lean into him. I already miss the connection we had when we were alone upstairs. We can't really be ourselves with their families around. I know I should make him move his hand, but we're at the back of the group and no one can see. Besides, this little touch is comforting. It's almost as if he's letting me know that he, too, wishes we didn't have anything to hide.

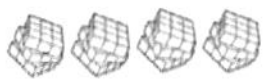

Dinner is filled with analysis of today's scrambles and discussion about who is moving on to the semi-finals tomorrow, and how well the guys know them and what they expect the outcomes to be. I'm able to return Sebastian's zip-up to him, claiming that the restaurant is warmer than the hotel was (although I do get ahead of the turtleneck thing by saying, "I kind of like how cozy my sweater feels like this, though"), and there aren't any invasive questions about the nature of our friendship, which surprises me considering my current hickey, but I'm not complaining. I'm glad when we all head back to the hotel, though. Even though dinner was fine, I'm ready to get back to our room and not be on edge anymore.

When we pile into the elevator, the guys engineer it so that they are circled around me, meaning that I don't have to stand next to any parents. It's sweet that they can tell I'm tired and agitated and are trying to protect me in their own way, but I have not forgotten that we are having a serious chat about public displays of staking their claim to me as soon as we're alone in our own room.

The elevator stops at our floor first and some of the parents have to exit the elevator to let us off, meaning that they're watching us walk down the hallway to our room. That we're sharing. Where someone gave me a stupid hickey.

As soon as the door to our room closes behind the last one inside, I round on them before they have a chance to distract me with their dicks.

"We need to talk." I keep my voice to a normal volume,

cognizant of the neighboring rooms, but I let all of the frustration and embarrassment I've felt this whole evening come through in my tone. "Look at this!"

I yank down the neck of my sweater to show them my hickey. "I wasn't cold tonight. I was hiding the fact that one of you gave me a hickey."

Sebastian is the first to speak. "I get it," he says, and I start to relax. Until he keeps talking. "It's not symmetrical. There's only one. We can fix that for you."

"The lack of symmetry is not the problem," I say through gritted teeth. "The problem is that it's here at all. And all of your parents saw it!" When they still don't say anything, I turn to Felix and Lukas. "Which one of you gave this to me?"

"Hmm," Felix hums, looking to Lukas and then back to me. I wonder if they really aren't sure, or if they're just being assholes and refusing to tell me.

"Hickeys are not okay," I say slowly. "You promised no PDA this weekend."

"It's not PDA," Lukas is quick to point out. "It happened here in the room."

"But then it left the room when I did, and I only even knew about it because *your mother pointed it out to me.*" My volume is rising, and I can't help it. For being such smart guys, they sure do miss a lot of things when it comes to people and feelings.

"Oh. Okay." Lukas rubs up the hair at the base of his neck and stares down at the carpet as if that's going to give him the answers.

They all just stand there for a minute, contemplating the floor, before Elliot quietly slips off his shoes and slides his room slippers onto his feet. I'm sure he held out as long as he could, so I can't even be annoyed, but it's the cue the guys need to break the spell and begin to move silently around the room. No one looks at me or speaks as they get ready for bed. I can't tell if they're pissed or sad or embarrassed, so I don't even know if they understand that we're having a fight. Do they just not know how to act, or are they pretending it's not happening?

The room fills with tension the longer none of them speak. It's so much worse than the sexual tension I felt with them last night, and it needs to burst soon because I'm not sure how much longer I can handle this.

I shut myself in the bathroom to get ready for bed and try to wash away the day. By the time my face is clean, I'm barely even angry anymore. I'm just ... drained. Even looking in the mirror and seeing the hickey as I braid my hair back off my face, I'm having trouble mustering up any of the outrage I felt earlier, instead feeling guilty for upsetting them even though I do feel it was valid for me to be mad.

I feel like I kicked them when they were down. Today was stressful for them. Sebastian flipped the equator on one of his scrambles and Felix DNFed on his blindfolded event, so even though they are still competing in many of the events tomorrow, they did take some losses and have to be feeling bummed about that. And then here I come, yelling at them over a hickey that can be covered by a turtleneck.

My apology dies on my lips when I exit the bathroom and see all four of them shoved into one bed together, their elbows knocking into each other. That can't be comfortable. Are they expecting me to join them?

"What are you planning now?" It comes out sounding accusatory, and all their faces fall as they swivel in my direction. I feel another pang of guilt, and open my mouth to issue the apology I lost upon seeing them, but Lukas speaks before I can.

"We can all sleep in this bed," he says, his voice flat and

his eyes trained on a spot on the wall. "You can have the other bed to yourself since there's no trundle bed available."

"We promise, we did call and ask," says Sebastian, earnestly. "It's just that the hotel is full, with our competition and the other conventions here too this weekend, so they don't have any extra trundles."

"Guys, no. That's not what I want." I plop on the edge of the empty bed, facing them. If there was an ounce of anger still left in me, it's gone. Seeing them looking this dejected and pathetic, I want to gather them all up and tell them everything will be okay. "I'm sorry I got so angry. I just felt embarrassed to have all of your parents see a hickey on my neck."

Now Lukas pins me with a stare. "You're ... embarrassed by us?" he says.

"What? No! No, not at all!" As if I didn't already feel bad enough, now I feel like pond scum. "I just don't want to be seen as one of those girls."

"What girls?" Sebastian looks to his friends in case they understand what I'm talking about, but they all look as lost as he is.

"The ones who only chase boys and don't really have any other goals or aspirations." I try to find the words to explain my complicated relationship with, well, relationships. "You all know how important school is to me. I want to graduate with honors, and have a job lined up already so as soon as I'm done with school, I can hit the ground running as a journalist. I'm not one of those girls who's in school as much to hook up and party as to get an education, and I hate the idea of anyone thinking I'm anything other than a professional, competent person."

Felix blinks owlishly at me, speaking slowly as he tries to understand. "And me giving you a hickey makes you feel like you aren't a professional, competent person?"

Aha, so it was him. "Did you mean to mark me?" I point to my neck and the hickey that is clearly on display with my hair pulled back.

"Yes," says Felix, immediately and with confidence.

"And you didn't stop to think everyone would see it when I went downstairs?" For such smart guys, they really are dumb sometimes.

"So you *are* embarrassed by us." Sebastian looks so dejected, and my guilt pings again, but I shove it down. I need to make them understand that it's not about them at all, it's about peoples' perception of me.

"If I were embarrassed by you, why would I be here with you? Hanging out with you in front of an entire ICF competition? Or spend the day with your families?"

"You're not embarrassed by us, but you don't want anyone to know anything that is going on between us," says Elliot, as if he's talking himself through this idea that I'm presenting to him. "That feels a lot like you're embarrassed."

Suddenly, I'm absolutely exhausted. I slump down on the bed, flinging an arm over my face to cover my eyes.

"It's not you that's the embarrassing part. It's everything else. Knowing that people are thinking about me having sex? And the whole sex list thing in general is pretty humiliating. Don't you guys remember how embarrassed I was when you first found it and realized I hadn't ever done anything besides kiss a guy?" I uncover my eyes and turn onto my side so I can look at them. "Anyway, it's a moot point now, because I'm pretty sure they know about us. At least Andrea does, and I'm sure she probably told the rest of your families."

"And this makes you mad," says Felix, studying my face.

"Well, it doesn't make me happy. I don't want to be defined by who I'm sleeping with. When girls are just seen as someone's girlfriend or hookup, people treat them like they're … less than. Like that's all they are, all they're good for."

"And my mom made you feel like that? Like fucking us is all you're good for?" Lukas's face is a mixture of surprise and anger as he reaches for his phone.

"No!" I launch myself off my bed to yank the phone from his hand and end up landing sprawled out on top of them, spread out across their legs.

Chapter Twenty

None of the guys say anything as I snatch Lukas's phone from him, clutching it to my chest.

"Your mom didn't do anything wrong." The last thing I need is Lukas calling his mother to yell at her for making me feel cheap, when she actually kind of saved me from even further embarrassment.

Tossing Lukas's phone across to the now-empty bed, I straddle Lukas's lap, placing my hands on either side of his face. I can feel him hardening beneath me in spite of the unsexy situation we are in, and it brings my mind right back to dry-humping Felix earlier today, and the not-so-dry humping that followed.

Not the time, brain. I look into Lukas's eyes, saying it again. "She didn't make me feel less than. She was actually pretty chill about the hickey, just gave me a head's up so I could cover it. Your mom is great."

"Maybe we don't talk about my mom when you're on top of me?" His erection twitches underneath me, and he looks away from me, staring off into the middle distance. I wonder if he's trying to will away his hard-on by mentally going through all the digits of pi or something.

I see an opening to get rid of some of the tension that's been clouding the room since we returned from dinner and I started a fight. "Oh? Am I making you uncomfortable?" I roll my hips slightly to tease him.

"More like rock hard," says Lukas, breathless, his hands clenched in the covers at his sides.

I lean forward and kiss him gently. "Let me show you how not embarrassed I am by all of you."

I tease him again with another roll of my hips and set my glasses on the nightstand before reaching between us and pulling his cock out of his boxers. I should make a rule that they can only wear boxers when I'm around, it's so much more convenient than real pants.

He's not quite as thick as Felix, but he's a little longer, and somehow he's still growing as I stroke him.

Flicking my eyes up to his, I continue coaxing his cock even harder and say, "You might have to walk me through how you like it, but Sebastian and Elliot did a good job teaching me the basics."

He nods, his jaw tight, as I scoot back enough to lean down and take him in my mouth.

"I like it when you use your tongue to play with the head, and use your hand to gently roll my balls," he says. His voice is gruff with arousal as he takes my hand and wraps it around his shaft, showing me the amount of pressure he prefers. "When you wrap your hand around me, don't be scared to be a little rough."

Well, if he's going to give such clear instructions, the least I can do is reward him by listening and blowing him exactly the way he likes.

The noises Lukas makes as I lick and flick my tongue over the head of his cock are turning me on way more than I ever would have expected. I never thought giving pleasure would feel just as good as receiving it.

"You look like you'd like someone to touch you," says Elliot. "Can I help you out?"

"Yes, please," I say, popping off of Lukas's cock just long enough to answer.

He climbs off the bed and moves to the foot of it, giving everyone a little more room. Lukas spreads his legs a little wider, giving me more space as well.

Elliot wraps his hands around my thighs and tugs, forcing me to lie on my stomach with my legs stretched behind me. It's not the easiest position for me to be in to give a blow job, but I push up onto my elbows and make do. He climbs onto the bed, straddling thighs, and palms my ass, massaging and lifting as he settles in over me. His palms are warm even through the thin fabric of my sleep shorts. And I hold my breath, waiting for the moment that his thumbs reach down beneath the hem to touch my bare skin, and hopefully slide through my folds to find my center.

But he doesn't. Elliot just keeps massaging the globes of my ass, bringing them together and then separating them, sometimes letting his thumbs slip under the hem of my shorts to pull my cheeks apart, but never getting anywhere close to where I want to be touched. My breath catches as the weight of his hard cock rests across my ass. It feels naughty, the way he slides his cock along the crack of my ass, squeezing my cheeks around his girth.

His refusal to actually touch me where I want is maddening, and I decide that if Elliot won't satisfy me, then I'll pass that same frustration on to Lukas. Maybe he'll tell Elliot to stop teasing me.

"A little rougher," says Lukas after I've teased him with the barest of kisses around the head of his cock, avoiding the very tip. "Wrap your lips around my dick and suck me."

Lukas grabs my braid and tugs, pulling my head back to give himself a better view of me bobbing on the tip of his cock. It's incredibly hot, seeing him looking down at me as he pulls my hair to control how far down I can go, and between that and Elliot's cock dragging along my ass, I'm so wet I'm probably going to have to throw these sleep shorts away later.

"Can I fuck you?" asks Elliot, his hands leaving my ass only to run up my back along my spine. When he runs his hands back down, they catch on my hips and pull me into his heavy length. "Or are you too sore?"

I hum an "mm-hmm" that comes out more like a moan, and thrust back against him as best I can in this position and with him sitting on the back of my legs. I hope he understands, because I'm not taking my lips off Lukas's cock. I'm determined to do a good job by him since I abandoned playing with him earlier to fuck Felix.

Elliot swings a leg off of me, wedging his knee between my legs and spreading them so he can kneel between them. He lifts my hips and Sebastian shoves a pillow under them, keeping them elevated. I hear the tearing of the condom wrapper, and wish I could watch him roll it on. It was incredible sexy watching Felix stroke himself when he put one on earlier. But I also don't want to stop what I'm doing to Lukas, because the way he's groaning and thrusting shallowly against my mouth is easily as sexy as, if not sexier than, seeing Elliot slide a hand down the length of his cock.

I'm not so focused on the cock in my mouth that I don't feel the soft pull of my shorts and panties being tugged to the side though, or the slight weight of Elliot's cock as he runs the tip up and down the length of my wet folds.

Elliot teases me twice, and I pass those teases right on to Lukas, who tightens his grip on my hair as if to remind me that he likes it rougher, and this is not rougher. Maybe he gives Elliot a look then, or maybe Elliot decides he's ready to stop toying with me, because he notches himself at my entrance and begins to ease into me, inch by inch. He groans, a sound of animalistic bliss that lasts until he's all the way inside, and it sends a wave of power through me. I've literally brought him to his knees just by existing.

"Fuck, you're so wonderful," says Elliot, running his hands up and down my sides.

I wouldn't have thought I'd like to give over control in this way, but even though I can't move, pinioned as I am on two cocks, I feel like I still hold all the power in this situation. And not having to think, just being able to enjoy this moment with my guys, is amazingly freeing.

Elliot's fingers dig into my hips, and he begins to move me on and off of his cock in time with each of his thrusts, pulling me off Lukas's cock and then pushing me back onto it. It's almost like Elliot is using me to fuck both himself and his best friend. So much connection between all of us, and it has warmth for these beautiful men racing through my body.

And right on the heels of that warmth is an orgasm, coming out of nowhere. Heat flushes through me, and tingles—so many tingles. My arms can't hold me up and I collapse forward. It's only Elliot's hands, still gripping my hips tightly and pulling me back into him as he groans out his own climax, that keep me from gagging on Lukas's cock as I ride the waves of pleasure Elliot is sending through me.

"You okay?" Lukas pulls me off his cock and brushes my hair back behind my ear.

My eyes are watering from the way I collapsed onto him, his cock hitting the back of my throat, and he wipes the tears from my cheeks with his thumbs. The way he's smiling down at me is so comforting, I could nearly drown in this look. There's pride and caring, and no judgement. It's wonderful.

"I'm great." And that's completely true. I'm not

panicking, or stressing about school or my future or my parents. I'm simply here, in this moment, something that doesn't happen to me very often. I look up at him as Elliot pulls out of me, leaving me feeling empty. "You didn't come yet."

"No." He wraps his hands around my upper arms, helping to lift me to an all-fours position. "I was hoping I could do that inside you."

I lean forward and capture Lukas's lips with mine. I'm half expecting him to pull back because my lips were just wrapped around his cock, but he doesn't seem to mind. I put every assurance I can into this kiss to let him know that I want this.

"Of course you can," I tell him. "I would love that."

Sebastian, still sitting next to us on the bed, covers my hand with his. "Would it be okay if I took Lukas's spot? I'm dying to get your mouth on me again."

I respond by reaching out to tug him in for a kiss as Lukas slips out from underneath me. "That works out, because I'm dying to get my mouth on you again."

Lukas moves into place behind me and slowly peels down my shorts. When they reach my knees, I almost topple over as I try to lift myself up to free my legs, but Lukas and Sebastian steady me, all of us laughing at the reminder that sex doesn't have to be serious all the time. Lukas grabs the pillow that was under me and tosses it aside, using his own knees to spread mine wider and grabbing my hips to position me so my ass is in the air when I lean down to take Sebastian into my mouth. I feel quite exposed, but I know I'm safe with them. They've never made me feel otherwise, and whatever Lukas is planning, I trust that I'm going to enjoy it.

Sebastian's hands are in my hair as Lukas trails kisses along the backs of my thighs and across my ass. I shiver, anticipating what's to come, but force myself to focus on Sebastian, licking up his cock and sucking hard on the tip before bobbing my head down farther, taking as much of him into my mouth as I can. Lukas starts massaging my ass, and based on what Elliot had done, I prepare myself for his cock to push inside me.

But it's not a cock I feel at my entrance. No, he slowly eases a finger inside my pussy, soaked from my orgasm. "Are you sure you're not too sore?"

I nibble gently along Sebastian's length as I say, "I'm definitely sure." Between Lukas's finger and the kisses he scattered across my skin, and the enjoyment I'm getting from sucking Sebastian off, I'm desperate for him to fill me properly.

"Only if you're sure." Lukas plants a kiss on each of my ass cheeks, and I hear the condom wrapper tear behind me.

I'm definitely sore, but not enough to have denied Lukas —or myself—this. He slides inside me with such care it's almost as though he thinks I'll break if he doesn't take his time.

But I'm not made of glass, and if he likes rough blow jobs, I'm betting he prefers not to have to approach sex cautiously. So I press back against him and clench my inner muscles around his cock to let him know I'm not fragile, that he can have his way with me. The maneuver elicits a groan from him.

"You're not playing fair," he says through gritted teeth, the pads of his fingers digging into my waist.

"What do you mean?" asks Sebastian, his head falling back against the headboard as I suck hard on the tip of his cock. "Fuck, Rebecca, that's good."

"She squeezed me with her pussy," says Lukas, not moving behind me. "How am I supposed to last when our girl is so tight?"

"Good girl, Rebecca." Felix leans over to plant a kiss on the top of my head, even as I swirl my tongue around the tip of Sebastian's cock. He's stroking his own dick leisurely, seemingly content to watch all of his friends have their turn.

"Fair is fair though, right, Sebastian?" asks Lukas, spreading my ass cheeks.

"Fair is fair," Sebastian confirms, one hand fisted in the sheet and the other holding the back of my head so I can't do something mean like pull off of him completely. Not that I would, but I kind of enjoy being held in place by him. This is a different side of Sebastian than the one I see when we have our clothes on, and I like seeing him control his experience a bit.

But there's a hint of teasing in his voice that I've never heard before. They're up to something. I don't know what it is, so I exert the only bit of control I have at the moment and clench my pussy around Lukas's cock again and swirl my tongue around Sebastian's tip.

Lukas groans and spreads my ass again, and I feel him run one of his thumbs around the rim of my asshole.

A surprised moan escapes me, and Sebastian presses down slightly on my head, ensuring that I stay focused on what I'm doing in spite of what Lukas has planned.

Lukas pulls out of me and swipes his thumb through the moisture coating my pussy, running it up to circle my back door again before repeating the motion. Once my juices are thoroughly spread, he slides his dick back into place, pressing his thumb against my asshole. My hips twitch, pressing back against his hand, and I feel the very tip of his thumb slip into my ass. This was not on the calendar for this weekend. Lukas is deviating from their schedule.

I feel more powerful than I have ever felt. These guys live and breathe by their calendar, and something I did made Lukas go off-book. Feeling like I could move mountains, I shift back against Lukas, encouraging him to press his thumb deeper into my ass. At the same time, I take as much of Sebastian as I can into my mouth and suck hard, hollowing out my cheeks and bobbing up and down on his cock.

"Fuck, Rebecca," growls Sebastian. His hips buck, and he clenches both fists in my hair and spurts hot, salty cum down the back of my throat.

Lukas pulls out of me and then slams himself back in, his thumb filling my asshole as his cock claims my pussy. My orgasm comes out of nowhere, ripping through me like a shockwave and sending pulses of the most incredible pleasure I've ever felt through every cell in my body. Lukas fucks me through the tremors, thrusting harder and faster until he shouts his release and collapses onto my back in his own orgasmic haze.

Felix, still next to me and stroking his own dick faster than before, uses his other hand to brush stray strands of hair back from my face. "Are you okay?"

"Oh, yeah," I pant. "I'm great. Incredible. That was ... I just need to lay here for a few minutes." My head is on Sebastian's lower belly, his softening cock right next to my face, and he strokes my hair as sleep threatens to overtake me. Three cocks on the day I lose my virginity might have been pushing it, but I'd wanted it so bad. I force my eyes open and look up at Felix. "I'm not sure I can take one more. I'm sorry."

"You never have to apologize for that." Felix leans down and places another kiss on my cheek, and it dimly occurs to me that the movement puts his face as close to Sebastian's penis as my own is. I wonder, vaguely, if that even registers for them. "Just rest."

"I need to ... get cleaned up." There's no way I can sleep in my shorts now, not after Elliot fucked me through them.

And I'm officially down to my last pair of panties. My choice is to either go bare now, or go bare during one of the days around other people. Not really much of a choice. I'm definitely going to have to run out to a store. Next time I'm going to have to keep in mind the way my body reacts around these guys and pack extra.

A lot extra.

"You rest," says Elliot from the other bed. He must have moved over there to watch Lukas fuck me. "I'll clean you up." He disappears into the bathroom to get a washcloth.

"Are you still mad about the hickey?" asks Lukas, rolling off of me to lay beside Sebastian.

"I'd forgotten about it until you just reminded me." I can't help but laugh a little, amazed that something that had infuriated me so much went right out of my head as soon as I was presented with a hard cock to suck on. "But don't do it again."

I can feel the unvoiced grumble going through the group, even as Elliot runs a warm washcloth over my face and then between my legs.

"At least, not somewhere visible without asking me first," I add. Because I might not mind if they mark me someplace that only they will see. That could be a sexy little secret just for us. And one day I might actually want to let them leave their brand on me where others can see it, and if I say now that they're not allowed to, I'll be eating my words.

And there are so many better things I could put in my mouth instead.

"Deal," agrees Sebastian, lifting me a little so he can slide out from under me.

I'd feel sad, but Lukas slips right into his abandoned spot, pulling me against him. I settle my head against his shoulder, cuddling his arm against my chest. It's a cozy, if a little chilly with my skin slightly damp from sweat and Elliot's washcloth, but Felix pulls the blankets over us and cuddles up to my back so I'm surrounded by their warmth.

I glance over to the other bed, where Sebastian and Elliot are both looking back at me.

"It's only Friday, and we already checked off all of the items for this weekend," comments Sebastian.

"And then some." The memory of Lukas's thumb in my ass sends a thrill through me, and another follows when I think about Felix sliding into me for the first time.

"Are you okay with everything that happened today?" asks Felix, kissing my shoulder. "With us taking your virginity? I don't like that we had to leave you alone so soon after."

"Of course." I didn't realize this was something they would still be worried about. "It was my idea, if you recall."

"Well, if you have any other ideas, please voice them immediately," says Lukas earnestly, and I let out a giggle.

"Will do." I've already got a few ideas forming, and some of them involve a lot more than a thumb.

Chapter Twenty-One

Today, I'm prepared for the parents to show up at breakfast.

I made sure to cover the hickey on my neck with makeup so it's not even noticeable. I hope they'll have completely forgotten about it. And I hope even more that they ask absolutely no questions about how the rest of our night was after we left them at the elevator.

I might be okay with the parents joining us for breakfast today, but the guys, apparently, are not.

We got here early enough to find two tables next to each other, but the idea of sitting separately from each other has them all cranky.

"I suppose we should sit at both tables to save them," says Felix with a deep sigh.

"Probably," agrees Sebastian. There is absolutely no excitement in his voice.

"Guys, it's fine, we can sit at two tables for one meal," I tell them. "You are not making your parents sit by themselves after they came all the way here to support you." I hate sounding like I'm telling them what to do, but really, they should just have breakfast with their parents and stop being whiny about it.

"You're right," Lukas sighs. "I just want us to all be able to sit together."

"Should we let the cubes decide who sits where?" asks Elliot.

"Maybe they're here and we can let them pick seats?" Lukas looks around as if they might show up any moment.

I roll my eyes and sit down at one of the tables. "I'm sitting here. Whoever's turn it is to sit with me is also sitting here. Easy peasy."

Lukas sets his tray on the other table. "It's Sebastian and Elliot's turn, so Felix and I are over here."

"I miss our dining room table," Felix grumbles, but he sets his tray next to Lukas's. "It would be tight, but it would fit all of us."

"We could look into a bigger table, or one that expands, so it wouldn't even be tight," suggests Sebastian.

"I like that idea. Let's put it on the to do list," Elliot agrees, setting his tray down next to mine at the other table.

"I like your table." After last weekend's tabletop activities, I've got more plans for that table. I'm attached to it. "I'm not sure you really need a new one."

Although, if they invite all of their parents over, there really wouldn't be enough room for everyone to sit comfortably, so maybe they would benefit from having an expanding one even if it does mean saying goodbye to the sex table.

"Why are you all sitting separately?" We all look up to see who's speaking, and see Calvin approach, eating yogurt as he's walking around.

"Our parents are here, and we needed enough seats for everyone," explains Elliot.

"Do you want to join us? We can steal another chair from somewhere," I offer. The guys might be annoyed with me for it, but he offered us a place yesterday so it's only fair to offer him one today.

"Maybe for a minute." But instead of sitting down, Calvin surveils the room, spinning in a slow circle as he spoons yogurt into his mouth.

"She's not here," says Sebastian, blowing on his coffee before sipping it gingerly.

"At least, we haven't seen her yet," adds Elliot, separating the contents of his fruit bowl out on a plate by type.

"I wasn't looking for anyone," denies Calvin. "Although, I was looking for you yesterday, but when I went up to your room it had the Do Not Disturb sign on the door. And you really sounded like you didn't want to be disturbed."

He grins and quirks and eyebrow at Elliot and Sebastian, and even though he's clearly just ribbing us and there's nothing creepy or malicious about it, my face heats instantly.

I was afraid last night that our neighbors in the rooms on either side of us might hear us fighting, but I'd never once considered that they might have overheard us making up. And the fact that one of their friends heard? I just want to bury myself right under this table.

Lukas stands suddenly, his thighs knocking against the table and nearly toppling his orange juice. "Mom! Dad! Good morning!"

He hurries to hug his mother, glancing over his shoulder at me. Is he concerned they heard and worried I'll be upset? That's sweet of him. Maybe some of what I said last night clicked after all.

"Good morning, everyone. Calvin, it's nice to see you," says Sebastian's mom, setting her tray right next to mine on the table.

"Uh, I gotta go. I'll see you back in the waiting area

later." Calvin hurries off, weaving through the tables. He has a banana sticking up out of one of his back pockets and a Monster energy drink sticking out of the other. I look around the room for the telltale flash of pink hair that is almost certainly the reason for his sudden departure, and sure enough, there's Patti over by the waffle makers.

Summer leans down to give me a hug from the side. "Good morning, Rebecca."

The hug is awkward, with me hugging her arm as it crosses right below my neck, but it's a sweet gesture on her part. Maybe they really have forgotten about the hickey and are starting to like me after all.

If that's the case, though, Elliot almost certainly undoes any progress I've made by offering an explanation for Calvin's Do Not Disturb comment that I was really hoping had gone unnoticed by the parents.

"Rebecca had the good idea to put out our Do Not Disturb sign out yesterday to make sure housekeeping didn't come again," he explains. "I had to re-sanitize the hotel room yesterday after they'd come through."

"That is a very good idea, Rebecca," says Mary. "I'm sure Elliot appreciates having one less thing to worry about, with the competition happening."

"Today's a big day, are you ready for it?" asks Elliot's dad.

The guys launch into a discussion of what times they'll need on the different events, mentioning all the variables for if other competitors make certain concessions with DNFs or flipped equators. Even for them the calculations and statistics have to be a challenge, with so many moving variables. It all goes right over my head. Math has never been my strongest subject.

The beeping of an alarm suddenly emanates from all the guys' pockets.

"We need to get to the waiting area," says Sebastian, adding my dishes to his tray before sliding my tray beneath his to carry to the dish drop-off.

As soon as we step into the hallway leading to the event space, we can feel the pre-competition tension ratchet up. The parents all hug the guys goodbye and wish them luck before they break off for the competitor's waiting area. I hesitate only briefly before also hugging them. Their parents certainly already know something is going on between me and their sons so there's no point in trying to play the "we're just friends, who don't touch each other at all ever" card anymore, and this is a big moment for my guys. I want to make sure they know I'm here for them and support them, no matter what the outcome of this competition.

The audience room is a lot fuller today than it was yesterday, and we have to sit farther back than we did before to find a block of empty seats large enough for our group.

"Did all these people come just for these final rounds of these events?" I ask.

Without even looking around, Jen says, "No, these are just the competitors who are no longer in the running."

Wow. I didn't realize there were this many competitors here, but I suppose they've all been sitting back in the competitors waiting area and filtering in and out for their events. Now that I look around though, there are a lot of them mindlessly solving different types of cubes as they chat with neighbors and wait for the events to begin.

Our group is tense as the first event is announced. When Elliot takes the stage, I have to fight the urge to stand up so I can see better and make sure he knows I'm here for him.

The first scramble goes well, and I can tell Elliot is

pleased with it by the way he runs his hands through his hair. The next two are also solid. Not splashy or record-breaking, but good enough times that it looks like he's in the top. Like he'd discussed at length at dinner last night, it all depends on the scramble times his competitors put up.

Even though I have my book with me, I don't open it once to read even a single page. I'm on the edge of my seat the entire time. A lot rides on these scrambles, and it would be so disappointing for the guys to not be able to go on to Worlds when they've worked so hard for this goal.

By the end of the competition, my back aches from leaning forward for so long. I don't know how the guys are dealing with all of this stress. I can barely handle it sitting in the audience. But when it's time for the awards, I'm one of the first to my feet to cheer for them. There's so much excitement in the air, and the guys deserve every ounce of this celebration.

The guys do great in their individual events, each of them winning first place, but when they announce the winner of the relay, they come in second. I can see how much this stings, especially when Stephen gives them a smug smile as he steps forward to accept the first place medal for his relay team.

The guys handle it so much more calmly than I would. Stephen is such a little ass. Has he never heard of good sportsmanship? The other team barely won. The timers say only by a nanosecond, but I guess in this sport it really comes down to that tiny difference in time.

I can tell they're disappointed in the outcome of this competition. Even taking first in their individual events isn't enough to soothe the sting of losing in the team relay, which is the event they all care the most about.

Fuck, how much of this is my fault? Will they be mad at me for distracting them between events when they should have been getting their heads in the game? The thought hadn't even occurred to me before now, and it really should have.

As soon as the awards are done, instead of going back into the competitor waiting area, the guys jump down from the front of the stage and come right down the aisle to us. All around us, the audience is chatting and moving toward the exit, so we move out into the aisle to let others out of our row and wait for the guys to reach us.

"Congratulations!" Their moms rush forward to hug them and share in their success.

I hang back and wait for my turn, even though I want to shove to the front and throw my arms around them. But I know I need to let their families come first. Not to mention, I'm still worried that maybe I'm the reason they weren't as successful as they could have been. If I wasn't here distracting them, would they have completed their scrambles in the two nanoseconds that would have led to them winning?

Lukas meets my eyes over his mom's shoulder as they hug. In fact, all of their eyes are on me, waiting behind their parents. Their gazes are intense, but I can't read their expressions to know if they're thinking "later tonight, we are going to have amazing celebration sex" or "we lost because you distracted us, so later tonight we're going to dump you."

No, not *dump*. You can't dump someone you're not in a relationship with. But that doesn't make the idea of them being done with me hurt any less.

"I'm sorry you didn't get first for your relay," I say when it's finally my turn for a hug, and they all wrap around me at once. "At least you can still go to Worlds for your individual events."

It feels so good to hold them after worrying about them up on stage all day. And there is no way I'm going to miss out on celebrating with them or comforting them after their loss, even if I did insist that we avoid any physical contact that could be construed by their parents as remotely sexual.

Besides, we're friends. Friends hug each other when they win or lose a competition. And their parents were hugging them all. It would be weird if I was the only one not hugging them.

They all pull back at the same time, and I feel the sudden loss of their warmth keenly.

"Actually," Sebastian corrects me, "because we podiumed, we're still technically allowed to compete in the Worlds relay event."

"We knew you'd make it," says Andrea, rubbing her son's shoulder soothingly. "That's why your dad already booked our hotels and flights."

"Always good to be prepared," says Sebastian's dad, nodding as if to himself.

I don't think any of the boys would disagree with him. They take planning ahead to extremes in ways I'll never tell their parents about.

"Even though we had every confidence that you'd win," says Felix's mom, "we should still go out somewhere nice for dinner tonight to celebrate."

"Actually, we're thinking of driving home tonight," says Lukas.

"But it's such a long drive!" Lukas's mom looks to her husband for backup.

Hank obliges. "You've had a long day, you deserve to kick back and enjoy yourselves."

"And we're all here right now, it'd be so nice to spend quality time together." Elliot's mom glances quickly to me, then back to her son.

Elliot shakes his head. "We don't have any events tomorrow, and we need to catch up on all of the homework we didn't get done because we're here," he says. "We can't risk our grades slipping."

"Besides," Lukas chimes in, "Rebecca has to work at the newspaper tomorrow. We don't want to wait until tomorrow to leave and then hit traffic and make her late. That could jeopardize her job."

The parents all turn to look at me, and I try to smile but it feels more like a grimace. I don't mind being the guys' excuse if they really do want to go home tonight, but I don't want their families to feel like I'm stealing their kids away.

"All right," says Felix's mom. "I supposed we can't argue with that logic. I just wish you could let go and have a little fun once in a while. You boys work so hard."

"But all of their hard work is going to pay off, and they're going to have a great life and be able to have all the fun they want after graduation," Jen says, laying a hand on Lukas's shoulder. "At least tell me you'll stop for food on the way home. You don't want Rebecca to starve before you get back to Boston."

"We'll take good care of her," Sebastian promises.

But the way he looks at me when he says it, I suspect he might be referring to more than just dinner tonight. His expression is soft, not at all the way you look at someone who is just your friend. It's very sweet, and in another life I'd be melting, having a guy look at me like that. But I'm getting tired of reminding them that we aren't dating.

On the upside, at least he's not looking at me like he's thinking about eating out in a non-restaurant sense. Given our audience, that would be even worse.

We agree to meet up with the parents after we're packed up to say goodbye, then make our way to the elevators. "Are you sure you don't want to stay here?" I ask as the doors open and we pile inside.

I know they booked another night when they made the

reservation, so clearly they'd intended to stay originally. Are they truly changing their plans to make sure I'm not late to work? Or because they didn't get first in their relay and they're tired of being around me, the reason they weren't as focused as they could have been? I'm not sure which idea I hate more. Obviously I don't want them to be angry with me, but I also don't want them to rearrange their plans on my account, especially given that traffic would have to be apocalyptically bad for us to get back late enough that I'd miss work. It makes me think of how my mom will drop everything to accommodate my father, and he takes complete advantage of her willingness to bend to his will. I would never intentionally take advantage of their kindness, but I don't want to end up on a slippery slope where all of us just come to expect that my schedule is more important than what they want.

"Yeah," says Felix, "we would rather sleep in our own beds."

"And it's better to be at home where we know everything is clean," adds Elliot.

"What should I do with my slippers?" They're super cute and fuzzy—not what I would pick out for myself, but they have been cozy to wear around the hotel room.

"We'll pack them up for Worlds," says Elliot, wrapping them in a bag and placing them in one of their suitcases.

They're planning for me to join them for Worlds? I suppose that means they're not blaming me for their second-place finish today. And it would give me a chance to continue my article series for class, which would be great, but they should ask me instead of just assuming that I'll join them.

Between the way Sebastian looked at me downstairs, and their assumption that I would join them for Worlds, we need to have a conversation about what's happening between us. Later though. Their parents are all downstairs waiting for us and if we take much longer, I fear they'll think we're fooling around up here before we drive home.

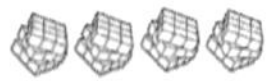

Back downstairs, their parents wait with us while valet pulls their car around.

"I know you're anxious to get home, but don't drive too fast," Jen tells Lukas, who nods solemnly.

"You all did a great job at this competition, and there's no sense rehashing everything. Just keep working towards Worlds," says Andrea.

"And Rebecca, you keep an eye on these guys. Don't let them work too hard," Summer tells me. Then, quietly enough that only I hear, she adds, "And don't forget to keep an eye out for signs. They'll lead you where you need to go." She gives me a wink and then steps back as the car arrives, saving me from having to figure out how the hell to respond to that cryptic statement.

"We'll be fine," says Elliot, loading our suitcases into the trunk.

Then there's one more round of hugs from the parents—even for me—and we're on the road back to Boston.

There's so much traffic, I'm glad Lukas is the one driving and not me. We're all quiet, not wanting to distract him at all as he navigates the busy streets.

As soon as we're out of the city, we pull off and grab a few wraps to go from a sandwich place just off the highway.

"What did you think of the competition?" asks Elliot, interlacing our fingers.

"It was really cool," I tell him. "I don't think I've seen so many people with such fast fingers in my life."

"I'm sorry we weren't the fastest ones there," says Sebastian. He sounds so disappointed, and I grab his hand in my free one.

"No! Don't you dare apologize for that. You all did a fantastic job, and I'm so proud of you. You're all faster than I could ever believe, even having seen you solve cubes a lot of times before this."

"Still, we weren't the best," Sebastian mutters, half to himself.

"Do you—" I start, then chicken out.

"Do we what?" Lukas asks, glancing at me in the rearview.

I sigh. "I'm just worried that I'm the reason you didn't take first. That I distracted you or something, and you couldn't focus as well as you normally would have because I was there. And I would feel really awful if that was the case."

All of them begin to protest at once. From the driver's seat, Lukas says, "You were absolutely not a distraction. Not at all. We loved having you there. It was awesome to go out to solve and see you out there watching. We didn't take first because we weren't fast enough, full stop."

"But if you hadn't spent so much time with me in between events, you could have been practicing more."

Felix turns all the way around in the passenger seat and takes my hand from Elliot, gripping it firmly as he says, "There is nowhere else we would have rather been between events than up in that room with you. What you gave us yesterday was worth more than any first-place medal."

I find it hard to believe that sex with me was a better prize than meeting their goal of first-place team at

Nationals, but when I try to protest they all shoot me down. "But—"

"No buts," Elliot says. "You being there meant a lot to us, and you were not a distraction."

"If anything, we probably did even better than we would have normally, because we wanted to impress you," Sebastian tells me, breaking some of the tension in the car as we all laugh.

"You always impress me," I tell them. "You're all amazing."

"I just realized," says Felix, letting go and twisting back to a more comfortable position, but keeping his head turned towards me. "We didn't introduce you to people like we said we would."

"Yeah, you only got to meet Calvin and Stephen," Sebastian says, Stephen's name coming out like it leaves a bad taste in his mouth.

"I liked Calvin, but Stephen was a real asshole. I hope he steps on a Lego right before he competes at Worlds." This makes all of them groan with imagined pain, even as they laugh. "Anyway, I'd actually kind of forgotten about that you were going to introduce me to people, to be honest." Between parents and hickeys and sex, I'd had other things on my mind.

"Well, Worlds is longer, so hopefully we'll have more time between events and then we can introduce you to people," says Elliot, completely convinced that I'm coming with them when they haven't even asked me yet.

I decide to just let it go for now. They've had a couple hard days, and we have a long drive ahead of us. Instead, I let them slip into a discussion about what they can do differently for Worlds, from practice sessions to items they need to remember to pack. It's sweet that they want me there, and I'm going to let them go on believing that I will be for a little while longer.

Chapter Twenty-Two

I'm startled awake by a tugging sensation. It's dark and still and there are hands on me. I immediately swing out, trying to protect myself.

"Shhh. It's just me," says Lukas, holding up his hands to calm me.

Mentally I recognize him, but my body is taking a little longer to calm down. My heart is racing and I'm still processing where I am.

"We wanted to carry you inside without waking you up," says Lukas, again trying to shove his hands between me and the seat. "We thought it would be romantic."

"Maybe next time, romantically wake me up instead." Even though they terrified me and as I'm not their girlfriend, I don't require romance, it's a sweet thought so I suppose I should give them some leeway for their intention.

But now that I'm awake, I'm not going to let him try to carry me. I'm fully capable of walking inside on my own.

I look up once I'm out of the car and realize we're at their house. "You could have dropped me back off at my dorm room." I would have thought them wanting to sleep in their own beds again meant they were ready to go back to their normal routine, and have a little break from all the extra people they've had to worry about this weekend.

"Then you wouldn't be here," says Sebastian, holding open the front door for me.

I can't help but smile as I step inside and see my purse already hanging on a hook by the door. I don't remember that hook being there last time I visited. And my suitcase and school bag sit right below it.

But I don't want the guys to see how much it means to me that they added a hook just for me. In a few months they're going to graduate and this whole arrangement will end, and it won't matter if I think it's sweet or not. I pull my phone out of my purse, letting my hair swing down to hide my face so they don't see all these thoughts flitting across it.

There are six missed calls from my mom from the past hour, and a long string of text messages asking where I am and why I'm not responding to her. I obviously can't wait until morning to respond, even though it's late.

"Is everything okay?" asks Felix, concern in his voice as he sets his hand on my shoulder.

I look up at him, preemptively exhausted from the conversation I'm about to have. "Yeah, I just need to call my mom."

"Okay. I'll bring your suitcase upstairs for when you're ready," says Felix.

"Thanks. I'll be up shortly." I go into the living room, preparing for the mental gymnastics I'm going to have to do for this conversation.

Mom is always so worried over Dad, and I'm so tired of pointing out to her how Dad takes advantage of her and doesn't respect her. She's making so many choices I hate and can't support that it makes it hard to listen to her complaining.

"We can wait for you," says Elliot, trying to hide a yawn.

"No, no, it's fine. I shouldn't be too long." *At least, I hope not.* There's no need to keep the guys up, especially when I napped in the car and they didn't.

Not to mention, I don't really want them to see how dependent my mom is on my dad. It's not a good look and she's not their problem, she's mine. I don't want them involved in something so personal either. If we were dating, maybe, but with the relationship we have, I don't need to bring them into it.

When they have all headed upstairs, I stretch out on the sofa. If I have to withstand this phone call, I might as well be comfy.

My mom picks up on the first ring. "Why did it take you so long to call me back?"

"What's wrong, Mom?" There's no sense in telling her about the speedcubing competition. She's never going to meet the guys, and she doesn't actually care about the reason, she only cares that I didn't answer when she wanted me to. And if I tell her I was sleeping, she won't care. If she's up with worry, she thinks I should be too.

"Your dad still isn't home from work," she complains, panic in her voice. "I've called him and texted him, but his phone is off. I called his office and no one is picking up. What if he was in an accident and he's hurt somewhere?"

I knew it would be something like this. It always is. "I'm sure he's fine and he'll be home soon." After he's done with whichever other woman he's sleeping with this week.

"No, I'm certain he's not fine. Otherwise he'd be home in his own bed already," she says. "I've called all of the local hospitals and he's not there, but when I called the police to report him missing, they said I had to wait. They're never helpful when I call. It's like they don't even care!"

I don't bother pointing out that she calls them almost every week to report him missing and he never is. He's always just avoiding coming home. I don't understand why, either. Mom is a complete doormat and does everything for him, thinks he walks on water. Yet Dad is always running around with other women behind her back. The last time I tried explaining to Mom why Dad wasn't coming home on time, she accused me of lying and trying to ruin her life.

"Is there anything else you can do in the meantime while you wait for him to come home?" I ask. Sometimes I can get her to distract herself. But tonight doesn't appear to be one of those times.

Felix peeks his head around the corner into the living room, rubbing his eyes and looking exhausted. "Everything okay?" he mouths.

"It's fine. I'll be up soon," I whisper back, blocking the phone with my hand so Mom doesn't hear me. Half-listening to her freak out about Dad is preferable to letting her know I'm spending time with a guy. Although she's so worked up about Dad not being home yet, and from my not having answered earlier, that I'm not sure she could be sidetracked at this point anyway.

Felix just nods a little and pads back up the stairs. I wish I could do the same, but Mom is still ranting and doesn't sound like she's ready to stop quite yet.

Suddenly, my mom's tone changes. "Oh, there, he's just pulling into the driveway," she says, her voice a mix of relief and excitement. "He probably just had a flat tire and I was worrying for nothing."

"Oh, good," I say, even though I'm completely over this conversation and was never once worried about his safety.

But I'm not sure Mom even hears me, because she's already hung up to go run out to my dad and fuss over him. She'll ignore the smell of another woman's perfume on him and heat up a plate of the dinner she made for him hours ago.

But it's not my problem. And I'm going to make sure that I'm never in that position, completely dependent on a man for my happiness. No matter how many times I've told her to walk away, she won't. She doesn't know how to exist without him, and she wouldn't have a way to support herself even if she did.

When I get to the top of the stairs, I can see my toiletry bag set out on the bathroom counter for me. That was very sweet of them to do. I get ready for bed as quietly as I can, wondering whose bed I'm supposed to be in tonight. I would assume Felix's since he's the one who came down to check on me earlier, but what if I'm wrong?

There's only one way I can think of to find out without waking one of them up.

I've put it off joining the group calendar long enough. I click the link to accept the invitation Lukas sent and pull it up. I was right, I'm scheduled to sleep in bed with Felix tonight. So I turn off the bathroom light and quietly cross the hall to his room, doing my best not to wake him up.

As soon as I pull the blankets over me, though, Felix reaches out and pulls me closer until he's molded around me, his soft breath ruffling my hair.

The next afternoon, the guys drop me off at work. I hug each of them goodbye in the parking lot and trail my suitcase behind me as I head inside.

The back of my neck prickles as I push the elevator call button. I can sense Brad approaching. I recognize the slap of those shoes and the whiff of arrogant cologne, but I refuse to turn around and acknowledge him.

I'm just stepping onto the elevator when Brad puts his hand between the doors to hold it for himself, stopping me from having this short ride in peace. His stupid face looks so smug as he follows me into the elevator, no hello or anything. Just the confidence that everyone will wait for him and everything will go his way.

I really don't like him. Or the way he side-eyes my suitcase.

As soon as the doors open at our floor, I exit the elevator, forcing myself to walk calmly to my desk so as not to give Brad the satisfaction of knowing he unnerves me. I stow my little suitcase under my desk as I did last time, but tuck it even farther back. No one asked any questions about it before, but a second time might make people ask questions I'm not prepared to answer.

I log into the computer I use and pull up my email. Maybe today will finally be the day that something gets assigned to me. There's only one email, which I open excitedly only to find it's just a note from HR thanking all of us interns. It features quotes from a few of the different departments calling out how appreciative they are of us, and there's a note at the bottom stating that we should be keeping an eye out for job openings so we could potentially continue on with this newspaper after graduation.

That's my dream, but right now it feels like the biggest hurdle. It doesn't escape my notice that my department is the only one without a quote from management. My professors all rave about the articles I'm writing for class, and if Carl just gave me a chance, I'm sure he'd see he should put me to better use than just brewing coffee and delivering paperwork.

But those are the only tasks I have for now, so I might as

well get busy with them. I make sure my suitcase is completely invisible under my desk and log out of the computer before making my way over to the break room. The coffee currently warming on the burner smells rancid, so I pour it out and start brewing a fresh pot while I restock everything. I pile the creamer and sugar packets high in their baskets, so even if the journalists take some, by my end of my shift it shouldn't be completely empty.

While that's done, I run over to see if Ashley needs help with anything, but apparently it's been a slow news day and there's nothing that needs delivering. With nothing else to do, I decide it's time to go get shot down by Carl again.

Obviously, I stop back by the break room on my way to his office and grab him a fresh coffee, fixing it just the way he likes it.

I knock on the half-open door as I enter. "Hi, Carl. I brought you some coffee, and was wondering if there's anything I can do to help with the next print run."

He glares up at me from his computer. For someone who is so renowned and good at what he does, he really is a complete grump. You'd think by now I'd stop wishing that he'd just once hint at offering me a smile, but it still disappoints me every time I'm greeted by that sour expression.

He leans over to peer past me. "Brad!" I recoil from the ferocity in his voice.

"Yeah, boss." Brad leans in the doorway, not even acknowledging that I'm standing right there.

"I have an assignment for you," says Carl, and my hopes soar before I realize he's talking to Brad, who has pushed past me to casually seat himself in the chair opposite Carl's desk. "You still have that contact down at the DOJ, right?"

"They fucking love me down there," says Brad smugly.

"Good. I need you to look into some allegations. FOIAs

obviously, but do it quiet, we don't want them spooked," says Carl, leaning back in his chair and steepling his hands over his stomach.

Brad leans forward in his own chair, his interest piqued. "What kind of allegations?" They look like two gossiping old ladies. Brad leans forward in his own chair.

Carl stares at me. "What are you still doing in here?" he barks. "Respect confidentiality and go do something useful."

I can't argue against confidentiality, especially if the conversation involves allegations and FOIA reports, so I shuffle back to my desk. Everything Carl would deem me useful for is done, so I might as well do schoolwork. The guys and I did some earlier today at the house, but I haven't had a chance yet to work on my next article for class. My professor has been loving my speedcubing series so far, and I want to put an even more community-focused spin on this next one after spending the weekend surrounded by cubers and their families. The way the guys found each other through cubing competitions, and their families have also become close, gives me a lot to work with. Found families are especially important for those who don't always fit in with mainstream society, and ICF is meeting this need for a specific subset of the population in a way that's not talked about nearly enough.

Once again, as soon as I walk into our dorm room, Ronnie sits up straighter on her bed and stares expectantly at me. There's another sandwich and a bag of chips sitting in the center of my desk.

I roll my eyes at her continued blatant attempt to hold

me hostage until I give her all the information she wants, but it's also a little funny. All she's missing is the interrogation spotlight, and I wouldn't put it past her to make one out of one of our desk lamps.

Shoving my suitcase into the corner, I make sure the wheels aren't touching anything else in the room and then plop down at my desk.

"Soooo," she drawls, ""how was your romantic weekend away?"

"It wasn't a romantic weekend away," I remind her. "It was the national ICF competition."

"It was a weekend away with your boyfriends, so it's automatically romantic," she says, waving off my explanation.

"They're not my boyfriends." How many times do I have to say it before she'll believe me?

I grab the sanitizing wipes I'd bought earlier in the week from my desk drawer and wipe down the entire desk and my hands. Then I open the sandwich wrapper and smooth it out to create a small plate, pouring chips onto one half while the sandwich sits on the other.

I look up to see Ronnie staring at me like I've done something weird.

"What?"

"Nothing." She sits back against the headboard with a smirk. "I've just never seen you do that, is all."

Never seen me do what, eat a sandwich? I try to remember if I've ever wiped down the desk before using it to eat off of, or ensured there is a defined line between two different foods so they're not touching. I suppose I haven't, at least not in front of Ronnie, but this is something the guys do—either because none of them like their foods touching or because they know that it bothers Elliot and they want to make his life easier—and I guess I've picked it up after two weekends in a row of sharing meals with them.

Shrugging my shoulder, I pop a chip in my mouth and sit down. It's not worth making a big deal out of it.

"So, how did your definitely-not-romantic getaway go?" Ronnie asks, fidgeting with the pages of the magazine beside her, but keeping all her attention focused on me.

"It was good," I say between bites. "The guys did well in their events. They didn't win first in the team relay, which was unfortunate, but they podiumed."

"They must be ecstatic."

"Mmmm." I tilt my head back and forth while I finish chewing to convey my meaning. "They're not unhappy, but they're disappointed to have come in second. They had some good solves, but some of the scrambles had a lot more layers or algorithms to memorize and they were pushing themselves to shorten their inspection times."

"Is it important to this conversation that I understand anything you just said?"

"No." I chuckle because I wouldn't have fully understood what I just said a couple of weeks ago.

"Okay, good, because I didn't," says Ronnie, checking her nails. "But it's cool that they did so well."

"I'm proud of them," I admit. I've told the guys that, but it's different admitting it out loud to someone else. Saying it to them feels a little like I'm doing it because I'm supposed to, even if it's the truth. Saying it to Ronnie feels more important, somehow. "They've worked hard for this."

"So, because they did so well, are they like the cool kids of that crowd?"

I've never stopped to think about if they're cool or not in their cubing circles. I would think so, being both talented and also sweet and kind and caring. But I don't really know.

I also don't really care. They're good friends to each

other and respectful to everyone, even that asshole Stephen. It doesn't matter to me if they're the life of the party or not. I don't even like parties.

"The guys definitely knew a lot of the other competitors, but I only really saw them talk to two of them," I say. "Most of their social time with the others probably happened backstage, so I didn't get to see how they interact with the other competitors."

I also don't really care. They're good friends to each other and respectful to everyone, even that asshole Stephen. It doesn't matter to me if they're the life of the party or not. I don't even like parties.

"And how did they interact with you when there was nobody around to see? Did your cube get solved, by chance?" she asks, wiggling her eyebrows suggestively.

The comment startles a laugh out of me, causing me to nearly spit out my most recent bite. I throw a chip at her in retaliation.

The chip lands right down her shirt between her boobs. Unphased, she reaches right in there, pulls it out, and pops it in her mouth.

"You're incorrigible." I shake my head, not surprised that Ronnie would just casually eat a boob chip like that.

"You mispronounced 'fun.'" Ronnie grins and scoots closer to the edge of the bed and me.

There's no way I'm going to win with a comeback to that comment, so I simply take another bite of my sandwich. It's not as good at the ones the guys make, but I'm hungry.

"Oh, come on, that was funny." Ronnie pouts. "What's not funny is the way you won't give me any details."

"You don't like the satisfaction being drawn out? Being teased?" I say with mock seriousness as I eat another chip.

A laugh bursts out of her. "Look at you! Making a

sexual joke! I rather like this side of you. These guys are really good for you."

"They've certainly been helpful and inspirational for my column series for class," I agree.

"And your list," she adds.

If Ronnie knew just how helpful and inspirational they were being in that department, she'd never shut up about it. Just thinking about the things we've enjoyed together has me blushing, which does not go unnoticed.

"Speaking of the list. How far down it are you?" she pushes, a teasing note still in her voice, but it's obvious she wants this girl talk so badly.

"Pretty far." I know I'm going to have to give her something more than that, but I don't want to go into all the sexy details. It's private, and I like it being just between me and my guys.

"Pretty far or all the way?"

I want to hide my face so badly, but I have chip grease on my hands so I just pick at my sandwich crust and don't say anything. My refusal to answer or meet her eye tells her all she needs to know.

She squeals and leaps off the bed to hug me from behind. "Congratulations!"

"It's not a big deal." Or at least, I don't want to treat it like a big deal.

"If it was a big deal though, how big are we talking?" Ronnie slowly moves her hands apart in front of me.

Laughing, I slap her hands away so I can finish eating the sandwich she got me. She's so ridiculous, and I love her for immediately making it a joke so I'm not feeling quite so put on the spot. She always knows how to lighten the mood when I get too serious.

"No, it can't have been that big," says Ronnie in a fake shocked voice. "That's two, maybe three feet."

"Like I said, incorrigible." I take a bite, hoping the conversation will drop and Ronnie will find literally anything else to talk about now that I'm home.

"Fun," she corrects me again. "I'm fun."

"If you say so."

"I do." She checks her phone. "Trevor is downstairs, so I have to go, but you eat up. I'm sure you need to refuel after all the calories you burned this weekend." At the last minute before she closes the door behind her, she pokes her heads back in and adds, "With your *boyfriends*."

I throw another chip at her, but it bounces off the door as she closes it, and I can hear her cackling all the way down the hall.

That girl. I swear, her friendship is the best and worst thing that's ever happened to me.

Chapter Twenty-Three

All week, Ronnie has made no secret of her opinion that I should give the guys a true chance with a real relationship. Unfortunately, all her little comments are having the exact opposite effect. By the time the guys text me Friday morning about our weekend plans, I've already decided I'm not going to see them this weekend.

When are you coming over tonight? Lukas texts.

We could also pick you up if that's easier, Elliot adds.

I've got an answer already prepared for this, something I know they'll believe and respect. *I'm actually really behind on homework and studying because we were gone last weekend. I'm going to have to stay home and catch up so I don't jeopardize my GPA.*

Ronnie keeps making a big deal out of them being my first, and how that makes them special and shouldn't I give them a chance to really try dating, but the fact that they were my first is even more reason for me to hesitate. My mom was not my dad's first, but he was hers, and she's always let that give him entirely too much power over her, holding on so tight to him because as far as she's concerned, he's her one and only even if he doesn't feel the same. I've seen how much that imbalance has fucked up my mom's life. I'm determined not to let that happen to me. I might have let them screw me, but there's no way I'm going to let them screw me over.

You could do homework here, Sebastian protests.

Elliot tries to bribe me my appealing to my stomach. *We could all work in the dining room and you'd have plenty of snacks.*

And good coffee, adds Sebastian.

We could pick you up after our poker game so you'd have a little bit of alone study time and then we could do the group study time, Lukas suggests.

I really need to be able to need to focus for this stuff. So it's better if I stay home.

Felix has a solution for that. *Is it math? We can help if it's math.*

No, it's a research essay for history. I've done the research already and I feel bad lying to them, but this is the only way I can think of to get them to let it go. It's not that I don't want to see them, it's just complicated.

What about if we just have a small movie night on Saturday? Elliot offers.

Your brain will need a break, says Sebastian.

I'm frustrated that they aren't letting this go. *I might have to go in for an extra shift at the newspaper.* It's a weak argument, and I'm sure they'll see through it, but it's not *not* true. There could be breaking news, and they might need me to come in to make the coffee so the journalists can cover it.

Fuck, that thought is depressing. I want to be the journalist covering the breaking news, not the invisible intern making sure Brad and his colleagues have enough French vanilla creamer.

I'll let you know if the weekend frees up though, I tell

them, before they can brainstorm yet another idea to get me to come spend the weekend with them. If they keep suggesting, at some point I might break down and agree, but I really need to put some distance between us so I don't do something stupid like start to fall for them.

Little dots appear and then disappear a few times.

Finally, Lukas sends a reply. *Okay. But if you do want a break, just text us and we can come get you.*

And maybe we can all hang out next weekend? Elliot asks. *We haven't seen you all week, we miss you.*

I can't break a promise I don't make, so I stay noncommittal, even though it makes me sad to think about going more than another week without seeing them. *Yeah, maybe,* I reply. *If next week doesn't throw too much work at me.*

The guys are silent for the rest of the day, only sending me a goodnight text. I appreciate that they respect me prioritizing studying over socializing, but I find myself checking my phone off and on all day, hoping to see a text from them.

But every text that comes in—and there are a lot of them —is from my mother. Mostly worrying about Dad not telling her if he'll be home on time tonight, and overanalyzing every two-word response he sends when she asks him something, when he bothers to respond at all. She's planning all these things that she thinks will make him happy, even though I know for a fact she hates most of them. It makes me so sad and angry to see how she's completely lost her sense of self to being the wife of a man who doesn't even notice she exists.

And I'm annoyed with myself that every time my phone dings with a text, my heart leaps with the hope that it'll be from one of the guys, and then falls when every time, it's just my mom again. By the time Ronnie waltzes into the room to get ready to go out for the night, I've decided that I'm going to have to break things off with them. I already know they're getting too attached to me, and I need to put an end to this before any of us gets hurt.

The next evening, Ronnie is getting ready for a date with Trevor, and I'm finishing up an assignment, when my phone goes wild with text notifications. I sigh, sure it's going to be my mother again. She's been calling and texting me all day, devastated that my dad didn't want to go with her to see some action movie that he'll love and she'll hate. Instead, he left at 10:30 a.m. without saying goodbye or telling her where he'd be, who he'd be with, or when he'd be back.

But it's not my mom. It's the guys.

Lukas: *Did you get enough homework done to have a movie break?*

Felix: *Did you get called into work?*

Elliot: *We could come pick you up.*

Sebastian: *We're making pasta and homemade garlic bread.*

The texts all come in one right after the other, and Ronnie glances over at me with an eyebrow raised. "Are those your not-boyfriend boyfriends?" she asks, leaning into the mirror to check her lipstick line. It's perfect as always.

"They're not my boyfriends," I say for the billionth time, but my eyes are focused on my phone. I know I'm going to have to respond or they'll just keep texting, but I really don't want to.

"So you keep telling me." Ronnie blows me a kiss as she

grabs her purse. "All right, I'm heading out. Have fun with your guys tonight. Love ya!"

I don't bother to correct her on her way out the door. If I tell her what I've decided to do, she'll stay home and try to talk me out of it, and I don't want to ruin her night like I'm about to ruin mine.

Sorry, I can't tonight, I text back, then turn off the volume on my phone and place it screen-side down on my desk.

Grabbing the book we're reading in my lit class, I climb into bed and curl up to read ahead. But I can't focus on the words. All I can think about is how much more enjoyable it was to listen to Lukas and Felix read my schoolwork to me. Even if they did end up distracting me.

Or maybe I distracted them. Either way, it was truly magical. And if I go through with my plan, I'll never experience that again.

After fifteen minutes, I give up and check my phone.

They've sent pictures of themselves holding up plates of delicious-looking pasta. My stomach growls, reminding me that I skipped dinner tonight because I didn't want to go to the cafeteria alone.

Looks yummy, I type. Both the pasta and the guys.

I waver, willing myself to put the phone down so I don't give in and ask them to come pick me up. And I know they would. They'd probably just abandon their meal and jump right in the car.

Well, Elliot would probably make them wrap their plates and put all the leftovers in containers first, but then they'd be right on their way.

But I'm going to hold strong. I hit send, then put the phone in my desk drawer where I can't see it and pull my laptop into bed with me to work on the last story in the series I'm working on for class. If I'm going to be thinking about them anyway, I might as do the one last thing on my plate that involves them so I can wipe the slate clean and move on with my life.

I pour every bit of affection I have for them onto the page. My appreciation for sports like speedcubing for giving a home and family to these brilliant people who might not be as comfortable in mainstream society, yet once they're given the space and friends they need, they absolutely thrive.

I stay up way too late, but when I'm finally done, I know it's the best thing I've ever written. I send it in early to my professor, then close the laptop and blink tears from my eyes. I'm going to get an A on this assignment, but I don't even care.

There's one last thing I need to do, and it hurts. My entire chest feels like my heart is being carved out of my body, but I force myself to climb out of bed and retrieve my phone from the drawer. I read back over my mom's texts from last night and today, imagining myself in ten, fifteen, twenty years, sitting alone at the dining room table at the guys' house, surrounded by congealing plates of pasta and garlic bread that I lovingly prepared for my cubers, who never bothered to tell me they wouldn't be home for dinner. In my mind, I text them, asking where they are, but they don't answer. Instead, I get a notification from my news app. A new article from *The New York Times*, written by Brad, who in this imaginary future left the *Tribune* and became the biggest of big-shot reporters. His byline taunts me. *That should have been me.* I click off my phone and gather up the plates, scraping cold globs of lasagna into the trash, washing the dishes, putting away all remnants of the love and care the guys are ignoring, just like my father always has.

I blink back to reality, scrubbing my sleeve over the tears

streaking my face. I can't let that be my future. I won't let it be.

I swipe my phone open and delete our group conversation. Then I block all four of their numbers.

This is for the best. I'm protecting all of us. The longer we keep doing this, the more they'll expect me to put my life on hold to spend time with them, to skip class to go to watch them compete. If I don't put an end to it now, I'll eventually find myself dropping out of school, leaving the newspaper, and becoming my mother all over again. I can't let a few orgasms and a hook on the wall derail my life. My education and career have to come first.

Chapter Twenty-Four

"Oh em gee, the most amazing thing happened!" squeals Ronnie, flinging open the door to our dorm room.

I just groan and roll over under my blankets. I should get up and show interest in whatever happened to her, but I'm pretty sure I'm sick. My entire body feels heavy and achy, and my eyes won't stop watering. I didn't go down to breakfast this morning because I don't want to infect anyone in case it's contagious. I'm not even hungry anyway.

"Oh no! Honey, what's wrong?" Ronnie rushes over to my bedside and puts her hand on my forehead. "Are you not feeling okay? Your not-boyfriends brought you home like this?"

"I didn't go over to their house." It's a lot of pressure looking Ronnie in the eye, so I look past her shoulder to the TV, where I've found the space show the guys and I have been watching at our movie nights. Now that I'm actually paying more attention to it, it's not that bad. It's actually kind of comforting to have it on, even though it also hurts to remember that time with them.

"I thought they were picking you up," says Ronnie, confused. "They were texting you when I left yesterday."

"They were, but I didn't go over." I roll away from her, not wanting to talk about it. Ronnie was so hoping I would make them my real boyfriends, and I don't want to see her look of disappointment when I tell her we're done.

Ronnie sits back on her heels, aghast.

"Did they break up with you? I'll kill them." She looks around the room as if she'll find a battleaxe in the corner to run off to bash in the guys' front door with.

"You can't dump someone you're not dating." Another tear drips down my cheek. I hate that I miss them and I hate being weak in front of my friend. This was the right choice for me. This was a clean break and we're all going to be better for it in the end.

"Those assholes!" Ronnie stands and starts pacing the little floorspace we have, radiating rage and looking like she wants to hit something.

"They're not assholes. They're good guys." For now, anyway. I don't want to stick around and watch them change into assholes like they inevitably will, like all men do.

"No, they're not," she spits out. "Not if this is the way they're treating you. They fucked you and left you, that makes them assholes."

My phone vibrates on the nightstand with an incoming message.

"Is that them?" Ronnie grabs for my phone, but even sick, I'm able to get to it faster than she can.

"I blocked their numbers," I say in a small voice as I turn over my phone. It's Mom. My dad apparently didn't come home last night. I click the phone off and stick it under my pillow, not able to deal with her drama right now.

"Good for you." Ronnie still looks pissed, but like she's trying to overcome it when she kneels down at my side again. "I'm sorry I wasn't here for you last night. You should have called me."

"I didn't want to ruin your good time." And I wanted to be left alone. I need to be okay with being along if I'm going to buckle down and see my goals to fruition.

"I'm not having a good time if you're at home crying." She shucks off her shoes and then lifts the covers, forcing me to scoot over as she climbs into my bed.

"No," I protest, "I'm sick, I might be contagious."

She looks down at me with a mixture of pity and vague amusement. "Sweetie, you're not sick, you're heartbroken. Now, what is this terrible show that we're watching?"

I'm not heartbroken, because I'm the one who cut things off with them, not the other way around. Besides, I can't be heartbroken over the end of something that wasn't even a relationship. But I know I won't be able to convince her of that, and if she wants to risk getting sick, that's her choice. I warned her. "It's about a bunch of people living on a spaceship," I mumble, curling up next to Ronnie. I can practice being alone later. Right now, it's nice to have her snuggled up next to me.

"It sounds dumb. So catch me up. What's everyone's name?"

It's been two weeks, and my brain still feels fuzzy and out of sorts. Could the guys have changed my brain chemistry when they fucked me so I'm no longer my focused, career-driven self? I shouldn't miss them this much. I barely know them. It's only been a few weeks.

My journalism professor praised my last speedcubing

article, saying it's the type of human interest-meets-sports story that more newspapers should be running.

I should be glowing from his words, but all I could do was force a smile and thank him. This is not like me. I need to reassert myself into my own life. Even if it's super hard to actually care about any of it right now, I'm still saving myself from a lifetime of heartache.

Although it doesn't help that the ICF World Championships are coming up this week, and I can't stop watching the promo videos. Ronnie slaps my phone out of my hand every time she catches me, and has even threatened to take it away so I don't have to see "those assholes."

At least my professor's praise kicked my ass into gear long enough for me to send his note and the article to Carl. If my professor thinks more newspapers should be running articles like mine, then I might as well start at the one I'm interning at. Besides, I need to move my focus from my not-boyfriends back to my career, where it belongs.

It's weird coming into the newspaper on Sunday afternoons from my dorm instead of from the guys' house, without my overnight bag. My purse looks lonely and small tucked down under my desk by itself.

As I log in on the computer to check for any emails, I glance across the bullpen to Carl's office. The door is open, and I can hear his regular bursts of laughter as he sits in there talking to Brad.

No emails. Not surprising.

I cast another glance at Carl's office. I want to swoop in there as soon as Brad leaves and ask what he thinks of the article I emailed him on Friday. It's been long enough that he should have had plenty of time to read it.

Resetting the break room takes very little time. All of these little tasks I can do with very little brainpower, and I keep peeking out the door to check on Carl's office. I don't want to miss an opportunity before he gets sucked into another meeting. Although from the sound of his laughter, he doesn't appear to actually be working in there. But he's the boss, so he can do whatever he wants, I guess.

Since no one is around and I'm waiting for the coffee to finish brewing, I pull out my phone and check to see if ICF has put out any new promos.

There's a new video featuring Sebastian. It's not even a choice. My finger clicks on it automatically. It's not even a choice.

"The best advice I could give to someone who wants to solve a cube is simply to decide what they want all of the colors to be on each side, and then break it down step by step to get there," he says. "You just have to follow those easy steps, or layers, then you'll have solved the cube. It's not hard."

A sound escapes me that's half laugh, half sob. Of course he sees it so simply. Just decide you want to do it, and then do it. All there is to it. But the thing is, he's not wrong. I mean, he's wrong about just anyone being able to solve a cube so easily; your brain has to be wired a certain way for that, I think. But in a broad sense, he's right. If I want something in life, like a successful career in journalism, I just need to decide what steps it takes and then follow them. No deviation.

Ignoring the brewing coffee, I march up to Carl's office. I can't keep waiting around for my boss to notice me. I need to take things into my own hands.

Before I have a chance to knock, I freeze.

"And then she says, speedcubing is about found family and that's one of the most important things in life," says Carl, choking out the words through fits of laughter.

"It's like she has no idea what's really going on in the

world," agrees Brad, shaking his head and matching Carl laugh for laugh. "Has she ever read a newspaper?"

"She thinks it's a fucking sport!" Carl laughs even louder. They can probably hear him on the other side of the bullpen.

They're obviously talking about me. About my article. Did he share it with Brad? He couldn't be bothered to reply to me about it, but he can forward it to that asshole for a laugh?

The door swings open in front of me, and it takes me a moment to realize I've pushed it open. I didn't even realize my hand had reached out.

"Fuck, Rebecca, get in here," says Carl, wiping the tears of laughter from his eyes. "I didn't think you had a joke like this in you."

Flames of rage lick at my skin. "It's not a joke," I grit out.

"Come on, you can't be serious. This is a real newspaper. You can't expect us to run a fluff piece like that." Carl waves his hand toward the computer screen, where my article is pulled up.

"I'm completely serious," I tell him, my nails digging into my palms. I can't believe I'm standing here having this conversation. I knew it was a long shot that he'd actually run the article, as much as he dislikes me, but I hoped he'd at least give me some real feedback. I never once thought he would take it as a joke.

Or make fun of me to my face in front of a coworker. Especially one as awful as Brad.

"And to think she slept with them to get that story," Brad sneers, looking at me as if I'm as big a joke as he apparently thinks the article is.

"Oh, now, wait a minute," says Carl, sitting up straighter in his chair and getting serious. "Did you sleep with these speedcubers to get this story, young lady?"

I freeze, my brain refusing to provide me with the words to deny it. "I. Uh. I didn't—" The guys did help with the story, and I was fooling around with them, but the two things have nothing to do with one another. But how do I explain that to my boss? Why should I *have* to explain that to him?

All traces of amusement have disappeared from Carl's face. "That is a violation of ethics, Rebecca. You say you want to be a reporter? Well, reporters don't trade sex for information. You're fired. Clean out your desk and leave. Now."

"Not much of a loss there," says Brad, crossing one ankle over his knee and leaning back to look at me. "She's a shit writer anyway. Way too many emotions. And she never fills the creamer basket enough."

Too many emotions? A shit writer? I want to punch Brad in the face. But I have approximately half a second before my tears spill over, so I do the cowardly thing and run away.

I yank my purse out from under my desk and weave blindly through the bullpen to the stairs. No way am I going to stand there and wait for the elevator. Everyone overheard what just happened, and if they somehow missed it, it won't be long before they know. Carl wasn't trying to be quiet about the fact that he was making fun of me before, and he's not going to be quiet about the fact that I've been fired and why. I'm sure Brad, his lecherous little yes-man, will help him spread the word all over the paper.

At least I have confirmation that Brad definitely saw me kissing the guys goodbye in the parking lot the first time they dropped me off. Yet another way men can ruin my life. I'll just add it to the list.

Now I have to embarrass myself even more, sitting here waiting for the next bus, trying not to cry in front of strangers on the street. Even worse, though, is that being fired means no more internship, and likely no work-study credit. Even if it doesn't end up as a failing grade, I've planned out the credit hours I need each semester to graduate, and if I don't get these hours I'll have to cram them in somewhere else down the road.

I'd sent Carl that article because my professor thought it was good, that it was worth it, and it just cost me my future. Now I'll have a ruined GPA, have to find another internship and maybe take an extra semester to do it, and that recommendation letter I was hoping to have from a Pulitzer Prize winner is clearly out the window. How am I going to land another internship? Even if this doesn't get shared around the newspaper community right away, any paper I apply to will want to call Carl for a reference, and pretty soon every editor in Boston will think I slept with my sources to get an inside scoop.

By the time I make it back to my dorm, I feel even more mentally drained than I have in the past two weeks since blocking the guys' numbers. I just want to crash out on my bed and pretend I never took the risk.

As soon as I open the door though, I scream and my hand flies up to cover my eyes. I was not prepared to walk in to the sight of my roommate splayed out naked on her bed with a toy between her thighs.

Chapter Twenty-Five

"Oh god!" Ronnie and I both shout. She follows it with, "I thought you were at your internship!" as I take a step backward into the door, which snicks closed against my back. I spin around and fumble at the handle with my eyes squeezed shut, but when I manage to get the door open again she shrieks, "No! Close it!"

I do as she says, pressing my forehead against the wood and cursing every single thing that has ever happened in my life to bring me to this moment.

Behind me, I hear Ronnie say, I assume into her phone, "I gotta go. I'll call you later."

"Is it safe to open my eyes now?" I ask tentatively after a few more moments.

"Yes, yes, oh, god. Sorry about that." When I open one eye and look over my shoulder, Ronnie is standing in the middle of the room wearing an oversized T-shirt and stuffing her legs into a pair of sweatpants. "I was, um, on the phone with Trevor."

"Yeah, I figured that part out." I know most people in a dorm probably masturbate when they have the room to themselves, but I never thought Ronnie would be one of them when she sees Trevor almost every weekend.

I vow to always knock on our door when I'm coming home unexpectedly from now on. And maybe just generally, to be on the safe side.

Now that the adrenaline is beginning to ebb, something else is prickling at the back of my mind. It's … envy. I'm jealous that Ronnie has someone to be so open with about her sexuality, and I once again have no one. And I hate being jealous of my best friend, because she deserves love and good sex and a solid partner. And anyway, I made the choice to not have those things, so I have no right to be envious.

Dropping my purse on the floor, I flop onto my bed and crawl up to my pillow. Maybe I can just sleep the whole rest of the semester and then I don't have to deal with any of this ever again. Or I can give up on everything, move back home, find a job walking dogs or painting crosswalks or something else that will ensure I don't have to interact with other humans. That sounds like a nice plan right now.

"Oh, honey, is my coochie that terrible to see?" Ronnie brushes my hair back from my face.

"Please wash your hands first?" I say, batting her hand away. I know she was making a joke, but I don't want her vagina-hands touching my hair and face.

"I was using a toy, not my hands." She rolls her eyes, but puts on hand sanitizer. "And we'd barely gotten started."

"I'm sorry that I interrupted." Now I feel even worse. I remember what it was like when the guys would get me worked up and all I wanted to do was come, and now I've made it so Ronnie can't finish.

"If you're home early from work with your eyes all swollen from crying, I'm guessing there's a reason for it. Never be sorry for needing a friend. You know I'm always here to support you." This time when Ronnie brushes back my hair, I don't flinch away. "Now tell me what happened."

"I got fired," I say into my pillow. I've always been the best, the hardest worker. Never in a million years could I have imagined that I'd get fired from anything.

Briefly, I explain everything that happened at work tonight. It's embarrassing, and I start crying again as soon as I start talking, but at least having Ronnie next to me is comforting.

Except that she's not who I really want to be comforting me. I love Ronnie so much, and I'm grateful that she's here, but hers isn't the shoulder I'm aching to cry on.

Which makes me cry even more.

"Okay, here's what we're going to do. We're going to call the HR department there and complain," says Ronnie.

"There's no point. I knew the rules, and I broke them anyway." If I hadn't sent Carl the article and asked for the paper to consider running it, I would have been fine. But I got overconfident, and never expected anyone to know about my relationship with the guys. Although I still stand by the fact that I wrote an amazing article and the community should read it.

"Maybe a little, but what Carl and Brad did was worse. He had absolutely no right to treat you like that, especially in front of that other asshole."

"I'll never get a job as a reporter." I gave up the guys so I could focus on my career, and then I ruined that and now I'm left with absolutely nothing. "Carl knows too many people, and he'll give me a shit reference. No one will want to hire me."

"You don't know that," says Ronnie, but I can tell she knows I'm probably right.

Rolling over, I frown up at her. "They'll ask why I was fired, and he'll say I broke the ethics code."

"Hmm, I suppose that is a little hard to spin."

"And the World Championships are this week," I stare past Ronnie to the ceiling. I feel empty. Maybe she was right. Maybe my heart is broken.

"Have you been watching those promos again?" Now Ronnie isn't consoling, she's annoyed. "I told you to stop. They were assholes and you deserve better."

"I can't help it." I pull the pillow out from under my head to hold over my face.

"Don't make me play mom and threaten to take away your phone," she says. She'd really do it too. "Now, I'm going to take a shower. Don't do anything stupid while I'm gone."

Once she leaves, I throw the pillow farther down the bed and just rest my head against the mattress as I stare up at the ceiling for a good ten minutes. I have no motivation to work or study. My career is in jeopardy and I see no way to get it back on track. I can reach out to my advisor, but it's not like they'll be able to do much, if they even want to given that I'm the one who broke the rules. No legit newspaper will want to work with me once they find out why Carl let me go.

My phone rings from deep within my purse. It's probably my mom, but I really don't have the energy to pick up it up and talk to her right now. I'm already feeling bad for myself. There's no way I can help keep her spirits buoyed right now too.

Ronnie comes back in, looking much calmer with her hair wrapped in a towel. The phone rings again as she enters, and again I let it go to voicemail.

She's just shucked her bathrobe and is standing there topless, digging through her drawer for a bra, when it rings a third time.

"Do you want me to just turn it off?" asks Ronnie, seeing that I'm making absolutely no move to answer it.

"Sure." I really don't care right now.

She digs my phone out of my purse, but freezes when she looks at the screen. Instead of turning it off, she answers it, staring at me.

"Hello, this is Rebecca's phone."

I sit up. I'm not opposed to Ronnie answering my phone, but her face has gone white with concern.

"Yes, thank you for calling. We'll be there as soon as we can." She hangs up and looks at me, her face ashen. "That was the hospital. You mom's been in an accident. She just arrived in an ambulance."

Ronnie swings open our door, still shirtless, and yells up the hall, "Courtney! We need your car, now!"

"No! I'm going out tonight!" Courtney calls back down the hall.

"Bitch, this is an emergency! We're going to the hospital!"

"Why? You having a baby?" calls a different voice.

Ronnie doesn't answer, just pops back into the room and throws on a tank.

Our door swings open again, and Courtney stands there in a party outfit, only half her makeup done.

"Here are the keys." She holds them out by the disco ball keychain. "I hope everything's okay."

"Me too. Thank you." Ronnie smacks a kiss right onto Courtney's cheek. "Come on, Rebecca."

"Thanks," I mumble to Courtney as I hurry behind Ronnie.

I want to feel grateful to Courtney for letting us borrow her car, but there's no room in me for anything but guilt for letting my phone ring so many times without answering it. And for all the times lately that I've ignored it when it really was my mom calling. I haven't had the energy to deal with her problems on top of my own, but now for all I know she could die thinking I don't care enough to answer her calls.

I'm a terrible daughter. I've left her to be taken to the hospital alone, without anyone there with her for support. I don't even know what to expect because I didn't even take the call myself. I made my best friend do it because I couldn't be bothered.

Ronnie drops me off in front of the ER, telling me to go inside and find my mom while she parks. I rush in and give my mom's name at the desk.

"I'm her daughter, someone called and said she was in an accident." Everything is a confusing blur as a nurse ushers me to a curtained bay.

I fling the curtain aside and see my mother stretched out on a bed with a blanket over her, her arm strapped to her chest. Her face is bruised and scraped. "Mom! I'm so sorry, I got here as fast as I could. What happened?"

"Oh, it's not too bad. I don't know why they called you," says Mom, waving her good hand dismissively. Pointing to her purse on a chair, she says, "Can you try calling your father again for me?"

"Where is Dad?" My father is a dick and a cheating liar, but surely he would at least show up to the hospital to be with my mom when she's been hurt.

"Or better yet, why don't you call him from your phone? I'm sure he'll answer you. Tell him not to worry. That I'm going to be fine."

"You don't look fine. Why isn't Dad here? What exactly happened?" The only reason she could want me to call from my phone is if he isn't answering any calls from her.

"I'm sure he'll arrive soon," Mom insists. "Just as soon as you tell him what's happening."

"But I don't know what's happening!" The guilt I felt

earlier is beginning to fade, being replaced with an irritation I try not to show. This woman is maddening, but she's injured and has just been through something traumatic. She doesn't need me yelling at her.

"Hi, are you the daughter?" asks a male nurse, stepping through the curtain into my mom's bay.

"Yes, I'm Rebecca. Can you tell me what happened?" Since my mom clearly won't.

"Neighbors called an ambulance, stating that your mom fell while chasing a car," says the nurse, looking over a chart. "Looks like she fell with her arm stretched out, which tore her rotator cuff, and she has a full-thickness tendon tear. There are also a couple of cracks on her ribs, there are some minor lacerations to her face from the road, and we're going to monitor her for a concussion."

"Okay, but what does that mean exactly?" I'm hung up on the part where she fell while chasing a car. What on Earth was she doing that for?

"She'll need surgery on her shoulder, but right now the head injury is the more pressing concern," explains the nurse.

The curtain is shoved aside, and Ronnie stands in the opening, panting. "Okay, I'm here. What's happening?" She leans over to rest her hands on her knees.

The nurse ducks out as I point Ronnie to the empty chair, which she sinks into to catch her breath. "Mom was chasing a car and now she needs surgery." I figure the simplest explanation is the best. "The real question is, why the hell you were chasing a car, Mom?"

"That doesn't matter," she insists. "Just call your dad. Once he gets here, everything is going to be fine."

I barely manage to stop my eyes from rolling. "Can you hang out here for a minute?" I ask Ronnie. "I'll be right back. Don't let them take her to surgery without me."

Ronnie nods and stands up, moving over to Mom's bedside. She takes her hand and talks quietly with her as I step out past the curtains. Once I'm far enough from Mom's room that she won't overhear my conversation, I call Dad. It takes a few attempts, but he finally answers.

"Mom's in the hospital, where are you?" I say without greeting when he finally picks up.

"She's not my problem anymore," says Dad, clearly distracted.

"What do you mean? She's your wife, not a problem." This has always been his attitude, but I've never heard him come right out and say it before.

"Not for much longer," says Dad. "I told her I was moving out of the house, and she flipped out. Started running after me. I tell you, it's flattering, but I can do better."

My father is leaving? He told my mom he's leaving her, and she's back there insisting that he's going to come to the hospital and be with her? Great. One of my parents is an asshole and the other is delusional. This isn't news to me, but this is a new level of bullshit, even for them.

"So, just so I'm clear. You told Mom you were leaving her, you got in your car and drove away, Mom tried to *run after your car*, and she fell and hurt herself badly enough that she needs surgery, and you did ... nothing?" Maybe if I spell it out for him he'll realize what an asshole he is.

"I told her I was done, that means she's not my problem anymore. Besides, I had a date tonight. Which you disrupted with your constant calling, by the way." He sounds annoyed. His daughter calls to tell him his wife is in the hospital having surgery, and he's annoyed because it's interrupting his date with another woman.

The man is one hell of a piece of work.

"Sorry to bother you," I bite out, then hang up.

I can't believe that asshole. Mom dedicates her entire life to taking care of him and meeting all his needs and loving him, and this is how he treats her? She could have had a whole life of her own, a career, *friends*, but now she's left with nothing and no one.

Well, she has me, but I clearly haven't been as supportive as I should have been lately. I silently promise to do better by her.

"Rebecca," calls Ronnie, peeking out from between the curtains. "They're here to take your mom to surgery."

I hurry back over to talk to the doctors, determined to ask all the questions and be the best daughter I can be.

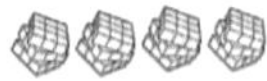

"All right, the surgery was a success," says the surgeon when they come out to meet me in the waiting room a few hours later. "You'll be able to see your mom soon. A nurse will come out once she's been taken back to her room and let you know the number."

"Thank you," I say, but the surgeon is already walking away, ready for their next case.

"That was stressful," says Ronnie, slumping down into a chair. She's been pacing and prowling around the waiting room, which was stressing me out, so I'm glad she's finally sitting. "At least we know she's going to be okay."

"Yeah, now we'll just have to deal with the mess that is her life." I rub the sleep from my eyes. I'm exhausted and emotionally drained. "I'm not surprised Dad left, but she's going to need a lot of help dealing with that emotionally. That's going to be worse than the recovery from surgery."

"Just so you know, that's not all on you," says Ronnie,

slinging her arm around my shoulders to pull me closer. "She needs therapy."

"I doubt she'll go." Not unless the therapist will promise to help her get Dad back. "Dad has always been her entire life, and now he's abandoned her. I don't know what she's going to do."

"Whatever she wants," says Ronnie with confidence. "Besides, he was always the worst. She's better off this way."

"True, he never met another woman he didn't want to sleep with." That's my dad: womanizer, and solid reason not to trust men.

"Well, yeah, but I was more thinking because he never supported your mom. Not emotionally at least. And a good guy, he'll always support the dreams of the woman he loves." Ronnie stands and stretches as if she didn't just say something so incredibly romantic it makes my heart ache. "Do you want me to stay the night with you here?"

"No, I'll be fine. There's probably only one chair in the room to sleep in anyway." I stand and pull Ronnie in for a hug. I really do appreciate her being here beside me through this, and everything else the past few weeks have thrown at me. "Besides, no use in us both getting uncomfortable sleep while listening to my mom complain that we're not my dad."

She gives me a sympathetic look as she squeezes my arm. "All right, I'll go return Courtney's car and come back tomorrow with fresh clothes for you."

"Thanks." I stand there, watching Ronnie walk away. While I'm in a really sucky situation, I'm glad I have my best friend by my side.

The hospital room chair is even worse than I imagined. Not that I'd be getting any sleep even if it was the most comfortable thing ever. Mom doesn't want to rest at all. She wants to leave and try to go find Dad herself to convince him to come back to her. She's saying all sorts of ridiculous things, insisting that this has happened before and he always comes back when she grovels, which I find surprising. Not because I think it's out of character for her—it's absolutely not—but because the most likely reason is that whatever girl he left Mom for realized he was trash and kicked him out. But it's mainly a surprise because I didn't know about any of this. She never told me.

"Mom, you can't go find Dad right now. You just had surgery," I explain for at least the sixth time. "The doctors aren't just going to let you leave."

"But I need to be with him. I'll sign myself out against medical advice. I have to go explain to him why he's making a mistake. What is he going to do without me? Who will make him dinner and fold his laundry?" She tries to swing her legs out of the bed, but I block her and push them back onto the mattress. We've been doing this dance every few hours all night. They said her concussion was very mild, but I'm tempted to ask them to check again because she's obviously not thinking clearly. Unfortunately, I know it's not a head injury that's causing this behavior. This is just my mom.

"Knock, knock," says Ronnie from the doorway.

"You don't have to knock." Ronnie has already seen the worst of my family. If she hasn't run yet, I doubt she will.

"I brought you some clean clothes." She hands me a bag.

"I love you." I am definitely starting to feel ripe. I'd love a shower, but that can wait a while longer. Clean clothes, though, will help a lot.

When I come out of changing in the bathroom, Ronnie is listening patiently to my mom at her bedside. I wish I could get Mom to calm down that much, but she seems to get agitated whenever she talks to me.

"All right, well, I have class, but text me if you need anything," says Ronnie, pulling me into a big hug.

"Thanks again." I hug her back. I'm so exhausted, but she's gotten my mom settled enough that maybe I'll get a little bit of a break.

But as soon as she's gone, Mom goes back to demanding I give her back her phone. I've asked the nurses' station to keep it for me because if it's in the room, she'll try to get out of bed to get to it. And all she does once she has it is try to call Dad. I'm afraid he'll try to get a restraining order if she keeps it up.

"How about this," I say, trying to get her to focus on me. "If Dad calls or texts me, I'll ask him to come visit." I highly doubt he'll do either of those things, but at least it's a promise I can keep.

"All right. He'll call soon," says Mom, nodding to herself. "I'm sure he's worried sick about where I am."

"I'm going to go grab a coffee. I'll be right back, okay?" I slowly back toward the door, half convinced she's going to try to follow me, but her head bobs in agreement. I'll have to trust her because it's been possibly the longest night of my life, and I need coffee. There's no way around it.

I let the nurses' station know I'm stepping away and she's alone in the room, then make my way down to the cafeteria. The first sip of coffee is ... a disappointment. It's worse than the hotel coffee we had at Nationals. But at least it's caffeine.

Although each sip makes me think yet again of the amazing coffee the guys brewed each morning that I stayed with them. And then I remember that they should be leaving soon for Worlds, if they haven't already. Events start tomorrow, and they'll want to get there early to adjust to the different time zone.

It's probably better for them that I won't be there this time. I won't distract them. They'll need to stay focused to achieve not only their personal bests, but also the titles of World Champions. This is everything they've ever worked for.

Meanwhile, I'm heading back up to the hospital room to take care of my mother and drink crappy coffee, with absolutely zero possibilities for my own career. Once everything is sorted with Mom, I'm going to have to make an appointment with my academic advisor and get his help sorting things out.

Actually, no, I decide as I wait for the elevator. I'm not going to wait. This is my career. I can take care of Mom and solve the problem of my future at the same time.

I quickly type out an email to my advisor on my phone, explaining the gist of the situation and requesting his help in landing a new internship and asking my options for replacing the credits that I will now be missing for this semester.

There's a lot of commotion on Mom's floor as I step off the elevators, and it's rather disorienting to hear so much noise on the normally quiet floor.

As I turn the corner to my mom's hallway, though, I realize the disturbance is coming from Mom's room. I toss my still-full coffee in the trash and race ahead, praying that whatever it is, it's nothing too terrible.

Chapter Twenty-Six

My prayers, it seems, are going unanswered. A nurse stops me as I approach the room. "You can't go in there right now," she says.

"That's my mom."

"I know, and we're doing everything we can. I just need to you to be patient while we help her, okay?" The nurse ushers me back from the doorway, and I crane my neck to see inside. There's a group of nurses and physicians surrounding her bed, telling her to lay still while they do whatever it is that they're doing.

It feels like hours, but it's probably only minutes before they're wheeling her out of the room, an oxygen mask on her face, a tube coming out of her chest, and her wrists strapped to the bed. Her eyes look wild, but hazy.

The last nurse to come out stops in front of me. "We're taking her to surgery. Her moving around seems to have broken off a small piece of her rib, which has punctured one of her lungs. We need to remove the sliver of bone and repair the lung."

"Is she going to be okay?" Lungs are important. She needs them to breathe. My mom and I have had our struggles and we're not as close as I wish I could be with my mother, but I don't want her to die or have anything bad happen to her.

"We're going to do everything we can," says the nurse, already glancing back toward where his colleagues disappeared down a hallway. "We're hopeful that it will be a straightforward procedure, but we'll have to see what it looks like when the doctor gets in there. Do you want me to walk you down to the waiting room?"

I shake my head. "I remember where it is." If he needs to be in the operating room with my mom, I'd rather he be there than with me.

"All right." He's already walking away. "Check in with the receptionist when you get down there. She'll get you the case number."

All the nurses around me have gone back to their jobs, caring for the other patients. This is normal for them, but it's life-changing for me. I wander in a daze down to the waiting room, where the receptionist points me to the same area I sat in last night with Ronnie.

Pulling out my phone, I text Ronnie. *Mom is back in surgery. Broken rib punctured a lung.*

Oh shit! Ronnie texts back almost immediately. *Want me to come sit with you?*

I check the time. Ronnie has class soon and I don't want her to miss it because of me. She already has a tendency to be late, and her professor doesn't love her as a result. She doesn't need to miss a whole class.

It's okay, you have class. I'm sure everything will be okay. Hopefully. *I'll keep you updated.*

And I'll keep my fingers crossed. I'm sorry everything is hitting you one thing after another, she tells me.

Not much I can do. I'm going to just sit and play on my phone while I wait for an update from the surgery. And maybe keep an eye on the updates from the upcoming World Championship. Because if I'm going to suffer and be miserable, I might as well make it worse.

No speedcubers though! It's as if she can read my mind. *Those assholes don't deserve a second of your thoughts or energy after what they did. They can rot in hell as far I'm concerned.*

I feel bad that I've just let her think they were the ones to end things, but at this point so much time has passed that I don't feel like I can tell her the truth now. And it doesn't really matter who ended it. It's over, and I'll have to find a way to make my peace with that. *No promises.* I wish I could promise, but no matter how much I've tried to focus on school and work, I can't stop thinking about them.

I'm just as bad as Mom. Worse, maybe, obsessing over multiple guys. But I refuse to let them become my entire personality. I will get over this. Eventually.

That doesn't stop me from occasionally picking up my phone and opening up an internet browser window, typing the guys' names into it so I can torture myself with their pictures and the Worlds promos. But if I'm going to avoid my mother's fate, I need to stop. I know I need to stop.

But after I just look one last time to see when their first event is for the competition.

A familiar voice calls out my name. "Rebecca! Baby! Are you okay?" I look up to see Lukas hurrying across the waiting room. He scoops me into his arms, and over his shoulder I see Felix, Elliot, and Sebastian, all of them looking as worried as Lukas.

I'm completely stunned, and for a moment I just stand there in shock as Lukas holds me. But I'm so tired and stressed, and it feels so good to be swallowed up in his arms. I've missed them so much. I know I should be strong and push him away, tell them to leave me alone, but I can't make myself do it.

"You should have called us." Felix wraps his arms around both me and Lukas.

What are they even doing here? I ghosted these guys. They shouldn't be here. How did they even find me?

Sebastian runs a hand over my hair. "Tell us what we can do to help," he says.

"Have the doctors come out to give you an update yet on how everything is going?" asks Elliot, taking one of my hands in both of his.

"Uh." I can see the receptionist watching us, probably wondering if she should call security. I give her a little wave and smile to let her know I'm okay. "What are you doing here? Shouldn't you be on your way to Seattle?"

"We've been worried about you," Felix tells me, running a hand along my jawline and cupping it gently around the back of my neck. "You haven't been answering our calls and texts, we didn't know what was going on."

"We came to your campus. We're sorry, we didn't mean to stalk you, but we didn't know what else to do," says Sebastian.

"I blocked your numbers," I say softly. I'd ghosted them specifically because I didn't want to do the hard thing and end things with them to their faces. I'd taken the coward's way out because I knew I wouldn't be able to say it to their faces. "We'd gotten through my list. I figured it was best if we just stopped seeing each other. I didn't know how to tell you."

"Well, it hurt," murmurs Felix, dropping his hand and taking a step back, like he's afraid I'll push him away. "I can't believe you just cut us out like that without saying anything. I know you didn't want to call what we were doing dating, but what we had was special, at least to us.

We thought you knew that. We never thought you'd just disappear on us without even saying goodbye." The others nod their agreement. Their pain is etched across their faces, and my heart twists seeing and knowing I put it there.

"Even if you don't want us anymore the way we were, we still want to be your friend," says Lukas.

"It'll be hard, but we want you in our lives, however you're comfortable being there," says Elliot.

Fuck, I miss them.

Tears are brimming behind my eyelids, but I blink them away as something occurs to me. "Wait, so you went to my school, but how did you know I was here?"

"Your roommate, Ronnie," says Lukas.

"Ronnie told you where I am?" That doesn't sound like her. Ronnie keeps referring to them as "the assholes" every time she catches me watching videos of them.

"Well," hedges Sebastian, "not at first."

"Definitely not at first," agrees Elliot, his eyes wide. "At first, she ran over to us at warp speed and yelled at us. A lot."

Okay, that sounds much more like her.

Felix shudders. "She's quite terrifying."

I crack a grin at that, imagining the scene.

"We explained everything to her," he continues.

"And we're sure you had your reasons for not telling her the whole story, and we're sorry for telling her. Now she's mad at you and made us promise to tell you that you're, quote, 'in for it later,'" says Lukas. "We're also sorry she's mad at you because of us."

Fuck. I'm definitely going to have a lot of explaining to do to Ronnie. That's going to be a rough conversation.

"We really are sorry, but we explained to Ronnie," says Felix.

"The whole thing was very confusing." Sebastian brings the conversation back around to the story.

"Yes, it was very confusing," agrees Felix. "But we explained to Ronnie that we hadn't broken up with you."

"You couldn't have. We weren't dating," I say, my voice so small I'm not sure they'll even hear it.

"And we did get Ronnie to promise not to take her anger out on you until your mom is doing better," Elliot says.

They didn't hear me. It's probably for the best.

I shake my head, forcing myself to focus on the basics. "Okay, so now I understand how you knew where I was, but that still doesn't explain why you're here."

"Because your mom is in the hospital and you shouldn't be here alone," says Sebastian. Confusion knits his brows together as he tries to figure out why I don't understand.

"But shouldn't you be leaving today for Worlds?" I glance at the clock on the wall, calculating how much time I might have with them before they absolutely need to leave, even as I'm telling myself I have no right to want them to stay after everything I've put them through.

"You're more important," says Lukas, taking my hand and leading me back to my seat.

"I'm not. You might not get another chance at the title." They've worked most of their lives to get to this moment and they can't give it up. Not for me, or for anyone.

"The only title we want is one from you," says Felix, sitting on my other side and taking my hand.

"Rebecca?" says a nurse, coming out to find me. She pauses briefly when she sees that I'm deep in conversation with the guys, but then comes over. "Your mom came through fantastically. You can head back up to the room whenever you're ready."

"Why don't you lead the way," says Elliot, offering me a hand and pulling me to my feet.

We ride the elevator up to my mom's floor and they follow me down the hall to her room. As soon as we're outside her door though, the guys hang back.

"You go in and check on your mom, we'll wait out here," says Elliot.

"Thank you," I whisper, watching them walk away.

I can't believe they're here, that they showed up for me like this. It's both a comfort and a hurt that they're here. I've missed them so much, but now I'm going to have to watch them walk away again. I'm not sure my heart can take it.

"Hey, Mom, how are you feeling? Any pain or discomfort?" I ask stepping into the room. "The nurse said the procedure went well."

"Has your dad called back yet?" asks Mom, her voice a little raspy.

"What?" She just got out of surgery to repair a punctured lung, and this is her first question?

"You called your dad earlier. Did he call back yet? Is he worried about me?"

I've spent all night by her side and this morning, and she doesn't even care that I'm here. That I'm missing classes to support her. All she can think about is my asshole father.

"No, he hasn't."

"He's going to," says Mom confidently. "But call him again just in case. He'll want to know I came out of the surgery okay. He'll be worried."

"Mom, I—" I start to explain that I'm not doing that, and he's not worried about her, only ever about himself, but she cuts me off.

"Who's out there?" asks Mom, trying to see around me. "Who's outside my door?"

I turn around and see the guys hovering just outside the door.

"Sorry," Sebastian says, taking a few steps back. "We didn't know she could see us."

"Rebecca! Who's out there?" Mom asks again.

"Do you … want to come in and meet my mom?" I say with a deep sigh. I'm so embarrassed the guys I like are about to see my mother like this, but I don't see way around it.

I lead them into the room. "Mom, these are my friends." The guys all look from me to each other, but I keep going, "Lukas, Sebastian, Felix, and Elliot."

"Nice to meet you," says Lukas. He, Sebastian, and Felix wave. Elliot tucks his hands in his pockets.

"Four of them? That's good," says Mom, not even acknowledging them. "At least one of them will always be able to take care of you."

I bite my tongue and force myself to stay civil. "I can take care of myself," I point out. I've always taken care of myself. Mom certainly never took care of me.

"But of course, all four of us will always take care of her if she wants it," agrees Sebastian, and I shoot him a dirty look. He meets my gaze. "I said, if you want it."

"I can take care of myself," I say again. It comes out harsher than I intend, but I'm just so tired right now and just the thought of relying on someone else, as I sit here looking at my mother in her hospital bed, broken because of how much her identity is tied to my father, makes me want to scream.

The guys nod, looking like little puppies I just kicked. As if I wasn't already feeling shitty enough about everything, now I feel even worse for hurting them.

"We'll just … wait in the hall. If you need anything,

we're right here," says Lukas, gesturing for the others to follow him. They all file out, but the tension in the room stays.

I feel like an asshole. And it's Mom who put me in this position.

"You should be nicer to them," she admonishes me, "You'll never find a man to take care of you if you're mean to every man you meet, and you're not supposed to take care of yourself. That's not how it's supposed to be. The men are supposed to take care of their women."

I can't take it anymore. All these years of watching her do this to herself, the past weeks of hurt and heartbreak, and the past twenty-four hours of worry and exhaustion, coalesce into one giant glob of emotion in the center of my chest, and I snap.

"No!" My voice is loud in the tiny room, but I'm not going to temper myself for her anymore. "That is it! I'm going to be the best goddamn reporter you've ever seen, and I will support myself. I will not throw away my life like you have by expecting someone else to take care of me and never giving myself an opportunity to be the one to do it. I won't tie myself to another person so tightly that I don't know who I am without them. I won't be like you." I take a deep breath. "Dad left you, and he's not coming back! Even if he does come back, you shouldn't let him!"

"He loves me." Mom shakes her head. She's not even listening to me. I don't think she's heard a single word that's left my mouth.

"No, he doesn't. Those guys out there," I point toward the hallway, "they're missing Worlds to be here with me right now, but Dad wouldn't even miss happy hour for you."

"That's not true. He just has to work late a lot. He works so hard to support me," says Mom. Her delusional refusal to see the truth runs so deep, I'm not sure she'll ever be able to climb out of the hole she's in.

"No, he doesn't. And that's not what love is. It's not whatever you and Dad have." My words falter as everything I've experienced over the past weeks since meeting the guys plays out in my mind, clicking things into place like a perfectly-solved cube.

Love.

That's what the guys feel for me. They're here even though I didn't call them. Supporting me even when I told them I don't need them. Putting me above their own goals in a way I'm not sure I would have done for them if the tables were reversed.

Well, that ends now.

I stare at my mom for a beat, as she stubbornly continues to insist that my father loves her and that as soon as he's able, he'll be here. She's still talking when I turn and leave the room.

The guys are standing outside her door, looking uncomfortable. They've heard everything, I'm sure, but we don't have time to worry about that right now. I reach for them.

"Do we still have time to make it?"

"Make it where? Do you need us to run out and get something for you?" asks Lukas, standing up from where he was leaning against the wall.

"To Worlds," I tell him, starting for the elevators. They don't follow, and after a few steps I turn back.

"But your mom is in the hospital," Sebastian points out, brushing his hair off his forehead. "Is she being released?"

"She's going to be fine. She doesn't want me here, and I don't want to be here anymore."

"I can't hear what you're saying, Rebecca. Speak up," calls Mom from her hospital bed.

"I'm leaving," I call back into the room. "Call me once you're in therapy."

There's no way I can help her. She needs someone more than me. A professional who can help her realize that she's put her entire life on hold for a man who doesn't love her, and help her figure out how to start it over and actually live it.

Meanwhile, I've got four beautiful, wonderful men who love me, and have been showing me that for weeks. They deserve so much better than me, but if I'm who they want, I'm going to help them achieve their dreams.

That doesn't mean I'm going to let mine go, but for now, we have a world championship to get to.

"Are you sure?" asks Felix, glancing back at my mom.

"I am. Let's go." I start walking down the hallway and when I get to the elevator and look behind, they're still hovering outside Mom's room, looking uncertain. "Come on!"

As soon as I push the elevator call button, I can hear them hurrying to catch up. They're going to have to hurry a lot more than that though, if we're going to make it in time.

"We're so glad you made it," says Lukas's mom the next morning, wrapping her son in a hug and then hugging all the other guys, then me.

"Sorry we're so late," I say, embarrassed that they probably all know how badly I've behaved these last two weeks. "It's my fault."

It hurts to admit that, but it's true. And if I'm going to

treat the guys fairly, I need to be able to acknowledge where I've gone wrong.

"There's no way you could have planned what happened to your mom," says Sebastian's mother, stopping me before I can say anything else. "We're just glad she's doing well enough for you to be here."

Hmm. It's odd that she's only commenting on our being late due to Mom's hospitalization. I look over at the guys, who all have a slight pink tinge to their cheeks. I don't think they've told their families what I'd done. How I ghosted them. If they had, their parents would certainly hate me and not want me to be here.

"What time did you get in?" asks Elliot's dad.

"We didn't get to the hotel until well after midnight," says Elliot, stifling a yawn.

Lukas's dad frowns. "That's not enough sleep."

"Well, we got you registered," Lukas's mom tells them, handing out their lanyards.

The guys shuffle along to the competitor waiting area and I follow their parents to the audience viewing area. It's even more crowded than Nationals and it's only the first day. I'm sure it'll get even more packed before the world champions are named.

"Thanks for checking them in," I say, as we settle into our seats. "It helped to sleep in a few extra minutes."

"You're welcome. We're family, we're here to help. Besides, they needed all the sleep they can get if they're going to win this week," Mary says, smiling.

Her words are sweet, but fill me with guilt. It's my fault they arrived so late. If it weren't for me, they would have arrived early yesterday, checked in, and gotten a full night's sleep last night. We were all so exhausted, we didn't fool around at all once we got here. Just crashed into bed. I think Elliot even considered skipping some of his cleaning steps.

He didn't do it, but he really looked like he was thinking about it.

The guys all make it to the next day of competition, but by the time we're heading up to the hotel room at the end of the day, they're all rather subdued with exhaustion.

"At least you'll have some good material for your class article," says Lukas as we step off the elevator onto our floor.

I wince. I haven't told them yet about everything that happened at my work.

"I actually already turned it in. My professor loved it, so I sent it to my editor at the newspaper," I explain, taking a deep breath to help mentally prepare myself for the next part.

"That's awesome!" says Felix, pulling out the key card to open our door.

"Of course he loved it, you're a great writer," Elliot agrees.

"I got fired." I let the words tumble out as we go inside, and I drop onto the bed to stare up at the ceiling.

"I'm confused," says Sebastian, sitting down next to me so he can lean over and look down at me. "Did your editor not read it? He has to read it to know how wonderful it is. How would you showing him an article you wrote get you fired?"

"Oh, he did," I assure him. I don't want to tell him that I didn't get fired because of the article, but because I was fooling around with them and one of the other reporters figured it out.

"Will you send it to us so we can read it?" asks Elliot, taking off the shoes I'd left on and replacing them with my hotel slippers.

My mind had been too distracted, but not Elliot's. Even when I miss something, he takes care of it, without complaining.

"Thank you," I tell him, reaching out to squeeze his hand. He smiles down at me. "You want to read the article from class that got me fired?"

"Of course," says Lukas immediately, taking off his outside shoes and sliding on his room slippers. "We want to support you, and be involved in your life."

"And we meant it when we told your mom that we would always support your goals," adds Felix.

I'd thought they meant it in the way Mom had earlier, that they would financially support me and keep me. That's why I'd been so pissed and snapped at them. But of course they mean that they'll always support my goals. They're better guys than I've ever given them credit for.

"Well, my advisor is working on finding me a new internship, so hopefully I'll be back in a newsroom for the fall semester at least. There's nothing you can do in that department, but I appreciate the thought."

"You know we'd do anything to help you," says Sebastian, leaning in to kiss me.

It's so sweet, and I want to sink into the feeling. Or maybe cry. I've missed them so much. I never should have let Ronnie's teasing freak me out so much that I threw this away.

For the first time in my life, I think that maybe I can have both a career and love. I can let someone else care for me without losing a piece of myself.

"And support you," says Elliot, turning my chin so he can capture my lips with his own.

"I should have said this a long time ago," I say when we pull apart, "but I was an idiot and didn't realize what was happening."

"What was happening?" Felix asks, leaning in for a kiss of his own.

I look around at each of them in turn. "I was falling in

love with you." I grin at the looks of shock on all their faces. "I love you. All of you. And I'm sorry it took me so long to realize it."

I pull them towards me, and we all fall together in a tangle of limbs on the bed. Suddenly, no one seems to be very tired anymore.

Epilogue

The sun is beating down and I feel sweaty and gross from lugging my suitcase down to the parking lot.

"We could have helped you bring this down," says Lukas, stepping out of the car.

"I know, but I had the time." I kiss each of them hello, even though there are other students and families milling around, packing up their own cars for the summer break.

"Is this the last of it?" confirms Felix, lifting my suitcase into the trunk.

"It is. I hope you're not regretting your offer already," I say, sliding into the backseat between Felix and Lukas.

"Not at all," says Lukas taking my hand.

The ride over to their house—now our house—is quick, and it feels good to walk into their house and know that it's mine too. I hadn't wanted to move back home. I need some space from Mom while she goes to therapy, and I haven't heard from Dad since the hospital, so it's not like I could have stayed with him even if I wanted to.

"This is where we keep mail," explains Elliot, pointing out a new rack on the entryway wall. Each section has a little label on it with one of their names.

The bottom basket is labeled "Rebecca", which sends a thrill through me. First my own hook, now my own mail basket. They really are trying to make me feel at home here, as if I didn't always.

"I have mail already?" I pull out the envelope that's sitting in my basket and rip it open. Maybe it's a little welcome letter from them. Or a list of rules on how to keep the house clean. Or a printed schedule of the bed rotation for the month.

It's none of those things. It's not even from the guys. My eyes rove over the page, confused. I reread it.

It's a job offer from a company I definitely haven't applied for.

"What's this?" I'm so confused.

Felix turns the paper so he can glance at it, and immediately grins. "She got it."

The other guys all cheer, throwing their arms around me and kissing me. I kiss them back, but I'm still lost.

"But I didn't apply here."

"We did, though," says Elliot, blushing.

"It was overstepping, and we know that," adds Sebastian. "And we're sorry. But also not sorry."

"You were looking for a reporter position and we read the article you sent us," says Lukas. "We just knew we had to send it in to *Speedcubing Today*."

Elliot taps a finger on the letter. "And look, they loved it!" he crows.

"You sent my article in to a company and didn't tell me?"

"Are you mad?" asks Felix. "We knew it was a possibility. We just thought it was worth the risk."

Part of me wants to be upset that they did this without telling me, but my advisor still hasn't found me a new internship, and here my guys have literally landed me a job

—not just an internship, but an actual *job*—in my career field. It's not hard-hitting news, but it's still a field I'm interested in because my boyfriends are speedcubing superstars.

"Only if they just gave me the job because I'm the girlfriend of four speedcubing World Champions," I say with a smile. They all shake their heads emphatically.

"No, they wouldn't do that," insists Sebastian.

"You deserve it because you're talented," adds Lukas.

"Thank you." I pull Lukas in for a kiss. "I love you."

Now that we're living together, I can do that whenever I want. And the idea that they can do the same has me smiling through the kiss.

Bonus Scene

Thank you so much for reading *Bro Smooth*.

Didn't get enough of the guys' fast fingers? Check out this spicy little scene from Rebecca's first night officially living with her four speedcubing boyfriends.

If you can't wait for the next obscure-sport reverse harem in The Bro Series, keep an eye out for *Bro Awesome*:

A struggling business administrator, Wren, takes the only job she can find—with a trick shot team. The entire company is a joke, but she's determined to turn things around for them. What she didn't count on is her three sexy bosses making everything harder with their constant flirting.

About the Author

Alby Blake is a grant award winning, midwest romance author who spends her days researching ways to embarrass her characters and trying to drink as much tea as possible. If she's not writing, she may be in the garden or admiring her cats.

Also by Alby Blake

Captured by a Knight

Welded Hearts

Love in Hiding

Bro Amazing